MW00626510

MY BROTHERS KEEPER

"A TIME IN THE LIFE OF BEST FRIENDS"

Written by

Michael Shane Dabney

© 2013

Special thanks to my Book Cover Designer Paul Patton Jr. , my Photographer Howard Rowell Sr. and my Publisher Carrie Jemii for pulling it all together.

Dedication...

—❧—

Ehis book is first dedicated to two very special people of my life. My daughter Jazzmin and my son Stephen.

Jazzmin, I love you with all of my heart and soul. More than you could ever know or realize. I am so happy and proud of the great and strong woman you have become, and I pray God continues to bless you for the rest of your life.

Stephen (RIP), you have been gone now for some time, but you are forever in my, your sister, family and friends lives though your memories. Nothing and no one could ever take your place and you are truly missed.

I would also like to dedicate this book to all who have been an influence in my life, those who have given me the courage to pursue this dream and take that leap of faith to keep going and FINISH.

Last but definitely not the least, I dedicate this book to a special person. One, who has shown me that I can truly love and be loved no matter how many past hurts I've had. Maybe one day, I'll truly open back up for that love and be able to have my life complete again.

Enjoy......

CHAPTER

1

Marcus "A fallen Angel"

—✦—

Unable to sleep…

I stare up at the ceiling thinking to myself *damn another restless night*! I'm tired, tired of tossing and turning. I look over at the clock sitting on my nightstand, 3:40am; it glares its lights at me as if to say hi! Knowing I have to be up by six to catch my flight to Washington DC by nine, I have to find some way of getting some sleep. I continue laying there where sleep eludes me…realizing I'm fighting a losing battle, I get up out of my bed to get a glass of brandy thinking it will help me relax just enough to fall asleep. I get my drink and walk over to the bay window of my condo. As I look out onto the skyline of the city it never ceases to amaze me how beautiful and peaceful the city looks at night, especially from 40 floors up. I always think of how dirty and corrupted the city is sometimes but from this high up you would never notice. I continue staring out into the abyss due to the restless night that I'm having and it happens, the worst night of my life enters my thoughts again, not that it really goes anywhere but this time the memory of my wife ,Brenda, comes to me so strong it's as if she is standing right next to me.

Brenda…my wife…the love of my life for six wonderful but oh so short years. She was more than my wife and mother of our daughter. She was my lover, my world, the air that I breathed, and simply put she completed me. I still don't know how I wake up every day without her. I still can't believe she was taken away from us so soon.

Flashback…

August 15, 2001 8:00pm

It was late and I was sitting in my office working on the finishing touches of my business proposal for JSW Entertainment to have them buy add space in my magazine the following day. I was wrapping things up when I received a call that would not only change my life but the life of everyone I knew and loved.

Phone rings…"Hello".

"Mr. Bass?"

"Yes, how may I help you?"

"I am sorry to be the one to call you like this but there has been a terrible accident you need to get to the hospital right away".

"Jason is this you, man you know I got my presentation to finish so I'm not in the mood for jokes especially one like this" Thinking it was one of my boys, Jason Gray, because he was always playing jokes, I tried to brush it off, but the detective had different plans.

"I'm sorry Mr. Bass but I don't know a Jason, and this is no joke.

"What are you talking about what accident?"

"Again, I'm sorry to be the one to tell you but this over the phone, but your wife has been in a serious accident, and you need to get to the hospital right away."

I froze. My heart started pounding as if it was going to explode. I couldn't breathe, couldn't move, it was like I was in a trance. The detective called my name over and over, unable to get a response. When I came too, he suggested that I allow an officer to take me to the hospital; I told him that I can drive but not knowing that he just called my name multiple times, assumed I was in no condition to drive myself. He stated that he had a car already in route to pick me up and I was to meet him out front, plus driving myself, would take forever in the Chicago traffic. I reluctantly agreed and figured that by going with an officer would be faster with sirens and lights blaring. I made my way to the front of my office just as the officer arrived. I don't know what happened but seeing the squad car caused a rush of anxiety to rise up in me. I felt nauseous needing to throw up. My legs felt like jello not being able to hold me up. The officer rushed over to me and helped me into his car. The officer got me secured in my seat and quickly sped off. The drive to the hospital was a blur. I don't even remember pulling into the emergency room parking lot. Upon arriving at Johns Hopkins emergency entrance, I was immediately met by a nurse who was informed I was on my way.

While rushing into the emergency room in a panic, yelling at the top of my lungs.

"Where's my wife, what's going on with her, where's Brenda?"

A doctor came rushing up to me trying to speak to me as calmly as he could,

"Mr. Bass your wife was in a very bad accident, we had to operate immediately." The doctor spoke,

"I want to see her, I want to see my wife, when can I see my wife?"

"Mr. Bass we are doing all we can right now but please go with a nurse and fill out some paper work, I will be out to talk to you just as soon as I can but I have to get back in the operating room."

Reluctantly I went with the nurse, filled out all of the paperwork which seemed to take an eternity. As I was finishing up the paperwork, a detective walked up and introduced himself to me. With all of the confusion on the phone he didn't have time to tell me his name or I just didn't hear it whichever the case.

"Mr. Bass my name is detective Roberts and I have been assigned to your wife's case. Mr. Bass I am very sorry that we have to meet under these circumstances."

"How did this happen?"

"Apparently your wife was driving home from what seemed like the grocery store, I could tell this because of the groceries in the back seat, when she came upon a stop light. Apparently the light was red and while she was waiting for it to change, a driver who was in high-speed pursuit by the police slammed her into from behind."

"Wait, I don't understand, please explain how if she was hit from behind, that impact causes her to be in such a bad condition?"

"The impact was so extreme that it forced her up out of her seatbelt and through the windshield where she suffered severe head trauma amongst other wounds."

Hearing the words come out of his mouth made me weak in my legs weak again, almost falling in fact. The detective noticed I was unable to stand and helped me into a chair. I put my hands in my head in bewilderment. Karla Williams, another doctor at the hospital and one of my dearest friends was walking by and came over to me.

"Hey Marcus, what are you doing here, what's wrong?

"Brenda was in a very bad accident and now is in surgery. Karla, the doctor doesn't know if she is going to make it or not."

"Brenda is a very strong woman and she knows that she has you and Jazzmin to live for so she will fight with all of her might to stay alive." Karla keeping the cool head she usually has said calmy.

"You're right my baby is strong, and she won't give up no matter what. That's what I love about her, her fight, her strong will. But, I'm scared to death, if she doesn't make it through, what am I going to tell Jazz?"

"The truth Marcus, the truth, she deserves that. By the way where is Jazzmin"?

"She's with my mother, that's where Brenda was going when this happened."

Just then the doctor came into the waiting room in a rush, I jumped up and looked at him and he had this scared look in his eyes.

"Is she ok, is my wife going to make it?"

"She has suffered massive head trauma due to the impact of the blow to the head. She has swelling of the brain, also a lot of internal bleeding due to a blood vessel in the brain had ruptured. Now we were able to stop the bleeding, but the swelling was more difficult. We had to place a small bolt in her skull to allow her brain to breath. Right now, she is out of surgery but not out of the woods, it will be touch and go for the next 24 to 48 hours. If she makes it through that she has a good chance of a full recovery, but I must tell you Mr. Bass, due to the severity of her condition she has a very difficult and uphill battle ahead of her. I'm truly sorry!"

Again, I froze, just hearing the fact that there's a possibility that Brenda may be taken away from me, I just couldn't handle it. Karla, noticing my knees were buckling, led me to a chair. I sat there with my head in my hands staring into emptiness. With everything hitting me at one time I didn't realize how much energy it took out of me because I passed out. When I came too I saw my mother and my baby girl right next to me.

"When did you two get here?"

"We've been here for only a few minutes and didn't want to wake you. Karla filled me in on what's going on, do you need anything son?"

"Yeah ma............ a miracle" I said.

 "She's in God's hands son and my Father knows what's best for her............. and you" my mother being a very religious woman said softly.

I looked down at my daughter who was sleeping on one of the couches in the room and just tried to figure out what I was going to tell her when she woke up out of what seemed to be beautiful sleep she was having.

"Does she know?" I asked my mother.

"No, she was asleep when Karla called the house and I just put her in the car and came here, luckily she didn't wake up".

At that moment Karla came in and told us they had a room prepared for us to go into so we could get away from the rest of the chaos in the emergency waiting room. Plus, this would allow us to be alone. I didn't want to move but I knew it would be best if I had them in a separate room, this way we were together and my mother and daughter could get some rest in peace. The room Karla took us into was like a studio apartment it had a couch that let out into a bed and a couple of chairs in it with a T.V. it also had a small refrigerator and a bathroom. I let out the couch, put Jazz in it and told my mother to lay in it with her.

"No son, she needs her father with her so when she wakes up she knows you are there and always will be".

It must have worked because when I laid down I fell fast asleep. Only to be awakened shortly after by Karla and the other doctor who operated on Brenda.

I jumped up out of the bed…

"What's wrong?" Even though I already knew by the look on Karla's face" not being able to look at me in the eye.

She was gone, my wife, the mother of my child had been taken away from us in a blink of an eye. I went to my mother who was lying on the other side of Jazzmin and touched her. She woke and saw it in my eyes.

"She's gone isn't she?"

Before I could answer, my daughter woke up and said

"Who's gone daddy"

I couldn't get the words out of my mouth for the tears that had begun to flow.

"Daddy what's wrong" Jazzmin begins to cry

My mother sat Jazzmin up onto her lap and began to tell her what happened to her mother?

"Jazzmin, honey, your mother was in a terrible accident tonight and although the doctors tried their best they couldn't save her"

"What do you mean nana?" as my daughter began to cry. "Where's momma, I want my mommy!!!

At that moment she jumped into my arms crying uncontrollably.

"Baby girl, the doctors did all they could do but it wasn't enough, they did their best, they really did but mommy is no longer with us, I'm so sorry baby girl" I tried my best to console her and explain the best I could how the doctors worked on her and did all they could to save her, but it wasn't good enough. I had to explain to my four-year-old daughter how her mother would no longer be in our lives.

"I don't understand daddy, why couldn't they save mommy and where is she gone?"

"Baby girl, momma is gone to be with God now". My heart felt so heavy as she asked me the heartening question. Jazzmin buried her head into my chest, continuing to cry unconsolably. That was the hardest thing I ever had to do and I vowed to never allow my daughter go through any more pain like that again.

I just knew that on the day of Brenda's funeral Jazzmin was going to be uncontrollable with tears of sorrow for her mother but to my surprise she was calmer and stronger than I could ever imagined. After Brenda was laid to rest, I turned to Jazzmin.

"Well it's just you and me now babygirl." My daughter in her youthful stage looked me square in the eyes,

"No daddy, mommy is still here" as she pointed to my heart. That brought tears of joy to my eyes knowing that I have such a strong daughter, just as strong as Brenda.

Back to reality…

That was 10 years ago now and it still feels like it happened yesterday. As I stood there thinking about how everything turned out, I couldn't help but think of how Jazzmin is turning out a lot like Brenda. She is growing into a beautiful young woman and only at the age of 14. I still can't believe how strong she has been through all of this.

CHAPTER

2

Marcus "Life Must Goes On"

I looked at the digital clock on the VCR, it read 5:15. I didn't realize I had been standing at the window for almost an hour and a half. I thought I might as well take a shower and get ready for my flight. I turned to go into the kitchen to put my glass in the sink, realizing I hadn't taken one sip after all, I chuckled. After putting my glass in the sink, I turned to walk down the hallway to my bedroom, as I walked I couldn't help but notice, staring straight at me, the portrait of Brenda holding Jazzmin when she was a newborn. I paused in front of the picture; looking as if she was smiling at me with those deep brown eyes, with those dimples that I loved so much. It was if she was smiling in approval of how I was raising our daughter. I think to myself, although she has been gone for a long time, I can still feel her essence in our home. I closer to the picture and with my two fingers kissed them and placed them on her lips. I speak out loud;

"Thank you, baby-girl, for giving me the most beautiful and precious gift anyone could ever give. I vow to never (in my power) allow her to go through pain like that again".

I felt a tear forming in my eye; I wipe it away and head for the shower. I went into the bathroom and began to run my water so I could take a shower. While my water was heating up I turned on the radio because I knew that the "Tom Joyner Morning Show" was on and I just had to listen to my boy Jay Anthony Brown murder another hit. When he performs those songs all I do is laugh my ass off, thinking his writers are geniuses. I turn the radio to his station; he was already jamming with one of my favorite old school joints "Sweet November" by one of my favorite groups of all time The Deele. I wondered what ever happened to the rest of the members because Babyface was a successful singer, songwriter, producer, and arranger and along with LA Reid had a successful record producing company. Oh well that's life, they come and they go is all I could think. I stepped into the shower, it was a little hotter than normal but I like it hot and I got used to it quickly. I began singing with the song and was jamming if I do say so myself until I forgot that my voice was not the alto voice it used to be when I was youngster but now a major baritone as I tried to hit the high notes my voice cracked. I laughed out loud and thought oh well I'm a magazine owner not a singer. I paused "*a magazine owner*" I thought, man who would have figured that I would turn out like this the CEO/Founder of "*Urban Couture*" one of the largest urban based magazines in the country outside of Essence, Ebony. I stayed in the shower allowing the water to sooth and soak into me as my thoughts traveled to the presentation I was about to make. I couldn't help but think that life has turned out pretty good and all I wished for was Brenda to be here to share it with Jazz and me. I finished and got out of the shower, doing so I checked myself in the mirror to make sure my head was still clean-shaven from the night before. I thought to myself in a moment of laughter thank God I had skills to cut my own hair because as much as I cut it I would be spending much cheddar having someone else keep it up. Out of the bathroom I began putting on my baby oil gel and lotion, a combination Brenda always loved. She would touch me and tell me my skin was so soft and how much she loved it. This is the one thing that I make sure I keep up not only is it a good thing but it's a way of having her with me always. I finished getting dressed I checked the clock which showed 6:30. I had plenty of time before my driver was scheduled to pick me up at 7:30. I double checked my things to make sure I wasn't forgetting anything. I looked in my briefcase, checked off my portfolio, my layouts, the ad space, and the proposal. Something was missing though, oh (snapping my finger) my picture of Brenda holding Jazzmin when she was just two years old that I always carry with me no matter where I go. I forgot that I had to take it out to replace the frame because of the idiot baggage handlers broke the other one throwing my luggage around. Handle with care my ass; I thought; I know better now not to put any breakable items of value in my luggage. Luckily I was able to find another beautiful frame to put the picture in and it just happened to be Brenda's favorite color, burnt orange. Just then the phone rang and I looked at the clock 6:45. Who in the hell could be calling me at this hour?

I answer...

"Hello".

" What's up man?", Braden Withers, one of my boys spoke.

"Hey man I know it's early and you still have to get yourself ready but I just wanted to wish you luck today on your presentation."

"Thanks man, and what are you doing up at this hour, you could have called me later, you know how cranky you are in the morning when you don't get your full 10 hours of sleep" I said chuckling.

"Forget you man (Braden trying to sound serious knowing I'm right), Anyway; I just wanted to wish you well and see how you are doing. You know what day this is right?"

"Yeah man how can I ever forget the day my wife was taken away, that's' something I will never forget."

"Marcus I don't mean to dredge up bad memories, I just wanted to make sure you were ok."

"Thanks, but besides not getting much sleep I'm actually ok."

"Good, now how is my God daughter doing and where is she going to be while you are away?"

"She is staying with my mom and she is great. You know something? I couldn't have asked for a better daughter, I thank God for her daily."

"Yeah I know she's great; anyway, why you didn't ask me to keep her you know I love spending time with her especially since I don't get to see my own that much anymore?"

"I know you love her but I didn't want to bother you and besides she's in a school program for the summer and it's right down the street from my mom's so I just thought it best since she doesn't drive much anymore."

"Yeah you are right and besides I don't like getting up any earlier than I have too anyway. Good luck and call me when you touch down in DC, oh before I let you go have you talked to Darius?"

"No why?"

"Man, he is going through it again with Trish."

"Not again!"

"Yeah again, I told him not to marry her ass, hell we all did, but he wouldn't listen and went ahead and married her anyway. Now look at him… Miserable!"

"Well, you were right about that, but, no I haven't talked to him and I won't until I get back but let me go so I can finish up and get out of here, my driver will be here in a half hour so I gotta go."

"Alright dude, holla at me when you get back."

"Will do, peace."

"Peace!"

My thoughts trail back to Brenda, sadness come over me as I think this is the day (August 15, 2001) she died, looking at her picture, I tell her "I miss you so much baby and I love you still and always." I kiss her picture then put it in my briefcase.

7:15 packed, bags at the door, ready to go, just one more thing

Ring…..Ring…..Ring…..

"Hello!"

"Hi momma!"

"Hi son, how are you?"

"I'm ok, ready to go."

"Well I know you will do well but I still asked my Father in heaven to watch over you and to let His will be that you are successful on this business trip."

"Thanks mom, is Jazz a wake?"

"Yes she is eating breakfast let me get her, Jazzmin your dads on the phone."

"Hi daddy" she says with great enthusiasm.

"Hi baby how's my favorite girl doing?"

"Daaaad I'm your only girl" as she sings the word.

"I know I know, so how are you?"

"I'm fine, when are you coming back?"

"I'm not scheduled to be back until the day after tomorrow."

"Cool, so that means I can stay at Nana's over the weekend huh?"

"Yeah I guess so since it will be Friday when I return. Anyway, I just called to say I love you very much and to be good while I'm away and lastly I will call you every night ok?"

"Ok daddy, I love you too."

"I love you too pumpkin, bye, bye for now baby."

"Daaaad (She cooed); You know I don't like goodbye's; say talk to you later that way I know you will."

"Ok, ok I forget sometimes honey, talk to you later and be good for grandma."

"I will daddy, talk to you later, here's grandma."

"Ok son you better get out of there so you won't be late."

"I won't, besides I have a driver taking me to the airport."

"Ok good, then you be safe and call us as soon as you get…where are you going again?"

"Washington DC!"

"Oh yeah Washington DC, call us as soon as the plane lands so I know you are safe ok and tell the President I said hello?"

Laughing hysterically, "Sure Ma I'll do just that, ok now let me go, love you ma!"

"Love you too son and I'm so very proud of you."

"Thanks ma."

"Bye, talk to you later."

I think to myself what a wonderful support system I have. Although my father has been gone for a long time and my mother and I were all we had. It feels so good that we still are so close. I'm so glad Jazzmin has my mom here in her life. I don't know what I would have done if my mother wasn't around. I begin walking my things to my front door and I couldn't help but think of my conversation with Braden about Darius. I'll never understand why people get married out of fear of losing that person when they may not be meant for them in the first place. Oh well I hope he and Trish work things out this time but we'll see. Since I had a few minutes to spare I decided to give him a quick call to check on him before I left for my flight. When I did I heard all hell breaking loose between him and Trish.

"Hello" Darius speaks.

"Hey man what's up, just wanted to quickly give you a call and see how things are going" hearing a lot of commotion in the background.

"Man, I'm cool just dealing with some things right now, I'll have to hit you later, Dammit Trish stop!!"

"Uhm are you two ok?"

"Yeah we will be if she would just stop hitting me."

"Tell me who she is?" I hear Trish speaking.

"Who's who? Yo' Marcus let me get off of here and handle this."

"Alright man, handle your business; I'll hit you when I come back from DC."

"Ok cool, have a safe flight."

Darius abruptly hangs up the phone and I can only imagine what's going on at his house now and what it's about but knowing D and what I heard Trish say, it's about another woman. Damn I can only hope he wore a condom (chuckling).

CHAPTER

3

Darius "Busted or Am I"

Darius Davenport has always been a ladies' man. Women flocked to him. He's 6'1", athletic, dark skin, bald head and could play the hell out of some basketball. BUT!! One problem! He's never satisfied with just one woman. Even when he was "supposed" to be committed to someone he always had a side dip. That is until Trish Montegue walked into his life. She's 5'9", athletic, red bone, long hair which flowed just passed her shoulders AND she was a college hoop star (which is what drew him to her). We, his boys, could never figure out just what it was about this one that made him do things that he normally would have never done. It's not like he hadn't had women like her before but something about her was different. Maybe it was the fact that she treated him the same way he did the rest of his women. At times she would not call him back when he called. She canceled dates with him never rescheduling. She would also date other men while they were "dating". Yeah, she was a challenge, which was the reason why he asked her to marry him we think or was it the fear of losing her to some other guy. I still think back to the night another guy answered her phone when he called. Damn! He was pissed, he went ballistic and next thing you know they were engaged. I still wonder to this day if it was all a trap set for him or what, but she has him now so I guess we'll never know. I almost can't believe they have been married now for 10 years but I guess the children played a large role in it. Darius has always wanted to make in in the music business and had a couple acts in high school but nothing truly came of that. But he strived to make it anyway and now a self-made millionaire record producer who is the founder and CEO of D-Nice Records. He built his record company from the ground up to a multimillion-dollar company. Yeah I could say that he's living the dream but the only thing that's keeping him from truly living it is the inability to stay faithful.

"Hello" Darius speaks

"Hey man what's up, just wanted to quickly give you a call and see how things are going" hearing a lot of commotion in the background

"Man, I'm cool just dealing with some things right now, I'll have to hit you later, Dammit Trish stop!!"

"Uhm are you two ok?"

"Yeah we will be if she would just stop hitting me."

"Tell me who she is!" I hear Trish speaking.

"Who's who? Hey Marcus let me get off of here and handle this."

"Alright man, handle your business; I'll hit you when I come back from DC."

"Ok cool, have a safe flight" hanging up abruptly.

"Don't play dumb with me Darius who's the bitch you've been fucking and don't' even try to lie because she called and left a message on the answering machine. I guess she thought I wasn't home or hell for all I know probably didn't care!"

"Trish I don't know who you are talking about." trying to lie my way out of it knowing full well Trish was talking about my new intern I hired.

"Oh you don't huh well apparently she not only knows you but she said you two were together Saturday night when you told me you were in the studio working on some music for your latest group."

"Trish for the last time I don't know who this woman is and I was at the studio working, if you don't believe me call the studio and ask." knowing she would do just that I took precautions to ensure that my bases were covered, thinking back "was I working? Yeah, I was working on this hot new intern that I hired. I probably shouldn't have hired her because she didn't have a clue as to what the music business was about but hell let's face it, she was fine and had a body to kill for."

"Darius…. Darius…. DARIUS! You hear me, stop acting like you don't and tell me who the bitch is?"

"Baby like I said before I don't know who or what you are talking about." picking up the phone on the table, and holding it in Trish's direction, "Here call the studio and check for yourself. I won't say a word while you talk and when they tell you that I was there, you'll feel real stupid."

Trish taking the phone and putting it on the receiver knowing even although she don't believe him, she knows he is not stupid enough to hand her the phone not having covered his tracks.

"Darius I'm getting tired of these phone calls from women saying they spent this time with you and that they didn't know you were married. I'm sick and tired of it. I don't know how much more of this I am going to take."

"Baby come on, I know that I messed up in the past, but that's the past. We've went through counseling behind it. I realized how much I hurt you and I promised you then as I am continuing to do right now, I am not messing around with anyone nor am I going too. You and the kids mean too much to me to lose you all."

"Darius I want so badly to trust you and I don't want to lose you either but it's hard when these women keep calling or looking at me funny when I come into your office. I just can't take it anymore. I just don't want to go through the same situation that happened 5 years ago, you do remember what happened right and how that one night almost cost us everything." Trish talking about a stint of infidelity that not only almost ended their marriage but her and the kids' lives as well.

"Yes I remember all too well and I promise you that nothing like that will ever happen again." Darius thinking back to what happened in what seemed like just yesterday.

5 years earlier

One Saturday night I was in the recording studio working with one of my up-and-coming new groups "Back to Soul", the session was taking a long time due to the fact they were having difficulties with the vocal harmony. This was getting to the point of going over budget and we were running out of time before the deadline to go into full production.

"Ok fellas we gotta get this track right tonight because we go into production tomorrow. I don't care how long it takes we gotta get it done."

"Mr. Davenport, we're trying but something just don't seem right."

"Larry why don't you and Kevin switch vocals and see how that goes, I think that it will work out just fine."

"Ok we'll try that."

"Alright, here we go, One, two" …. Beep, my intercom buzzer sounded with the voice of my assistant Terry on the other end interrupting the session."

"Terry, you know not to interrupt me while I'm in a recording session?"

"I'm sorry Darius but this is urgent."

"Terry unless it's my wife or kids calling you know it's not that urgent."

"Well if you saw what I'm looking at you would think so, just come to the reception area and take a look for yourself"

"Man, this better damn well be important or you're so fired tonight."

"You just might give me a raise after this."

"I'm on my way, hey fellas, take five and work on switching the harmony around like I said and see if you can get it to work better."

Getting up from my chair and leaving the booth. I get on the elevator to go to the lobby and see what's going on. Exiting the elevator, entering the lobby, I noticed the police standing there.

"Are you Darius Davenport?"

"Yes!"

"Do you know a Cassandra Haywood" Thinking oh shit….and appearing a little nervous

"Yes I know her, why, what's the problem?"

"Well we received a call from a Mrs. Davenport about a woman trying to get into her home with a weapon. When we arrived on the scene Ms. Haywood was screaming at the top of her lungs stating that she was not giving you up and was going to kill Mrs. Davenport and apparently your kids. She was waving a gun and banging on the door telling her to open it up. We told her to freeze and put down the weapon but she refused and turned the weapon towards us."

"Oh my God, is she dead?"

"Thankfully no, the officer just wounded her and she is at the hospital handcuffed to the bed."

"What about my wife and kids are they ok?"

"Yes they are fine; luckily she was not able to get in to do any harm."

"Ok I'm a little confused, why are you here now" breathing a sigh of relief.

"Because on the way to the hospital she kept saying that you are the cause of this and you promised her that you were going to leave your wife and kids for her. She also claimed she is pregnant by you and that she will stop at nothing to get you."

"Oh wow…..I can't believe this!"

"So, the affair is true I take it?"

"Unfortunately, yes, but it was only for a short while and when I realized that she was crazy I ended things but I didn't think she was insane."

"Mr. Davenport, take my advice on this, it doesn't take long for someone to get like this. In the meantime, you will have to come to the station to give a formal report so we can have accurate documentation of everything before we formally charge her."

"May I ask what you are charging her with?"

"Attempted murder, attempted home invasion, aggravated battery because she did damage to one of your vehicles, that's it for now but more charges could come depending on the district attorney."

"Wow, I can't believe it, I just can't believe it. Terry, tell the group that I had to go, don't tell them why just say I had an emergency and that I will be back as soon as I can. If I'm not back in an hour let them go home but tell them to stay by the phone."

"Ok boss, I'll take care of it."

Snapping back to reality

Taking Trish by the hand and sitting her down on the rust-colored leather couch.

"Trish, I know what you are talking about and I know how messed up things had gotten but baby you got to believe me when I say that will never ever happen again I swear."

"I so want to believe you Darius, but I just don't know?"

"Trish, baby, listen, from the bottom of my heart I mean it. I won't do that again, I can't lose you or the kids. I don't know what I'd do without y'all."

"It better not be happening all over again, you know what I said in therapy."

"Yes I remember all too well trust me, you said you'd leave me and take the kids and half of the business if I messed up again."

"That's right and I meant what I said too, so don't try me."

"I'm not baby, I'm not" pulling her close feeling that I dodged another bullet..........this time!!

CHAPTER

4

Darius "Back in trouble again"

I knew I was in trouble from the moment our eyes met. She came in for the internship interview. She had on this sharp business outfit but I knew she wasn't out to get the internship solely based on her knowledge of the music business because the outfit was cut as low and high as humanly possible without being illegal. Hell, I wasn't thinking with my head, well at least not with the one that matters anyway.

It was very hot that day. I knew this because the central air in the office was screaming. Due to the fact my two partners were out of town on business I had to deal with hiring an intern, which meant interviewing college kids who probably didn't take the music business as seriously as they should. I know they didn't take it as seriously as I did. All I know is I had made a deal with Trenicia (Tre) and Zantell (Zan), my business partners to try again at taking on an intern to show them the ropes of the record business. In spite of what happened the last time they both said that it would be good for public relations if I did so that way I could begin to expand my company and work with larger and more popular artists. Needless to say, I was dreading the interviews, remembering how I was in college. Hell, I don't know to this day how I graduated and Summa Cum Laude. To my surprise, the interviews were going pretty well and I had in mind who I was going to hire. Mitch Carpenter, a young kid in his junior year of college from the south side of Chicago getting his bachelor's, studying piano and music history at University of Illinois Chicago, he reminded me a lot of myself at that age. We spent most of the interview just talking and finding out we liked a lot of the same things. Mitch had an old school mentality and knowledge to go with it. He believed in acts actually performing the music and singing it, not using technology to do it for them. Yeah I liked him from the start and thought that he will work out great. I was all ready to call him back to let him know that he has the internship when my assistant Terry buzzed

"Darius your last interview is here" my assistant Terry said.

"I told you I was done interviewing and I decided on Mitch.

"I think you may want to reconsider."

"Why?"

"All you need to do is come to the lobby and see for yourself."

Reluctantly I did just that.

"This better not be a waste of my time" I said, huffing.

"Have I ever led you wrong?"

"Well?"

"Ok, ok, ok that was one time." Terry speaking of the time his leading got me busted with Trish.

"Ok I'm on my way" and hung up the phone.

I left my office heading towards the lobby. I felt this uneasiness in the pit of my stomach. I couldn't figure out what was going on, but my body already knew what my eyes were about to find out. As I turned the corner that lead into the lobby I noticed what seemed to be every male in my company along with a couple of female employees all in the lobby, all in a huddle as if they were playing football and was about to run a play. They were hovered over something or someone so I couldn't see, but soon will find out what all the commotion was about. I stood there watching for a few minutes taking in just how my money was going down the drain as my employees stood around on the clock. Just then my assistant Terry turned and caught me looking at the commotion and he noticed that I was not happy at all. Terry knew as well as all of my employees how I felt about just lounging around and not being productive. I was even more of a stickler for business etiquette or lack thereof. Terry must have known I was fuming because at that moment he said

"Ok guys and girls let's get back to work"

Just at that moment they all (in unison) turned to look at me, seeing how pissed off I was, and getting more so by the second. They scattered back to their areas like roaches when the lights come on. When what seemed like smoke clearing my lobby I saw all too well the reason my lobby was packed with my employees. Sitting in the middle of our very cushioned lobby chairs I had custom made for our Afro centric lobby was a vision of pure heaven. She was a smooth dark skinned, full figured and I mean full figured woman that has the body that would make Vivica Fox take notice. She has shoulder length hair that was in a flipped style. She had some bedroom eyes that would melt the heart of any hard-core thug. The lips of pure melons looking so soft and supple. Lastly, she had these dimples that would make Steve Harvey jealous. I knew she was here for the interview not because she had on this sharp black pin stripped pant suit with a white collard blouse which was open three buttons down and with pearls on the outside of the blouse but because my assistant Terry was drooling so hard I almost had to give him a babies bib. As I walked over to introduce myself, she immediately stood to greet me. I would say she was about 5'6" to my 6'1" frame, she came up to the middle of my chest. When she stood, I noticed one more thing, her body, and all I could think to myself was damn!

I reached out my hand to greet her and she reciprocated the gesture and shook my hand.

"Hello I'm Darius Davenport!"

"Zenobia, Zenobia Bentley!"

"Welcome to D-Nice Records!"

As we shook hands it seemed like an eternity went by because Terry cleared his throat and it took us out of our trance we were in. I took my hand away and looked at him. He had this look on his face as if to say uh oh not again. Thinking that I had plans for Ms. Bentley other than her being a possible intern, but at first I didn't have any plans for her other than to just interview her for the intern position, but as everyone knows plans do change. As I began to escort Ms. Bentley back towards my office I couldn't help but notice how she was checking me out. I knew this because as I was heading towards my office I turned to show her where the lady's room was just in case she needed it, when I saw her looking at my ass. She seemed to be embarrassed, but not because she was looking but at the fact she was caught. I couldn't help being flattered that she was checking me out and thought to myself that this was going to be a very interesting interview. As we made our way to my office, I offered her a seat and I sat behind my mahogany desk Trish purchased for me as a gift for going into business for myself.

"Please have a seat Ms. Bentley" I said gesturing towards a chair in front of my desk.

"Please call me Zen."

"Ok, Zen I must say that's a very beautiful and interesting name so where did you say it derived from?"

"Well my mother loved Africa and decided to look up exotic names when I was born and here I am. I did some research on it and it's a Latin word and it means those who have a deep desire to be creative, expressive, very passionate and romantic people"

"Hmm I see, that's very nice so what brings you to D-Nice RECORDS?"

"Well I saw on campus that you were offering internships in your company and I wanted the opportunity to gain insight on how a record is put together from the bottom to the top. Also, with me attaining my double degree in Business and Marketing I feel I could be a true asset to your company."

"I see, well first off I must tell you that this internship is not traditional. It pays, but not enough to live off of and the hours will be grueling. Please know, the record industry is not a typical 9 to 5 kind of job.

You may work some early hours, late hours, or combinations of the two, do you think you can handle that?"

"I *know* I can Mr. Davenport if given the chance!"

"I like your confidence, but I will be totally honest with you, I already had someone in mind as to who I was going to hire for the internship."

"Mr. Davenport, I know I almost missed out on the interviews coming as late as I did. I also understand that you may have someone else in mind, but I had to take my chances" Zenobia stood and walked over to my side of the desk, leaning over allowing her blouse to open a little wider showing her cleavage, looking very seductive "I know that if given the opportunity I can make this internship worth your while and trust me you won't regret allowing me to be your intern."

Thinking to myself, she's saying one thing with her mouth but I knew she was meaning something totally different with her advances, but boy I didn't know just how much of a difference she was thinking.

"Ms. Bentley, sorry Zen, this is highly inappropriate for an interview and I would appreciate it if you would return to your seat so we can continue" Zenobia appearing very embarrassed returned to the other side of my desk.

"I am so sorry about the way I came onto you but honestly I felt so attracted to you and I thought I felt the vibe from you so I took a chance. I am so sorry Mr. Davenport and I do hope that this in no way influences you in a negative way with considering me for the internship because I am very qualified for the job and would love the chance to prove it to you".

After I looked over her credentials seeing she did have certain skills different from Mitch and we talked further I told her that she made my decision that much more difficult but I will consider her for an internship. I let her know I would have to run it by my business partners and I will let her know what my decision will be one way or another.

I got up to escort Zen to the front lobby. As we were walking towards my office door, she stopped abruptly, turning towards me, still having that look of shame on her face. She said…

"Please forgive me for my forwardness and if given the opportunity you won't regret giving me the chance."

"Zen listen; let me say this and hopefully I can ease your mind a little. What you did was very inappropriate and yes I should have ended the interview right then and there, but honestly after talking with you longer, looking at your credentials and getting to know you a little better, I see you in a different light. I must admit you really changed my mind. That's the only reason why I continued with the interview deciding against my better judgment and just escorting you to the door but I'm glad I didn't."

Zen smiled an uneasy smile then began heading towards the lobby. As we reached the lobby, I could see the look on Terry's face as if to say that he knew I was going to hire her. When Zenobia exited the lobby and I turned to go back to my office Terry couldn't help but open his mouth.

"So are you going to hire her boss?" saying that with a grin on his face.

"I don't know, but I will say this she has made my decision hard."

"I bet she did!" He said smirking

"Terry it's not like that, honestly she did come on to me but I shut her down and after that I got the chance to know more about her and her qualifications in marketing and advertising. I found that she is a very bright girl and has a real future but I did let her know that's not the way to go about things. Honestly she as well as Mitch are both very qualified to be interns, I like the fact they both bring something different to the table that's why I'm going to have a difficult time in making my decision, that's why I am bringing in Tre and Zan to help me make my decision."

I headed back to my office, once there I couldn't help but think of what just took place. All I could say to myself was that it's going to be a long summer. After getting back to my office I contacted Tre and Zan since they were in LA on business to let them know how the interviews went and what my thoughts were on the two candidates. I told them I hadn't made the decision if I were going with just the one or both and after hearing the qualifications of both candidates, they agreed to what I was thinking. I was hesitant to tell them the situation bout Zenobia but I had to since I knew it was right for them to know what was going on and that I was not thinking with my little head. They admitted that they had reservations about it and since they would be back in a couple days suggested I wait to hire either candidate until returned. This would allow them to have an opportunity to sit down with Mitch and especially Zenobia just to make sure they are on the same page. They went on to say if we decided to go with Zenobia they made sure I knew they will keep an eye on her and make sure they keep her busy so she does not have a reason at all to be alone with me. I thanked them for their input and also got an update on the trip and they stated that things are progressing well and will give me a full update once they return to Chicago. After hanging up the phone with them I sat back and reflected…reflected on the drama I caused not long ago. I knew that I couldn't let that happen again. I just hope I'm stronger this time around…I gotta be.

CHAPTER

5

Marcus "The Deal"

Ok, got all my stuff together just one last check of things, portfolio, ad layout, suit, extra cloths, picture of Brenda and Jazzmin hmm what am I missing oh shoot, gotta turn off my alarm, I remember the last time I came home and my neighbor told me that my alarm clock ran constantly and kept them up all weekend long. As I turned to go back to my bedroom and made sure I had turned off my alarm, my door buzzer sounded

"Hello?"

"Your car is here for you sir," the front desk security officer said.

"Ok I will be down in a few minutes."

"Ok I will inform him you will be right down."

Looking at my watch reading 7:15 good he's early I thought as I took one last look over my condo to make sure that everything was in order. I was just about to walk out of the door just when I stopped in my tracks and said a small prayer.

"God I know I don't talk to you like I should and I am trying to do better at that but I do thank you for all you have done for me. I know how I was acting after you took Brenda from me but I know that you forgave me for it and have blessed me tenfold from that point on. I thank you for Jazzmin and I couldn't ask for a better daughter in the world. I ask that you allow me to have a safe trip to DC and that everything goes well with my meeting. But most of all I ask that you watch over Jazzmin and momma until I return. In Jesus name, Amen"

I turned the security alarm on, grabbed my bags and headed for the elevator.

Once down in the lobby I noticed that the sun was shining bright through the lobby windows.

"George, how are you doing this morning?" I asked the security guard at the desk.

"Oh, I can't complain Mr. Bass how are you doing on this fine day?"

"George, what have we discussed? It's Marcus I'm not all formal, but I am blessed and feeling very good today if I do say so myself."

"Where are you off to this time?"

"DC. I have a big presentation and if all goes well my magazine could go global."

"Well, I wish you nothing but the best and just to let you know that I truly appreciate you and thank you for not treating me as just a worker but a human being."

"Well George my mother always told me that it does not matter what a person does for a living he/she is still a person and should be treated with nothing but respect because they are earning a living honestly just like you are."

"Your mother seems like a lovely lady, may I ask you this, you always talk about your mother but you never talk about your father. I know I am being nosy but I'm just an old man and I couldn't help but notice it, don't you and your father get along?" apparently a sad look came over my face, which George picked up on it "Marcus I'm sorry if I was out of line, I didn't mean to say something wrong."

"No, George you didn't, it's just that I lost my father a long time ago as a kid and it's hard for me to talk about it sometimes that's all don't worry about it. Hey when I get back I will sit down with you and tell you the whole story but right now I have to go catch a plane."

"Ok Marcus I will be right here" he said, smiling.

"See you later George!"

"Bye Marcus."

Outside the driver was waiting on me with the door open. He took my luggage and put it inside the car.

"Hello sir" he said as he took my bags.

"Thank you."

"So, you are off to O'Hare."

"Yes!"

"And your plane leaves at 9:00am correct?"

"That's correct."

"Good we have plenty of time to get you there."

"Yeah I know" that's what I loved about living on the North side of Chicago because O'Hare wasn't far away and I've made it there in 45 minutes with heavy traffic so I wasn't worried at all.

As the driver was heading out of the front of my building I turned on Tom Joyner show and the song "So Alone" by Men at Large was playing and I couldn't help but close my eyes and think of Bren'. I sat quietly with my eyes closed just thinking about her "I really do love you I thought, ask God if you wouldn't mind to let things go well for me if you don't mind".

All of a sudden, the driver said…

"I will do that sir."

A little startled, I said "Huh?"

"You asked me to ask God to let things go well for you."

"Oh, sorry I didn't know I was talking out loud."

"Oh, sorry sir."

"It's ok don't worry about it."

As we drove on I reflected over and over how lucky and blessed I am to have such a wonderful support system around me and I couldn't ask for more a lovely daughter who is growing more and more every day. A mother who loves me unconditionally no matter what and friends that not only cares about me but speak the truth no matter what goes on. Yeah I can say that I am truly a lucky and blessed man.

Finally at the airport I looked at my watch and it read 7:45. Record time. I got out of the car, the driver helped me with my bags. I took a deep breath, thinking to myself here we go again (with the baggage handlers) but I wasn't going to let anything worry me on this trip. I went into the check in area to get my ticket that was already waiting for me because Teresa my secretary (who was a wonder) had already made my reservations.

Arriving at the counter to check in, I presented my identification to the clerk

"Ok Mr. Bass here are your tickets and you are on flight 1969 of American Airlines exiting out of Gate B-2 and your flight is on time"

"Thank you very much"

I looked at my watch and it said 8:15 a whole 45 minutes until I leave and I just realized that I hadn't ate a thing. I decided to go to a small café and get a cup of coffee and a poppy seed muffin. Man, I love those things but I don't allow myself to have too many since they are way too fattening and I know I don't want to go back down that road again. Ever since I lost almost 70 pounds and got back down to a slim 215, I was not in the market to gain weight again.

As I sat there sipping on my coffee and eating my muffin I couldn't help but notice this beautiful caramel brown skinned sistah with long dark brown hair that was just past her shoulders. It was cut into a style like the late R&B singer Aaliyah and was beautiful. She had on a dark blue business suite with some dark blue stiletto heeled shoes and a briefcase to her side reading a copy of my magazine that just came off the presses this week. I glanced over, I couldn't help but smile in delight at my hard work. I must have been staring hard because she noticed me looking and smiled at me. I smiled back and asked, "Are you enjoying the magazine?"

"Yes I am as a matter of fact, I am a subscriber. Do you read the magazine?"

Laughing lightly "Well I should say I do since I am the founder and CEO of the magazine."

"You're kidding?"

"No, I'm not."

"Yeah right, you're just saying that to talk to me."

"Hmm you think so huh, so how can I prove it to you?" I could tell she didn't belie me and she was looking as if to say, "here we go again another broke brotha trying to lay claim for something they didn't do."

"Hmm well if you are the CEO then you would have a business card or something to show who you are?"

"As a matter of fact, I do," I said, standing to pull it out of my personally engraved cardholder to hand to her

As she took it and read it, I could see the embarrassment on her face as she saw the deep purple and black card with the gold lettering on it that said,

Marcus Bass

Founder / CEO

Urban Couture Magazine

P.O. Box 2469

Chicago, IL 60125

(773) 555 – 4585 Office

(773) 555 – 5785 Cell

(773) 555 – 4588 Fax

marcusbass@urbancouture.com

Looking rather flushed, she apologized,

"I'm so sorry Mr. Bass I am truly a fan of your work and I honestly thought that you were this fly by night brotha trying to take credit for what is a wonderful piece of work just to talk to me."

"It's ok I get that quite a bit since I don't dress like I own something like that."

"I just feel so stupid I can't believe that I just thought that about you."

"Really it's ok, I pretty much figured that you thought that and I would have too if it were reversed Mrs.?"

"It's Ms., Ms. Johnson, Kim Johnson!"

"Well it's very nice to meet you Ms. Johnson."

"Please, call me Kim."

"Ok Kim and I'm Marcus."

"Yeah I read that" she said, chuckling, holding up my card, we both laughed.

"So, what brings you out this time of the morning Kim?"

"I am on my way to DC for this convention that my partner got me into."

"Funny I'm on my way to DC too, what do you do if you don't mind me asking?"

"Well I have my own consulting firm that I run with my longtime friend and business partner Danielle Nichols."

"Sounds interesting, I would love to know more about it but I have to go get on this plane."

"Yeah I hear you and as much as I don't like to fly I have no choice since I have to be at this convention that starts at 1:00pm."

"I understand that, well it was very nice to have met you Ms. Johnson, sorry Kim."

"It was nice meeting you too Marcus, and maybe if you are not too tied up maybe we can meet for a drink while in DC. By the way how long are you going to be there?"

"I'll be there 'til Friday working on this deal with "Jump" athletic apparel."

"Sounds interesting?"

"Well you have my card so I guess I will be hearing from you sometime in the next couple days?"

"And that you will."

With that, we left to go to our perspective planes. As I walked, I noticed that she was behind me and I turned around

"Are you following me?"

"Actually no, my flight leaves at 9:00 from gate B-2, flight 1969."

"Really, you're kidding well it's a funny coincidence that mine is the same flight."

"Really?"

"Really, I'm not kidding" pulling out my ticket to show her.

"Wow this is a coincidence because we are not only on the same flight but I noticed that you are in first class and so am I right next to you" pulling out her ticket to show me and we both just laughed at how incredibly ironic this is.

"Well I guess we can continue our conversation from the café?"

"Yes we can and I'm glad that I have you to sit next to instead of someone else who would be annoying to me."

"Yeah me too!"

We continued to walk to our gate together and I couldn't help but think of how much she favored Brenda. I didn't want to freak out or anything but it was so amazing how much they favored. You know they say we all have twins out there somewhere. I remember growing up people would assume that I am someone else all the time. Made me think back to when this girl ran down the street hollering another guy's name but coming directly at me and when she got to me she said I wasn't him. Of course, I knew this but it was one of those things. Interesting thing is I did meet the guy and we did favor but I thought that I looked better ha ha ha. As we boarded the plane and took our seats, we continued our conversation. She told me more about her finance consulting firm and how it had been a lifelong dream of hers to own her own business and after a lot of sweat, tears, struggles and strife's she now has her dream and it was well worth all the pain she went through to get where she is. She continued telling me how she loves to help those in need and started this firm along with her partner to help those in the urban community and the lesser fortunate about finance and how to manage their money and not live beyond their means. She also told me of how she is a big community volunteer and loves to do it and gives donations every year to different organizations.

I didn't want to get too much into her business about all of the pain she went through but I must admit I was very curious as to what was going on with her. Our flight didn't take long only a couple of hours but as we talked it seemed as if it took just minutes because her conversation was nothing of what I've encountered from some of the other women I've ran across in recent years. She had a good; no great head on her shoulders, she was well driven, knew what she wanted out of life and how she was going to go about getting it and not allowing anything to stop her this time.

As the captain informed us to prepare for landing I couldn't help but think of how much I was attracted to this woman and that I couldn't wait to get my meeting over and for her to get her conference end so we could see one another.

"So where are you staying while in DC?" I asked.

"I am staying at the Holiday Inn Express by the airport."

"Interesting!"

"Oh…wait don't tell me, you are staying at the Holiday Inn too?"

"Although that would be nice, no I'm not, I'm staying at the Chateau Marriott just across the street from the Express."

"Well now that is interesting, well would you like to share a cab together?"

"Actually, I have a car waiting on me, Mr. Mead the owner of "Jump Athletics" who I'm here to meet sent one for me but you are more than welcome to join me?"

"I'd love too."

"Good so let's go."

We went to claim our luggage and walked towards the exit I couldn't help to think of the irony of how things are with Kim and a smile came across my face. As we rode in the town car that Mr. Mead sent for me I noticed there was a bottle of Champaign and so I asked her if she would join me in a glass? She had no problem with that and as we enjoyed a glass together I noticed that it must have begun to go to Kim's head because she began to get a little frisky and started to snuggle up close to me. I enjoyed it very much and started to get close myself but then we arrived at her hotel.

"Well miss Kim it was truly a pleasure spending this time with you."

"Oh no the pleasure will be all mine when you pick me up for dinner later."

"Is that so?"

"Marcus I don't usually do this but I honestly feel very attracted to you and I want to see you again."

"It's funny because I was thinking the same thing at the airport and I want to see you too so we will definitely have to get together later on after our perspective engagements."

"Well, I will call you later when I am done and we can work out the details then."

"That will be very lovely, bye, bye for now Kim."

"For now, Marcus!"

I got out of the car and walked her to the entrance of the hotel; she turned to me and gave me a huge kiss. It took me by surprise but I didn't resist and I'm glad I didn't because she turned out to be a helluva kisser.

"WOW! That was real nice, what made you do that?"

"I have wanted to kiss your full lips for some time now, I just didn't have the nerve but I think the Champaign helped and I wanted to taste your lips just in case I didn't get the chance to see you again."

"Now what makes you say that, we will see one another tonight if I have anything to say about it."

"I know but I just wanted a precursor to this evening."

"Hmm well I'm not mad at you at all, and on that note you have a wonderful conference and give me a call when you are done."

"I will do that."

"Later!"

Arriving at my hotel, and entering the lobby, as I approached the front desk, I noticed a gorgeous honey brown sistah working behind the desk and as she looked up, smiled, and asked if she could help me? I told her who I was and that I had reservations and she checked me in and informed me that I had a message waiting. It was a message from Mr. Mead,

"Marcus if you are reading this that means you made it to DC safely. I hope you find your accommodations just fine and I look forward to our

meeting this afternoon. My driver will be there at 2:30 to pick you up for our meeting at 3:00 that will be plenty of time for you to get here. So get to your suite and relax and I'll see you soon.

Edwin"

I felt real good that he is taking this much interest in showing me so much love and had only known me through the expo and a couple of publications he read while he was in Chicago on business. As I turned to go towards the elevator all I could think was this was going to be a good day I could feel it. Upon exiting the elevator on my floor, I couldn't help but notice how luxurious the hotel was and it was filled with all kinds of black art. My room was a gorgeous executive suite on the 20th floor hell it was an apartment. It had a full kitchen with a dining area, a full bathroom with a Jacuzzi tub and a stand-up shower encased in glass, a huge king size bed for me to fully relax, and it even had an office area so I could do my work and get totally prepared for my meeting. I went over to the window and looked out into the city and I could see the capital building from my room, which I thought was wonderful. Just when I turned to pick up my phone to call momma and Jazz to tell them I made it ok my hotel room phone rang.

"Hello?"

"Marcus," a male's voice said.

"Yes this is he, who is this?"

"This is Edwin, I was just calling to make sure you made it alright and you are getting settled in."

"Yes I am, actually I just got into my room a few minutes ago and was admiring the room and the view. I could get used to this for sure."

"Well if things go well you will just have to get used to it. I didn't want to bother you I will let you get yourself together and I am looking forward to our meeting this afternoon. I'll see you then."

"Ok, and I'm looking forward to it too so I will see you at your office a little later."

"Ok Marcus bye for now."

"Bye Mr. Mead."

"It's Edwin!"

"Ok Edwin, bye for now."

I hung up the phone, I couldn't help but get a little uneasiness in my stomach. Although I was confident in my presentation, something seemed a little too easy about this. Edwin seemed a little too eager for our meeting and I didn't know how to handle it just yet. I mean I've had plenty of meetings and presentations but this one almost seemed as if the contracts were signed already. Oh well I thought, my magazine is doing well and I know my presentation is on point so I'm not worried about anything. I almost got caught up in the moment when my phone rang again.

"Hello?"

"Daaaaaddddddyyyyyyy!" Jazzmin said enthusiastically.

"Hey baby girl."

"Are you in Washington DC yet?"

"Yes I am baby girl and I was just about to call you and grandma."

"When did you get there?"

"Just a little bit ago, just put my bags down. What are you doing?"

"Nothing really, me and grandma are about to go get some Chinese for lunch."

"You and your Chinese food, do you ever get enough of eating that?"

"Nope, I love it. I miss you daddy!"

I could feel my heart melting…

"I miss you too baby girl but you know I'm on business otherwise you would be here with me right?" I always hated leaving her when I went out of town. Ever since Brenda died, we have not been as much as a couple of days apart and I did not want it any other way.

"Yeah I know, just remember to bring me a souvenir," she said while chuckling.

"Ok baby girl, now where is grandma?"

"She's right here looking at me wanting me to get off the phone."

"Well hand her the phone."

"Oh ok, I love you daddy."

"I love you too babygirl."

"Here's Nanna."

"Hey son."

"Hey ma, how are you doing?"

"Oh, I'm fine son; you know I am in heaven whenever Jazzmin comes over."

"Yeah I do and I'm so glad that she has you in her life."

"Me too, so how was your flight?"

"It was wonderful mom; it didn't take that long either just a couple of hours, besides the person I sat next to helped make it seem quicker too."

"That's good I'm glad you made it safely."

"Yeah me too, and Mr. Mead already has hooked me up ma, I mean the room is off the hook, it not only has a full kitchen with a dining area, but a full bathroom with a Jacuzzi tub and a stand-up shower encased in glass, a huge king size bed for me to fully relax, and it even has an office area so I could do my work and get totally prepared for my meeting."

"Wow baby that sounds real nice he must really like you."

"Well from the sounds of things I hope so."

"Well I'm not worried because I already said a prayer for you and asked my Heavenly Father to watch over you while you are on this trip and that His will be done and let it be that you are successful on this trip."

My mom was always a very religious woman and I'm glad that Jazzmin has her in her life to show her another side of life especially in the area of church because ever since Bren passed I hadn't gotten up the strength to go back to church.

"Thanks ma and I truly appreciate it."

"No problem son now I'm going to let you go so you can relax and get ready for your presentation."

"Ok ma, I love you."

"Love you too son talk to you later."

"Later ma."

As I hung up the phone; I couldn't help but smile because of how blessed I am to have two of the most wonderful women in my life. As I glanced around the room, I looked at the clock and it read 12:00 noon so I figured I would lay out my suit for my presentation and get me a quick nap so I can be fresh. After laying out my suit and my materials, I decided to take a shower to relax and lay down.

CHAPTER

6

Marcus "Pre-meeting Jitters"

Aagghhh…….(stretching) as I was waking from a nice nap. I noticed that the clock by the bed read 1:30pm. I thought to myself that I have to get up and get dressed so I can be ready for my meeting with Mr. Mead at 3:00pm. Just as I was about to begin my prep to get myself together for my meeting, the phone rang.

"Hello?"

"Hi Marcus."

"Kim?"

"Yes it's me, I wanted to say hi and wish you luck on your presentation this afternoon."

Elated, I said "Thank you very much, I truly appreciate that, also I'm glad you called because I wanted to hear your voice before I left, also to set up a time when we could get together and have dinner and talk some more."

"I'm sitting here at this convention right now honestly not able to concentrate on anything because I couldn't get you and our first encounter out of my head."

"I know what you mean, and I am looking forward to seeing you later on. Do you think 7:00pm would be a good time to meet up?"

"Sounds good to me, I know I'll be done here at 4:00pm and that will give me plenty of time to freshen up and put on something nice for you."

"Hmm, I'm sure that anything you put on will be just fine by me."

"Where shall we meet up?"

"Actually, I will pick you up, Mr. Mead has given me total access to his driver for the time I'm here, so I will pick you up at 7pm in front of your door."

"Ok sounds great and just so you know I'm not one of those women who keeps her man waiting, I'll be downstairs promptly at seven if not shortly before."

"Her man huh, is that right?"

"Oh, I'm sorry did I say that, I don't mean to come off presumptuous!"

"Yes you did, but it's ok I understood what you meant, in fact it sounded kinda nice."

"Well I'm blushing now, so I'm going to let you go and will be looking forward to seeing you soon."

"Me too, see you soon Kim."

"Ta ta for now."

Just as I hung up the phone, and was heading for the shower, my phone rang again. I thought to myself man, is this grand central station or what.

"Hello?"

"Marcus, how are you feeling, did you get some rest?"

"Hello Edwin, yes I did in fact, I was just about to jump in the shower and get refreshed so I can meet you in a short while, what can I do for you?"

"That's why I'm calling, are you a spontaneous person?"

"Yeah I like to think I'm somewhat spontaneous (thinking of what took place between Kim and I), why you ask?"

"I was thinking, instead of meeting me at the office, surrounded by these four walls, going over ideas and crunching numbers. Why don't we meet for dinner, that way you can meet my wife and we can mix a little business with some great pleasure?"

"Oh, wow ok, well I did make dinner plans with a young lady I just happen to meet would it be ok if I bring her along?"

"That's perfect bring her along and that way it would be a double date."

"Ok, I think that would be nice and I know she would be game."

"Good, let's say we meet up at 7:30; just tell my driver when he picks you up to bring you to the restaurant he already knows where it is."

"Sounds good to me because I was going to pick her up at seven anyway."

"Cool, it's a date, so now you can enjoy yourself and get a little more rest, oh and FYI bring your dancing shoes!"

"Huh?"

"Yeah man bring your dancing shoes, my whole plan is to show you a wonderful time while you're here in my city."

"Ok I gotcha, I'll do just that."

"Marcus, let me apologize for the switch but I figured this would be better and a bit more comfortable."

"No apologies needed, in fact I kinda like it this way."

"Cool, so I'll see you around 7:30."

"Ok, see you then."

I hang up but the butterflies remain, but it's not one's of something negative it's more like something positive is about to happen. I wonder can this be real, I mean it seems as though I've have the contract without doing any presenting of my materials. Wow what a good feeling, oh well now that I have plenty of time what am I to do with myself I wonder.

CHAPTER

Marcus "Time on My Hands"

Thinking to myself, since I have all this time on my hands and this is my first time in Washington DC. I figured that I would take advantage of it and the driver Mr. Mead provided for me. I called the driver and told him to pick me up 2:30.

A little while later I received a call from the front desk informing me that my driver had arrived. When I arrived in the lobby I noticed the driver from earlier this morning a slender, caramel colored, African American male with a bit of salt and pepper hair but more pepper than salt. He had on a black suite with a white shirt and tie with a chauffer's hat on and sunglasses. I told the driver that I have a few hours to kill and would love a tour of the city. He of course suggested I go see all the monuments and the capital, which wouldn't take too long unless I wanted to get out and walk around. I said, "nah I'm cool with looking around for now." As we pulled out of the hotel parking lot I noticed that the sun was shining extra bright, as if it was shining just for me. I looked up in the sky and just marveled at how beautiful

God is and all His Glory. I closed my eyes and said a small prayer

"Thank you Lord for blessing me through all of my endeavors, I couldn't have done any of this by myself especially since you called Brenda home. So Father I give you all thanks and praise for all that you have done and all you are going to do in my life. Please watch over momma and Jazz while I'm away and allow everything to go well in my stay here in DC. In Jesus Christ name Amen."

As we drove down the street it was amazing how the venue changed more as we drove. On TV, it seemed as though they showed nothing but the good neighborhoods in DC, well I guess they don't want the rest of the country to know how bad it is there since it is our nation's capital. The drive to where the monuments were didn't take too long about a half hour in traffic. I thought to myself this is nothing like Chicago's traffic, I could get used to this. We drove around and the driver was pointing out different monuments to me and telling me who they were. I saw the Lincoln memorial, the Jefferson, the Washington, and the war memorials. I didn't plan on getting out but as we drove by the Lincoln memorial I couldn't help but think how it must have been to have been there while our great civil rights leader Dr. Martin Luther King Jr. delivered his great "I have a dream" speech. I asked the driver to get me as close as he could and park so I can go see where he (Martin Luther King) stood as he delivered his speech. He obliged me and was able to find a spot real close. I got out of the car and headed towards the monument. I arrived at the Lincoln Monument and as I walked up the steps, I couldn't help but think that many years ago one of our great African American leaders stood here and delivered one of the most powerful speeches of our lifetime. As I arrived at the top of the steps, I turned around to face the Washington Monument, as I did the hair on the back of my neck stood up and this feeling of his spirit came over me. At that moment I looked down, realizing I was standing in the exact spot he stood. The cement blocks under my feet had words on them and it read

I HAVE A DREAM
MARTIN LUTHER KING JR
THE MARCH ON WASHINGTON
FOR JOBS AND FREEDOM
AUGUST 28, 1963

As I looked out a tear formed in my right eye, not of sorrow, but of the pain, struggle, sacrifice, joy, fulfillment, success, happiness and most of all pride of all that our people have endured during those times. I couldn't help but think to myself that I too have a dream and thanks to God I am living my dream. As I walked down those steps, I couldn't help but feel a sense of pride for my people who came before me, who paved the way for me to be in the position I am today and I know it's up to me and others to continue this fight and pay it forward for those to come after us. When I arrived back at the car my driver whom I never knew his name nor even asked was standing outside the car having a smoke and drinking a Pepsi.

"I need to give these damn things up" he said as if he could read my mind about my distain for smokers.

"Hey that's on you but I never could bring myself to pick up the habit not even a taste. I had too many family members' die off from smoking so I just never picked up that habit."

"I hear you" he said as he put out the cigarette, he went on to say. "My father marched with Dr. Martin Luther King Jr. and he would tell me stories all the time about how it was back then and what our people went through" he went on to say how, "It's a shame now that our younger generation tend to take things for granted or feel like they have a self-entitlement to something that they have not even earned."

"I understand where you're coming from, that's why I'm raising my daughter in a way where she not only knows where she came from but she learns the importance of responsibility at an early age. I tell her all the time nothing in life is free. I tell her all the time if someone gives you something for free then they can take it away from you, but if you earn it then no one can take it away. By the way with everything going on I never got a chance to ask your name."

"It's Willie, Willie G. Briggs"

"Are you serious right now?"

"Yes why you say that sir"

"You're not going to believe this but that's my mother's name before she married my father. Would you happen to have family in Illinois?"

"I can't say that I do but I have family all over. I will have to look into that, you know how small this world is, so you never know."

"Yeah I know all too well how small it is."

"Well Mr. Bass" Willie trying to get back on track of business.

"It's Marcus, please!"

"Ok, Marcus, it's only four o'clock what do you want to do now?"

"I would like to see Howard University."

"Ok Howard it is and if you don't mind me asking is this your first time in D.C.?"

"Yeah it is can you tell?"

(chuckling) "Yeah I could tell, but I wanted to take you to a couple places I think you would appreciate while you're in town, is that ok with you and don't worry it's nowhere dangerous, contrary to what other people may think I love my job so I am not going to jeopardize it for anything in the world."

"Yeah that's cool I trust that you will take good care of me."

"May I ask where you're visiting us from?" looking at me through the rearview mirror.

"Chicago!"

"Wow Chicago!" Willie's eyes lighting up from what seems to me joy to know someone from Chicago. "I hear they call it the windy city, tell me is it really that windy there?"

"Man, is it, especially in the winter with the cold coming off the lakefront, yeah that name is truly earned. I remember one time being downtown doing some shopping and I was about to turn onto Michigan Ave from 4th street. When I did the wind was so strong it almost knocked me over."

"Wow, see I've never been there and had always wanted to go because of what I've heard."

"Oh, and what did you hear?"

"Oh, you know the usual, that the city is known for the best pizza and barbeque oh and can you tell me what house music is?" Willie coming off like a school kid who just got a new game and is so excited about learning more about how to play it.

Laughing hysterically "House music is, well it's a type of feel-good music that when you hear it, it makes you want to get up and dance and dance your troubles away. There are many variations to it. There's what you call deep house which is on a slower side but you can groove to it. Artist like James Brown has tracks that we call "deep house" then there's what I call "Juke" and it's a very upbeat track with a lot of base and it almost forces you to get up and dance. One of the most famous local artists known for his music is "Farley Jack Master Funk" yeah he knows how to get it in and make you get up."

"Oh, ok kind of like our music here, see we're known for Go-go music, do you remember the song called Da butt?"

"Oh my God yeah, I remember that, man that was my joint back in the day."

"Well that sound comes from DC and yeah I can understand where you're coming from because when you hear it you want to, no you HAVE to get up and groove."

"Yeah I hear you I love that and I love to dance."

"Well good, and we stood here long enough talking let's get in the car and start this journey."

We got back into the car, he asked me what kind of music I like listening too and of course I told him I'm old school to my heart and being from Chicago the house music capital of the world gotta have some of that. He said good and then put in some EWF (Earth Wind & Fire) and I was in heaven from then on. As we drove I couldn't help but notice all the beautiful scenery that D.C. had to offer, just when I was about to ask him where we were, he stopped and I noticed that we were in front of the Martin Luther King Jr. National Memorial. My mouth dropped open in the amazement of the pure beauty of what the Alpha Phi Alpha fraternity inc. had done in honor of their fellow brother. Again a warm feeling came over me, and I thought to myself how blessed I am. Willie parked the car, and we walked up to the memorial and he showed me where things began and where the groundwork first started. He also told me that he once lived down the block and was able to watch as the idea of the memorial come into reality. He said that it was a struggle financially for a while, and some people did not want this memorial to go up. Saying things like "He's not a president so why does he get his own memorial." All he said he could do was watch how no matter what people said or tried to do God would not allow this dream to die and fade away, so here we are standing on a piece of history.

Again, I was in awe of everything and taken aback to all that we have went through and still have to go through to prove that we belong here and have earned the right to be here in America. All we ever asked for is a chance, that's all. As we walked around the monument I couldn't get over the size of it.

"Wow, this is huge and very impressive."

"Yes it is, it stands about 30 feet tall and it's made out of granite from china called "The Stone of Hope.""

I just stood there in pure amazement of the craftsmanship of it all. I knew I had to do more research on it and find out how things were done, hmm maybe do a piece in my magazine for black history month.

"Well Willie, I love this but I need to get ready and get back to the hotel so I can get ready for tonight."

"Ok and I'm sorry for taking so long with this."

"Oh no please don't apologize because this is something that I truly enjoyed and will be bringing my daughter back to see, so I thank you for this and I hope when I come back you and I can sit down and talk more."

"That would be great Mr. Bass, oh sorry I mean Marcus, sorry hazard of the job!"

"It's ok and I look forward to it."

We drove, back to the hotel I felt more and more at ease about why and what I was here for. Again, all I could say is "Thank you Lord for Blessing me." As we pulled up to my hotel I realized that I didn't get to go to Howard University but thought that I'll be here for a couple more days so I'll make sure I get there.

"Well I can say it has been a wonderful time with you Willie and I appreciate you driving me around."

"It's my pleasure Marcus and I can say that you have been one of the nicest persons I've had in a long while."

"Thank you Willie that means a lot, I try to treat everyone as if I'm looking in a mirror. So, if I want to be treated right I have to treat others right first."

"That's a good policy to live by and I will do that myself just picture myself on the other end. Well take it easy and I'll be back for you promptly at seven o'clock maybe just a little before."

"Cool looking forward to it, see you soon."

I enter the lobby doors and head towards the elevator. I enter the elevator and press the button for the 20th floor and as the door closes, I begin to reflect on my day thus far and begin to look forward to my night.

Arriving on my floor, I walk down the long hallway to my room. I enter my suite and the first thing I do is look at the clock on the nightstand reading 5:15pm. Knowing that gives me plenty of time to take a shower and change into my suit. I pulled out my presentation and gave it a quick look over just to make sure that everything was on point. Then I went to the bathroom to start my shower. I turned on the water to let it heat up because hotel water takes too long as it is (I thought to myself). As I stepped into the stand-up glass shower, I am in heaven because of the five showerheads that are spewing out nice hot water. I stayed in there for what seemed like an eternity but had to get out and get myself together. As I exited the shower, I look in the mirror to make sure my face and head is all-good. I leave the bathroom and put on my lotion & gel, as I do that I look at the clock and it reads 6:00pm. I thought to myself wow I did stay in the shower longer than normal, but I guess I can't blame myself because that shower was wonderful. I put on my slacks, socks, shirt & tie and decide to call my favorite girls.

Ring......Ring.....Ring......Ring....

"Hello, you have reached the Bass Residence, sorry no one is able to come to the phone but if you leave your name, number and message someone will be sure to give you a call as soon as possible............ beep."

"Hey ma, it's Marcus, I was just…!"

"Hello, son!"

"Hey ma, I thought you were gone and I was just leaving a message."

(Mom laughing) "Child your daughter has me going tonight, we're in there baking cookies and I was up to my elbows in flower that's why it took me so long to get to the phone, I'm sorry son."

"Oh no ma it's ok I was just wanting to call and check on you two and speak to Jazz before I left for the evening."

"Oh ok, and how was the meeting son, and did you wow him with your presentation."

"That's just it ma, we haven't had it yet, he moved the meeting from his office as a general meeting to a dinner meeting. I'm going to meet him at "McCormick & Schmicks" It's a seafood restaurant."

"Oh, ok well it sounds as though he already want to do business with you and this will be a celebratory dinner"

"Hmm from your mouth to Gods ears ma."

"I told you that my Father has this all in His hands."

"That you did ma, that you did."

"Ok let me get Jazz…Jazzmin your dads on the phone"(Mom yelling into the kitchen)

(Jazzmin comes to the phone)

"Hi daddy guess what, we're making my favorite, chocolate chip cookies!"

"Hi baby girl, yeah mom told me that you have her up to her elbows in flour, are you giving her a hard time?"

"No daddy, I just asked her if we could make cookies tonight and she said that it was ok, I'm being good I promise."

(Chuckling) "Ok, ok, I believe you honey, well I just wanted to check on you and say goodnight because I will be heading to dinner soon and I know it will be late when I return and I may not be able to call you because it will be late."

"Oh, ok that's fine daddy, I hope you have fun there and don't do all business, what is that you told me before something about business and playing don't mix or something?"

(Laughing hard now) "No I said that all business and no play makes for a dull day, you are so funny, thank you for keeping me smiling honey. Ok go and finish your cookies and I'll finish getting dressed. I love you for life baby girl."

"I love you for life too daddy, here's nanna."

"Hey son, are you ready for your dinner date?"

"Yeah I am ma, and you know the next time I come out here I'm bringing you and Jazzmin for a vacation."

"Ooooo that would be so nice, I've never been to Washington D.C. before!"

"Yeah I was thinking earlier that I'm going to bring Jazz out but I said why not make it a family trip and we all come back out. There's so much that you should see and for her to learn about our history that history books don't tell."

"Child don't I know it, well you go ahead and get yourself together and I'm going to get back into this kitchen and finish these cookies with Jazzmin. I love you son and have a good time tonight."

"Love you too ma and thank you for always being there in my corner no matter what."

"Where else would I be, I'm so proud of you Marcus I really am, ok now go before I get emotional."

"Ok ok I'm going; I'll give you two a call in the morning. Goodnight ma and love you."

"Love you too son and good night."

CHAPTER

8

Marcus "The Meeting"

6:20 the clock on the table reads

Hhaaahhhh...............I breathe a sigh of relief as I prepare myself for the evening's events. Funny thing is I have no clue what's in store for me because Edwin has thrown me off a little with the sudden change of venue. But it's ok I've always considered myself a chameleon anyway, always able to adapt and change with the flow of the tide. So, I think to myself, bring it on I'm ready. Just as I was going deeper into my own thoughts my room phone rings.

"Hello?"

"Well hello handsome, how are you feeling right about now?"

(Wow such a lovely voice I thought as I heard Kim's voice come through the speaker)

"Well hello to you too gorgeous, and I'm feeling very well and how are you?"

"Oh, I'm fabulous now that the conference is over and I get to see one of the most handsome men I've met in a long time."

"Ok, ok stop it you're trying to make me blush, and it's working."

"You can't help me for speaking the truth right?"

"Well, I don't know about that but I do say thank you for the consideration, are you about ready to go?"

"Yes I am, I'm just finishing putting the last-minute touches together, because I want to look extra good for you tonight."

"Well first of all you look great just the way you are and you don't have to do anything extra for me, by the way our plans have changed slightly."

"Oh" Kim curious as to know what.

"Yes, when I got off the phone with you, Edwin called me."

"I was going to ask you how things went but I didn't want to seem too eager and wanted you to bring it up."

"Well that's what I have to tell you, we didn't have the meeting yet."

"Yet?" Kim sounding confused.

"Yeah yet (I couldn't help but chuckle a little), He called and wanted to make it a dinner meeting where I am going to meet his wife and he told me to put on my dancing shoes too."

"Oh, wow sounds interesting, so if we're going to dinner and dancing is what I have on going to be ok?"

(Although not knowing what she has on exactly)

"Yes you should be fine, he did tell me we're going to a restaurant called "McCormick & Schmicks", and afterwards to a place called "Lux Lounge.""

"Ooohh I've heard of both of those and from what I know they are real nice, I think that the lounge has like three or four levels to them with different types of music."

"Yeah I looked it up and that's exactly what it has, so I'm excited about it."

"Wow, Marcus this sounds real nice, I'm so happy for you."

"Me too, but the deal isn't done yet. I can't count the chickens just yet so I'll flow with everything and see how it goes. So my driver is to be here before seven and I will be over to pick you up ok?"

"Hmm I have an idea, since I'm dressed, why don't I take the shuttle over to your hotel and wait for the driver in your room. That is if it's ok with you?"

(Feeling a little heat rise in my chest)

"Sure that would be lovely, I'm in room 2800 the executive suite."

"Ok I'll see you in a few minutes."

"Looking forward to it."

I'll admit when she said she would come over to my room I got heated because of my attraction to her and I haven't felt this way in a long time. I look at the clock and it read 6:30 so she should be here in a few minutes, this gives me time to put things at the door that I need to take with me.

6:40 the doorbell rings and I open the door to a vision of pure loveliness.

"Wow, well hello beautiful" Kim wearing a beautiful black bell bottom pant suit, with a purple cow neck blouse that flowed in the front not showing anything but leaving to the imagination, a nice sterling silver necklace that hits just below her cup line flowing into the blouse with matching earrings, accompanied by a small black Gucci hand bag.

"Well hello yourself, I see that great minds think alike in the color scheme of our outfits."

I was wearing a black five button down suit, one from the Steve Harvey Collection with the button on the cuff and on the split in the back of the jacket, along with a purple shirt with a black and purple tie and cuff links to match. I had on my sterling cross necklace that Brenda gave me that I always wear with my Citizen's watch and bracelet to match.

"Yes, I see, so what made you wear my favorite color Ms. Johnson?"

"Well Mr. Bass, this happens to be my favorite color as well (smiling)."

"Hmm interesting, I see right off we have a few things in common, why don't you come in."

Kim enters the suite and is amazed at the décor and size of the suite

"Wow I must say that Mr. Mead must like you to bring you here and provide such luxurious accommodations as this."

"Yeah I can say that I was thoroughly surprised when I first entered into my suite and when I talked to him I told him I could definitely get used to this and he said that I should get used to it, leading me to think that this will not be my last time out to DC."

"Well from the sounds of things it won't be and after reading your work I can see why he should like you and want to do business with you"

Kim goes over towards the window and gazes out into the city and see's the capital lit up.

"This is truly beautiful Marcus and oh so romantic"

I walk up behind her as she looks out the window

"Yes I know it truly is Kim, (I take Kim gently by her shoulders and turn her to face me).

"I must admit that I've been wanting to do this ever since we left each other this morning" I gently place a kiss on her nice, luscious and full lips and she eagerly return the passion that I am giving off, she moans in delight.

"Mmmm, very nice" (as our lips part).

"Yes, just as I remembered and I like very much."

"So do I...wheewww so do I, is it getting warm in here or is it just me?"

"Well I can say that it is us for sure."

"Well we will have to put things on ice for now because it is about time to go and I don't want to mess anything up for you by making you late for your dinner meeting."

Although I knew better too and I agreed that we should put things on hold for now, yeah for now that is.

"Yes we shall chill for now and hopefully pick things up where we leave them right here."

"Hmm Mr. Bass are you asking me to come back to your room after your dinner meeting?"

"Kim, I'll be frankly honest with you, yes I am but I'm not just asking for a one-night stand with you, I want to have a true romantic evening with you and if we make love in the process then that's what it will be "love making", so yes I am asking for you to come join me in a night cap."

"Well I will admit this, I was kinda hoping you would because I want to spend as much time with you as I possibly can before we go back to Chicago and go on with our lives and you forget all about me." Kim poking her lips out as if she was sad.

"Oh really, so you think I'd forget about you huh, well I think it could be the other way around Ms. Johnson."

"Oh I doubt that Mr. Bass because you have sparked something within me that I have not felt in quite some time so I know I won't forget you, I was just hoping you'd say that so I feel better now."

I smile and we give a nice embrace and we kiss again oh so gently and just when we were about to get hot and heavy my room phone rings.

"Aaahh saved by the bell (smiling)."

"Hello?"

"Marcus, it's Willie I am downstairs for you sir?"

"Thank you Willie, we'll be right down."

"We?" Willie sounding puzzled.

"You'll see!"

"Ok, I will see you in a few minutes."

We hang up the phone and I gather my things that I need. I reach over and place my fingers on my lips and kiss the picture of Brenda and Jazzmin and say a small silent prayer. Kim awaiting patiently allows me to finish what I was doing and then speaks her what was on her mind.

"You know Marcus, normally a woman could be upset or feel a bit of jealousy at what you did but I for one admire you for your strength and courage. Also it shows me that you love deeply and I like that about you."

"Kim I cannot lie to you, yes I love deeply and she was my wife and I still love her deeply, but I know she wouldn't want me to be alone for the rest of my life. So, let's be clear, there is no replacing her nor is there no holding anyone to her standard because one thing she taught me is that she was her own woman and there will be no other after her. I've never compared any other woman to her nor will I. Just so you know there is no competition so you don't have anything to worry about, ok?"

"Ok Marcus I believe you" Kim feeling a little more at ease.

"Good now let's go get our eat and dance on."

I gather what I need for my presentation. We leave my room and head towards the elevator, as we walk our hands unintentionally come together.

For the first time in a very long time, it feels right and I don't feel guilty as I have in the past as if I'm cheating on Bren. We reach the elevator door and I press the button and she turns and gives me a smile that just tells me that even if it's just for tonight she's in my corner no matter what and I smile back. Exiting the elevator, I see Willie standing there waiting on me and he has a look of surprise when he saw Kim on my arm.

"Good evening Marcus, good to see you again and may I say you have a lovely date for the evening."

"Good evening Willie and thank you, I do have a lovely date don't I? This is Kim Johnson and baby this is Mr. Briggs, Willie to be exact."

"How do you do Ma'am!"

"Oh, please call me Kim, and I'm doing just fine how are you doing Mr. Briggs?"

"Ok now you call me Willie, and I'm doing well myself"

"Well Mr. Meade has reservations at the McCormick & Schmicks restaurant at 7:30 and from what I know it's not too far from here."

"I know he informed me, and no it's not, it will only take us about 15 minutes even with traffic so we'll be there in plenty of time."

Willie opens the door for us and we enter the town car, I notice that there's a bottle of Champagne with a card attached to it and it reads

Good evening Marcus, I wanted to start the night off right with a bottle of champagne as a small token of my appreciation for everything that will transpire this evening. Let's enjoy the night and the looks of a long-lasting relationship.

EdWin

"Wow I must say that he's winning me over."

"Well he should because you're worth it Marcus."

"I can't help but think that all the hard work, sweat, tears, and most of all sacrifice that it took for me to get my magazine off the ground that now it's truly paying off."

"Believe me I can understand where you're coming from and starting your own business is not easy at all so here's to you and your continued success."

We toast and have a small sip of champagne as we ride to the restaurant. Kim snuggles up close to me and she whispers in my ear.

"I liked it when you called me baby."

"Did I do that, oh I'm sorry I didn't mean to be presumptuous." Chuckling!

"Oh no Marcus you were not presumptuous at all, it was and is flattering for you to think of me that way, it actually gave me goose bumps."

"Well I do feel that right now and I know that we just met but I feel so very comfortable with you that I can let down my guard and just be me with no inhibitions."

"I feel the same way and I'll tell you a secret, I've had this warm feeling inside of me, that things between us is just so right and I don't want it to end but I will admit that it's a little scary to feel this way this fast."

"Oh, wow I thought I was the only one feeling this way, so I guess I'm not in this alone huh?"

"Nope you're not."

"Good, so let's just enjoy the evening and let things happen and see where they go deal?"

"Deal!"

"We're here" (Willie says as he pulls up in front of this gorgeous restaurant).

Willie gets out of the driver's side and come open our door, I look at my watch and it read 7:25, yep he said it would take just about 15 minutes I thought to myself. As we exited the car the attendant at the door opened it for us and welcomed us to the restaurant. The maître-d asked us if we had reservations and before I could open my mouth to let him know we're here to meet someone, Edwin comes from around the corner and greets us.

"Well, well, well, finally we meet again, how are you doing Marcus?"

"I'm doing wonderful, Edwin."

"Please call me Ed."

"Ok, Ed it is and this is my lovely date Ms. Kim Johnson."

"Nice to make your acquaintance, come with me I have a room reserved for us so we can be comfortable and relax as we should be."

Edwin leads us towards this private dining area that is nothing short of magnificent. It has elegant chandeliers, and the lighting is not to light nor to dark where you can't see the person in front of you. The chairs and tables are not what you normally see in a regular restaurant; these were more like lounge tables and chairs something more comfortable and allowed you to feel more at home. As we approached, a lovely woman with an elegant three quarter off white colored dress, with a short crop hair do, and stiletto heels on. She reaches out for my hand and Edwin introduces us.

"Honey this is the man I have been telling you about, this is Marcus Bass founder of "Urban Couture Magazine" an up-and-coming magazine that is not only geared for the urban side of life but all facets of life, culture, fashion, sports. You name it he speaks on it, that's why I wanted him out here."

"Nice to meet you Ma'am."

"Oh please, I'm Sheila."

"Ok Sheila, this is my date Ms. Kim Johnson, she has her own financial consulting firm back in Chicago."

"Oh really, well it's nice to meet you Kim, and may I say girl you are wearing that outfit."

"I was thinking the same thing about you and those shoes."

Edwin and I couldn't help but look at each other as if to say "women!" while chuckling.

"Marcus, so Ed tells me that the two of you are going to be doing a lot of business together."

Me looking and feeling very surprised but overjoyed at her statement, respond in cool and smooth manor.

"Well, that's what I'm hoping for and hopefully after my presentation we will be able to form a long-lasting relationship."

(Edwin interjecting) "Marcus I want to put your mind at ease about something. I already had decided to have your magazine as the main focal point of our advertising. You see after we met in Chicago a few months ago I came back home and started doing some digging around and wanted to see what you were about but most of all I wanted to see what others thought of you. I know I could have just told you this over the phone but I wanted to do things in person. Marcus, the deal is done between you and I, all we have to do is work out the details of the finances and the ball will be rolling. I already know I want to take out add space in the front inside cover and back and spaces intermingled in your magazine. Also I have already devised a plan to have a complete special edition magazine coverage of my company "Jump Athletics" with certain pro athletes that I have already contracted with and informed them your magazine is the one they will be featured in. So yes I have done my homework and tonight I brought you here to celebrate and to toast the future of a wonderful relationship."

"Wow, I am truly speechless, I don't know what to say, here I am thinking that I have to be completely prepared and have my presentation as tight as I can get it without flaws, all the while you have already blessed me with the work. How can I thank you?"

"Just continue staying true to you, your magazine, your staff, your customers, and most of all your readers and that will be thanks enough."

"Well you got that because I know if I cannot be true to those things I won't be true to myself and then my magazine will suffer so I give you my word that I will not change but just get better."

"A toast (everyone lifting their champagne glasses that was pre-poured) to the marriage of Urban-Couture and Jump Athletics and a very long and lucrative relationship"

(Cheers all around).

"So, Marcus did I have you going or what?"

"Yeah you did, I was thinking that something was up because it almost seemed to easy but I felt that I have a good product and my presentation was tight so I had nothing to worry about, but you know how it is when they say when something seems too good to be true it usually is?"

"Yeah I know but one thing I was taught at an early age by a fellow family friend and I'm going to teach it to you. When you believe in yourself, have faith in God NOTHING is too good to be true because He can deliver the things that you may think are impossible but you have to believe that He can and will."

"Yeah I definitely hear you and my mother says things like that all the time, like "There's nothing too hard for my God to overcome, also if God brings you to it He'll bring you through it."

"Sounds to me like you have a wonderful mother there."

"Yeah she's my world outside my daughter."

"Oh yeah you do have a daughter don't you, well we have a daughter and a son and the next time you both come out you'll have to bring her."

(I catch the subtle hint but going with the flow)

"Yeah we'll have to do just that, now what's good on the menu because my adrenaline was pumping so hard it had me starving (chuckling out loud)?

"Man this is one of our favorite restaurants and we come here at least twice a month sometimes more, and we've tried everything on the menu and I can honestly say that there's nothing on the menu that we don't like."

"Hmm well I've always wanted to try oysters on the half shell?"

"Ok that's one of our favorites, now I will say this they are an aphrodisiac so be careful (Kim and I look at one another and just smile as if to say we don't need an aphrodisiac), but I'll have an order come out and you try it and let me know what you think."

A few minutes later, we have the appetizers come and we eat the oysters, and to my surprise, they are very good. We have another order of them and then have our meal. Where I order a full lobster tail with twice-baked cheddar sour crème potato, and a house salad with Ranch and French dressing, Kim orders bake tilapia with rice pilaf and a Cesar salad while Edwin orders an 18 ounce Porterhouse steak with all the trimmings and Sheila orders Filet mignon with a baked sweet potato and a salad. After dinner is over and we have had laughs and drinks, Edwin asks if we were ready for some dancing. I tell him yes we are and he gets the check and we head for the door. Outside the air is nice and crisp, not too cool but just with a hint of chill on it to where it allows you to breathe in easy.

"Are we off to the Lux Lounge (I ask Edwin)?"

"Yes we are, this is one of the newest, hip, elegant spots in DC and what I like about it the most besides the different levels of music. You have to be dressed nicely to be admitted in, they don't allow any gear that would bring unwanted attention there. They have one of the top security companies in the place so you and your lady will feel secure. They have different things going on each night so you cannot say you will be bored going to it. I think you're going to like it very much. Oh and one more thing, I know the owner very well and I told him I have a friend coming in from Chicago who loves house music and steppin' so he told me he has one level hooked up for the night with just that type of music."

"Ok just when I thought you couldn't impress me anymore you go and do this, yeah I'm ready to do some damage on a floor so let's go."

Kim and I enter into the car and Willie drives us to the lounge. I must say it was truly a beautiful sight to see. It had white pillars on the outside with a white 3D image of the name over the entrance. As we entered, I was just amazed at the décor. The wood flooring was immaculate, and it shined so bright you could almost see yourself in it. It had several bars so you wouldn't wait to long for your drink order. The spacing in the lounge was just right. Too often you go to a place and it's too crowded and you can't move which can make for a very frustrating night. We walked around the place for a bit just to take it all in. I noticed that Kim was holding onto me kind of tight, as if she was marking her territory. I didn't mind at all because in my own way I was marking mine. Yeah I knew dudes were jocking but I didn't care because Kim was one of the most gorgeous women there. The music was nice and I notice that although there were different areas of music none of the rooms were overpowering and you could enjoy the music you wanted without interference. As we made our way to the level where Edwin had the owner set up a night of House and Step for Kim and I. I couldn't help but see that it was roped off, I thought to myself ok what's going on and what has Edwin done this time. There was a security guard at the entrance and he stopped us from entering (at first, before Edwin spoke).

"Excuse me but my name is Edwin Meade and I believe this is our room for the evening."

"I'm sorry sir but I will need to see some identification (the security guard asks)."

"No Problem" as Edwin shows him his ID.

"Thank you sir and welcome to the Lux, my boss will be with you shortly, he said to make sure you and your guest are comfortable. The bar is fully stocked and you have open access to it, please enjoy your stay."

"Thank you sir I believe we will."

"Uhm Edwin, did he say that we have "open access" to the bar?"

"Yes he did!"

"Well where I'm from that means the drinks are on the house?"

"Very perceptive my friend, I told you I'm going to show you a wonderful time and I don't want you to go back to Chicago saying you didn't have a good time here in my chocolate city."

"Well I'll be honest with you, even without the dinner and now dancing I still have had a great time here in your city. This just puts icing on the cake that's all."

"Well my friend I'm glad you feel that way because I want this to not be the last time you come here."

"Oh, trust me I know it won't be."

The ladies excuse themselves to go to the rest room and this gives Edwin and I a chance to really talk a bit. I want to know how long he had in his mind that he was going to work with me.

"Ok so tell me, just when did you make your decision to go with my magazine?"

"You wanna know the truth?"

"Uh yeah that's why I asked (chuckling giving him a dumb look)."

"Well, I've seen a few of your publications and then when we ran into one another at the expo in Chicago you had this vibe that I liked. I knew from doing some research that you took care of your clients and that you didn't allow a lot of BS into your magazine and you don't print anything that is not true in that you have not done your homework on first."

"Wow impressive I must say and yes you are correct, I do, do my homework and make sure that everything I put in my magazine is the truth, after all that's what my readers have come to be accustomed too and they deserve at least that."

"So now you know."

"Yeah I do, but I guess I am more so wondering why you didn't say something sooner?"

"Like I said I wanted to get you out here and see you in a different atmosphere other than work and see if the vibe I was feeling was right on the money and my friend I can say it is."

"One thing I've always said and live by is that I'm real all the time and I don't fake for no one, either take me as I am or leave me alone because everyone is not for everybody."

"You're so correct there, hey let's get a drink, what will you have?"

"Hmm let's see I'm feeling like a brandy night tonight, so let's start there."

"Cool my kind of guy, I love me some brandy and they have the best here, Cognac."

"Now that's what I'm talking about!"

As we get our drinks, the ladies' reappear looking at us as if we started the party without them.

"Uhm hhmm" both Sheila and Kim clear their throats as if they are parched. Edwin and I laugh a little because we already had their glasses ready but they didn't know it. Edwin leads in another toast.

"A toast to a wonderful night, a wonderful friendship, and a great working relationship."

"Oh, and to the future, no matter what it brings or where it takes us as long as we're happy and keeping it real."

Everyone one chimes in "Here here!"

After sipping on the Cognac, we sit down for just a bit and take in the freshness of the room and the place. I can tell that Edwin has really outdone himself with everything from the town car to the suite, to the dinner and now the Lounge, again I think how lucky and blessed I am after all the hard work and sacrifice that went into my magazine. I think to myself that this is truly paying off. I couldn't help but think of Brenda and wish she could be here with me, but I knew she was spiritually there all the way. I must have drifted off into la la land because Kim nudged me kind of hard and I snapped out of it.

"Baby are you ok, Kim asks me?"

"Yes baby I am, I was just reflecting on things, I tend to get caught up sometimes in my own thoughts and find myself somewhere else in my mind."

"Well I could tell that you were somewhere else because I called your name a couple times wanting to dance."

"I'm sorry sweetie, sure I'd love to dance, now you can step right?"

"Oh boy please (she says joyfully) I will dance circles around you."

"Is that right?"

"Yes that's right, what you don't believe me, well let's get on the floor."

"Lead the way pretty lady, ok y'all watch and see how it's done in the Chi."

Edwin and Sheila looked on as Kim and I took to the floor. I allowed Kim to "think" she had me on the floor just for a little while. I'll admit that she moves like an exotic dancer, her hips were speaking another language and I couldn't help but notice how she me mesmerized with her body language. As we turned and dipped I decided to show her how I really get down. I turned her with my right hand and then released her only to catch her with my left hand. I spun her around and just when she was about to face me I dipped myself, and spun around three times, and came back up and caught her in rhythm, which put a smile on her face and I could tell she was thoroughly impressed.

"Wow, that was very nice Marcus, I must say."

"Why thank you my lady, I told you that you can't touch me out here, although I will say I may have underestimated you just a tad bit because you are a wonderful dancer and your body is talking to me right now."

"Hmm is it now, well what is she saying to you?"

"She's saying to me that she can't wait to leave and get back to my suite and finish this night out."

"Very perceptive Mr. Bass and although I am enjoying myself tremendously I will love it when we're alone and I can spend some good time with you, just the two of us."

"Yes I can't wait either."

As we were exiting the dance floor, I noticed Edwin talking to a gentleman. I figured that he must have been the owner because no one else was in this room but us and the security guard wouldn't let anyone else in. Kim and I came to the table and Edwin introduced us.

"Marcus I want you to meet Charles Browin the owner of Lux."

"Nice to meet you sir and let me express what a wonderful place."

"Thank you very much, I am very proud of this one, we just opened it not long ago and have three other locations, one in Philadelphia, Delaware and Atlanta. We are looking to expand elsewhere like Chicago, New York and LA but have not found the right place for it just yet. Also, we need to have some backing in those areas as well but don't know anyone there as of yet."

"Well now you know one person in Chicago and I have always wanted a nice place like this to go to in Chicago. Yes we have some of the best clubs but they tend to be a little on the young side. Also, the dress codes have truly laxed and I don't care for them anymore."

"Well Marcus while you're in town we should get together and talk about things, Edwin tells me you own your own magazine there in Chicago?"

"Yes I do it's called "Urban Couture" and I'm always looking to expanding its fan base, that is one reason for me being in D.C."

"Sounds good, I will have to check out your magazine and who knows we may be able to help one another out."

"Well funny you should say that, I have my presentation in the car and I always carry a couple of our best publications as well as our latest one with me just in case. I'm always in network mode, before we leave I will make sure you get a copy of it."

"Sounds real good, well I'm going to let you enjoy your evening and I look forward to talking with you before you leave D.C."

"I'm looking forward to it too."

"Nice meeting you Marcus, Edwin it's always a pleasure, and ladies enjoy your evening."

"We will thank you."

Charles leaves to tend to other business around the Lounge. I look at Marcus with this I can't believe what just took place look, and he looks back at me with this it's just business look on his face.

"Ok man what's up for real?" I ask Edwin.

"I told you before I want to get you out here but what I didn't tell you was that I wanted you out here for than just my business. Just think if he comes to Chicago with a Lux Lounge you could write about it and give it pub and be an intricate part in making it hot."

"Yeah that would be nice to have something like this there, also I'd want to talk to him about playing music from time to time."

"Don't tell me you DJ too?"

Laughing "Yeah I've done it in the past and I still have my equipment and keep up with all the latest music. I just haven't found the right venue to try and get back into it on a part time basis. Music is my release and I can express myself through it, so yeah this could be an opportunity to do that in."

"Well I'll be damn look how God works; you came here for one thing and have the possibilities of another."

"Yeah look at how God's working (also thinking of Kim too), well I think we're going to call it a night."

"Oh man come on it's only 11:30pm."

"Yeah I know but we want to spend some time together that's all and besides we're both a little tired from the flight and being up all day too."

"Yeah plane ride my ass, I know what you're going to do but hey if I had a lady on my arm like that I'd be thinking the same thing."

"Uhm you do have a lady like that on your arm dude" I interject.

Edwin laughing "Man you know what I mean."

"Yeah I do, so we're going to get out of here and enjoy the rest of our night. Sheila it is truly a pleasure meeting you and I hope we all see one another again real soon."

"It is a pleasure and Kim I enjoyed meeting you too and thanks for the information about your firm, I'll be in touch."

"Thank you girl and the pleasure is mine as well, talk to you soon."

"Oh, Marcus before you leave don't forget to give Charles your info and the magazine so you two can meet up."

"Oh, I'm in top of it don't worry, I rarely miss an opportunity for new business, I'll be in touch with you tomorrow."

"Ok bruh, have a good night."

"Oh, I plan on it, good night you two"

As Kim and I leave our private room, I run into the owner and ask him if he would be able to follow me to my car to get him the information he requested. He said he was able to and we left out to go to my car. As we got there I opened the door for Kim to get in and pulled out my portfolio. I handed Mr. Browin a couple magazines I had as well as my business portfolio. I could tell he was already impressed with the layout of the hard work that my staff puts into it. He then asked me when I was leaving DC. I told him that I was supposed to leave Friday morning but Edwin changed my plans so I'll be here through the weekend. He was happy about that and wanted to set up a time to meet with me while I'm here. I said that will be fine and we parted ways for now. As I entered the town car and sat back in my seat, Kim curled up into me again and it felt so good. It's been a long time since I've allowed another woman to be this close to me for any length of time. I didn't know what was happening or going to happen but I wanted to just go with the flow of things for once in a long while. Willie drove us back to my hotel, we were all but ready to be alone where we can just enjoy one another.

"Here we are sir, I mean Marcus."

"It's ok Willie I know it's an occupational hazard."

"What can I say, I try to keep it professional at all times."

"And you do a wonderful job."

We exited the car I turned to him and gave him a two C-notes and he looked at it as if to have never seen one before let alone two.

"What's this for Marcus?"

"Hey, I take care of people who take care of me and today you took great care of me so I like to return the blessing."

"Thank you very much, and what time shall I pick you up for the airport?"

"Well now that plan has changed, I am not leaving until Sunday now, Edwin wants to meet up for a couple things and I met the owner of Lux and he wants to meet up before I leave to discuss a possible business venture."

"Sounds great, well I guess I will see you on Sunday then."

"Oh see that's where you're wrong my friend, I asked Edwin to make sure I have you for the entire weekend so you can show me around and if need be take my baby around while I conduct business." Kim standing in ear shot heard what I had said to Willie and all she could do is smile.

"Sounds great to me, I look forward to it."

"Ok good so go home and get some rest and I'll call you in the morning when we're ready to get up and get out, cool?"

"Cool by me, well goodnight Marcus and again it's been a true pleasure meeting you."

"Willie the pleasure is all mines."

Willie and I shook hands and I turned to face Kim, she was standing there looking so wonderful. All I could say to myself was this was a great day and looks to be a great ending to an already great day.

"Are you ready to go Ms. Johnson?"

"Indeed I am Mr. Bass."

"Well let's go then" As I took her arm in mine we entered the hotel lobby and walked towards the elevator doors. All I could think was that this is a dream and I'm going to wake up from it. As I pushed the button for the elevator door to open, it was as if she could read my mind because she turned to me and said.

"This must be a dream."

"Wow you were you reading my mind?"

"Why would you say that."

"Because I was just thinking of how this is a dream and I was going to wake up."

Kim laughing "Yeah I know what you mean, I mean Marcus I'll be honest with you, this has never happened to me and I almost don't know how to handle it. I mean being out to dinner with you and then to the Lounge is one thing but we're about to be alone and I feel like a schoolgirl being alone with a boy for the first time. Almost like I don't know what to do."

"Well I can understand where you're coming from and I will not do anything that you do not want to do, that's my word."

"Thank you Marcus that makes me feel so special."

The elevator door opens and we enter, she leans into me and I place my arm around her. It seemed as though the elevator took an eternity to get to my floor but it finally opened on the 20th floor. We exit the elevator and walk to my suite which was at the end of the hallway. I reach for my room key and was about to put it in the door when I turned to Kim.

"Give me your word that no matter what happens tonight, there will be no regrets and this will not be the last time we see one another."

"Deal!"

"No Kim give me your word."

Kim looking me straight in the eye "Ok Marcus I give you my word."

I reach and pull Kim's chin up so our lips could meet and give her a nice, soft, brief kiss on the lips. I turn, put the key in the door and we enter.

9

Marcus & Kim "Best Night of Our Lives"

We enter the room, the smell of a fragrance I picked up called "butt naked" exuded throughout the room. I chuckled at the thought of the fragrance because that is exactly what I intended to do, get but naked. But I didn't want to rush anything, so I took my time with Kim and as Keith Sweat said in his song I wanted make this night "Last forever". Also, I had a cd of a jazz blend I made which helps me relax after a long hard day. I go to the CD player and put it in and press play.

"Mmmm I love the fragrance, what is it?"

"You're not gonna believe me when I tell you what it is."

"Try me?"

"It's called "Butt Naked", I know, I know, I didn't buy it for the name I actually love the smell."

Kim laughing, "I believe you but it is sort of ironic right about now isn't it."

"That it is, would you like it if I helped you get a bit more comfortable?"

"Mmmm and just what do you have in mind Mr. Bass?"

"Well close your eyes and I'll show you. I want to take you on a ride of full ecstasy to which you never want to return from."

"I have a confession…no one has ever been able to do that…are you sure you can help me reach that height?"

"Most definitely and after tonight if I have my way it will only get better."

"Mmmm please don't tease me like that" Kim moans softly.

"Oh baby, trust me, teasing you is the last thing I'm about to do."

I go to Kim and take her by her hand, I lead her to the center of the room. I ask her to stand very still as I prepare her flight. She looks at me with a bewildered look, not knowing what I had in store for her. I tell her to close her eyes and just let the music and fragrance sooth her mental thoughts. She obliges me telling me she feels at ease in my hands. Although I don't want to leave her presence in any way I go to the front closet to retrieve the overnight bag she brought with her that she thought I did not see. I take it and enter into the bathroom where I start running water in the Jacuzzi bathtub. I put bath oil and bubble bath in the water allowing it to simmer through the water. I come back to Kim as she stands there looking rather nervous as to what I'm preparing.

"Are you ok my love?"

"Yes, but I must admit I'm a little nervous… is that water I hear?" hearing the water running in the Jacuzzi tub.

"Yes it is, I am preparing our bath…I want to fulfill your fantasy and try my best to do what no other man has done or ever will do."

"Well, you don't have a tall order to fill because I've not had that many men to do anything such as this."

"Well, let me be your tour guide to the land called fantasy."

"Be gentle with me Marcus."

"Ms. Kimberly Johnson, you are in the best of hands."

I take Kim and bring her closer to me, so close she feel my breath on her skin, I begin undressing her. First with her blazer, I take it off and place it on the desk chair, then slowly take her hands and raise them above her head, slowly lifting her blouse above her head, shoulders and hands I place it on the chair with the blazer…..I can tell she's feeling a little skittish….as she said she feels like a school girl. I get on one knee and I ask her to put her hands on my shoulders for balance as I take off her stiletto heels. She complies and I one by one remove her heels from her feet. I then unbutton her slacks and slowly lower her pants down towards her ankles carefully taking each leg out one at a time. I place the pants on the chair along with the blazer and blouse. I whisper:

"Are you ok my love?"

"Yes…but…damn, you are driving me crazy….all I want to do is jump into you right now."

"Trust me my love all good things come in time and patience."

"I trust you Marcus, I trust you."

"Good!"

As I continue, I surprise her by unsnapping her bra with one hand and she chuckles.

"Pro at this are we?"

"I've had some practice over my lifetime."

I continue with the removal of her bra and I am standing in amazement at the sheer beauty of her body and almost catch myself staring too hard. But I catch my composure and remove her panty hose as well as her laced boy cut panties. All the while undressing her to her surprise I undress myself as well. I come to her and take her hands in mine and place them around my neck as I place my hands around her waist. I pull her closer to me as I gently begin kissing her lips. Before we get too caught up in the moment I lead Kim to the Jacuzzi where I've placed candles around for just enough lighting. I help Kim enter the warm soothing water and as I sit down I help lower her into the water and back into my chest. We sit there for what seems to be an eternity.

"Mmmm I can do this forever."

"Sshhhhh, don't speak, let your thoughts take you away."

"They already have Marcus."

"That's what I like to hear."

After moments of soaking, and enjoying one another, I take Kim and bathe her. I then help her out of the Jacuzzi and dry her off gently. I then lead her to the bedroom where I have warm massage oil waiting. I lay her down on her stomach and begin to give her a full body massage. She moans in delight as my strong, firm, yet gentle hands caress and stroke every inch of her body. Just when she thinks that the night could not get any better I turn her over and slide between her thick, well-shaped, and very well-toned legs. I ease up to her resting on my arms and tell her that WE are going to make love with each other, but first I must have desert. I begin kissing her from the top of her head lowering myself towards her love box. I continue to her neck then to her supple breast where her mounds rise with delight and her nipples stand erect waiting for some undivided attention, so I oblige them. As I continue tracing her beautiful body and finding my way towards her pierced belly button I play with it with my pierced tongue just for a moment. Moving lower towards the center of her melting pot I gently kiss and spread her legs, I kiss her inner thighs and move up towards her love box. I hear Kim moan in delight as she is truly enjoying the pleasure I am providing. I begin tasting the sweet nectar of her and the more I gyrate my tongue, twirling it around and around Kim moans more and more. She gets to a point of explosion, just when she can't take anymore I move my body up onto hers. As I move over onto her gently as I can, she feels my manhood throbbing, she continues to rise in sheer delight, she arches her back to prepare to receive me. I enter her soft, wet, warm love box and she lets out a gasp as if she's been waiting all her life for this moment. As we begin to move in a rhythm only a maestro who conducts a beautiful and harmonious symphony can enjoy, we find ourselves having an out of body experience, with what seems as seconds passing by and time almost stand still it happens, we explode into the most orgasmic ecstasy only few could ever dream of. After what is the most wonderful and explosive moments either of us have had I pull Kim into me and hold her close, I gently kiss Kim on her forehead and tell her I can stay here forever and she agrees as we fall blissfully off to sleep in each other's arms not muttering another sound.

CHAPTER

10

Marcus "Braden past comes back to haunt him"

Sleeping peacefully without a care in the world, I am startled by my phone ringing at an ungodly hour of the morning. I was very hesitant to answer because it was a number I did not recognize. Remembering the last times an unknown number called me; I instantly began to wonder what's wrong and is Ma and Jazz ok. The last time I got a phone call like this my Brenda had been in a bad accident and was severely hurt, only soon to be taken away from me but little did I know this was not about me but something that will turn lives upside down. As I answered the phone and heard the woman's voice an uneasiness came over my stomach

"Hello?"

"Is this Marcus?" A woman asks.

"Yes this is Marcus, who is this?"

"It's Kandi!"

"Kandi, Kandi Evans, Braden's Ex Kandi?" knowing now who it is, the uneasy feeling in the pit of his stomach gets worse.

 "Wow you had to say it like that huh?"

"I'm sorry but I wanted to make sure I'm talking to the right person. You do know what time it is right, so I have to get my bearings; wow it's been years?" (As I sit up in bed).

"I know almost 20 to be exact."

"Yeah I know, it's good to hear your voice, how have you been and how did you ever find me?"

"I've been good for the most part and I am a fan of your work first of all and I called your office and told your secretary who I was and that it was an emergency that I get in touch with you, How have you been Marcus?"

"I've been blessed, Kandi, I've wanted to say this for a long time and I don't mean to dredge up the past but I am truly sorry about that day and the role I played in it."

"Marcus, funny you should bring that up because that's part of the reason why I called. I forgive you now and forgave you then. It wasn't your fault; you were just being a friend and a loyal one at that. I know Braden put you and the rest of the guys in an awkward position and you did what you thought was best."

"True and I'm glad you see it that way because that's how it was, hell it didn't happen to me and I've regretted it my damn self. Funny thing is Braden and I were talking about you not long ago and we spoke of that day. He said that he truly made a huge mistake and all he wanted to do was apologize to you, but he knew you wouldn't talk to him."

"Marcus at that time I didn't want to speak to him or anyone who knew him. I truly hated him at that time but I have moved on and grown from it, I've gotten married and traveled the world."

"Wow that's good to hear, and it seems as though you're very happy, so I have to ask what's up with the phone call at (looking at the clock) six in the morning (looking over at Kim sleeping soundly)."

"Well (Kandi pausing)…I have something to tell you."

"Uh oh, uhm I am not the father (trying to make light of the uneasy tone of the conversation), I'm sorry ok I'm listening."

"You always did have jokes Marcus but it's kinda funny how you said that and this is not easy to say so bear with me for a moment."

"Ok cool, no worries, what's up K?"

Kandi laughing "I always thought it funny and cute how you called everyone by the first Letter of their name and I see you still do it."

"Yeah I guess old habits die hard, but for real, why you prolonging this?"

"I am huh, well, here goes. On that Saturday back then when all that mess happened and you took me home?"

"Yeah boy what a day, I remember it all too well, wished it never happened, but what about it."

"Well, Braden had his news to tell me right, I mean about his decision to be with another woman, well he wasn't the only one who had big news to share as well."

"Uhm Kandi, you're making me nervous, what are you talking about?"

"I'm talking about the news I was going to tell him.........Marcus... .....I...I...I was pregnant then!"

"WHAT! (I yell quickly and then turn to make sure I didn't wake Kim)...and of course you never told him otherwise I'd had known." (I go back to a whispering voice)

"I know, I know and I feel bad about it, I had just found out myself and I was going to tell him but I was so hurt at the time that all I could think about was getting as far away from him and as fast as I could. I didn't want to see him anymore because of the way he hurt me."

"Damn so what happened, I mean did you keep the baby or............?"

"Yeah I kept it, I mean him, Braden, his name is Braden, Braden Withers II to be exact."

I get up and walking towards the window in sheer shock.

"Oh wooooooooow, are you for real, Braden has a son? Damn!!! So, what made you call and tell me this now after all this time and why not call him?"

"I know it's been a long time and I honestly didn't plan on telling him anything but I'm faced with a dilemma and he needs to know he has a son."

"Why Kandi, why now after all this time you decide to tell him now, I mean it's been almost 20 years and out of the blue you call me and drop this bombshell on me. What could be the reason now instead of just living out the rest of your life with the secret and again why call me, why not call Braden?"

"Marcus, please don't be mad at me, but I don't have his contact information anymore, so I don't know how to get a hold of him and you said if I needed anything to call you remember?"

Remembering that fateful day when I told Kandi those words.

"Yes I remember Kandi, I remember all too well, that was one of the worst days of my life and it wasn't even about me."

"Well the reason why I'm contacting you now is because (as Kandi starts to cry)."

"Kandi, come on now, what's wrong, why the tears."

"Marcus, this is so hard, my son, our son has Leukemia and could die from it. The doctors say that he needs a bone marrow transplant and for some reason my blood type won't work. So, they asked me about his father and I told them that he's not a part of his life. They said to reach out to him so they can do some testing to see if he's a match to help Braden out, besides I think it's time he knew his father."

"OH WOOOOWWW, Kandi...I'm sorry but you wait this long before telling someone?"

"I know, I know, I mean I hate myself for it, I thought I'd punish Braden for what he did to me and never tell him about his son but now I know that wasn't a good idea."

"Kandi...damn, so what's going on now, what do you need me to do?"

"After that day, I threw away everything that reminded me of Braden and I didn't want anything else to do with him."

"Uhm but you were pregnant and you kept him, AND you named him after Braden so I would say you didn't throw everything away and besides that's a helluva reminder of Braden don't you think?"

"Yeah I know and honestly I thought about aborting him but I'm glad I didn't because he's the most precious thing that has ever happened to me."

"Ok, ok, ok, I'm trying to wrap my head around this whole thing. So you need to get in touch with Braden and tell him right?"

"Yes, well, that's the reason why I am calling you, I was wondering if you could talk to him for me and after that then maybe we could talk. I mean it's been so long I don't know how he would react to this. I mean I know he has other kids and he loves them a lot and I'm a little scared to talk to him right now for fear of rejection."

"Fear of rejection, really Kandi, I'm sorry but I really don't mean to sound so sarcastic but?"

"Yes, but not for me, I don't care about me, but for Braden Jr. I don't want him to reject his son."

"Kandi, I'm going to ask you something and please don't take offense to it, but are you sure he's Braden's?"

"Yes Marcus I'm sure, I mean I know this is a bombshell and it's been a long time."

"Yes it is and has."

"But I'm telling the truth, besides they would have to do a DNA test anyway to make sure his blood is a good match anyway."

"Oh wow, I feel like I'm on a Maury Povich show for real right now. All I can see going through my head is "you are not the father", but I will talk to him and try my best to smooth the road for you the best way I can, but I'm not making any promises. It won't be easy, and I don't know how he will react to this news, especially since it isn't on the best of terms with your son, but all I can do is talk to him, no promises."

"Thank you Marcus, that's all I can ask for, and I'm truly sorry for putting you in the middle of this but I didn't know who else to call."

"Yeah I know, that's the story of my life it seems, for some reason everyone seems to find it easy to call and talk to me and tell me their life's story so to speak" chuckling trying to make light of the situation.

"Well I know why, it's because you are a caring person and you have that charisma that makes it easy for people to just open up to you, that's one thing I noticed about you all those years ago. That's why I was more comfortable opening up to you then and I still feel the same way now. It's like you're A Brother's Keeper."

"Gee thanks I appreciate it but it still don't make my job any easier, but I'll do it. Is this a good number to get in touch with you on?"

"Yes this is my cell, so please lock it in and call me when you talk to him and let me know as soon as possible ok?"

"Ok, I will, and Kandi?"

"Yes!"

"Don't be a stranger from here on out, no matter what happens ok, things like this shouldn't keep you away?"

"Ok, I won't… and Marcus…thank you."

"You're welcome; I'll talk to you soon."

"Bye Marcus."

"Bye Kandi."

I hang up from speaking with Kandi and just stare out into the morning. The cloudiness and rain don't help with the news that was just laid on me. All I could think was wow Braden has a son he don't know about who's in bad shape. Why me, why do I have to be the one to carry burdens of others, I don't get it, but it seems as though everyone else knows but me. I continue staring out into nothingness when I hear Kim's voice and not realizing she's standing right behind me, it startles me a bit.

"Baby is everything ok?"

"Whoa, you scared me a bit."

"Sorry honey, I didn't mean too" as Kim wraps her arms around me.

"It's alright…to be honest…no I'm not ok…but I will be in time."

"What's wrong baby…would you care to talk about it?"

"Well I don't know how much of the phone call you heard but it was someone from my past."

"Really, well I wasn't' trying to listen but yes I did hear part of it. I just woke up and realized you weren't there, that's when I saw you over at the window…baby…may I ask who it was?"

"It was a woman that one of my best friends "Braden" used to date and I haven't spoken to her since I dropped her off almost 20 years ago"

"Wow that long ago…baby why now…why did she contact you out of the blue now?"

"Are you sure you want to hear this story, I mean we just met and I don't want to burden you with my situations" Kim taking my hand and caressing it, trying to reassure me and give me some sort of comfort.

"Baby I know we just met but if you allow me too, I'll be here for you for the rest of your life and I mean it, I'm not going anywhere."

"Oookkk…I think you need to sit down because what I have to tell you…once you hear it…you may faint from the shock."

Kim walks over and sits on the bed. I sit beside her and begin telling her the entire story of what happened 20 years ago up until this phone call. As I tell Kim the story of how one day, one decision altered the lives of all of us and changed history as we know it. She sits there with her mouth wide open the whole time in disbelief. As I tell her the story I find myself drifting back into the past.….reliving the entire story all over again.

CHAPTER

11

Braden "The Break-up"

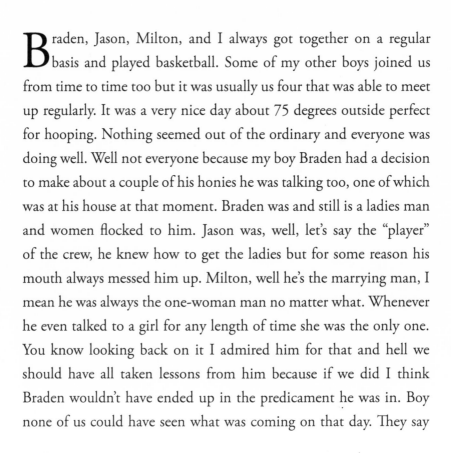

Braden, Jason, Milton, and I always got together on a regular basis and played basketball. Some of my other boys joined us from time to time too but it was usually us four that was able to meet up regularly. It was a very nice day about 75 degrees outside perfect for hooping. Nothing seemed out of the ordinary and everyone was doing well. Well not everyone because my boy Braden had a decision to make about a couple of his honies he was talking too, one of which was at his house at that moment. Braden was and still is a ladies man and women flocked to him. Jason was, well, let's say the "player" of the crew, he knew how to get the ladies but for some reason his mouth always messed him up. Milton, well he's the marrying man, I mean he was always the one-woman man no matter what. Whenever he even talked to a girl for any length of time she was the only one. You know looking back on it I admired him for that and hell we should have all taken lessons from him because if we did I think Braden wouldn't have ended up in the predicament he was in. Boy none of us could have seen what was coming on that day. They say that fireworks don't always happen in July. Right!!!

"Hello?"

"Yo B, we hoopin today?" I asked Braden.

"Yeah man I was waiting on Milton and Jason to get back with me on the time, hold on that's Milton on the other line now."

Braden clicks over and takes the call...................

"I'm back, yeah Milton said we are hoopin at 2."

"Cool that will give me just enough time to get my run in and get something to eat."

"Marcus can I talk to you about something?"

"Yeah man you know it, what's up?"

"Kandi is here and you know what we talked about before right?"

"Yeah I remember so have you decided to tell her this weekend that you are not going to be with her and that you chose another woman over her? Man are you sure you're doing the right thing?"

"Honestly I don't know if I am doing the right thing or not. I mean I care for her but I think I care for Gabrielle more, that's why I wrote the letter to her to explain how I feel. Dude this shit is hard."

"Tell me about it, but you know I'm your boy and I got your back, hell we all do, no matter what but you have to make a decision because you have two wonderful women who both have fallen for you."

"Yeah I know y'all do, y'all always had my back and I'm glad too but.........(sighs)........yeah I know and that's what sucks the most."

"Hey where's Kandi anyway?"

"She went to the store with Katrina, that's why I'm able to talk to you about it right now."

"Oh ok, well you better tell her and soon bro before something blows up in your face."

"Yeah I know and I think when I take Kandi home on Sunday I'll sit down with her and tell her that way she's at her house and not here and I don't run the risk of anything getting destroyed."

"Man I'm shaking my head right now, are you serious right now, you're more worried about your stuff being broken than breaking the heart of a woman who loves you.........man that's on the cold side."

"I know but what am I to do?"

"Tell her B, tell her, she deserves the truth and not to be prolonged anymore."

"You're right, as always, man good to know you look out for a brotha."

"You know I'm here my brotha."

"My brother's Keeper, yeah you are that."

Later on as Milton, Jason, Braden, and I were on the basketball court around the corner from Braden's house hoopin' it up; Katrina, Jason's girl, comes over wanting to speak to him. We take a break and sit on the court cracking jokes on each other's game as they spoke to one another.

"What's up Katrina?"

"You're not gonna believe this, Kandi found a letter that Braden wrote to some woman named Gabriell telling her how he loves her and wants to be with her and other stuff, she's pissed off and ready to explode. I think y'all need to get home right now."

"Oh shit! Are you serious… wait, you're telling me she found a letter, what letter and why was she going through his stuff anyway?"

"She said she was looking for something to right on when she found it, and of course read it."

"Yeah right she was just being nosy that's all, man I tell you y'all women sometimes."

"Hey, don't put that off on all women, I don't do that stuff."

"Uhm…remember…I caught you going through my drawers too and you gave me some bullshit excuse about looking for something so don't even try it."

"Ok, ok that was one time and I haven't done it since."

"So, what is she doing now?"

"When I left she was sitting on the couch crying and tearing up pictures that she found of him and her together."

"Oh, wow damn, ok let me tell Braden so he can get home" Jason smirking to Katrina.

As Katrina walks away, Jason turns around with that squeamish grin he has when he knows he has the goods on someone and can't wait to spill the beans.

"What's up Jason, what did Katrina want" Braden speaking to Jason.

"Maaaaaaaan you better get home."

"Why what's up man?"

"Dude Kandi found a letter that you wrote to Gabriell."

"OH SHIT!!!!!" Braden jumps up off the concrete.

"Dude what letter?" Milton and I asked in unison.

"It's a letter I wrote to Gabriell telling her that I want to be with her and no one else."

"Dude I told you to tell her before something like this was going to happen, see I knew it?" I told Braden

"Marcus I don't need the I told you so speech right now, and besides I was going to tell her Sunday but I knew she wouldn't take it well so I was waiting for that right time to tell her."

"Man are you for real" Milton asks shaking his head "So what are you going to do now?"

"I don't know but I better get to the house. Y'all coming with me right just in case?"

"Yeah just in case she's destroying your house, I can't miss this" Jason laughing.

"Man forget you, I just want witnesses just in case she comes at me foul."

"Damn man, I'm speechless right now" I said.

"Yeah me too and I got butterflies in my stomach" Braden replied.

As we walk back towards the house, we try to figure out how Braden was going to handle this situation with Kandi. We each enter the house first Milton, then Jason, then me, then Braden. Before we knew anything Kandi come storming out of the kitchen, rushing past all of us damn near knocking us over and jumps into Braden's face.

"YOU BASTARD!!!... how are you going to do me like this. Who in the hell is Gabrielle and when was you going to tell me about her and the fact that you're in love with her?"

"Kandi, why were you going through my shit?" Braden trying to sound angry.

"I can't believe that you did this to me. Are you serious…after all we've been through…you go and confess your love for another bitch…so when were you going to tell me Braden…huh…when…?" Braden standing there frozen like a dear caught in the headlights of a car.

"Answer me you bastard!"

"I was going to tell you Sunday when I took you home but just didn't know how to."

"I can't believe this shit…how dare you did this to me?" Kandi begins to cry hysterically.

"All I can say is I'm sorry, but I didn't mean to hurt you, I really do care for you" Braden reaching out trying to hold Kandi and console her.

"Don't touch me you bastard", Kandi jerking away from Braden "I want to go home."

"Ok I'll take you home."

"NO, I don't want you taking me anywhere."

Kandi walking back into the kitchen where the rest of us were and we all jump when she comes in, turns to me, and asks me to take her home. At that moment Braden walks into the kitchen

I stand there with a dumbfounded look on my face because I don't know what to do and look over at Braden and he gives me the nod to take her home.

"Yeah I'll take you."

Kandi gathers here things and walks out the door. I follow shortly behind her and help her get into Braden's Camaro. Braden comes out to say something to Kandi but she jumps in and slams the door in his face and begins to cry. Braden comes over to my side of the car.

"Man get her home safe please" Braden said while looking directly at Kandi as if to think this is the last time he'll see her again.

"Yeah I got you…sigh…not trying to beat a dead horse but…man I warned you about this" I said as I put my hand on his shoulder.

"Yeah I know but I can't do anything about it now…damn bro…I wonder am I making the right decision or not?"

"Well my brotha, I don't know, but regardless, if you are or not…as it stands…it has to play out and we may never know. Look let me go and get her home so I can get back myself" Braden and I give each other a pound as I turn to get into the car. When I get into the car and start it up Braden continues to stand there. As I pull off I look into my rear-view mirror at Braden who is still standing in the middle of the street truly not realizing he made the biggest mistake of his life, one that he will soon regret. It's bad enough that the drive to Kandi's house, which was in Decatur IL, which was a long hour drive as it is but with a woman who was crying hysterically and me not knowing exactly what to say, was going to make it even longer. I thought about trying to comfort her and do what I can to somewhat ease her pain but I knew nothing I was going to say would help. But surprisingly she calmed down and spoke.

"Marcus, can I ask you a question?"

"Yeah sure."

"Do you know about this other woman?"

Feeling a little uneasy about this line of questioning and where it could possibly lead too, I answered anyway.

"Yeah I know about her."

"Does everyone know?"

Sigh…"unfortunately yes… everyone, well with the exception of Katrina of course."

"So why didn't someone tell me about this sooner?"

"Kandi look…the thing is…sigh…this was between you and Braden and I for one didn't feel as though it was my place to get in the middle of it."

"But you and Braden are boys and you were always around when I came over, so if you couldn't tell me why wouldn't you tell him to tell me before I found the letter?"

"Well actually I did tell him in a way, I told him that he will have to make a decision soon because he had two wonderful women and that they both were not going to hold out too much longer for him to make a decision as to whether or not he's going to be with one or the other."

"But what's wrong with me, why didn't he want to be with me?"

"Sweetie, that's a question only he can answer, to be honest with you I told him I think he should be with you but I can't make up his mind for him, all I know is you are a wonderful woman and I'm sorry that I was somewhat in the middle of it all."

"I feel like such a fool, I can't believe that he did this to me"

"Please don't because you are nothing like that"

Kandi goes silent again and that's how the rest of the ride goes…in silence. As I pull up to Kandi's house I notice that her look on her face has changed. It's almost as if she knows the future and that he (Braden) will regret that he made the wrong choice in this matter. I get out and open the car door and let Kandi out. She gives me a hug for what seems like the last time I'll see her again and says to me.

"I'm sorry for blaming you for part of this, I was just angry. You are a good friend and will always be my friend."

"Thank you very much and I'm sorry too for all of this. I wish it didn't have to happen but there's nothing we can change about it now. Take care and if you need anything just give me a call."

"You're right, there's nothing we can do to change it. Life goes on right? Well thank you for bringing me home, I truly appreciate it. Take care of yourself too and get home safe, bye." Kandi turns to walk up the drive only to take a few steps and turn around just before I was about to get into the car.

"Marcus?"

"Yes" As I am about to get into the car

"Stay the way you are and don't ever change ok?"

"I'll try!"

"Bye!"

Kandi turns and walks up the driveway of her beautiful two-story home and enters her house. She looks back one more time to notice I was waiting for her to get in the house. She waves to me as I pull out of her driveway to head home. I was thinking to myself that was the last time I was going to see her again. The drive home was kind of solemn and it made me think about a lot of things that has taken place and things going on in my own life. I usually drive with music playing but I couldn't seem to make myself listen to anything but my thoughts. I guess this was a lesson for all of us to learn; we just had to figure out what it meant for each one of us individually. As I pulled up in front of Braden's home I sat there for a few minutes to collect my thoughts. I wondered if I should even tell him about the conversation Kandi and I had or not. I mean I don't want to betray anything between him and I and I know he's going to ask me but I think it may be best not to say anything. Apparently he saw me pull up and not get out of the car so he came knocking on the window

"What's up B?"

"Man, that was crazy but how is she?"

"Really B…you're gonna ask how a woman is after breaking her heart?"

"You're right man and I'm not trying to sound insensitive but I just don't know what to say right now. Man, I really cared for her, hell still do and I hate that it happened this way but that don't mean I don't give a damn about her."

"I know man but seeing her like that and then the drive to take her home was worse."

"Did she say anything?"

"Nope, just cried all the way home" After everything that went down, the ride to her house, the strange vibe I got from Kandi, the long ride home with my own thoughts, after all that...I guess I made the decision not to tell...well in a way Braden made it for me he just didn't know it.

"Man, I really fucked up didn't I?"

"You're my boy and all but man to man...my opinion...yeah I think so but who knows it could all work out for the best. I mean you can go off with Gabrielle and be just has happy and live a full life I don't know. But what I do know is, I just dropped off a very hurt and brokenhearted woman and we may never know if she recovers from this."

"Damn!" Braden said letting out a deep sigh.

"Damn is right!" I said not knowing what else to say...hell what else could be said at that point.

After a few awkward moments of silence, I broke in and said, "Where is everyone?"

"After everything happened and you left with Kandi, Katrina was upset too because they are best friends. So, she told Jason to take her to his house and Milton had to leave to check on his mom so it was just me here thinking about everything. Man, she tore up every picture that we took together."

"Dude…Really…Can you blame her, I mean, come on what would you do if you were in her shoes. B it's time for all of us to take stock in our lives and get things together because I don't ever want to be caught up in the middle of something like that again."

"Yeah you're right…my bad. I didn't mean to drag you in the middle of this."

"I know but it is what it is, hey look I'm gonna head home and chill, I'll hit you later on to check on you."

"Thanks Marcus I appreciate it and thanks for being there when I need you.

"Hey what are brothers for right?"

"Right!"

"Peace!"

Braden and I give each other that manly handshake and hug and I turn to leave and go to my apartment which is only around the corner, thank God because I didn't feel like driving anywhere else. As I walked home though I couldn't get the last look on Kandi's face as I was leaving. There was something there but I couldn't put my finger on it…

I pause for a moment snapping back to the present in my mind. I look at Kim and she's still sitting there silent, mouth wide open, eyes bugged out from the shock of what she just heard.

"That's it, that's the whole story, lock, stock and barrel." I say to her.

"Wow what a story."

"Yeah tell me about it, the bad part is…it's all true."

"Yeah I see and honestly if someone else would have told me that I wouldn't have believed it. Ok so I know the story of the past but why did she contact you now after all this time."

"She just informed me that on the day I dropped her off she had a secret of her own. The secret was that she just found out she was pregnant and was going to tell Braden that weekend but then all hell broke loose so she decided not to tell him."

"Oh, damn that's truly messed up."

"Tell me about it."

"So again, why now…why call you of all people and tell you this?"

"Because I told her that I would always be her friend and so I guess she took me at my word and here we are and on top of it she drops a bombshell by telling me that her son is dying from leukemia and is need of a bone marrow transplant."

"Oh, wow Marcus, are you for real, I mean after all that has happened she comes to you now and lays this bomb on you?"

"Yeah…she does…amazing isn't it"

"Why now, why you and why not Braden, I mean I know you're a wonderful person I can already tell you are and a great listener but damn…this is a blow for real"

"I know baby, I know, I know…sigh…but I know what I have to

do…just don't know how to do it. I have to call Braden and tell him I need to talk to him as soon as I get home. I would tell him this over the phone but this is something best said in person. Besides I think it's best to be there when I tell him just in case he needs me. Damn this is going to be hard."

"Baby no matter what, I'm here with you and for you, I want you to know this ok?"

"Thank you baby, I appreciate it" I give Kim a kiss on the lips. "I gotta call B."

"Ok, well I'm gonna go ahead and start getting myself together, would you mind if I take a shower"

"Not at all…the only thing bad about that is I can't join you right now but it's ok, I have to do this and I'm gonna start getting some breakfast together, are you hungry?"

"Yes…breakfast does sound good right about now, yes please and thank you."

"Ok cool well you go ahead and get in the bathroom and I'll do what I gotta do out here"

I sat there in a daze, knowing I had to call Braden and inform him I had something to tell him but can't tell him what it is and why I can't tell him, damn this shit sucks. Oh well that's what friends are for and he's my boy so I gotta do what I gotta do, I just hope he understands why I have to do it this way.

CHAPTER

12

Braden "Reality hits home"

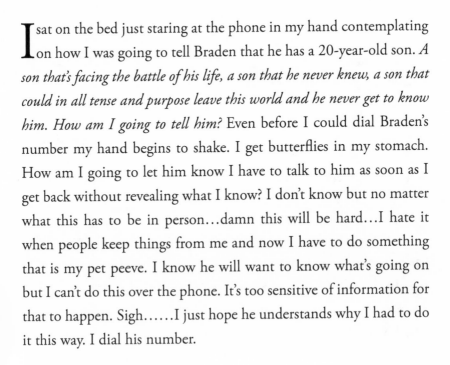

I sat on the bed just staring at the phone in my hand contemplating on how I was going to tell Braden that he has a 20-year-old son. *A son that's facing the battle of his life, a son that he never knew, a son that could in all tense and purpose leave this world and he never get to know him. How am I going to tell him?* Even before I could dial Braden's number my hand begins to shake. I get butterflies in my stomach. How am I going to let him know I have to talk to him as soon as I get back without revealing what I know? I don't know but no matter what this has to be in person…damn this will be hard…I hate it when people keep things from me and now I have to do something that is my pet peeve. I know he will want to know what's going on but I can't do this over the phone. It's too sensitive of information for that to happen. Sigh……I just hope he understands why I had to do it this way. I dial his number.

Braden answer's…

"What up dude, how's DC?"

"What up man, DC is great I'll have to tell you all about it another time."

"Cool, I can't wait to hear all about it...wait...man what's up why you calling this early in the morning?" Looking at the time and realizing it's early.

"B, I don't know how to even go into this, and I'm not going to do it over the phone but I just want you to know that as soon as I get back home we gotta talk face to face ok?"

"Yeah man, but what's going on, you sound like you seen a ghost."

"Well you can say that in a sense."

"Bruh you got me concerned right now, what's going on?"

"I'm not gonna tell you everything but I'll say this, remember who we were talking about the other day, talking about the women we regret not marrying and such?"

"Yeah you told me about Shandi and I told you about Kandi, why what's up?"

"Well let's just say one of our past has come back to the present."

"Wow you heard from Shandi, dude from the sound of her I'd love to meet her."

"No it's not Shandi."

"Nnnoooo...you bullshittin...are you for real" Braden sounding shocked.

"Very real."

"Kandi…Kandi called you?" Braden getting even more excited.

"Yeah she did." Trying to play things down.

"How did she sound…what did she want…wait… why now after what 20 years?"

"She sounds pretty good and that's what I need to talk to you about bro, but honestly I can't do it over the phone."

"Wow dude really, don't do me like this, what did she say and how is she, man I have so many questions, is she still mad at me, does she hate me, is she married, does she have kids, what man tell me what?"

"B, all I can say is this, what I have to tell you will change your outlook on life, but real talk I'll hit you when I get home so we can talk face to face. Believe me B this is nothing to speak of over the phone and you know I'd tell you if it were, just trust me ok?"

"Alright man, I trust you, so I'll be cool and wait, but I gotta know, how did she sound?"

"She sounded good, really good" trying to make light of what bomb has just been dropped on me.

"Cool, man I do miss her and would love to talk to her again."

"Really, so what would you do if she wanted to talk to you?"

"Does she man, really, does she want to talk" Braden sounding excited.

"Well yeah she does but I have to talk to you first."

"Why man, why do you have to talk to me first, what is she dying or something?" Braden trying hard to get me to talk about this but I know I can't, not over the phone.

"B, I'll talk to you when I get home that's my word, just make sure you're available no questions."

"Ok man I'll leave it alone, so you're flying back Friday right?"

"No, I had a change of plans and I'm coming back on Sunday."

"You mean to tell me I have to wait another three days in order for us to have a sit down? Man, that's not right."

"Sorry bro but things went extra well for me out here, in fact so well that I may have a couple business ventures to talk to you about but I have to meet with another guy first. Also, there's someone I met, that I want to introduce you too so you'll just have to wait." I said chuckling.

"You're cold man, cold…but it's cool, and congrats, I'm happy for you."

"Thanks man, but let me holla at you later, I gotta get up and get me something to eat."

"Ok, thanks for making me twist in the wind the entire weekend, appreciate it" Braden said laughing.

"Sorry man but I needed to hit you and let you know now so you won't be busy on Sunday."

"It's cool, but for real, thanks for letting me know about Kandi, man she's been on my mind hard lately and I can't figure out why."

Thinking now I know why but know I can't say anything just yet.

"Yeah I know man it's like that sometimes, when people are on your mind heavy all you want to do is reach out to them. Well maybe you'll get to do that one day soon."

"Yeah maybe, hey, have a good one and get at me as soon as you touch down."

"Ok Peace!"

"Peace!"

Braden and I get off the phone and I just sit on the bed holding the phone not knowing what's going to happen or how Braden is going to take this news. Life is funny sometimes, when you think everything is going well something comes along and knocks you for a loop and just the opposite, when you think nothing else could get worse all of a sudden your life makes a major turn and things look up for you. I guess that's what they call the circle of life right, life and death what a vicious circle to be in. Gotta get up and get us something to eat and make changes to flights and such, I have a busy day ahead of me.

CHAPTER

13

Jason "Speechless"

J ason's my guy and all but sometimes I wonder what head he thinks with. He always seems to get himself into trouble and it's usually with or over a woman. He just can't seem to keep the right head thinking straight. It seems as though every time I get a call from him it's always about some woman he done screwed over. I wish this dude would get his life together and maybe one day he will but that's a day we'll all want to see.

"Hello/"

"MARCUS..." he yelled into the phone and sounded as if he was crying.

"Jason...is that you?"

"Yeah it's me."

"Dude what's going on with you?"

"Man, you're not going to believe this, that, that, that bitch!"

"Dude what bitch are you talking about this time?"

"Man, this is no time for jokes, I can't believe that she did this to me, damn, I'm gonna kill her ass."

"Jason calm down first of all and tell me what's going on with you."

"Remember that chick I was messing with down the street?"

"Yeah, what's her name?" I was trying to think…sort of.

"Mercedes!"

"Oh yeah, I remember now, Mercedes, that's right because we used to tease you about her name being something of elegance but her attitude was more like a broke down Buick (laughing my ass off)"

"This ain't funny, I'm gonna kill this heifer."

"Ok, ok, ok my bad, but why are you talking about doing something that's gonna get you locked up for the rest of your life?"

"Simple, she broke into my apartment and took all of my court documents, my clippers, pictures, and my extra phone and put them all in a tub of water ruining them. Not to mention she took all of my cloths and poured bleach ALL OVER THEM. Man, I'm so pissed right now."

"Dude I told you to stop dealing with those ghetto hoe's especially the ones living down the block from you; that was never a smart idea on your part bro."

"I know you told me this but this is not a time for the "I told you so" speech, what am I gonna do, man she just messed things up for me right now. Oh, and on top of that she busted out my window last week when I was over Shontell's house."

"What…..ok, ok, ok are you sure she's the one who did it and how did you know it was her? By the way how did she know where Shontell lived anyway, didn't you tell me she lived across town on the South side and didn't have a car?"

"Yeah she does but apparently she had a friend help her and follow me there and that's when she did it."

"Ok but how do you know she is the one who did your car in?" remembering the day it happened because I had to go pick Jason's ass up

"SHE TOLD ME!"

"You don't have to yell at me, I'm not the one who's sleeping around with all kinds of women, making them believe that they are the only one, making them fall in love with your ass, promising them the world and having babies left and right."

"Hey man you don't have to bring up all of that, I love all my kids and am proud of every one of them."

"Dude you should be, Hell you have enough to start your own football team and have a bench. (Laughing hysterically now), how many is it 12, 13, what I lost count?"

"Dude it's 15 and I didn't call to talk about that"

"Damn 15, shit where did the other two come from."

"Remember Bridgette?"

"Oh damn I forgot about her, wait, wasn't she supposed to be a one nighter?"

"Yeah, well that one nighter turned into not one but twin 18 year old's (Jason rolling his eyes)."

"Oh damn man that sucks dude, so back to Mercedes, so what are you going to do? You know you can't afford to go to prison, you struggle enough as it is trying to take care of the mouths you have, what's gonna happen if you go to prison, then your kids will really be fucked?"

"Yeah I know, but man I'm so pissed right now I don't know what I'm gonna do."

"I hear ya, but you better think things through before you do something crazy, and from now on you better start wrapping things up before you have another one or worse contract something you can't get rid of or hell HIV and then what you gonna do."

"Marcus!...I really didn't call for all of this."

"Uhm, so why did you call because you know I'm gonna give it to you straight?"

"I just called to ask you if I could borrow a few bucks to get me some gear so I can go on this interview for the CTA on Monday?"

"You have an interview, what happened to your other job at the post office?"

"Not what, who?"

"Not again, man, are you serious?"

"Yeah man, right in the mail room, I couldn't help it, she was fine, but she was also my supervisor"

"Wait, hold up, you mean to tell me you got with your supervisor, and then what dumped her?"

"No, I didn't dump her, she wanted a relationship and I told her I couldn't"

(Shaking my head at the phone)

"Man, you will never learn will you, I don't know what I'm gonna do with you. But yeah you can borrow and I mean BORROW a few bucks to get you an outfit for your interview but it will have to wait until I get home from DC."

"DC, what's in DC?"

"I came out to close a deal for my magazine."

"Oh, ok cool, I forgot you were going out there, wait wasn't you supposed to come back tomorrow?"

"Yeah I was but plans changed bruh, and now I have an opportunity to not only do some advertising for another company out here but possibly become a partner in a club that will be coming to Chicago called LUX. It's off the chain and I met the owner while I was out last night and he wants to discuss bringing one to Chicago and I meet with him Saturday, so Kim and I are not flying back til' Sunday morning"

"Kim, who's Kim?" Jason not missing a beat.

"Man, this is my new baby."

"Ok you go all the way to DC to meet someone? You couldn't meet anyone here in Chicago?"

"Aaahh see that's where you're wrong, she does live in Chicago she came out here on business too."

"Oh wow, cool, so wait, you just met her and she's your baby? Come on man, is the loving that good?"

"Well to be honest, yeah it is but that's not the reason, I mean she's wonderful, we have a lot in common, she's fun, and loves to dance, and well it's more than I can put into words."

"Dude…are you saying you're in love with her?"

"I'm not saying that but I can say that for the first time in a long time I want to see where things go with her and I."

"That's cool, I'm happy for you, personally I got tired of seeing you mope around here looking like a lost puppy."

"See if I were there I'd kick your ass for that, you know how it's been for me, don't play."

"Yeah I do man but damn it's been what 10 years and you haven't dated anyone seriously since Brenda?"

"I know, I know, but there hasn't been anyone who I clicked with since Bren, not until now I mean. I don't know what's gonna happen, all I know is I'm happy right now, and she's a wonderful woman. So, I want to see where it goes. Hey man, I'm gonna have to let you go, I'm trying to cook breakfast for us."

"Mmmm Oh ok so you're pulling out all the stops huh, cooking breakfast, she must be fine for you to do that?"

"Well to answer your question yes she is fine, but that's not it and you know I'm not just into looks, she has to have a great head on her shoulders and must and I mean MUST be about her business."

"Yeah I know, you've always been picky, so I get you, go ahead and do your thang and let me know when you get back and again thanks man I appreciate it."

"No problem man, I can't let my boy go out like that so I got you when I get back, we'll go to the mall when I get home."

"Ooohh can we go to Evergreen Plaza?"

"Don't you mean Ever "black" Plaza, hell no, I'm not going to that ghetto ass place. Dude I'll take you to one of my spots where I get my suits."

"Man, your spots are too expensive, I can't afford them."

"That's why this is a loan and you can pay me back in small installments, look don't you want to look nice for your interview?"

"I guess, but man."

"Man nothing, you need this after all you've been through (trying not to laugh)"

"I hear you snickering and it's not funny."

"Shit the hell it ain't, you always get yourself into this mess and expect us (your boys) to get you out, uhm remember the court situation?"

"Yeah, yeah, yeah you don't have to remind me, hell I'm trying to forget."

"See that's all I'm trying to say, man you better straighten up for real, ok well I'm out, and I'll holla at you on Sunday."

"Peace!"

"Peace J!"

I hang up the phone and my head starts to spin from all the information that has hit me within the last couple hours. I think to myself God why did you give me this "whatever it is" where people come to me all the time. Sometimes I wonder who I can go to when I need someone to talk to or a shoulder to cry on hell anything. Sigh... oh well I guess that's just the way I'm made but I'm ok with it and I love helping people anyway so I guess I'm doing somewhat what I'm supposed to be doing. I continue making breakfast when Kim walks into the kitchen looking scrumptious herself.

"Mmmm Good morning again baby."

"Good morning beautiful did you have a nice shower?"

"Yes oh God yes I did, I have to get me one like that."

"Yeah I hear you, I'm already going to contact my contractor and see if I can have that done to my bathroom hopefully with minimal damage."

"Baby, is everything ok, I mean I heard you yell a couple times and I wanted to make sure you were ok from earlier?"

"Yes baby I'm fine, that was just one of my boys Jason who got himself into some more mess with another female. I tell you, that dude is going to run into the completely wrong one, one day and it's over."

"Wow is it like that with him?"

"Not always but it seems as though he can't get away from the ghetto and he's talented, the guy can do just about anything but he don't want to settle down and focus on one thing and make it work."

"Maybe you can help him out?"

"Oh, baby don't get me started, I have tried before, hell WE ALL have but he just don't want to stick with any one thing."

"Well maybe one day he will, hmmm by the way it smells so good in here. I didn't know you were a cook too. You know you can spoil a girl with good loving and now if your cooking is good I may just have to keep you"

"Hmmm really, and what makes you think that's not my plan all along Ms. Johnson?"

"Hmm really, so what are you saying Mr. Bass, are you trying to keep me?"

"Well let's just say that I want to see where things go with us, I'm not trying to rush anything but I like how I feel right now and how I feel about you, so yeah I want to see what happens."

"Well, I'm game, and from the looks at the food I will be a very happy woman in about a half hour" Kim smiling at the turkey sausage, smothered potatoes with onions & green peppers, pancakes, biscuits & gravy, eggs with cheese and juice I was preparing.

"Well, I aim to please Ms. Johnson, I aim to please"

(Kim putting her arms around my neck and giving me a soft kiss)

"That you do and did last night......wheewww that you did."

"I'm glad you enjoyed it as much as I did."

"Oh yes you can definitely say that, ok so I've heard about Braden and now Jason, how many other close friends do you have?"

"I don't have that many close friends but there's Braden and Jason as you know, then there's Darius, now he's another trip sometimes and then there's my boy Milton, he's a quiet one, and he's one who's been going through some hard times since his wife has been tripping on him. Lastly there's my guy Jonathan, him and I aren't that close but I became his friend through Darius, but we're real cool though."

"Oh ok, so Darius, that's an interesting name and it seems as though I've heard his name before."

"Have you heard of D-Nice Records?"

"Yeah I have."

"Well he's the founding owner, built it from the ground up."

"Oh ok, that's where I know his name. My niece just got an internship there."

"Oh ok, cool that's a good thing."

"Mmmm well I wouldn't say all that"

"Huh, why not, your niece is taking the initiative to do something with her life right?"

"Yeah that's true but she is, how can I say it, well I'll just put it out there, I mean I love my niece and everything but she's a gold digger and she heard about the scandal that went on there with one of the big executives or what people think they know of it anyway. So, she wanted to go and find out for herself is she could land one."

"Are you serious, wow?"

"Yeah, quite serious and I told her that's not the best way to go about things but she won't listen to me. And she has a good head on her shoulders, very smart and talented but she can be lazy and want a man to take care of her."

"See that's truly fucked up, and it gives hard working women a bad name."

"Yeah I know, but she's doing her as she calls it, ok look I don't want to talk about her, I want to sit down with you and enjoy this lovely breakfast and see what else is to come."

"Well after breakfast, I want you to go to your room and get your things and come back here, I have to change our flights from Friday, to Sunday, then from there we're going out on the town and site see and do whatever else we can get into"

"Sounds good to me"

We sit down to the table, I took her hand and said grace, when I was done she had a smile on her face as if she was pleased that I talk to God. Yeah I do talk to God just not as I used too and my heart is over joy at all the blessings that I can't help but talk to Him. I think to myself that this is going to be a wonderful weekend.

CHAPTER

14

Darius "How could I let it happen again"

Darius was sitting in his office, trying to get some work done but not being able to accomplish much. Not because he had so much on his mind but it's kind of hard to focus when you have your hot new female intern underneath your desk performing….well let's just say she's putting in work but not the kind he hired her for. Just when he thought he could complete his mission there's a knock on his door. He forgot he had a meeting with his two business partners Zan and Tre to discuss plans for the two new interns especially since originally they were going to take only one and not two.

Knock, knock, knock

"Stop……Zenobia, stop, someone at my door" Forcing Zenobia pausing the job she was performing." Come in" I say as I finish gathering myself and my composure, hoping they don't notice anything.

"Darius, we need to have a meeting about the interns you hired." Zan says!

"Yes Darius, I thought you were going to wait until we got back to further discuss bringing on two interns instead of just one. Why on earth did you go ahead and hire both and I thought you were going to discuss it with us first?" Tre chimes in.

"Hello ladies, it's nice to see you first of all, welcome back from your trip to Cali. Did you have a nice time out there?" Trying to make light of the situation that they feel I put them in.

"Yes we did, and yes we accomplished what we set out to do, which is lock in another artist and get the radio station to do some syndication for our other artist, so answer our question Darius" Zan getting back to the point.

"Yes, I was gonna go with Mitch only but honestly when I took a look at Ms. Bentley's information and talking with her I saw that there's a way for us to have both candidates for internship."

"Mmmm hmmm are you sure you just looked at her "information" and nothing else?" Zan looking at him with a side grin.

"Zan, come on now, you know me."

"Yes I do know you that's why I'm asking. Look Darius I care about you and I've been here with you through thick and thin and I'd hate to see things go wrong for you again and this time they may not end up coming out ok for you and I for one don't want that."

"Yes Darius, we don't want that and we're not saying that this woman isn't legit, all we're saying is, just be careful this time." Tre chips in her two cents worth.

"Ladies, I do understand where you're coming from and I will be careful this time. I promise I won't let my little head cloud the judgment of my big head. Believe me I do not want to go through what I went through before and I won't take you two through any of that again, I promise." feeling as though he just jumped out of the frying pan into the fire.

"Ok Darius, we'll see!" They both said simultaneously.

"Wow y'all seem as though you don't believe me?"

"Darius, it's not that we don't want to believe you but Terry told us how Ms. Bentley looked and if she's half of what he said then you can be in some trouble that's all." Tre says with hesitation and concern in her voice.

"Tre, I know what you mean and yes I must say she is very beautiful, but when you get to know her and read her bio I think you'll change your mind about her."

"Again, we'll see, anywho, so where is she, isn't she supposed to be in right now it's already past 9:30?"

"She did come in but I sent her out to get some Garrett's popcorn for me, I have a sweet tooth right now and a craving for my Chicago mix of caramel and cheese."

Tre and Zan both start laughing because they know how much I love that popcorn.

"Boy you are gonna have so many but call her and have her pick me up some too but I want the kind with the cashews in them." Tre says taking advantage of the situation.

"Oh wow, just a few minutes ago y'all wanted to dog her out but now want her to get you some popcorn. I'll see if I can catch her and have her bring some back. Anything you want Zan?"

"Nahh I'm good, I'm back to my workouts and I have my Zumba class later on and we weigh in today so the last thing I want to do is add extra pounds before my workout."

"Ok, well if y'all don't mind I want to get back to what I was doing." trying to rush them out the door so he can get Zenobia out from under his desk.

"Hmm it don't seem like you're doing much if you ask me"

"Well I am thank you very much, y'all want to get paid right, well I gotta get this budget worked out for the next fiscal year and see if I am going to give raises or not this year." thinking I just may dodge this bullet after all.

"Uh huh ok, all I know is we've done very well this year and I want my money." Tre Laughing and high fiving Zan.

"I know that's right girl, shoot we put in extra work so I know we'll be just fine."

"Ok, ok, ok ladies, are y'all done? Let me get back to it and I'll see you guys for lunch when we take the new interns out for a meet and greet."

"Ok Darius but can we make it at 1pm, I have a conference call at 12 and I know it's going to be at least 30 minutes but no more than 45?"

I was actually thinking that's a great idea since I have to get his new intern from under my desk and over to Garrett's to get the popcorn. I can only thank God that my office is downtown already and Garrett's isn't too far from here.

"Yeah that's cool, I have a few things to wrap up myself so one it is, goodbye ladies and please close the door so I can get some work done without interruption." Really wanting to get Zenobia from under my desk without getting caught.

"Ok boss, we'll leave you to your "work, see you at one" they both say as they exit my office.

Zan and Tre close the door and all I could think to myself is that was a close one. Maybe they're right, maybe I should play this above the belt and not get involved with Ms. Bentley, but would she just accept it now that she's been in this uncompromising position? I wonder?

"Ok Zenobia, you heard the ladies, off to Garrett's you go." saying as I reach in my pocket to grab some money for the popcorn.

"Uhm, how am I going to get out of your office without being seen by your assistant Terry?" Zenobia looking confused.

"Well see that door right there (Pointing to the one at the north end of the office that looks like just a wall of hats), that's a doorway that leads to a stairwell. The stairwell leads to the back door to the street. No one will see you, trust me."

"Wow, so you have this figured out already huh, I guess you've done this before right?"

"Well let's just say I've had some issues before where I had to make a quick exit but was caught up in my office and almost didn't get away. So, I had it installed and not many people know about it and you can't get in from the outside"

"Wow, I'm curious to know what kind of situations you were in."

"Well that's something of my past and not many people know that either and I'm gonna keep it that way."

"Ok, I won't push, I'll go get the popcorn, but please don't just have me run your errands for you, that's not why I want to be here." Zenobia deviously thinking other things. She heads towards the secret door, waiting on me to open it and let her out.

"I know and I wouldn't ask normally but this is a pinch so just help me out this time and I won't forget you."

"Oh, I know you won't forget me, I know that for sure." she says as I push the button to open the door and let her out.

Zan exits through the door and it closes behind her. Although I feel I've gotten away with it this time, an uneasy feeling sits in my stomach from her statement "I know you won't forget me", for some reason I have a feeling that she's not gonna make things easy for me but not quite sure how.

CHAPTER

15

Darius "What did I get myself into this time"

Isat there working on the budget and other contracts I had to look over for some prospective artist. I couldn't help but think of how I got myself into the trouble before that almost cost me not only my wife and kids but my business as well. I know better and I know what I have to do so I have to make sure that Ms. Bentley stays on the right track and keep her so busy that she has no time to think about me or what just took place.

"Wheewww almost done with that now I need to talk to Terry about some things." Reaching for his phone to call Terry to have him come into his office.

"Terry!"

"Yeah boss!"

"Can you come on here for a sec?"

"On my way." getting up to go into Darius's office he glances at Zenobia's desk notices that she's not there and hasn't been for a while now. Puzzled he wonders where she could be. He gets a look on his face as if to say, "Oh Shit, here we go again."

"Knock, knock, hey boss what's up?" asking as he enters Darius's office and sees the bewildered look on his face.

"Sit down please I have something to talk to you about."

"What's going on Darius, you don't look good? By the way have you seen Zenobia, I need her to do a few things for me?" Terry asked nervously.

"That's why I asked you into my office. Terry, I have a problem that I need your help with. Remember when I got into that trouble a couple years ago and what I did afterwards?"

"Yeah I remember" Terry thinking boy do I remember, remembering the affair Darius had and how it not only almost cost him everything. "You had a meeting with the entire staff and came clean about the affair you had and how it almost cost you this company. You vowed not to let anything interfere with the business anymore and had all of us sign a confidentiality agreement, wanting reassurance that we would not talk to the media or anyone else. I'll admit when that happened it concerned me a little, made it seem as if you didn't trust us, especially me."

"Terry, I know that you were feeling as if I didn't trust you and some of the other staff members had expressed that very thought but I assure you it's not that I didn't trust y'all, I had to do what I had to do to cover myself for one and the company. One thing you should know about this business, it's just that, business, and you have to

CYA no matter who it may be from. Look I'm not trying to dredge up old memories but I do need you and I need for you to keep it strictly between us, I mean it, well for now at least until I or we can figure out what to do."

"Boss, you're making me a little nervous, tell me what's up, what's going on or shall I guess?"

"I would say guess but I don't want you to gloat."

"You hit that didn't you?" Terry smirked.

"NO... I didn't "hit it" well not in the sense you're referring too. But she was in here just a little while ago, the same time Tre and Zan came into my office."

"WHAT...wait, she was here and they didn't say anything to her or make her leave?"

"Well they didn't know she was here?"

"I don't get it." Terry looking very puzzled.

"Think about it."

"Oh damn, you mean to tell me...I mean come on boss she was... Darius, no you didn't...please tell me you didn't have her under your desk?"

"I wish I could, boy do I wish I could... but I can't." Darius lets out a deep sigh. "Now I don't know what to do because when I sent her on a run to get some Garretts popcorn, I told her that I won't forget her for not speaking about this and she looked at me with a weird look and said and I quote." I know you won't forget me, I'm sure of that", as soon as she said it I got this uneasy feeling in my stomach and now

I don't know what to do because I think she's going to do something or try to hold it over my head."

"Ok, wait, but I didn't see her leave your office, how did she get out?" having a very puzzled look on his face.

"There!" Darius pointing to the wall with the hats on it, pressing the button underneath his desk, the "wall" with the hats open up to show his private exit way. Terry stands up and walks over to the door with his mouth wide open in utter shock at what he saw.

"Oh my God, are you serious, man when did you install this? More importantly why did you install it?"

"I had it installed when I went through that bullshit with that gangster who was trying to muscle in on my business. I needed a way to get out of here and no one knowing about it. I had a contractor work on it throughout the night that way no one knew about it. It took a while but I was able to get it finished. That's how she got out of here without anyone seeing her leave my office."

"Damn...I remember that mess but I didn't know you had this installed, man this is tight, I love it. So where does it lead too?"

"It leads to the back side of the building where no one can see you leave. You can't enter either because I had it made so it has no handle for you to get in...so once you're out, you're out."

"Darius...ok talk to me, for real what's up, I mean if she was here and you two didn't do anything, what's the big deal?"

"See that's why I reminded you about the confidentiality agreement, I want you to remember I need for you to keep things to yourself and that they will not surface ANYWHERE…and to tell you the truth she was under my desk performing a job that I can't pay for legally."

"Boss, I thought you said you weren't going to do anything anymore after the last situation?"

"I know man I know but remember the day she came in for her interview, when all of you were gawking at her in the lobby?"

"Yeah I do, that's when you told me she came onto you, wait did you do something then?"

"No, but I did think to myself it could be that easy. And you know my philosophy if it's that easy then it's that greasy and will slip through your fingers faster than water going down a fall, so here I am now with this dilemma and like I said I'm not feeling too good about it."

"Ok so if no one knew she was here, no one knew you two did anything, and there's no semen, there is no semen right, I mean we don't want another "Bill Clinton" accident?"

"Terry!!"

"Hey, I have to ask right, so again no semen right?"

"Right!"

"Well there's no evidence she was here so you should have nothing to worry about, I think you'll be fine."

"Yeah I'm thinking that too but still I don't know, I mean something with her just don't sit right with me. I mean women throw themselves at me all the time, but it seems as though she has another agenda in mind and I think I'm the rat that's about to be caught in her trap."

"Well my brotha I told you to stop being that rat, but for some reason you won't listen and always chase the cheese."

"Look…now isn't a time for an "I told you so" speech so please spare me ok?"

"Ok ok…so what do you want me to do?"

"I want you to keep her busy and out of my hair."

"Uhm but you're bald, you don't have any hair." Terry laughs hysterically.

"Ha, ha, ha you're funny; you know what the hell I mean. I need for you to keep her so busy that she has no time to think about me and doing anything to me period."

"Ok I'll do what I can but don't you think she'll think something when you are avoiding her?"

"See that's just it, I'm not going to directly avoid her, I'm going to do it indirectly."

"Huh, I don't get it, how can you not indirectly avoid someone?"

"See I'm going to be around and have her do things, hell I'm even going to talk with her, but I'm never going to be alone with her. Anytime you see her coming or heading into my office you make sure you get in here with any kind of excuse to speak with me and you have to do it alone that way she can't stay in here with me got it?"

"Oh ok, I got you, this way she can't say you're avoiding her by not being around, cool, that's smart."

"Yeah I guess, but hell the smart play was to never get involved with her period, but I didn't and now I have to head this train wreck off before it leaves the station and picks up momentum."

"Don't worry boss I got your back, with or without the agreement, I told you I'm here for the long haul."

"Thanks man I truly appreciate it." smiling an uneasy smile.

"No problem, now if you don't mind I need to get back to my office, I have Mitch doing a couple things for me and I need to check on him."

"Oh ok cool, and how is he working out?"

"Well it's only his first few days but he's doing well and he seems eager to learn more and more, I will say you need to spend some time with him seriously and that can help out with your other problem."

"Yeah I plan too, I just want him to learn from the ground up so to speak before he comes to hang with me, that way he can appreciate what it takes to run a successful music company and learn that it's not all glitz and glory."

"I hear you and I think he's going to work out well. Oh, and do you plan on hiring one of the interns this time out?"

"I know I haven't done it in the past but I think I will this time, who knows if we can get beyond this situation with Zenobia maybe she could come on too but we'll see."

"Alright boss, we'll see but man for real, brotha to brotha just be careful, I'd hate to see you get into something this time you can't get out of."

"Ok, I hear you, and understand. I'm going to be more careful I promise."

"Cool, oh and stop saying you promise because I for one know that's a bunch of bull."

"Yeah, yeah, yeah you think you know me don't you?"

"Just a little bro, but I do know one thing, you better keep your head on straight and I'm not talking about your "little" one either…Ok, I'm out, gotta go check on Mitch I'll talk to you later on."

"Oh ok cool, hey one more thing, now that Zan and Tre are back we're going to have a companywide lunch at 1pm to welcome Mitch and Zenobia to our team at least temporary."

"Cool, are we having Harold's Chicken this time?"

"Yeah we are and we're having J&J's too because I love their fried Shrimp"

"Cool, that's what's up, well I'll see you at One boss."

"Peace…hey shut my door on your way out, I need to make a call and I don't want to be disturbed."

"Ok, is everything ok?"

"Yeah I just need to call one of my boys and I don't want to be interrupted that's all."

"Ok cool, see you later."

As Terry exits and closes the door, I think to myself that I just dodged a bullet or I hope I did. I can't go through another episode like before and I can only think about what Trish said that she'd leave me and take my kids and half of my business. I can't have that. Losing half my business is one thing but not having my kids is another. Damn I need to talk to Marcus but don't want to disturb him while he's out of town so I'll call Braden to find out if he's talked to him and see what's going on.

CHAPTER

16

Darius & Braden "It will all work out"

᪥

Darius picks up the phone to call Braden because he knows that by talking to one of his boys with a sensible head can and will help him put things in better perspective. When he calls Braden though to talk about his own problems he doesn't realize that Braden is going through his own and needs to vent too.

"Darius, what up man, I was just thinking about you, what's going on?"

"What up bro, not much just trying to get these interns in line with their assignments."

"Oh, ok cool, how many do you have this time?"

"Two, a male and a female."

"Uh oh, did you say a female, man are you crazy?"

"Man, I know, I know, but it's cool, I'm making sure she's busy and out of my hair."

"Is she fine?"

"Fine don't even describe her man, I mean she's Vivica Fox, Janet Jackson, Aaliyah all wrapped up into one with a side of Trina."

"Daaayyyuuummmnnn, awe hell I know you're in trouble now."

"Damn!...doesn't anyone have faith in me?"

"Come on Darius, you know your track record hasn't been too good and after what happened last time I just knew Trish was going to leave you high and dry but she stayed, which I'm happy about but still dude you have to make sure you mind your P's and Q's this time."

"Yeah I know, and I'm gonna be good for real this time" I hate lying to my boy but until I get this situation with Zenobia under control I have to keep it quiet "Anywho I called to ask you have you spoken to Marcus, I haven't heard from him since he left for DC?"

"Yeah I talked to him earlier this morning; he called me and told me he's not coming back until Sunday now."

"Sunday...Why Sunday?"

"Well apparently things went better than expected out there for him, which I'm glad of so he has another meeting that popped up, oh and he met someone while out there."

"What...are you for real, I mean damn it's been what 10 years since Brenda's passing and he hasn't given anyone a serious look since. So what do you know about her?"

"All I know is her name is Kim and she has some company I think a consulting firm or something like that, he says she's all that and for the first time, since Brenda, he sounds real happy."

"Wow that's cool, I'm glad for him, I was wondering because I know we were supposed to get together tomorrow to go over more add layouts for his magazine. I have to run a special promotion with him. I have ideas about getting new, raw talent in here and see what I can do to build their career from the ground up, you know like we used to do when I first started out."

"Yeah I remember, boy those were the days, hey remember Eric aka "Cool Doc E", man that dude could spit a rhyme of the top of his head like no one's business. Man, I wish he could have gotten going, but I guess getting married and having kids will do it to the best of them."

"Yeah I know, he and James were my boys and they could have gone places but shit happens right. Hey look, when you hear from Marcus let him know I need to talk to him asap ok?"

"Yeah I will, especially since he has to talk to me as soon as he gets back anyway. Man, you're not going to believe who popped back up in the picture and wants to talk to me?"

"Who!"

"Kandi"

"Hell nah, for real, what in the hell could she want now after what 20 years, I mean for real, it can't be a child can it, I mean I know she hated you after all that happened but damn do you think she hated you this much to keep a child from you?"

"Man I don't know, all I know is Marcus said he needs to talk to me as soon as his plane touches down, so yeah I'm sitting here on pins and needles wondering what the hell is going on. I have been trying to play out all sorts of scenarios in my head but can't come up with anything that fits. I mean damn after 20 years she wants to talk. The only thing I could come up with honestly is that she's dying and wants to make a mends for things but hell she didn't do anything, it was all me so I don't know what it could be."

"Dude, I'm sitting here speechless, I have no idea either what it could be. I guess you'll have to find out when he gets home. By the way, how are the kids and is Gabrielle still trippin on things?"

"The kids are fine and you know Gabrielle, she has her good days and her bad days. Lately though she's trippin on the fact that I want the kids more and we have to go back to court. She thinks I'm just trying to lower my child support payments. I told her that I don't care about that and I don't plan on changing anything."

"I hear you but you do know if you keep the kids more then she will have to re-do the child support order because they will be with you for an extended period of time."

"I know that's a possibility and that's something that my lawyer brought up but I told her I don't plan on changing anything. I just want to see my kids more than I do now that's all."

"Braden, I get it but you know better than anyone, dealing with her has not been easy. Marcus told me about the time when you two went to drop the kids off in Ohio and she snapped at the door, he said that they were crying and you were begging her not to discuss things in front of the kids but she, as usual, didn't care. Man he said his heart was broken and that your drive home was longer than always."

"Yeah I remember and that drive home was rough, I mean he had to take over driving because I couldn't do it. Look, I don't want to talk about that anymore, all I know is I have to fight for my kids' sake so I have to do what I have to do."

"Speaking of fight, are you getting the position with your accounting company you've been interviewing for?"

"Well I'm glad you asked my brotha, because I did get the word just today, they called me in and sat me down and told me that I will be the chief financial officer and it comes with a hefty raise of $25,000 a year with a signing bonus of $10,000."

"WOOOOWWW Congratulations man, I'm so happy for you, so when do we celebrate?"

"Thanks man, and honestly I am happy too but with the news Marcus got me thinking about I almost forgot about it. But we'll have to celebrate next weekend because on Monday they are flying me out to the parent company in California for training."

"Training, what do you have to train on, you know the job right?"

"Yeah I know the financial part of it but I'll be in charge of not only this branches financials but also in charge of the entire corporation and I'll be over seeing all five branches financials and staff, that's why they are paying me so much loot. I'll have an expense account because I'll be flying at least twice a month and staying gone for probably two weeks out of that month so yeah I'll be humping."

"Damn I'll say, so that will put a damper on our hoop times won't it?"

"Yeah just a little but we'll get it in though, because you know how much I love sticking it to y'all."

"Ha, ha, ha ok you got lucky once and now you are a ghetto super star."

"Yeah you know how it is, anyway, I'll tell Marcus you need to speak to him if he doesn't get to you first, and man, keep your head clear ok?" Laughing!

"Yeah I will dude, you do the same."

"Ok, Later!"

I hang up and think to myself that my boy is going places. Wow a $25K raise with a $10K bonus. Damn that's nice but Kandi's back and wants to talk to him. I can't imagine what it is. I hope it's good news instead of bad but hell when a woman comes back into your life after you broke her heart wanting to talk it can't be good. I just hope for his sake it's not as serious as I'm thinking. Oh well I have my own issues to deal with and I gotta get a handle on it and fast.

CHAPTER

17

Darius "What in the hell am I doing"

I take time out to think about the events of the day and reflect on what I have to do and the decisions I must make for the sake of not only my business but my family.

"Wow, it's good to hear good news and I'm so happy for Braden, hell I'm happy for all my friends, well most of them (thinking about Jason and all his troubles it seems he continues to get himself into, but at the same time thinking how could he look at Jason when he keeps getting into them himself), Marcus a successful magazine owner, Braden now a successful accountant, Milton doing well as a head consultant for an insurance company, Jonathan a successful director for his own community outreach company, and me a successful record company owner. I can only think back to when we were all in high school back in Champaign/ Urbana, those were the days. It's funny how so many of us growing up together had so many dreams and goals and now living out our dreams."

I turn around to look at the bookshelf wall I had specially made to hold the awards and pictures of my family, the family I almost lost.

I think to myself "Damn, what in the hell am I doing, I do love my wife although we have our problems, and I can't imagine being without my kids. Why do I allow myself to get into this bullshit, I mean things aren't perfect and we didn't start off the best but we've been together now for a long time and I can't let anyone or anything get in the way of my marriage anymore. I have to make it clear that nothing can happen any further between Zenobia and myself and if she can't understand that then so be it she has to go."

I leaned back in his chair for what seems to be an eternity only to be startled by a knock on the door. When I turn around I see the last person I on earth I ever expected to ever darken my office again. Yeah that's right Cassandra Haywood!!!!

CHAPTER

18

Darius "A blast from the past, not always a good thing"

❦

"What the hell are you doing here?" I reach for my phone to call the police thinking she must have broken out of prison.

"Darius wait, don't call the police, I know I'm not supposed to be here but I had to see you."

"Cassandra, you know I have a restraining order on you. Wait, how in the hell are you out of prison, I know you got five years?"

"I know, I know, and I'm not here to cause you any trouble and I'm going to leave but I wanted to speak to you in person and I know if I called and tried to set up a meeting you wouldn't meet with me. Also, I'm out on parole for good behavior. I had to complete these classes while in prison and now I'm staying at a halfway house."

"Uhm if you're at a halfway house don't they have to know your every move?"

"Yes that's true but I was able to barter with someone to let me come see you just for a few minutes, that's all a few minutes is all I want or even ask for, so I beg of you please don't call the police on me, please?"

"Ok, but only for a few minutes, I mean a few minutes Cassandra, come on in." reluctantly I allow her to stay but only for a short while and as she walks into the office I keep the phone close by just in case I need to make a quick call not knowing what she's up to or why she's here.

"Can I sit down?"

"Sure, if you must, but get to it and be gone."

"Wow do you have to be so cold Darius, I mean I know what I did was wrong but you can't put the blame all on me. I loved and still love you Darius and I was angry then."

"Look, I know the part I played in all of this and believe me I regret every bit of it but that is in the past and I cannot go there again, I won't risk my family, my life nor my business again. I just can't do it."

"I know Darius and like I said I'm not here to cause any problems for you but there is something I have to tell you."

"What Cassandra, just what do you have to tell me?"

"Well when all that happened and I went to your house to, well you know what I was planning to do. I was mad and wanted you to leave your wife and family and come start a family with me."

"Yeah I know the police told me that you were pregnant and that you said the baby was mine but I always wondered how could you be when we used condoms every time."

"I know we did Darius but I must tell you that even though we used condoms and you thought that they were safe. What you didn't know is I poked a hole in all of them so I could get pregnant."

"WHAT THE HELL!!!!!" Darius balling up his fist as if he wants to pound Cassandra into his mahogany floors "So in other words you were just trying to trap me, wow and you come to me with this shit now."

"Well, I have to admit I did try too and I was pregnant but ended up losing the baby."

"Well thank God for small favors."

"You don't have to sound so happy about it Darius I really wanted your baby and for us to be a family."

"How Cassandra, how could we be a family when I already have a family, how in the world do you think I was gonna leave my family for you. I told you from the beginning that this wasn't but just a fling and made sure you knew it."

"I know but when we would go places and you would do things for me I thought that it could be more than what it was and so I took the chance to make sure of that but it didn't work that way and I ended up in prison."

"Yeah where you belonged, ok your time is about up, so all you came here for was to tell me that you were pregnant but you've lost the baby."

"No Darius that's not the only reason why I came here." Cassandra pauses and starts to cry.

"Oh, come on now save the tears baby and get to the point." Darius getting very irritated.

"Darius, I came here to tell you that when I was in the hospital and had lost the baby, they ran blood test on me to make sure I was ok and to check me out. But what they found just killed my soul."

"Ok what did they find out and what does it have to do with me."

"Darius I have HIV!" Cassandra now crying uncontrollably.

"Oh damn, I'm sorry to hear that but again what does that have to do with me, I don't have it."

"When's the last time you had a checkup Darius?"

"I don't need a checkup to know I don't have HIV and don't come to me with that bullshit about the possibilities either."

"Well just like me poking a hole in the condoms and the possibility of me getting pregnant for which I did there is a possibility that you could have HIV."

"Aww damn are you serious, I mean you come to me with this shit now after what 3 years, if you knew you had it why didn't you tell me right from the jump."

"I didn't know I had it Darius I swear, all I knew is when the doctor came in my room he told me he had seen something in my blood and had to send it off for testing to be sure, but by the time the results came back I was sitting in a cell and couldn't reach you. If I were to try and call you I knew you wouldn't take a collect call from me so I had no choice but to wait."

"I can't believe this, and now I'm supposed to think that I have HIV are you serious, so what am I to do now?"

"Get tested to make sure and believe me I hope you don't, I mean at first I was so mad at you that I wished you did but Darius I loved you then and I still do now and that's the last thing I wish upon you or anyone."

"Ok so now you've done your duty and you can leave and never come back to my office again."

"Darius you have to believe me when I say I didn't know and I wouldn't do this to you, not on purpose."

"I said you can leave now, I have things to do."

Cassandra gets up to leave and turns back to Darius one last time and says.

"I'm so sorry Darius I really am and I can only pray that you do not have this disease but please get tested so you'll know for sure."

"LEAVE!!!!"

Cassandra walks out of the office and closes the door, I get up and go to my window and just stare out into space. *I can't believe that bitch came in here first of all and to tell me she poked a hole in the condoms and then tell me she has HIV. I don't have it, I can't. Damn what am I gonna do if I do have it. I've been making love to Trish for the past few years and to think she........no I'm not gonna think that I can't think that. I gotta get tested no matter what. Damn!!*"

Darius picks up his phone and calls his doctor to make an emergency appointment to get tested then falls back into his chair and sobs alone.

"What have I done?"

CHAPTER

19

Kim "Caught In the Middle"

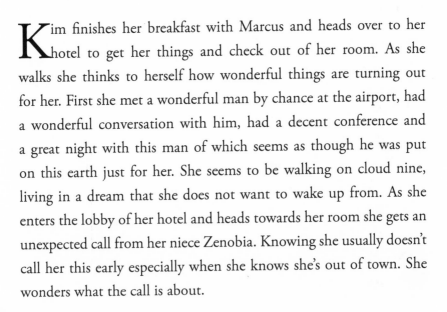

Kim finishes her breakfast with Marcus and heads over to her hotel to get her things and check out of her room. As she walks she thinks to herself how wonderful things are turning out for her. First she met a wonderful man by chance at the airport, had a wonderful conversation with him, had a decent conference and a great night with this man of which seems as though he was put on this earth just for her. She seems to be walking on cloud nine, living in a dream that she does not want to wake up from. As she enters the lobby of her hotel and heads towards her room she gets an unexpected call from her niece Zenobia. Knowing she usually doesn't call her this early especially when she knows she's out of town. She wonders what the call is about.

"Hello Zenobia, how are you doing?"

"Hey Auntie…I'm good…How are you and how is things going for you in D.C.?"

"I'm doing well, very well in fact, so what do I owe he pleasure of hearing your voice this morning miss?"

"Well I miss you and I wanted to hear your voice, besides I am out running an errand for my boss so I wanted to give you a call, is that ok with you?"

Hearing a different tone in her voice Kim asks her the question.

"Hmmm ok so tell me what's going on, and I mean what's really going on?"

"Whaaaaat, c'mon auntie you know how I love to talk to you and get advice from you."

"There it is you got into something and now you want me to help you get out of it right?"

"Well sort of, I mean I'm not into anything yet but I could be, I mean, uhm well it's like this, remember my new internship I have the one with the record company?"

"Yeah I remember you telling me that you were going to try and land you a baller, I do remember that?"

"Well let's just say that I may have landed the biggest fish of all."

"Ok now you got me curious, what are you talking about?"

"Let's just say that if all goes well I will be sitting pretty on the arm of the owner of the company."

"Zen are you serious....you do know he's married right.........and what did you do......you've only been there what three days how can you land him in three days?"

"Well remember the suit I borrowed from you the one with the low-cut blouse?"

"Yeah I remember it why, and what does that have to do with anything?"

"Well let's just say that I worked that suit to get his attention and it worked, well almost."

"Ok I'm confused, how did it almost work?"

"I used it to get his attention and when I went back to his office for the interview I went for it, I came onto him."

"YOU DID WHAT!!"

"I came onto him, BUT he shot me down cold and I'll admit that it hurt my feelings. But after he told me that's not what he's about and told me to sit down we talked and he conducted a proper interview. He did like what I'm studying in school so he offered me the internship anyway."

"See I told you that all you had to do is use your brains and not your body and you can go further in life than you realize. People will respect you more for it, ok so what's with the you may have landed the biggest fish of all speech."

"Well as it turns out he was, well is attracted to me and this morning I came into his office when no one was there and we did a little something in his office."

"Oh my goodness, no you didn't, I thought you said that he shot you down."

"Yeah I know but he did reveal to me that day that he did find me attractive but he couldn't go any further than that."

"So again please tell me how did it get to you and him doing a "little something" in his office, I mean if he said that and you left how did it come to this?"

"Well like I said as I came in this morning I was wearing a nice, fitted skirt, with my five-inch pumps with my blouse that ruffles in the front and he gave me that look and made a comment on my outfit so I went for it again. I told him that if nothing else could happen I wanted to show my appreciation for the internship. He asked me how can I do that and I pushed his chair out and leaned down before him and unzipped his pants."

"Zenobia, no you didn't, Oh my God, I can't believe you really went after Darius that way."

"Uhm how did you know his name is Darius?"

Kim feeling as though she just got busted cheating on her husband told Zenobia that this world is very small and the guy she met while coming to D.C. is one of his friends and they hit it off, She also told her that she told him about her and what she was going to the record company to do.

"Oh, wow so you're messing around with his friend, that's too freaky, well we both can get paid huh auntie I knew I got it from somewhere......Hhhaaaayyy!"

"Wait just a minute young lady, I, unlike you, am not trying to trap anyone and ours was a chance meeting. I didn't set out to do anything it just happened so let's get that straight."

"I know you're not like that I was just trying to make my situation seem a little better that's all."

"You were about to tell me what's going on and why you're in this situation?"

"Like I said I was in front of him, pants unzipped and everything. I was just getting into the job when we were disturbed by I guess his business partners because they came in and was talking about how they enjoyed their trip to California and how they signed a new artist and stuff."

"I'm confused, how did they talk to him and you were there too, didn't they see you?"

"See that's the beauty of it, he has this huge gorgeous mahogany desk and I fit right up underneath it, they didn't know I was there."

"Oh, wow I'm just speechless right now, you went there for the wrong reason, you got shot down, then you go for it anyway, and now you're under the man's desk. Did I miss anything?"

"Auntie Kim....that's not fair!" Kim pouting.

"Oh, really and how is it not fair, you set yourself up for this one, so what's the problem now and how did you get out of there?"

"See that's the beauty of it too, because after they left he told me to go on an errand to get some Garretts popcorn for him and that's what I'm doing now."

"Ok but I don't get it still what are you so giddy about, I mean If they didn't see you and didn't know you were there what's the deal?"

"Weeellll that's what I'm getting too, remember that digital recorder you told me to keep in my purse from the time I was harassed by that police officer?"

"yeah I remember, why what does that have to do with it?"

"Well I had my purse with me and when I had to get up under his desk I must have bumped it and it started recording and it recorded the entire encounter between him and I as well as his partners."

"Please tell me you're going to erase that tape?"

"Nope, I'm gonna keep it just in case."

"Just in case what Zenobia, really, what are you going to do with it?"

"I don't know just yet but I want to keep it just in case I ever need it for anything.......anything like maybe telling his wife about us."

"Zenobia you are delusional there is no "us" between you and him, it was something that happened that shouldn't have. You are playing with fire and you better be careful before this time you get burned for real."

"I know what I'm doing and I'm not going to do anything with it right away, hell I may not even use it but I just want to keep it just in case I ever need to use it that's all, no harm no foul right?"

"Wrong! there is harm in that, that's like a ticking time bomb just waiting to explode, take my advice and delete it now before it does explode and you're one of the casualties from it."

"I don't know Auntie I'll think about it, I just don't want to be used like a piece of meat and then discarded."

"Wait, how can you say that when you went there with the sole purpose of "landing a baller" as you call it, so how could you get angry if he does treat you like a piece of meat. Hell the way you're acting you are a piece of meat?"

"That's cold Auntie, that's real cold."

"Hey, I'm calling it like I see it, I'm sorry but that's what's wrong with a lot of our women today they always want to use their body to get what they want and then wonder why men don't respect them or treat them as equals. You see how I am and how I conduct myself right, well look at me, I met a great guy by chance and I didn't have to put out to do it or sucker him into anything, this was a chance meeting that has turned out great for the both of us."

"I know Auntie I know, but what am I to do now, I can't turn back the clock as if it didn't happen."

"True, but you can reverse the karma that is headed your way by deleting the recording because if you don't, watch out, karma will come back and bite you in the ass believe me I know. Look you're my only niece and I love you. I just want you to be careful that's all and get things in your life the right way. You are beautiful, have a great body, and a great mind to go with it but you have to use it intelligently and not the other way around."

"Maybe you're right, I know what I have to do and I'll do it."

"You promise?"

"Yes I promise!"

"Good now let me get my things together and check out of this hotel, I'll talk to you when I get back on Sunday."

"Sunday, wait weren't you supposed to come back Friday, I thought we were going to the movies?"

"Yeah well my plans have changed, and that's what I'm talking about when you do things the right way, good things happen. I was invited to stay here for the weekend with my baby and come back on Sunday."

"Your baby! but you've only known him for what less than 24 hours right?"

"This is true but it feels right and I want to see what happens and enjoy the ride."

"Oh ok so you can do it but I can't huh?"

"Well the difference between you and I is this, I didn't set out to get him and even better, he's not married."

"But did you tell him about…you know…?"

Kim knowing what Zenobia is referring to…she lets out a heavy sigh and her voice lowers.

"No…not yet…but I will…I have too, this is something I cannot keep from him, especially if this goes any further than this weekend. I just don't think I want to ruin what we have right now ok, so when you do meet him I don't want you to bring up anything ok?"

"Ok and I won't I promise, I just don't want him to hurt you like Uncle Larry did."

"For some reason I don't think he's like that, I mean all his friends come to him with their problems and he handles it like a champ so I don't think he will do anything to hurt me. Besides he has went through a lot in his life as well so what happened to me pales in comparison."

"Ok ok, I'll let it go, well, have fun and call me when you come in on Sunday so we can go to the movies ok?"

"Ok, and Zen?"

"Yeah?"

"Delete it!"

"Ok I will."

"I love you very much, always remember that."

"I know Auntie and I love you too, Bye."

"Goodbye!"

After Kim hangs up from talking to Zenobia, she sits on the bed in silence allowing her thoughts to consume her. Thinking of how she was going to tell Marcus about her past. Wondering how he was going to take the news that she knew she had to tell him. Not many knew of her past and she wanted to keep it that way but she knew full well that it would come back up someday but she didn't think it would be so soon.

Kim gets up from the bed and go into the bathroom. She takes a good long hard look in the mirror and begins to cry. After what seems like an eternity of tears she calms down and begins to clean herself up from the tears that had begun to flow. She knew she couldn't let Marcus see her this way so she wanted to put on a good face for him and not let anything ruin her time with him no matter what. She knows she has to tell him and soon but this is too soon.

After gathering herself together and her cloths she left her room and in some ways wanted to leave her past right there in the hotel room but she knew she couldn't. As she walked towards the elevator all she could think about was what she told her niece about karma and how it can come back to bite you and bite hard. She just hoped that this isn't karma coming back to bite her.

CHAPTER

20

Marcus & Kim "Is it too good to be true"

While Kim was gone to go get her things from her hotel, I began making changes to my hotel room extending the stay through the weekend. To my surprise Edwin had already booked me through the weekend. I could only think that he was very sure of himself and that I was gonna be there for the weekend but hey it was ok with me. Things are going great, I have a beautiful lady on my arm and I am about to make what looks like another connection for a business venture, so I'm all good. As I called the airline to change my flight they had informed me that my flight was not scheduled to leave until Sunday morning, all I could think of was that damn Edwin but I can't be mad at him. I told them I need to add a passenger onto my ticket and make sure we were in sitting next to one another.

After that was done, I began straightening things up around my room and had gotten done with that only to realize that Kim hadn't returned yet. I wondered what was taking her a while but just figured that it was something with the room or maybe checkout. Either way I wasn't worried about it. I called Willie and told him that I would like for him to pick us up at noon so we could go see the city and he can take us to some of the places that I had missed and some places I've already been so Kim could enjoy it as well. He had no problem with that and said he'd be there at noon. So with a little time on my hands, I figured I'd get my cloths together and take a quick shower, well quick for me that is.

I got in the shower and boy did it feel good, I didn't realize how tight my body was but I guess from the stress of the presentation that never happened and the dancing and then the wonderful night with Kim I guess I put my body through the ringer. As I enjoyed my shower and got out to dry off I noticed that Kim still hadn't returned. Now I must say I'm getting a little concerned because I know it don't take more than a few minutes to check out of a hotel, well at least it shouldn't. So I figured I'd give her a call and see what's going on.

When I do though it goes to voice mail and that's very odd but I dismiss it anyway but I can't help but wonder in the back of my mind what's going on with her right now. Just as I am about to get more nervous she walks through the door but I could tell things aren't quite right with her. This makes me pause and step back and truly look her over and wonder what happened from the time she walked out of my room and seemed to be floating on air and now she seems to be walking in cement.

Of course, the concerned part of me wants to ask what's going on but I think it best if I see if she opens up and tells me. I just hope everything is ok, from the look on her face I can tell it's not but I won't push and I don't want anything to ruin this weekend for us. I know she'll tell me in her own time I just hope it's not too long.

"Hey baby, I was getting a little worried about you, I was thinking that it shouldn't take you that long to get your things from your room."

"I'm sorry honey I really am but when I got to my room I got a call from my niece, the one I told you about who has that internship at your friends company."

"Yeah, yeah I remember, is everything ok?"

"Yeah they seem fine, I mean she was telling me how things were there and how excited she was about the opportunity, we just talked and I didn't realize the time that's all. I'm sorry I didn't mean to make you worry."

Kim knowing full well the story but she knew she couldn't tell Marcus the truth about the conversation, not right now, so she did what she had to do to avoid any drama at this point.

"It's ok hon I understand, I was just wondering and then when I called you and it went to voice mail I was really wondering then."

"Oh, I'm sorry about that I was in the bathroom straightening myself up a bit before I came back over."

"Well I was hoping we'd take a shower together but after time went by, I changed my flight and straightened up in here I figured I'd go ahead and take a quick shower. Well maybe we can get to enjoy that shower together later on?"

"Yes that would be so lovely and maybe later on I could talk you into giving me another massage because I need it after last night's events."

"Hmm is that so, well I think I could hook you up with that, but right now I need for you to put your things in the closet and we need to get ready to go downstairs. Willie will be here in a few minutes to pick us up."

"Oh ok, so where are we off too Mr. Man?"

"Well I figured we'd take a tour of the city and go see the monuments and such and go to the Martin Luther King monument and then go see Howard University since I didn't get the chance too yesterday, then Willie told me he knows about a great soul food restaurant that he wanted me to try so we'll have a late lunch early dinner there and then come back here and relax, talk, listen to music or do whatever we desire. Does that sound ok with you Ms. Ma'am?"

"That sounds like you have everything under control so I'm just fine with that, but I did hear someone talking about an African festival going on so is it possible we can go to that if not today maybe tomorrow."

"Yeah that's cool, I love going to them when they are going on in the City but over the past couple years they have gotten smaller and it seems as though they have the same venues out there with the same merchandise and that can get a little boring but I'm sure they will have different things here so yeah that's cool we can do that."

"Thank you Marcus."

"Baby it's no big deal you don't have to thank me."

"I'm not just talking about the festival, I'm talking about everything, I mean you didn't know me at all and now we're spending all this time together, I mean, I just want to say thank you and I appreciate it."

"Baby, come here, it's my pleasure and trust me if you hadn't been here with me I would have went site seeing and came back to this hotel and did nothing"

"Ok I find that hard to believe, that you would just sit in the hotel room."

"It's true, I don't go out to much when I'm on the road because I don't trust people too often and so I find it safer to stick around the hotel. I mean I venture out during the day but not too far and when the night comes I'm back where I know I'm safe and besides I usually talk to my mom and my daughter until they go to sleep so that's my time spent on the road. Speaking of her, let me give them a quick call before we head out."

As Marcus calls Jazzmin and his mother I go over to the window, my thoughts of the conversation I had with Zenobia consume me. I knew I had to tell Marcus about my history, but just didn't know how I was going to do such a hard thing. I realized I like him very much and don't want to ruin anything. I was so caught up in my thoughts that I didn't hear Marcus call my name and walk up behind me.

"Babe, are you ok, I mean I called your name and you didn't respond?"

"Yes baby I'm fine but I will say I have a couple things on my mind."

"Well as you know I'm a good listener and you can tell me anything at least I hope you know you can tell me anything, right?"

"Yes I know and I will but it's just something I have to sort out but I promise I'll tell you ok, I just want to enjoy you and this weekend we have going on."

"Ok baby I'll let it go for now and I won't push so whenever you're ready I'm here."

"Thank you Marcus that means a lot."

"Ok, now it's 11:45 so let's make our way down to the lobby because I don't like to keep anyone waiting."

"Ok!"

We exit the room we walk down the hall hand in hand but it's different this time. Kim is holding my hand tighter as if she doesn't ever want to let go. This gets me to wondering what is really going on with her. I know I said I won't push but I can't help but wonder what is really going on. I guess I'll find out in due time, I just hope it's nothing that will affect the beginning of what we have going on here. I just hope...

We rode the elevator I could tell that things were different, tenser than before, although I wanted to ask the question....it took every fiber within me not to, so I let it go and just kept silent. As the elevator doors opened and we exited I saw Willie in the lobby waiting on us. I told him what the plan was for the day and that we wanted to make sure that we were back in time for him to enjoy his family. He said that would be fine but his wife and family knows he's working and that the chances of him being home late are probable. I told him that the most important thing in life is your family and that one should spend as much time with them as they can. So with that we agreed on cutting it short if we had to and finish up on Friday.

We drove down the interstate to where the monuments were there was an uneasy silence between Kim and I. She didn't curl up into me as she previously did and now I'm truly worried about her. I can't take it anymore and I have to know what's going on with her.

"Babe, what's wrong?"

"Sigh…Marcus I really don't want to get into this and take a chance of ruining our weekend with my drama, so I hope you can understand that I need this time to just be about us."

"But that's just it, if you're going through something it will affect our time and honey what you're going through is about us because as of now I'm with you and I don't want nor like seeing you in any pain, distress what so ever, so please baby let's talk about it and get it out of the way so we can enjoy our weekend together."

"Ok, but I hope you don't think less of me or my niece when I tell you what's going on."

"Your niece, what does she have to do with anything?"

"Well because I'm concerned about her and what she's doing at your friends company. I feel that I'm caught in the middle of this because she interns there and I now know you and I just feel horrible because I know her intentions and they're not good Marcus."

"Ok look, whatever your niece has going on she's a grown woman and it has nothing to do with you and it damn sure has nothing to do with me. So tell me what's going on with her?"

"Remember when I told you about how she knew about the scandal that happened there and how she wanted to go get her a "baller" as she put it?"

"Yeah I remember, why what did she do?"

"Well the main reason why I was taking so long getting back over to you was because she was telling me the story of how she had this interview with the president of the company and how she came onto him."

"What are you serious right now?"

"Yes I am, but the thing is he shut her down and she said that she just knew she had blown her chances of interning there so she was about to walk out but he stopped her and told her how inappropriate it was but looked at her credentials and continued the interview and found her worthy of a shot for the internship."

"Ok cool, but what's the problem, it sounds like things went well for her?"

"Yeah I know and that's the problem because only after being there for a couple days she found herself in an uncompromising position and almost got busted by his I think partners she said."

"Oh, that would be Trenicia and Zantel, yeah they helped him build it from the ground up, but how did they "almost" bust her?"

"Well she said that she came in early and went into his office and things got, well they got heated and she started to perform oral sex on him and apparently she didn't get going good enough when they came into the office."

"Wait you're telling me that just after a couple days she goes and does this and almost gets caught, so how does she get away?"

"Well that's the thing, she said she was under his desk when they came in and they were talking and of course she had to be still and quiet. But what she didn't know was and this is the worst part of it all. She didn't know that this little tape recorder she carries with her was turned on and recorded the entire thing."

"Oh my God are you for real, so now what, is she planning to do something with the tape?"

"Well at first she was but I told her not to do anything and to delete it, she said she will but I know her Marcus and I think she's gonna keep it just in case she needs to use it for some kind of leverage on him."

"Oh damn...shit...I can't believe this, so you're telling me that my boy is about to get caught up in some scandal all because of your niece and the fact that she "accidentally" recorded her having oral sex with him right. How do you know it was an accident, how do you know she didn't go into his office with the recorder already turned on to set him up like this, Wow I can't believe this, so what are you going to do about it?"

"Wait are you saying it's my fault or something?"

"No, I'm not but she is your niece and you did tell me that she had the intentions of going there with that purpose right?"

"Well yeah but I also told her not to do it, I mean come on I can't physically make her not do something because she's grown, see this is why I didn't want to tell you because I didn't want to ruin our weekend together."

"Baby look you didn't ruin anything for us, it's just that I now have to tell my boy what's going on and to make sure he gets things under control because this cannot happen again. If it does he could lose everything and I for one don't want that to happen to him."

"I know you don't and now I feel even worse because I have now dragged you into the middle of things where you don't need to be."

"It's ok, I got you, but we have to make sure your niece doesn't do anything that she will regret later on…sigh…wow what a mess. Ok question, why would I look at you any differently than I do now, you basically have nothing to do with it."

"Well, I thought that after how we met and things are going that you may have that opinion of me that's all."

Laughing…"come on honey do you really think I'm that shallow of a man, I mean for you to want to purposely get with me the way you are, you would have to go through some elaborate scheming to do it because I'm sure you had no clue as to who I was and second you would have spent a lot of money doing so to set something up like a company, a conference, a flight and a hotel to stay in. I mean I think I'm a good catch but damn I don't think that anyone would go to such depths to do something like that especially when all you had to do was come to my office or see me out somewhere and try to talk to me that way. I don't think you would do something so deliberate so you have nothing to worry about. Besides I already checked up on you anyway and found out that you and your company is legit."

"What, are you serious Marcus, you did a check on me?"

"Yes, just to make sure you're no stalker or someone who's trying to find a pay day."

"I can't believe you did that, I'm so mad at you right now." Kim folding her arms pouting.

"Gotcha!"…I start to laugh hysterically.

"Are you playing, so you didn't do any of that stuff?"

"Nope, I just wanted you to hear how foolish you were being right now about how I would look at you, I mean come on babe, that's your niece, it's not you and further more even if it were you I would have sniffed it out by now because one thing about me is I am a very good reader of people and I sniff out bullshit a mile away, so no you couldn't be on that and be with me, besides one thing my mother always says, what's done in the dark will always come to light."

"She sounds like a very wise woman, but I can't believe you did that to me Mr. Bass."

"Well I just want you to understand that I care for you and YOU, only and I'm not worried about your niece or your past because we all have them and it's what makes up the person we are today so I just want you to know you have nothing to worry about, ok?"

"Ok, wow, the moment when I think you're gonna think or do something like make me leave your life, you flip the script on me and do this, I don't know what to say."

"Just say that you will not talk about this anymore and you will enjoy the rest of this day and weekend with me and we'll look into things once we get back to Chicago."

"Ok I'll do it I will not talk about this anymore and I will enjoy the rest of this day and weekend with you and we'll look into things once we get back to Chicago."

"Cool, now let's enjoy this day and night because someone is in desperate need of a massage."

"Oooo Yes I am!"

"Wait I was talking about me!"

"Oh, so not fair!"

"Ha ha ha just kidding, I was referring to you hon and trust me when I lay hands on you, you'll go to heaven and not want to come back."

"Ooohh I hope so because I truly need this."

"Alright don't say I didn't warn you."

As we continued on with our day, things between us were a little lighter but not like the night before and I have to admit that has me concerned. I know she feels better about getting things off her chest but I, for some reason, sense there's more to the story that she's not telling me but I will let it go for now but I know me and I will get to the bottom of it. But I can't help but think about her niece and what she's planning to do and I gotta warn Darius and make sure he get his act together before he loses everything. Damn Darius I think to myself why can't you just keep your dick in your pants and only for your wife. As we enjoyed the monuments, the African art, the Martin Luther King Monument it seemed as though things were getting back to where they were the night before. But still that craw was sticking in the back of my neck that there were something Kim is just not telling me and it's eating away at me. All I could think to myself was it will come out, soon enough, it always comes out

After a rough start to our day on Thursday, Kim and I enjoyed the rest of it after all. Willie took us to a great soul food restaurant where they had my all-time favorite pies, Sweet Potato. I had mentioned to Willie that I would love to go to a place to get me some and he did not disappoint me. He took us to Henry's Soul Café where he said they have the best sweet potato pie on the planet. I had to admit that he had me curious as to how good they were. I have to say that I was not disappointed in the least and would have to go back to get me a couple for the flight home.

Now I know that my mom won't like the fact that I'm eating someone else's pies since she's been the only one who could make pies the way I love them. Now don't get me wrong many have tried but no one has come close to hers until now. Their menu was great and they had everything I loved from their homemade meatloaf platter to their pork chop platter and of course their fried chicken platter. I met with the owner and told him who I was and that I will have to do a write up in my magazine of course I'm always in business mode and don't miss out on too many opportunities when I come across them.

After leaving the restaurant I asked Willie to take us back to the hotel where we could just relax and enjoy the rest of the evening. I also told Willie that we won't be needing his services on Friday because we're going to take it easy and stay around the hotel. Knowing how things were today I wanted to just chill out with Kim and take it easy for a day and let things kind of simmer down. Besides I knew I had to set up the meeting with Mr. Browin for Saturday and also having to meet up with Edwin and his wife again for dinner at another soul food restaurant and he said they have live jazz bands there. So I figured we could use a day of resting and just enjoy us. Yeah that's the ticket, just enjoy us and no one else…for now.

CHAPTER

21

Braden "Sunday Can't Come Fast Enough"

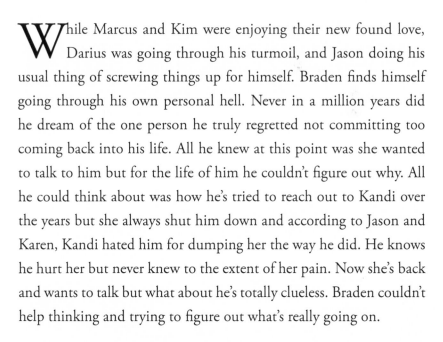

While Marcus and Kim were enjoying their new found love, Darius was going through his turmoil, and Jason doing his usual thing of screwing things up for himself. Braden finds himself going through his own personal hell. Never in a million years did he dream of the one person he truly regretted not committing too coming back into his life. All he knew at this point was she wanted to talk to him but for the life of him he couldn't figure out why. All he could think about was how he's tried to reach out to Kandi over the years but she always shut him down and according to Jason and Karen, Kandi hated him for dumping her the way he did. He knows he hurt her but never knew to the extent of her pain. Now she's back and wants to talk but what about he's totally clueless. Braden couldn't help thinking and trying to figure out what's really going on.

"Kandi, wow, Kandi Evans is back and she wants to talk but about what. I can't take this and now Marcus tells me I have to wait 'til

Sunday when he returns. That's a whole two days away, damn him, but what can I do I have no choice in the matter."

Thinking about what happened 20 years ago comes back to him like a flood and it's overwhelming and feels like he's going into a panic attack. Knowing he has to calm down but it's hard not knowing and having to wait on top of that.

But what could it be and why now, I just don't get it. The last time we spoke almost ten years ago wasn't bad but it wasn't totally good either, I remember calling her on a whim trying desperately one last time to reach out to her in hopes of forgiveness. I remember that she was so shocked that it was me calling especially at the time of night it was. Wow that night is so vivid it's like it happened yesterday.

Reminiscing…

"Hello?"

"Kandi."

"Yes who is this?"

"It's Braden!"

Silence… I could tell by the pause that she was in total disbelief that it was me calling her.

"Are you there?"

"Yes, yes I am, but why are you calling me and at this hour Braden?"

"First off I would ask of you not to hang up on me again please, I mean truthfully I can't believe that I'm actually talking to you right now?"

"Why Braden, why are you calling me, I've gone on with my life and I know you've gone on with yours and your wife, so why call me now?"

"I know you've gone on with your life and are happily married but for me it has not turned out the way I had thought it would."

"Well I'm sorry and I don't mean to sound cruel but that's not my problem, Braden you made your choice back then and it truly hurt me to my core but I had to move on because I knew you didn't want me."

"I know the way I handled things between us was wrong and I own it, I have no other choice but too. But I have been doing a lot of soul searching throughout these past few years and since my divorce."

"Divorce?"

"Yes, Gabrielle and I are no longer together"

"Well, I can't sit here and say that I'm unhappy about that but I will say that it seems as though Karma has come back to haunt you."

"Touché I deserve that one and I can't blame you for feeling the way you feel. I just want to know if there's any way in your heart you can forgive me and not hate me for things I've done?"

"Braden look, can I forgive you, yes, because if I don't then I'll be harboring ill feelings and I wouldn't be able to truly enjoy my own life. Do I hate you…well I'll be honest…at the time I did have hate in my heart for you and for some months after and I should still hate you but that's not within me to do…so no I don't hate you but I have to know one thing?"

"Sure, what is it?"

"Why wasn't I good enough for you, what did I do to make you not want to be with me? I mean I thought we had a good time together and I honestly gave up the opportunity to be with a few other men to be with you but only to have my heart broken. When my father passed away and you decided to go to your "cousins" place instead of being there with me I will admit that's when I first thought that things had changed between us. Even my family was wondering where you were, this great guy I had been talking about so much, why wasn't he here with me in my time of need. I had to lie to them and say that he had his own emergency that he was dealing with and couldn't be there with me physically but he was there with me mentally and called me on the phone. I hated lying to them but it was the only way I could stop all the questions from coming at me. I just couldn't take the fact that I knew that you thought going to your "cousins" place was more important than being with me. Braden can I ask you something and please be honest with me?"

"Ok sure and I'll be honest."

"Did you really go to your cousins or was it the fact you were going to see your now ex-wife?"

"Sigh.....I know I owe you the truth and although a big part of me doesn't want to say it and hurt you all over again but I owe you that much at least. Yes, I went to be with my now ex-wife as you put it. I had decided to ask her to marry me and knew I was going to break things off with you, I'm so sorry!"

"You know something, I figured that it was more than your "cousin" because how else would you not be there for me, Braden how could you." Kandi starting to cry.

Braden hears Kandi starting to cry. Although tears begin to flow from Kandi she tries to keep her emotions in check. Knowing this is a very difficult conversation Braden tries to ease the discomfort as much as he possibly could, but he feels that he's not doing a good job.

"At the time I thought I was doing the right thing but it turned out to truly be the wrong thing. I didn't realize how much we did not have in common and my marriage turned out to be a total disaster. I have no one to blame for my own pain and failure in that regards but me, I'm sorry and I didn't mean to drudge up all of this. Again I hope you can forgive me and I just hope that in some way we can be cordial towards one another, I'm not asking for you to be my friend but maybe if we were to bump into one another that we could at least exchange a nice hello instead of acting like total stranger."

"Braden, again, I forgive you and I'm truly sorry that you're going through your own hell. I can say that, yes, if we were to bump into one another I would say hello and it would be genuine. But I need to go back to sleep so I can get my kids up in the morning. Braden, there's one more thing I think you should know."

"What is that?" my voice begins to shake some from nerves.

"On that day that Marcus drove me home I felt so low and thought that no one could ever want to be with me let alone love me but Marcus was so caring and he genuinely wanted to make sure I was ok. Within all of the chaos he gave me hope that there is someone out there who would love me and want to be with me for the rest of my life. Now I know it because God has truly blessed me with a wonderful husband who loves and cherishes me to no end, I owe him a big thanks."

"Yeah I can see how that could happen because Marcus is that type of guy who does care and it's genuine, when he says he's a friend he truly means it. He doesn't say or do anything fake, I think it has a lot to do with how he grew up. I think that's one reason why I go to him so much for different things and advice is because I know he's going to give it to me straight."

"Yeah I can see that and he's a good friend, you're lucky to have had him then and now."

"Yeah that's true ok, I'll let you go back to sleep......... and Kandi."

"Yes Braden?"

"Thank you for allowing me this time, I truly appreciate it and thank you even more for not hating me."

"God doesn't hate you so how could I and with that you're welcome, goodnight Braden and take care of yourself."

"You do the same."

Braden hangs up the phone and tears flow down his face. The memory of everything that took place is exhausting. He can't help but think what a fool he was. He lost probably the best person he ever will have in his life and ended up with someone who became the worst. They say God gives us one chance to have our soul mate, the one He has designed just for us but if we lose them then we will forever search the world and never be truly happy. Braden wonders if he will ever find someone that can truly make him happy again. But first he has to wait and find out just what it is that Kandi wants to talk about and it's making him nervous more and more. Two more days until Marcus gets home and it's driving him crazy.

CHAPTER

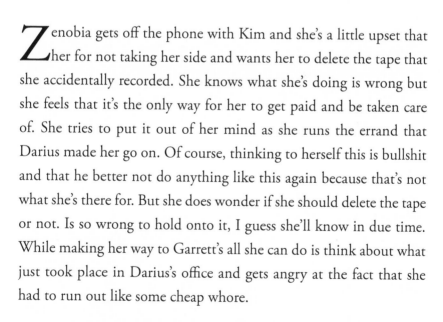

Zenobia "Out of the Frying pan, into the fire"

❖

enobia gets off the phone with Kim and she's a little upset that her for not taking her side and wants her to delete the tape that she accidentally recorded. She knows what she's doing is wrong but she feels that it's the only way for her to get paid and be taken care of. She tries to put it out of her mind as she runs the errand that Darius made her go on. Of course, thinking to herself this is bullshit and that he better not do anything like this again because that's not what she's there for. But she does wonder if she should delete the tape or not. Is so wrong to hold onto it, I guess she'll know in due time. While making her way to Garrett's all she can do is think about what just took place in Darius's office and gets angry at the fact that she had to run out like some cheap whore.

"I can't believe that he has me running this bullshit errand for him just so he won't get caught by his business partners. I should have just jumped out from under the desk but then I'd be out on my ass.

Damn but I'd have the tape recording though. Oh well I guess he had no choice in the matter and I didn't want to ruin things my first few days, hell I need more time to do what I have to do. But I think I'm going to hold onto that tape just in case he gets to acting funny in the office, hmm I may have to put in a call to his wife and let her know the deal. That will just the thing to remind him that he can't play me for a fool no matter what my intentions were. I know what Kim said is the right thing but I have to do what I have to do."

She places her order she receives a call from an unknown number. Knowing she usually doesn't answer unknown numbers, she thought that it may be Darius calling needing something. But what she didn't know was it was from one of the last person she needed to get a call from at this point.

"Hello!"

"Guurrrllll, how are you doing? I heard you got a job over at that record shop."

"Tracy?"

"Yeah girl, how you doing?"

"I'm fine and uhm when did you get out?"

"I got out a couple days ago and I heard about you and your lil record shop job."

"It's not a record shop, it's a record company where they record artist and make records and it's really not a job per se it's an internship."

"Oh well laddi da what's the difference you getting paid ain't you?"

"Yes I'm getting paid but it's not much, there are no benefits and it's only for six weeks."

"Oh, ok well I thought that you were gonna go over there and get you a husband or sugar daddy or something like that."

"Well yeah I did say that at first but I don't know if I'm gonna do that now, look Tracy what do you want because I have work to do?"

"I was just wondering how things are going since I hadn't heard from you in a while."

"I know you haven't and you know why though so don't play"

"I ain't playing and you also know you still owe me right, don't think I forgot about it?"

"Look I told you before that the screw up wasn't my fault and that I don't owe you anything. It wasn't my fault that you got caught up and ended up in jail so don't come at me like that."

"Look bitch...it is what it is but you still owe me the money I lost that night."

"No, I don't and I figured we're even anyway because you didn't tell me that the so called "baller" you were hooking me up with was a dope dealer. Shit he damn near raped me."

"Well, you're the one who said you wanted a baller right? You never specified what kind."

"Uhm Tracy I didn't want one who could and probably would kill me at the drop of a dime though, damn!"

"Well that's not my fault."

"Yes the hell it is your fault and if I didn't have my stun gun it would have been worse for me."

"Well I just wanted to know if you got hooked up yet or not?"

"Hooked up, what in the hell are you talking about?"

"Oh don't play, I know why you're at that record shop ooppss I mean "company" and it's not to learn how to make a CD."

"Regardless as to why I'm there it's none of your business and again I gotta go so you have a good one."

"Fine, bye then, but one more thing, don't get it twisted and forget where you came from, you're just a hood rat just like the rest of us. Just because you're in a fancy college don't make you any better than anyone else."

"Bye Tracy and don't worry about calling me again!"

"Bitch!"

"Back at you!" Zenobia hangs up the phone.

"Uuhhgggg I can't believe she had the nerve to call me after what almost happened to me. I should find her and kick her ass for hooking me up with that dealer. I want to get paid but damn not like the way he was wanting. Shit I gotta hurry up and get this stuff and get back to the office"

She got her purchase and headed back to the office all she could think was how things could have ended up if she didn't have protection, thank God for the stun gun. As she headed back into the office and was going toward her desk she runs into Terry and he has this weird look on his face as if he knows something she don't.

"Excuse me Ms. Bentley can you come into my office for a second?"

"Sure thing Mr. Thompson, I just need to give Mr. Davenport his package he wanted me to get."

"Oh, that's ok I can give it to him, I need to talk to you for a minute."

Realizing he's being very persistent I go into his office and find out what he wants.

"Please have a seat, I need to go over with you some of your duties that will take place over the next few weeks."

"Ok should I get a pen and paper and write this down?"

"No you won't need it because it will be on your daily calendar what you will have to do for the day. I just want to go over the overall responsibilities that you'll be doing while you're here for your internship. First thing you have to be on time and ready to go because we have deadlines for different things and I'm going to assign you and Mitch different tasks that you'll have to complete and they will be graded because this time around we're looking to hire one of you two so you have to be on your pees and ques. Second you will report to me and me only and I will go to Mr. Davenport if I need to on your behalf."

Zenobia getting this weird feeling that Terry is trying to block her from having any contact with Darius. But he can try all he want, she knows that she will get to him no matter what because she has some unfinished business to take care of.

"Third you will be helping out with the two new female artists we have and make sure that they are comfortable and have certain things in order when they are here and for when they go out on the road. For example, when they go out on the road it will be your responsibility to make sure their accommodations are properly made and that all the bookings are confirmed and things like that. It's not difficult but it can be tedious at times because if just one detail is missed then it can cost us a lot of money and that is something Mr. Davenport cannot and will not have trust me."

"Ok is there anything else I will have to do and will I ever get to work directly with Darius, I mean Mr. Davenport?" Zenobia fishing to see if he's blocking or if she's going to ever end up in a one on one again.

"That's the gist of it and as far as you working directly with Mr. Davenport you'll have a couple things that he'll handle with you but that's not towards the end of your internship after you've proven that you are serious about this.

"Oh ok, I was wondering because I think I could really learn a lot from him."

"I'm sure you can but he wants you and Mitch to learn things from the bottom to the top and not just go for the top right away. He wants you to truly appreciate what it takes to start and run a successful company."

"Ok, I don't mean nor want to be rude but if that's all, I need to get this popcorn into him."

"Oh I'll take it, I need for you to get to your desk and start completing a couple tasks that I already have for you."

Zenobia letting out a small sigh, knowing she's in for a fight to get to where she wants to be, gets up and go to her desk to start work on the tasks Terry has for her. All she knows is, this may end up being more difficult that she thought. When she gets to her desk she reaches inside her purse and remembers that the tape recorder is there and thinks that it may not be as difficult as she thinks after all.

CHAPTER

23

Marcus "New Business"

A fter having a nice first couple of days with minimal drama Kim and Marcus decide to take Friday for themselves and not do anything nor contact anyone. They spent the day just lounging around playing card games and enjoying the time alone. They ended the night with giving one another massages and just relaxed and went to bed. Rejuvenated Kim decides to get up early and surprise Marcus with her cooking skills and make him breakfast in bed.

"Good morning sleepy head." Kim says.

"Mmmm well good morning to you too Ms. Johnson, I see you're up already and what's that wonderful smell?"

"Well after that wonderful, relaxing, and peaceful day of just enjoying us yesterday I have a little more energy this morning. So I decided to get up and go to the store and get a few things to make you a special breakfast in bed."

"Wow I get breakfast in bed, now you know you better be careful because you can spoil a brotha with some good cooking. Uhm you can cook right?"

"I know you didn't go there Mr. Bass, yes I can cook." Kim laughing.

"Hey, I'm just making sure because I really don't want to have to visit the emergency room while in D.C."

"I see you got jokes this morning, well why don't you let me give you a taste of my goodies and then you tell me for yourself."

"I've already tasted your goodies and I loved every minute of it if I do say so myself."

"Mmmm Mr. Bass I see someone is being a little frisky this morning huh?"

"You did say "taste your goodies" right so I was just saying I've already had and loved them that's all."

"Although I loved you tasting my goodies, I'm not talking about me my love. I want you to taste what I prepared. So sit back and let me cater to you since you've been catering to me for the past few days."

"Yes ma'am I think I can do just that."

Kim gets up to finish preparing our breakfast, I lay there, mind going in a thousand different directions. I begin to think about mom and Jazzy of course and how they are doing but I know they are fine. I think about Darius and the drama he's facing. I think about Jason and his continued saga he has going on then there's Braden and the bombshell Kandi dropped on me. Sigh....what am I to do, I feel as though I have the weight of the world on my shoulders at times but hey that's the way it is right. Someone has to do it so why not me, but sometimes I wonder why me.

My thoughts shift to the meeting I have later on this afternoon with Mr. Browin to discuss him opening up a LUX Lounge in Chicago. I already know that would be a hit. Too many people contact me now wanting to go to a nice up-scale place without all the drama that goes along with having a nice evening out. Man, I wonder just what happened to the times of actually getting dressed up to go out, I mean you had to dress to impress in order to get into anything. Now all you see is women wearing or not wearing almost nothing at all and the men wearing their pants half down their ass.

It's a shame too, especially since the younger men really don't have a clue as to where the sagging pants come from. I guess I am truly getting old because I don't understand what women see in men who do that and I definitely don't understand why young men do it. Oh well I can only do my part and that's inform the public of what's going on. Although this has been an awesome trip I can't wait to get back to the windy city and begin to help my boys put out fires before they become infernos. Then there's Kim and her issues that she still hasn't opened up and shared with me. I still wonder…wonder what's going on with her and what she's hiding. I know she's hiding something but she acts like she's not and even though I tried to reassure her that nothing can be that bad she still won't open up to me. But yet I still have this gut feeling that it may be worse than I can imagine after all. I hate feeling this way but I have no choice, I was told a long time ago to trust your first gut instincts and I've always lived by that and it's panned out pretty well thus far. I know something's up, but just what, is yet to be seen. The good thing is I don't have that "runaway" feeling so I'll be patient for now. All I know is something has to give and soon.

While I'm engulfed in my thoughts I hear Kim talking to me.

"Baby, would you like milk, apple juice or orange juice?"

"Mmmm all three to be honest, I'm rather thirsty this morning."

"Oh I see, well I hope you're just as hungry too because I prepared for you an omelet with turkey sausage, sautéed onions and green and red peppers and pancakes with a touch of cinnamon in them I hope you like that?"

"Hmm girl was you reading my mind or what, I love all of those things and how did you know to put cinnamon in the pancakes?"

"Well it's something I grew up eating and I figured that you may like it."

"Wow so did I and that's the only way I truly like to eat them although going out to a restaurant you can't get them prepared like that believe me I tried."

"Well my dear you can have them whenever you like and it will be my pleasure to make them for you."

"Well I can definitely take you up on that offer and everything smells so good are you sure you don't need any help with anything?"

"Oh, trust me I got this, all you have to do is relax and let me take care of my man, that's all you have to do."

"You're man huh?"

"Oh, did I say that out loud?" Kim smiles in a blush

"Uhm yes you did say that out loud, but it's ok, sounds good rolling off those sweet lips of yours."

"Why thank you my dear I kinda like that myself, like when you called me your baby the other night, gave me goose bumps."

"I'll admit I liked that too so let's eat so we can get up and get ourselves together. We have a busy day ahead of us before we leave for home in the morning."

"Oh, do we now and what are we going to do today Mr. Bass?"

"Well after we eat I'm having Willie pick us up and he's going to drop me off at the Lux Lounge to meet with Mr. Browin and he's going to take you to the mall where you'll be meeting Sheila and have a girls afternoon while I conduct business."

"Oh is that right and how did you know that we were going to try and meet up?"

"When I contacted Mr. Browin I also hit up Edwin to discuss tonight's events. That's when he informed me that you and Sheila talked about getting together to do a little shopping for an outfit for tonight."

"Oh, ok so in other words he spilled the beans huh?"

"Spilled the beans on what hon?" finding out that she was trying to surprise me with a nice outfit for the night.

"Oh, come on, the fact that I wanted to find something special to wear for you on our last night in Washington D.C. now it's ruined."

"No, it's not babe because for one you haven't found anything and two and even better yet I have yet to see you in it so nothing's ruined ok. Look, let's eat and get ourselves together because I told Mr. Browin that I would meet him at 11 O'clock to go over the proposal he has in mind and talk about how I'm going to write up his club and introduce it to the Chicago."

"Ok, can you bless the food please?"

"It will be my pleasure."

I said grace, as I did that warm feeling came over me again as if things will be alright and I smiled. As we ate we just enjoyed one another and listened to the jazz station that was playing on the radio. I must admit that she's a very good cook. I was a bit surprised but pleasantly. After breakfast we got ourselves cleaned up and I had Willie meet us in the lobby. Gave him instructions on the day's events and made sure that he was available for tonight and surprised him with the idea of bringing his wife out to dinner with us. I wanted to show my appreciation for him and all that he has done taking great care of me while I was in D.C. he was flattered by it and agreed to the dinner. Well he didn't have much choice because I wasn't going to take no for an answer. When Willie had dropped me off at the Lux Lounge I get a call from Darius. Knowing I couldn't talk to him at that time I thought to ignore it and let it go to voice mail but something within me didn't let me do that.

"What's up D, how's life in the record business?"

"What's up Bass, you know it's busy as ever, how's things in D.C.?"

"Couldn't be better my brotha, so what do I owe the pleasure of this call?"

"Come on man can't I just call my boy and talk to him without wanting something?"

"Yeah sure but I don't think that this is one of those time especially since you almost got caught with a woman under your desk with your pants down and your dick in her mouth so no I don't think of this as one of those times." I said with a smirk.

"Dude how in the hell did you know about that, I haven't spoken to anyone about that, so?"

"You won't believe me when I tell you and I'm gonna have to cut this phone call short because I have a meeting but we'll pick it up when I'm done."

"Come on man don't leave me hanging like that, tell me how the hell you know about that?"

"Well let's just say that I find it ironically funny that I met the girl's aunt while coming to D.C."

"Wait, so you telling me that the new woman in your life is this chick's aunt?"

"Yeah, small world isn't it my brotha, see I told you to keep your cool and do right but I see you just don't want to listen. Look man we gotta pick this up later I gotta run but we will get into this because I have some information that's going to blow your mind."

"Wow really? What is it man don't leave me hanging like this."

"Oh, wow a play on words, you should have thought about that when you left your soldier hanging, I'm out I'll talk to you soon."

"Man, that's cold but ok I'll let it go for now but hit me a.s.a.p. peace."

"Peace!"

Damn I knew I should have let it go to voice mail but nnnoooo I had to answer. Now I have to get myself together before walking in these doors. Wow look how God works, He is so awesome and I can't thank Him enough.

As I walk in the doors of the Lux Lounge I just feel that this is the start of something big and I can be a part of it all. Bringing this fabulous venue to the Chicago area will be a great venture for me. I don't get in the doors good enough when I'm greeted by the same security guard that held our private room at bay. He looks at me as if he knew me but couldn't figure out from where.

"Hello, I'm here to see Mr. Browin."

"I'm sorry but the Lounge is closed at the moment."

"Yes I know but I have a meeting with him, my name is Marcus Bass, could you be so kind as to let him know I'm here for our meeting."

"Just one moment, Mr. Bass you say?"

"Yes, Marcus Bass, owner of."

I couldn't get the name of my magazine out fast enough just when Charles Browin came around the corner and saved me.

"Marcus, good to see you're a person who believes in being early rather than late, I can appreciate that, it says to me that you're about your business"

"Well thank you sir."

"Please call me Charles."

"Well thank you Charles and I live by the creed that to be early is on time, on time is late, and late is unacceptable. I got that from my boss when I was working a security job in college."

"Hmm very nice and I like that, I hope you don't mind me stealing that so I can use it for my employees. It seems as though they don't understand the concept of just because you're supposed to be in at 3:00pm doesn't mean you actually show up at that time to work. I tell you these young kids today seem to have no sense of time and consideration."

Laughing at his statement I couldn't help but agree.

"Yes I agree and they seem to think that you already owe them something and they don't have to work at what they get."

"Now you're preaching to the choir, you know something, when I was talking with Edwin about you and he said he had a wonderful vibe from you and hadn't really spent any time with you I honestly couldn't understand where he was coming from but now that I met you I can truly see it. You have that certain charisma that allows people to be comfortable and most importantly be themselves and it's a nice feeling."

"Wow, I'm honored and also taken aback by it but I'll take it, I give all thanks to God and my mother for me and how I am. Without them I wouldn't be where I am today"

"What about your father, didn't he play a role in your life" Charles sensing he seemed to hit a bad nerve apologized for reaching to far, "I'm sorry but I didn't bring up a bad memory did I?"

"Well, I honestly don't talk about it much but I can tell you. My father was killed at an early age from a drunk driver. He was walking down the street about to get into his car and come home and a driver who apparently had been drinking crossed four lanes of traffic and jumped the curb and ran him down."

"Oh, Marcus I'm so sorry, that must have been devastating, may I ask how old were you when this happened?"

"I was eight years old and my mother raised me alone ever since. I mean she tried to date and call herself getting me another father but none ever really worked out. So, one day I told her, I think I was about 13 or 14, that I don't need another father because no one could replace him. So, she never dated seriously again and it was just us from then on until my wife and daughter came into the picture."

"Oh, ok so you have a daughter that's good and how long have you and that lovely young lady been married?"

Laughing slightly because of the apparent confusion he does not know about.

"I'm not married to the young lady you saw me with, no I lost my wife 10 years ago due to her being hit from behind by a guy running from the police. You know something I'm surprised that I still drive seeing that all the bad things that has happened to those I love was because of a vehicle."

"Yes I can see how you would feel that way, so tell me the young lady you were with, is she someone special?"

Mr. Browin is being a tad bit nosy but I go along with it to see where it goes. He must have picked up on my detection and the facial look on my face because he then reassured me of why the questions.

"Ok Marcus, I can see the look in your eyes as to why I'm curious about your life and who you surround yourself with?"

"Very perceptive and yes I must say you have me intrigued, so tell me why the concern Charles?"

"Well it's like this, I run my business like a family, a strict family but a family none the less and I don't go into business with anyone I don't know or feel they have a good strong family value. You see in business you have to be very careful of whom you get into bed with because that person could wind up being the demise of you, your relationship, and your company all in one. So, I'm very careful as to who I am dealing with. So yes I ask a lot of personal questions and yes they tell me a lot about you but what tells me the most is not what you say when you answer it but how you say it. I pay attention to your tone, pitch, body language and your eyes to see if you're giving me the truth and I must say that although I heard what Edwin has said, oh and by the way speaks very highly of you. I still had to find out for myself just how you are and if I could truly trust not only his gut feelings but my own."

"Wow, I must say that I've never had anyone read me like that, usually I'm the one who does the reading and like you I'm rarely wrong about a person. So may I ask, what is your impression of me, I'm curious to know?"

"Well I must say that I see you as a go getter, one who is about his business, one who does what he needs and has to do to make it, one who rarely takes no for an answer unless it's no other resort. One who has good, strong family values and has love and compassion in what he takes on. Simply put you're a hustler by nature who loves from his soul."

"Wow…ok did it get hot in here or what, I feel like I'm in an interrogation room, I mean you read me like a book and I'm speechless right now."

"Marcus I'll tell you this, I've been in business with many different people in the 62 years of my life and I've learned through some good times and bad how to deal with people and read them very quickly so yes I can say I'm somewhat of an expert in that area and I like you I really do and you have a good head on your shoulders which brings me to our point of being here. I looked through your magazine and also did a Google search on you as well as your company just to get a feel of what others have said about you and I must say that everything I read is very nice. This is why I would love for you to help me bring Lux to Chicago and make it a success. I have people heading there already searching out locations and looking into what it would take for me to get it started but I need the word to get out that we're coming there and once we're there also to help publicize it and make it a huge success. Also, since I will not be able to be there full time due to the fact of my age and also that I'm living here would like to propose a partnership between you and I. I need someone who can be there, be my eyes and ears as to what's going on in the day-to-day business."

"Wow, I didn't expect this. I don't know what to say honestly but I truly am flattered that you would want me to be your business partner and help you get this off the ground."

"Well it's a simple yes to be honest with you but I always say go with your gut feeling on this and it will never lead you wrong."

"Hmm funny, as I was walking in here I had this feeling that this was going to be a wonderful venture but I didn't know to what extent but now I do. So, my answer is yes, yes I'll be your eyes and ears and together we'll make Lux a huge success and it will take the Windy City by storm."

"Good I'm glad you're on board, now all we have to do is some paperwork and get things finalized for our partnership and as long as everything checks out as I'm sure they will this will be the beginning of a wonderful and long-lasting relationship."

"That it will and I've gotten totally excited about this. Wow look how God works, I came out here for one thing and it turned into a couple more great things in my life. All I can do is give God the glory for all of this. Thank you Mr. Browin thank you very much for the opportunity and I won't let you down."

"You're welcome Marcus and please call me Charles from now on because we'll be in business together so no need for the formalities. Look I have a couple things I have to attend to but from what I know you're meeting Edwin this evening correct for one last meal before flying home tomorrow correct?"

Ok I was thinking to myself that this is to eerie that he knows so much about me and my business but I have heard that the smart business men and women of the world don't take too many chances they like to know everything about who and what their getting into so I wasn't too concerned.

"Yes we are meeting up later for dinner and listening to some jazz"

"Good, what I'll do if you don't mind, I'll stop by the B. Smiths and bring the paperwork for you to sign and have a celebratory drink with everyone before you fly out in the morning."

"That would be great. I heard that this place is real nice and I love me some Jazz too, so I'm looking forward to it. I'll admit that I'm a little bit overwhelmed by all of this but I'll be ok. I look forward to a long-lasting business relationship and the start of a true friendship as well."

"I too Marcus, I too, well I will let you go for now and will see you later on this evening."

"I look forward to it as well. Now I have to call for Willie to come get me and with all this going on I need to get me something to eat."

"Well do this, go to the bar and tell them to make you something of your choice while you wait on your driver to get here and tell them I said it's on the house."

"Thank you very much Charles I truly appreciate it, well I'll let you go take care of your other business and I'll see you later on tonight."

We stood up and shook hands I could feel that things are just right. Charles left and I went to one of the bars to place an order for some hot-wings, fried mushrooms, and a raspberry tea. Mmmm this was a great day and I couldn't wait to celebrate with Kim. I called Willie and told him that my meeting was done and he said it will take him about a half hour to get to me with the traffic and all. I told him that was fine since I was about to eat lunch. I asked him if he had anything and he hadn't at that point. I told him what I was having and he said that sounded great so I placed an order for him as well. I then text Kim and let her know I was done and that things went exceptionally well and we'll have some serious celebrating to do. As my food arrived it smelled so good and I was ready to dig in. I said grace thanking God for my food and most importantly everything that has happened in this trip. As I dug into my food I thought to myself that I would definitely have to have some great cooks in the Chicago Lux so people would really come out not only to party but to eat and socialize too. Yeah this is going to be a great venture, I can't wait.

I finished eating my food just in time for Willie to show up. I grabbed his food and went out to the car where he was waiting. I gave Willie his food and got in the car. Riding in the car as I left the Lux Lounge seemed as if I was floating on air. Willie asked me how things went with my meeting and I just chuckled and said that thing's went well, better than I expected. Willie asked me if I wanted to go to the mall where Kim was. I told him that I wanted to go back to the hotel to get some rest and get a few things in order. I did ask Willie about the ladies and their venture. He informed me that they seemed to be having a wonderful time and wanted him to come back to get them in a couple hours.

I told him that it was perfect timing and asked him if he knew of any good flower shops around and he told me he knew of a perfect one just on the way to the hotel. I had Willie stop there so I can get some flowers for Kim. I wanted to have them when she came back to our room. I wanted her to know that I truly appreciate how she's helped me relax and get through this weekend. I also wanted to let her know that I wanted us to continue what has begun to develop once back in Chicago. Yeah for the first time in a long time I'm going with my "gut feeling" as Charles stated and for the first time in a long time, since Brenda passed, just gonna roll with the flow of things.

We arrived at the flower shop where I was able to pick out some beautiful flowers for her. I also saw a cute teddy bear that had hug me on the feet. I thought that was so cute so I decided to pick that up too and get one for Jazzmin while I was at it. Upon leaving the flower shop I thought to myself that she's going to love these. Also I couldn't help but think of how blessed I've been since coming out to DC and chuckled at the fact that I think things went so well because God knew of all the hell I'm gonna have to deal with once I get back to the City.

Oh well that's life right, My Brother's Keeper, I keep telling myself. Yeah I guess I am in some ways because of all the fires I have to help put out but thinking to myself I wouldn't change a thing. Besides my boys have been there for me in my time of need so we all are brothers Keepers.

Yeah tonight is going to be special and one I'm going to remember and enjoy. Just as I was basking in the joy of the trip I got an unexpected call from one of my boys Milton. As I looked at the caller ID on my cell I couldn't help but wonder what in the world did he want because it's been a long time since we've talked. I immediately thought that this couldn't be good.

"Hello!"

"Marcus, I need to stop by and talk to you real bad, are you at home?"

"Milton what's up man, well no I'm not at home I'm still in DC right now on my business, what's up?"

"Man, I'm in a bind and I need your help. I need a place to crash for a bit just until I get some things worked out."

"Hold up, wait, what are you talking about, what's going on at your house."

"Well Sharon had flipped out and did some crazy mess and I don't know what to do."

Ok I'm tripping now because Milton is my boy and he's one of those brotha's who's quiet and keeps to himself and never and I mean NEVER gets into any mess so this is quite a shock coming from him.

"Ok what do you mean flipped out and what craziness has she done?"

"Well she's talking about divorce and has filed a restraining order against me falsely."

"WHAT THE HELL!!! wait a minute let me get my mind wrapped around this. Did you say divorce AND she filed a restraining order against you? But why I thought things between you and her were good?"

"Yeah they were at first for a while but then she just started flipping out on me for simple things and then she started to complain about finances. Ever since she lost her job she's been nitpicking about things and I don't know if I can take it much longer. I mean she gets on me if I come home later than usual. Accuses me of cheating if I want to go hoop with y'all, I mean man what am I to do?"

"Man, that's fucked up, but have you thought about counseling, I mean I think it works at least it did for me. After Brenda died I had so many feelings bottled up inside to the point I was about to explode but a good friend of mine told me that counseling is a good way to release that frustration and figure out what's really the problem. After I started counseling I found out that I was angry for all the wrong reasons and it has taught me a valuable lesson. Man, maybe that's what you two need to do."

"Marcus I wanted to go to counseling but she refuses to, claiming that I'm just trying to get her committed, saying that she's crazy."

"Well from what you're telling me she does sound a little coo coo, sorry man that was out of line."

"No, you're right but I don't know what to do now."

"Ok so why do you need to stay at my place."

"Well since she filed that report the police told me I had to stay away until the investigation has been completed."

"Oh, ok and how long do they think it will take for them to do that?"

"I don't know, they said that a social worker will have to get involved and everything."

"Oh shit, you know when they get involved it's not good for the father."

"Yeah tell me about it, but man I haven't done anything to her."

"Yeah man I know, I know you all too well and you wouldn't touch a hair on her and you really love those kids especially lil Jeremiah and he's not even yours."

"I know man, I know, damn."

"See that's what's wrong with some women now, they get a good man, don't know what to do with them and keep them happy but yet complain that whatever their doing isn't enough. It's a damn shame, then they wonder why their alone and bitter."

"Yeah you're preaching to the choir, but right now I have to do what the police told me to do so I just left without packing a thing. I don't have anything at all, hell I had to go to the store to get hygiene products because of how I left."

"Man, when this all take place if you don't mind me asking?"

"It started on Thursday and I left yesterday."

"Ok and you're just now calling me for a place, where did you stay last night?"

"At a hotel, I just needed a place to be alone and think of what to do. So that's why I'm calling now to see if it would be possible to crash at your place for a little while but I forgot you were out of town. I'm sorry to be laying this on you and I can find somewhere else to go."

"Man did you feel that?"

"What?" Milton sounding confused.

"That smack upside your head, dude you're trippin I have no problem with you staying with me but I won't be back until tomorrow."

"Oh, ok I can just go to a hotel again and stay til' you get home."

"See you speaking to fast, I was gonna tell you to just go to my building and let them know who you are. I'll call the front desk and tell them you're coming and to give you my extra key and pass code to get into my place. Take the second bedroom on the left when you get into my place and chill out until I get home and then we'll put our heads together and figure out something, cool?"

"Cool, thanks Marcus man I truly appreciate it, I figured you were the best choice since I've been having a bit of car trouble. My job is closest to you and just in case it goes out I can just catch the bus or walk. Again thanks, I'm glad you're able to come through."

"It's cool man just get over there and relax and we'll start working on things when I get back, now I hope you don't mind the other fellas knowing because we all need to come together and help you figure this out."

"No, I don't mind, in fact Braden and Darius know a lot of what's going on but not this. You're the first person I told. I just need to get my head together, I feel like I'm going to pop right now. I've never been so angry in my life. Man, she's talking about leaving and going back down south and I can't have that man, not being away from my kids like that."

"Yeah I feel you, I hate that I'm away from Jazzmin this long so I can't imagine what it would be like to be away from her for days, weeks or even months. Shit that would kill me for real."

"Uuhhgggg I don't even want to think about that right now. I just need to get through these next few days to find out what's going to happen and then make my next move."

"Ok man it's cool, let me go and I'll make the call and you should be ok."

"Cool and again thanks man."

"No problem, that's what friends are for."

"Yeah I hear ya, alright man I'll see you when you get back. What time do you fly into Chicago anyway?"

"I'll be flying in on the 12-noon flight which will get into Chicago at 1pm due to the time change"

"Oh, ok just want to make sure, ok thanks again and I'll see you tomorrow."

"Again, no problem and I'll see you in the morning, peace."

"Peace!"

Damn! Another one of my boys going through bullshit with his wife. Damn is marriage that hard now days? Hell should I even contemplate getting married again? I don't know but what I do know is I have to get my mind right before tonight and get in the celebration mood. But how could I be in a good mood when it seems as though all my friends' lives are crashing down around them. Damn this is hard sometimes but hey I know how to put on a face and go with the flow of things. They don't call me chameleon for nothing.

As we pulled up in front of my hotel, I got out and thanked Willie again for such great service. He asked me was everything ok and that he couldn't help but overhear a portion of my conversation. I told him that I'm fine but some of my friends are going through some things and I'll have to deal with once I get back home but right now I have other things to think about and take care of so I have to shelve things for now.

Willie asked what time should he pick us up and I told him 7pm and he confirmed it with me and said that he was on his way to pick up Kim and drop her back off, he said it shouldn't be no longer than about an hour. Again, I thanked him and walked into the hotel. As I entered the hotel lobby I made a call to my front desk and made sure they had Milton's name and that he has my permission to gain access to my home. All I could do is think of is how all of a sudden I'm tired. As I made my way to my room, I turned the lock, entered my room, and just collapsed on my bed. I thought to myself that this can be draining…and then passed out.

CHAPTER

24

Marcus "Sleep is a good thing"

❧

"**M**aaarrrcccuuuuusss.......Honeyyyyy, I see someone is being a sleepy head."

Being a little startled by Kim waking me up.

"Mmmm well hello baby, when did you get here?" Stretching...I answer in a groggily voice.

"I just got here and when I came in I saw the beautiful flowers and the teddy bears. They are so cute, are they for me?"

"Well one of them is and the other is for Jazz."

"Well as long as it's for Jazzmin I don't mind sharing with her." Kim said grinning sheepishly.

"Well I'm glad you don't mind because she's the one you'd have to share me with."

"Hmm I think I can handle that. Baby how long have you been

sleep?"

"What time is it?"

Kim Looking at the clock

"It's 4:30."

"Oh, wow I've been sleep all this time, Willie dropped me off at just about 12:15, my meeting didn't last long and I stayed there to eat. Baby they have some great food there and I said that I'm gonna have to make sure we have great cooks in Chicago when we open up."

"Uhm We, Chicago, open up, what's going on, am I missing something?"

"Well I'll say it like this; you're looking at the new partner for the Lux Lounge that will soon be coming to Chicago."

"What, Marcus are you for real, I thought that he just wanted to talk about advertising?"

"Well, he did want that but he also wanted to open one in Chicago and that's where I will do most of the advertising for it and pumping it up to make it a success."

"Baby when will he open it up, I'm getting excited for you and from the way we were treated the other night I can't wait to experience this in Chicago, hell we need a good upscale place that blacks can go too."

"Yeah tell me about it, I know he's not planning on getting it up and running for at least a year because he'd have to get a place, get all the permits and building up to code, hire people to do all the work to get it going then hire people to do the various jobs that will take place.

Babe it's going to be crazy cool once it's up and going. He's already talking about making it larger than the one here and having at least two more VIP Private Sections for special elite guest who are either in town or who fly into Chicago such as himself."

"Wow that sounds so wonderful, so how is it you're going to be a partner if you don't mind me asking?"

"Well he said that after meeting me and getting a good vibe. Talking with Edwin and also checking me out on Google and with talking with me this morning he said that he wanted me to be his eyes and ears in Chicago. I do know though he's going to do a background check on me because that's one thing he said he does for all employees before hiring them. Even though I'm not technically an employee I still know he's going to because one thing he said is this you have to know who you get into bed with in business. So, it's cool I don't mind at all because little does he know I'm already on top of checking him out to make sure that everything is on the up and up."

"Wow this seems like some eye spy type stuff going on but sounds exciting."

"Well in a way it is because you have to be careful who you deal with especially when it comes to business and money."

"Yeah I guess but sometimes you need to do that in life too because you can never be too sure of someone at times."

"Oh, are you talking about when I did a background check on you?"

"Marcus that wasn't funny then and it isn't funny now"

Kim trying to laugh it off.

"Ok, ok, ok I'll stop, but on another note how was the shopping adventure with Sheila?"

"It was great and the reason why I'm late getting back is because we went to a few more shops and I was able to find the right shoes and accessories for my outfit that you will see a little later."

"Mmmm I can't wait, so let me ask you this, how long will it take you to be ready?"

"Well since I want to make sure that I look a little extra special for you tonight I'd say about an hour and a half tops."

"Wow that long, sheesh, it will only take me about a half hour, boy I tell ya women." I say as I chuckle.

"Hey, hey, hey now it takes time to look as good as I do especially for her man."

"Well baby let me say this, you look good now and don't have to change a thing for me, I like you just the way you are."

"Well alrighty then Mr. Bass I like how you think.."

"Well, I just speaks the truth Ms. Johnson." sounding country.

"That you do, that you do. Well what would you like to do since we don't have to get ready for another hour or so?"

"I'd love to just lay her on the bed, set the alarm so we won't over sleep and have you curl up in my arms and rest for a while, I'm not as tired physically as I am mentally with all that's going on back at home."

"Mmmm sounds good to me and I honestly couldn't wait to get into your arms. I was thinking that all the while I was gone. And Marcus I know you have a lot to deal with once you get home but I hope you don't let it stress you too much."

"I won't baby and besides it's not that it's on me, I just have to help some friends out with their issues that's all."

"Yeah I understand that, I just want you to take care of yourself baby."

"Oh, trust me that I will, you have no worries in that area."

"Good that's what I want to hear."

"Well Ms. Johnson set the alarm and come to poppa."

"Mmmm I like the sound of that Big poppa."

We laid there dozing off all I could think of how things have truly gone for me and I'm happy about that but of course my mind drifted back to what's waiting for me back home.

CHAPTER

25

Marcus "All That Jazz"

B eep, beep, beep, beep, the alarm on the night stand goes off and the clock reads 5:30pm. I look at Kim sleeping soundly and realize that she was just as tired as I was. I slide out of bed and let her sleep a little while longer while I get up to take a shower and start getting myself together. Knowing I won't take long since I already ironed my clothing for tonight all I had to do was hop in and out of the shower and get myself together. I approached the glass door of the shower thinking to myself this standup glass shower with these multiple shower heads is going to feel oh so good when I get it installed in my place. I turn on the shower letting the water heat up as I look in the mirror and realize I need to shave. I start taking off my cloths and just when I bend over to take my lounge pants off I hear Kim in the back of me

"Mmmm mmm mmm that is such a lovely sight."

"Oh, is it now Ms. Johnson?" turning around to see Kim standing there stark naked.

"Oh, that it is Mr. Bass, would you mind if I join you in that shower you're getting ready to take?"

"Well seeing that you came in here all birthday suited up looking like a snickers bar, just satisfying, by all means please do."

We approach the shower door I hold it open for Kim and help her into the shower. Realizing it's a little too warm for her liking I turn down the heat but just as I did, the heat between us begins to rise. Kim stood under the water allowing it to sooth her heavenly bodacious body I couldn't help but take a step back and marvel of her figure. I have to say I love me a thick, voluptuous, in shape, curvy woman with everything in place. I couldn't help but try to in vision what her figure was. I had to say her supple breast had to be about a 40DD and her waist was looking like a 28 and her hips had to be about a 46 and that ass oh my goodness they say onions make you cry well she had a couple of them to say the least. I was in amazed, I think she knew it because when she caught me staring she called me over to her.

"Marcus, you look as if you've never seen me before."

"Well honestly I haven't, not like this, not in this light looking so scrumptious."

"You look as if you were sizing me up or something?"

"Well in fact I actually was." her not knowing she just read my mind.

"Hmm oh really and did you like your view?"

"Oh yes ma'am and then some." we get caught in a stare.

"Marcus?" she speaks breaking our silence.

"Yes Kim?"

"Would you make love to me?"

"Of course, let me get a towel and dry you off."

"No Marcus... I mean right here...right now."

I must admit that she surprised me just a bit. I know I'd be game to make love to her in the shower, hell anywhere but I honestly didn't think she'd be as open to something more on the risqué side, but I'm loving the fact that she's adventurous.

"It would be my pleasure and you just took the words right out of my mouth."

I went to Kim, took the towel she was holding and put it on the rack. Doing so allowed her hands to be free to do whatever she chooses to do with them. Standing in front of her, I take my hands and caress her face and gently place a kiss on her sweet lips. I feel her body quiver from the touch of our encounter. I kiss her deep, long, passionately, so much so I feel my manhood rise. Kim feels this too and surprises me a little by taking him in her hand and begins to stroke him. As we continue our deep passionate kiss. She strokes Jr. long and hard and when I think I'm about to make my next move she takes over and lowers herself allowing the water to hit her from all sides. She takes Jr. and begins to kiss him gently, licking him slowly, allowing her mouth to tease me with delight. She continues performing one of the best oral performances I've had in a long time. Not wanting me to reach my climax just yet she comes back to me and whispers in my ear.

"I've always wanted to make love in a shower, so TAKE ME DADDY!!"

At that moment I swear Jr. heard her more than my ears did because he became more erect and thickened up to a point I thought I was going to burst. I informed her I had no problem in obliging her desires. I took Kim and placed her back up against the glass wall of the shower that faced the mirror. I gently picked her up as she held onto my neck, allowing my manhood to enter into her love box, Kim let out a gasp of air in delight. I held her legs up with my arms allowing for no interference. As she rose up and down on me I couldn't help but get a view in the mirror. I thought to myself WOW what a beautiful sight of her voluptuous ass rising up and down allowing my manhood to appear and then disappear again. Kim looked at me then realized I was watching our love making happen live in the mirror. She wanted to enjoy our show we were performing for ourselves so I obliged her and turned her slightly so we could watch as we made love to one another. It was as if we were watching a live porno movie on set. That seemed to get our juices flowing ever more. I asked Kim

"Do you trust me?"

"Yes I trust you." looking a little nervous.

"Good, I'm going to do something to you I know you haven't had done."

"I'll admit I'm a little nervous now."

"Don't worry baby I got you, but what I'm going to do I want you to see all for yourself, I'm going to put on a show just for you."

"Mmmm ok I'll admit you have me curious as to what you're going to do."

"All you have to do is relax and enjoy your show."

As I slid Jr. out of her love box I turned Kim towards the back wall so she could face the mirror. I lifted her higher onto my shoulders and had her braced up against the wall. I then begin to taste the sweet nectar that was Kimberly Johnson. I could tell she was loving my craftsmanship and technique of tasting her sweet juices because she let go of my head and began to grab for anything on the wall that wasn't there. Just as it was getting wonderfully good for me I heard her voice

"Mmmmmaaarrrccuuuusss Ooohh mmmyyyy ggooodddd baabbyyy I'mmm about tooo, Ooohhh Maaarrrccuusss Oohh Marcus…Ohh Marcus…I'm….I'm….Oh my GOD…I'm Cumming…Oohh ssshhhhiiiittttt!!!"

All I could do at that point was continue devouring her until I had every last drop. I wanted to make sure that she thoroughly enjoyed this. As I felt her legs tighten up around my neck and thought she was going to break it I eased up and allowed the aftershocks to take over. I lowered her down from my neck and eased her into me allowing her body to collapse from the experience that just took place. I looked her in the eyes ever so softly and gave her a sweet kiss. She tried to speak but it was an exasperated sound.

"Mmmm baby, oh my goodness, I didn't think I could…I mean no one has ever…..how did you do what you did……damn!!"

"Mmmm yes you did taste oh so wonderful and didn't I tell you that I was a master at my craft. Hhmm I'll say it like this, the white boy may have invented it but I've mastered it."

"Well I can truly say that you did, oh my god, that you did."

"Mmmm don't you think we should shower up and get dressed before we run too late?"

"Ok, uhm I'm gonna ask you something and don't get mad at me."

"Ok what?"

"Don't laugh at me when I say this but, do we have to go out, can't we just stay in and continue what we're doing now?"

Laughing slightly because I honestly want to do the same thing but knowing I can't with the business deals on the table as they stand.

"Oh, baby trust and believe as much as I enjoyed this and I enjoy you period. I would love nothing more than to stay here and do things to you that Webster hasn't defined yet."

"Oh, my goodness I wish we could but I know that we can't and you have to meet with Edwin and Mr. Browin."

"That I do babe but I will say this, since this is our last night in D.C., at least for a little while, I will do my best to make the night short so we can come back here and pick up where we left off."

"I would love that but I don't want you to cut anything short on the account of me, I want you to woo them one last time while we're here that way they know they are truly getting the best person for their jobs."

"You know what woman, you keep up the way you are you're gonna make me fall in love with you."

"Mmmm really now, honestly, I feel the same way about you. I mean I'm not saying I'm there yet but I can easily see myself falling head over heels for you Marcus."

I take Kim by the chin and raise her face so her eyes meet mine

"Kim I'm not there yet either but I too can see myself falling for you and for the first time since Brenda died I wouldn't stop it when it comes."

"Oh, wow Marcus I just got all tingly inside."

"Nnaaahhh that's just the aftershock of my mastery at work." I start laughing hysterically.

"Oh hush that's not what it is."

"I know baby I know I'm just messing with you"

We giggled some and realized that we needed to get cleaned up and get out of the shower so we can get dressed for the night. I took the sponge and lathered it up, I washed Kim's lovely body from head to toe not missing a spot. She then returned the favor and we rinsed off together and I dried her off and helped her out of the shower. As she was exiting the bathroom she turned to me

"Yeah I think I can truly fall for you Marcus"

She exits the bathroom to begin getting dressed. I turned towards the mirror and began to lather my face with shaving cream and think to myself *"yeah I can fall for you too Kim" I say to myself.*

I shave and upon completion I realize that I haven't called mom or Jazzmin today. I leave out the bathroom and grab my cell. I make a call to my mom's house and talk to them letting them know how things are going and that what time I'll be home tomorrow. I apologize to them for making the call short but that I had to go to one last dinner meeting and I was running a tad bit late. Good thing I have a very understanding mother and daughter, they wished me well and then went back to baking some more chocolate chip cookies. As I hung up the phone I just basked in the glow of how lucky and blessed I am. I thought to myself that tonight was going to be a wonderful night. After getting dressed in what seemed to be record time I received a call from Willie that he and his wife were down in the lobby waiting on us. I told him to come on up to my suite and relax as we finish getting ready. He agreed and said they'll see us in a few minutes.

Shortly after a knock came through the door, I open the door for Willie and his wife.

"Good evening Willie how are you doing tonight?"

"Good evening Marcus, I'm doing very well thank you, how are you doing?"

"I'm doing and feeling rather good if I do say so myself, thank you very much."

"That's a wonderful thing, let me introduce you to my wife NiCole, baby this is Marcus Bass the guy I was telling you about."

"Nice to make your acquaintance Mrs. Briggs."

"Nice to make yours too and please call me NiCole."

"Ok NiCole it is and this is my baby Kim."

"Oh, hello Kim nice to meet you."

"It's very nice to meet you too and you have a wonderful husband. He took very good care of us and I for one am happy."

"Yes that's my Willie; he does the same at home. Tells me all the time that you have to treat people the way you want to be treated or otherwise that will come back on you."

"Yes it's true because you wouldn't want Karma coming back on you in a negative way, I tell my friends that back home all the time."

"Willie has been talking about you all weekend long of how you two hit it off and seemed like you had more of a friendship than a working relationship."

"I agree with you on that one, he was so easy to talk to and the only time we had any kind of incident was when he insisted on calling me Mr. Bass and I wouldn't have it"

Chuckling "yeah that's Willie for you, he told me that your mother's name was Briggs? I found that interesting because until I met Willie I never heard of that name before in my life."

"Yes her maiden name was Briggs and I told Willie that we have family in the East coast in Virginia and South Carolina."

"Hmm wouldn't that be something if you two were related?"

"Yeah it would be, but on that note we need to start heading out of here and to the restaurant. Willie knows already how I am about time so please lets go."

"That's so wonderful to hear, I'm so sick and tired of hearing how black folks are always being late for something unless it's free before 11pm at the club."

We all laughed in agreement and Kim and I gathered our things and we headed out the door. As we got to the car Willie and I opened the doors for our ladies and got in and headed to B. Smiths for a wonderful evening. I thought to myself again how blessed I am by God and how I am going to enjoy this evening.

As we approached B. Smiths I noticed there was a line to get in and I think that this must be a hot spot to go too. I wonder if we're ever going to get in and at that point I see Edwin walking up to the door in front of everyone and I think to myself that we're good. Willie parks the car and we exit and walk towards the restaurant just when I get a text from Edwin stating that as soon as we get there to come up to the front of the entrance because he has our table waiting. I text him back and let him know we just arrived and were walking up now. As we walk past people I notice that they are staring at us as if to say, "who in the hell do they think they are" in fact I heard a couple people say just those words, I thought to myself "damn it does feel good to have friends in high places". As we made it to the front entrance the maître de escorts us into the restaurant. The first thing I noticed was the live band playing jazz which I love and they were jamming. As we walked in Edwin met us at the front and he was smiling from ear to ear which made me think he's up to something.

"Marcus my man, how are you doing tonight?"

"I'm just fine Edwin, how are things with you?"

"I'm just wonderful and hello Kim it's very nice to see you again."

"Hello Edwin and the pleasure is mine."

"Hello Willie, I'm glad you and NiCole could make it."

"Hello sir, thank you for having us."

"Ok tonight I'm not sir I'm Edwin so cut the formalities."

"Ok I'm sorry about that."

"So where is Sheila?" as I interjected

"Oh, she's in our private room."

"Private room?" as I think mmm here we go again.

"Yes, see this restaurant has some rooms that you can reserve for private parties and since tonight was special and your last night in DC I wanted to make it a special one."

"Oh, ok so that's why you're grinning so much huh?"

"Actually no, I'm grinning because as you can see they have live music here."

"True I saw that and I love listening to me some good live jazz, hell live bands period. I often wonder what happened to the days when the group actually played the music they sang too. Like one of my favorite groups Mint Condition. Man, I have all their albums and love the fact that they play everything"

"Hmm now that's what I love to hear because my brotha I have a surprise for you."

"Uh oh, what do you have up your sleeve, I remember the last time you said that I met Charles and ended up in a wonderful business deal. Don't tell me you have something like that planned for tonight I don't know if I can take any more good news like that."

Edwin laughing hysterically.

"Nah my man it's just that I found out that your favorite group is performing tonight. See Ms. Smith the owner is a huge Mint

Condition fan and knows the band personally and whenever they are in town they always stop by and do a set or two, so you're in for a treat tonight."

"Oh wow, are you for real, man I haven't seen them in some years. I have missed the last couple times they came to the Chi because I had other engagements going on, man this is going to be great. Hey just to let you know Mr. Browin is going to stop by so I can sign some paperwork I hope you don't mind."

"No I don't, in fact he already contacted me to let me know he was going to stop by so I told him when he gets here to have the maître de escort him to our room so you two can handle business."

"Cool that's what's up, I appreciate it."

"No problem bro now let's enjoy the evening"

As we sit down and begin to enjoy the evening, I think to myself that I can truly get used to this. The music is grooving and I'm enjoying the conversation that's taking place across the table. Just as I think the night couldn't get better I heard the chimes of the keys on the board and the tenor voice of Stokley of my group Mint Condition started to play Pretty Brown Eyes. I couldn't help but sing along with them and I guess I was getting a little loud because I heard Kim in my ear.

"Mmmm Mr. Bass I see you are truly talented, I didn't know you could sing too."

"Well I can do a little sum sum for ya."

"I see well you know you'll have to sing to me one of these days right?"

"Mmmm it would be my pleasure."

Just at that moment I got a tap on my shoulder and turned to see Mr. Browin standing there.

"Hello Mr. Browin, how are you doing this evening?" as I stand to greet him.

"Hello Marcus, I'm doing wonderful and yourself?"

"I'm doing great if I do say so myself."

"That's good, that's good, is there somewhere we can go to take care of a couple things."

"Yes we can just step to another table and take care of things." I introduce him to everyone who didn't know him and excused ourselves so we could stepped over to another table to talk about the lounge and sign some paperwork. We sat down and butterflies entered into my stomach again. I almost couldn't believe that I was about to become part owner of a business such as the LUX. But I couldn't help but remember what my mother always has told me "Nothing is too hard for God and All things are possible for those who love the Lord and are called to His purpose" yeah that's so true as I thought to myself.

We conducted our business and I asked Charles if he were going to stay and he informed me that he was not able to because he had to get over to the LUX to put out a couple fires that has come up but he did say that he would be in touch with me real soon. As we walked back towards my table he excused himself and said he would stay but he had some business to take care of. He graciously offered to buy our first round of drinks and then left us for the evening. The night continued going off without a hitch. The music was slamming, the food was awesome and the company was (meaning Kim) was a dream. I thought to myself that I must be living in a dream but if I were I don't ever want to wake up. As the time got later and later I realized that Kim and I needed to be going so we can get back to our room and get some rest. Well actually finish what we started in the shower and then get some rest so we can get up and catch our flight by Noon.

"Well Edwin, although I'm having a lovely time I must say that we need to be getting back to our room so we can get some rest and catch our flight in the morning."

"Yeah man I feel you, we need to get going too, we don't like to keep the babysitter up too late and besides it's Church for us in the morning too."

"Oh, ok cool well say a prayer for us and our flight that we make it home safely."

"I will do that and I'm sure that God will bless your flight."

As we stood to say our goodbye's and exit the restaurant, I felt as if I was floating on air. I couldn't help but reflect on how things were going for me. Kim held my hand and it felt right, for the first time since Brenda it felt right with another woman being on my arm. I just took a look up in the night sky and saw a shooting star and it was as if Brenda sent an approval star just for me.

The ride in the car back to the hotel was very pleasant and surreal. It felt like the best is yet to come. We exited the car and the company of Willie and his lovely wife. Said our goodbye's and turned to walk into the hotel when a car honked its horn. I didn't realize that Edwin had followed us back to the hotel. As he got out I went towards him.

"Man did I forget something?"

"No man I just wanted to again thank you for coming out to DC and for the wonderful work that you are doing. I also wanted to say that I look forward to a long-lasting relationship not only in business but in life. It's good to truly meet a genuine person who has the same goals and business ethics as I do, it's really refreshing."

"I agree my brotha; it's rare to find another person, especially a black person who is truly about their business of building up and not tearing down. I like that in you and I'm glad God has allowed our paths to cross."

"So am I, so am I, also I had to give you this."

Edwin pulls out an envelope and hands it too me

"Man, what's this?"

"Open it!"

I open the envelope to find a check for the first full year's payment of ads in my magazine.

"Wow I didn't expect this; I don't know what to say."

"Just say that you'll continue doing what you do and that's all you need to say."

"You have my word on that."

And with that we shook hands and parted ways. As I turned to go into the hotel I noticed Kim standing there waiting for me looking ever so beautiful. All I wanted to do at that point was just finish off the night with her, get some rest and get up and fly home in the morning. I had fun in DC but home is where the heart is and Chicago is where my heart is and getting back to it is what must be done. Aaahh I think what a wonderful trip this turned out to be.

"Well Ms. Johnson what do you say we go up to our room and finish what we started?"

"Mmmm Mr. Bass you were reading my mind."

"Good lets go."

We walked into the entrance hand in hand and it felt so right, so right in deed. We got to the elevator door and I pressed the button. The door opened and we entered and Kim snuggled right up to me letting me know with her body that she's craving to finish what we started a few hours ago. As we exited the elevator and walked towards our room, Kim and I started the party a little early by kissing each other passionately, then I surprised her by picking her up in my arms and carrying her to the door. As she took out her key to enter the room, she slid the key in the lock and I opened the door. We entered our room, I put the do not disturb sign on the door and thought to myself this is where it all began and I knew that this is just the beginning. Round Two...Ding!!!!

CHAPTER

26

Marcus "Home Sweet Home"

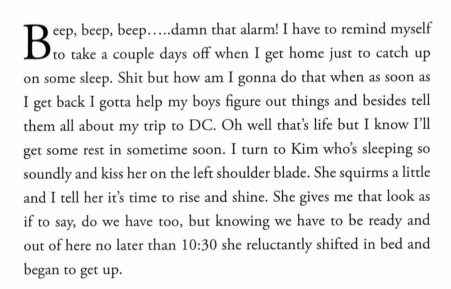

Beep, beep, beep.....damn that alarm! I have to remind myself to take a couple days off when I get home just to catch up on some sleep. Shit but how am I gonna do that when as soon as I get back I gotta help my boys figure out things and besides tell them all about my trip to DC. Oh well that's life but I know I'll get some rest in sometime soon. I turn to Kim who's sleeping so soundly and kiss her on the left shoulder blade. She squirms a little and I tell her it's time to rise and shine. She gives me that look as if to say, do we have too, but knowing we have to be ready and out of here no later than 10:30 she reluctantly shifted in bed and began to get up.

"Mmmm good morning Ms. Johnson."

"Good morning to you too Mr. Bass and I might add you were wonderful last night."

"I must say you were pretty amazing yourself, I didn't think you could do the things you did, I'm gonna check but I'm pretty sure there's a law against it but I won't be pressing any charges."

Kim moves closer to me and begins kissing me sweetly in different spots of my body.

"Well a girl can't show her man all her tricks in the first night right."

"Well I guess you're right and if that's just the sample I can't wait to get the full course."

"Mmmm that you will I promise that you will. What time do we have to be ready?"

"Willie will be here by 10:30 to pick us up and thank God we're only 15 minutes from the airport so we won't be rushing too much."

"Uhm so we have time to go for a round three huh?"

"Normally I would say yes but I did want us to get up, eat, get dressed and pack up the room and not rush with it so can I get a rain check on round three?"

"Although I want you right now I do understand but yes you can have a rain check on round three and I can't wait for that one too."

"Good because I can't wait either, now why don't you take a shower and I'll go down to the lobby to get us some breakfast."

"Cool, can you see if they have lemon poppy seed muffins please and if they do bring me one?"

"Oh, wow this is too freaky."

"What?"

"I love those muffins and I said even before I came here that if they did a drug test on them I'd fail from eating them all the time."

"Now that's funny." laughing

"Anything else you want Ms. Johnson?"

Kim giving me that, I want you and nothing else, look.

"Alright, alright I get that look so I will bring back the usual, I'll be back in a few."

I left Kim to get our breakfast and for her to start getting herself together. When I went to the lobby to get our breakfast the first thing I noticed was they did have the muffins so I grabbed two of them for us and some eggs, bacon and sausage, orange juice, apple juice and some fresh fruit so we can have a good breakfast. As I returned to the room Kim was surprisingly out of the shower with her traveling outfit on and almost ready to go. As we sat down at the table and enjoyed our breakfast. We didn't say much this morning just basking in the afterglow of things that took place. After breakfast I got in the shower and made it quick because I knew our time was getting shorter. After getting out of the shower I put on my sweat suite that I travel in and began to pack up the room. I made sure my clothes were packed, portfolio that I really didn't to use was put away, made sure Brenda's picture holding Jazzmin was in a safe place. Everything was at the door and it was 10:15. I did one last look around double checking to make sure I didn't leave anything. I almost forgot one thing though, every time I go somewhere and stay in a hotel I always leave behind a couple magazines just in case I get someone who likes to read and they may become a subscriber. Also, I leave a tip on the counter to thank the housekeeping staff for a wonderful stay and how they took care of me. After my last little things were done we exited the room. I looked at Kim

"Wow what a lovely time we had in this room, I'll never forget it."

"Neither will I and I look forward to coming back someday and who knows maybe to this room."

"That sounds like a plan Ms. Johnson."

"That it does."

As we walked towards the elevator and got on, I thought to myself she's right, it does sound like a good plan. So much so I already had plans on coming back out here with her but she don't know it yet. As the doors opened up and we exited into the lobby I saw Willie sitting in the lobby looking like he had a wonderful night with NiCole himself. I motioned to him that I was gonna give the hotel keys to the front desk and we can leave. As I approached the desk to give my keys, I did tell the clerk that I was going to keep one of the keys as I always do as a reminder of a special place I've been and want to go to again. The clerk smiled and said people do it all the time and not to worry because the keys are decoded as soon as we finish up the transaction anyway. I smiled and said thank you and we exited the hotel. The sun was shining bright again and it made me feel good. As we drove to the airport I could tell everyone was still tired by the yawning faces going on. Willie got us to the airport in great time. We exited the car and got our bags. I turned towards Willie

"Thank you Willie for a wonderful time and taking such good care of us I truly appreciate it."

"The pleasure was all mine Marcus, like I said before it's not often when I get to drive for someone like yourself who truly appreciates a working man no matter what profession he's in."

"You're correct, as long as it's legal it don't matter to me and with that I have a little something extra for you." I gave him the envelope and saw the astonishing look on his face.

"Wow Marcus, you didn't have to do this."

"Yes I did Willie, yes I did because you didn't have to spend as much time away from your family as you did to take care of me and my lady."

"But $500 Marcus, that's way too much."

"No, it's not and to be honest I wish it could be more but that's pretty much all the cash I had on me."

"I don't know what to say."

"Just say thank you and leave it at that. Oh, and that when I come back out."

"We, when we come back out" Kim interjects.

"Ok, ok, when we come back out I want to make sure that you are the one to drive us around and take care of us."

"Deal, let me give you my information so you'll have it."

"No need, because Edwin already gave it to me."

"Oh, ok well I didn't know."

"That's ok, I just wanted to make sure I had it so I could make sure to keep in touch. Also I will be passing it along to other people I know who come to DC for business so you will be getting calls from some people I know."

"Wow that's great I am truly thankful, well Marcus it was truly a pleasure."

"Yes it was Willie and please be sure to tell NiCole hello and goodbye for us and we'll be in touch."

"I'll do just that."

"Goodbye for now Willie."

"Goodbye for now Marcus and to you too Kim."

"Bye Willie and take care." Kim says.

We parted ways and entered into security I felt good and wasn't even gonna let security bother me today. We got through security in good time and waited for our flight to boar. When it arrived, we entered and got our seats, sat back holding hands and basking in a beautiful day.

"Well Ms. Johnson homeward bound we go."

"Yes Mr. Bass Chicago here we come."

"What a beautiful trip this turned out to be, for the both of us."

"I must truly say it turned out way better than I had ever could have planned. Right now, I'd be at home getting things together for Monday's meeting with my staff and letting them know how the conference went."

"Yeah well I'd be getting ready to shoot hoops with my boys and I know I'll get it in but I'm glad this turned out the way it did."

"Me too, so how long will the trip take?"

"Going back will be shorter since we're going across time zones and we're an hour behind so our trip is two hours and we'll be back at 1pm but in reality it's 2pm here."

"Oh, ok so I have you all to myself for a couple more hours at least huh?"

"Yes you do but you'll have more time like that I'm sure."

"Looking forward to it."

"As am I."

Kim snuggled up into me as the Captain gave the instructions to the flight attendants and we took off heading for home. Chicago here I come is all I thought and of course to put out fires that were simmering while I was gone and I hope nothing exploded. I could only hope.

As we rode home on the plane Kim snuggled more into me and fell asleep, I wish I could have slept but my mind was racing thinking about what took place over the past few days while in DC and what's unfolding at home. Here I am coming off a great weekend when all of my boys are going through their own personal hell. First things first though I have to get my babygirl and get her home and hug her tight. Then I have to start with Milton and figure out what he's going to do next about his situation. Sigh…then Braden wow, I don't know how I'm going to tell him that atomic bomb of news I have to tell him but I have to tell him. Darius and Jason is simple in comparison but they have to get it together too. Darius has to learn to keep his dick in his pants and so does Jason unless he's ready to settle down. I laugh to myself and wonder sometimes what I'm going to do with them but they're my boys and they've been there for me when I needed it so I know I have to be there for them now. Just when I was getting deeper into my thoughts I heard the captain call for the landing process. Aaahh home sweet home, Chicago has its ups and downs but its home. I hated to wake Kim but I knew I had to. As the plane landed we discussed when we were going to get together again. Knowing we both had a busy schedule to do since our time was thrown off by the extended trip. As we went to the luggage claim and gathered our bags we gave one another a wonderful and passionate kiss and said our goodbyes....for now. Although I hated to leave her I knew that I had to ease her into Jazzmin's life so I didn't want to rush things. As I was heading out to get into my town car that was waiting for me I notice that Kim was standing there waiting.

"Hey baby, is your ride coming?"

"I called my assistant and she said she was on her way but was stuck in traffic."

"Ok well did she say how long she'll be?"

"She said she's on the Dan-Ryan and traffic is touch and go."

"Oh damn, well you know if she's on the Ryan now and it's like that she's going to be another hour at least to get to you. Look my car is here and why don't you just get a ride with me. I can have him drop me off at my place and then take you to the Southside."

"Are you sure that's ok Marcus? I mean I can wait, I'll just go back inside and go up to one of the cafés and relax."

"First of all baby it's no problem and second who knows when she will show up and third you're tired like I am from the trip so if you can get home sooner the better you'll be."

"Sigh….well if you are ok with it."

"Baby this is fine and I'm sure the driver don't mind making a little extra money in the process."

She agreed and we got in the car and took off. She made a call to her assistant and told her to turn around and head home, telling her she has a ride. She said she'll see her in the morning for the staff meeting. As we drove to my place all I could think about was the weekend and how everything went. It felt good to have a great weekend that went off without a hitch and even better than I expected. We arrived at my building and the driver pulled up to the front entrance of my condo. I gave Kim a kiss and got out of the car letting her know I will talk to her a little later when we both are settled. I also told her to let me know when she arrived home safely so I won't worry. I gave the driver a few extra dollars to take Kim home and went into my building where George was waiting on me.

"Good afternoon Mr. Bass."

"George what did I tell you."

"Ok Marcus old habits."

Laughing "It's ok I understand, so how has your last few days been?"

"Oh, they've been just fine, I'm only here because one of the staff members called in and they couldn't fill the shift. How was your trip Marcus, did you knock them dead with your presentation?"

"Well George I'll put it like this, I'll be making a few more trips to D.C."

"That sounds great I'm so happy for you."

"Thanks George, but I'm tired and I need to get me some rest, but I promise to tell you all about it later."

"Ok I understand about trips like that so I'll wait to hear all about the good news you had. Oh, and just to let you know there's a Milton Cunningham in your place where you aware of that?"

"Yes I was, he's one of my boys who's going through some things and needed a place to crash for a while."

"Oh, ok I just wanted to make sure that no one did something they had no business doing. I know how you are about your privacy."

"Thanks George I appreciate it but it's all good." Chuckling thinking how protective George is about me and Jazzmin and I appreciate that.

"Oh, ok just want to make sure I didn't have to fire someone. Well you go on up and get your rest and I'll be here when you need me."

"Ok George and thank you for being there for me and Jazz, have a good day."

"Good day Marcus"

I left the lobby and headed for the elevator, I pressed the button for it to come. When the elevator came I pressed my floor and instantly thought of what's waiting on me…Milton…my boy but what he's going through I can't imagine. As the elevator reached the 40th floor I got out and headed to my place. I loved the fact that the whole floor only had me and one more couple on it, I was glad I didn't have to worry about too many neighbors. As I reached my door and put my key in I paused hoping everything will be ok with Milton…But I could only pray.

CHAPTER

27

Milton "What to do now"

Arriving at my condo, I opened my door, I noticed things were very quiet, almost two quiet. I walked down the hall towards my bedroom so I could put my bags away. I looked into my spare bedroom and noticed Milton was lying down. I thought about waking him but figured that he'd been through enough already and probably needed his rest besides this would give me a chance to make a couple phone calls to inform people I made it home safe. I returned to my bedroom and sat on the bed just when my phone rang. The caller ID said "Babygirl" and I smiled because my daughter beat me to the punch of calling her and my mother first.

"Hello baby girl"

"Hi daddy, are you home yet?"

"Yes I just walked in the door honey and was about to call you. How are you and your grandmother doing?"

"We're fine just sitting here watching tv and eating lunch."

"Oh, ok and what are you eating as if I need to ask?"

"Oh dad….you know my favorite"

"Let me guess….Chinese?"

"Yep sure is."

"You know something you're going to turn into a China doll one of these days. Let me talk to your grandmother real quick."

"Ok daaadd…(Jazzmin coos) oh and did you bring me something?"

"Yes I did bring you something and no I'm not gonna tell you what it is. You'll just have to wait to find out."

"Daadddd (I can hear Jazz pout)."

"Don't dad me, you'll have to wait."

"Ok, ok so when are you coming to get me?"

"I was thinking that you can stay over moms for the night and go to school in the morning and I'll pick you up after school."

"Yyaaayyy I was hoping you would let me stay over."

"Wait a minute I'm beginning to think you don't want to see your old man anymore."

"Daadddd you're not old and you know I can't wait to see you but it's that I don't get to see grandma that much and I like spending time with her."

"I know hon, it's ok, now put mom on the phone please."

"Ok, here she is."

"Hi son, I see you made it home safe and sound."

"That I did mom, has Jazz been too much trouble."

"Child no, you know I love my grandbaby and want to spend all the time I can with her."

"Yeah ma I know, well I told Jazz that she can stay with you and go to school in the morning and I'll pick her up afterwards."

"Oh, that's fine, I'll just make sure she gets there on time."

"I know mom and thank you, well I gotta run and get settled in because I have a few things to take care of.'"

"Wait how did the trip go, I want to hear all about it?"

"The trip went well ma, better than I could have ever expected but hold off 'til I pick Jazz up from school and I'll stop by and tell you all about it?"

"Oh, ok well I won't hold you up, get your rest and get settled in and I'll talk to you later son. I love you."

"I love you too ma and I will do just that."

"Bye son."

"Bye ma."

I get off the phone with the two most important people in my life and just smile. Then I think about how there is now a third. Speaking of the third I wonder how she's doing, I know she's not home yet so I'll give her a chance to get there, get settled in and call me. Right now I know I need to take a shower and get my bags unpacked. I always hated not unpacking when I got home. I know me if I didn't do it right away then it would be two weeks before I unpacked and that's not gonna happen. I go into my bathroom and look at my shower and think of how great it will be once I get my new shower in. I have to put in my reminders to call the contractor to see how it's going to be done. I don't care what the cost will be, well sort of, but I have to have that shower. I get out of my sweats and jump into the shower and it's hot and soothing. I feel as though I'm washing all of my cares and worries away even though I don't have many of the worries thank God.

I use this time to think about what's been going on with my boys since I've been gone especially with Braden. That's a talk I honestly dread having because I have no clue as to how he's going to take the news of the fact that not only does he have a son but his son is dying. My heart breaks for Braden Jr. and what he is going through especially not knowing his father. I couldn't imagine not having Jazzmin in my life and her going through something like this and not knowing me. Wow…I feel tears come to my eyes and it's not a good feeling, that's why I have to have this talk with Braden so he can get tested to make sure he's a match for his son so he can help him out.

I stay in the shower so long that my water starts to get lukewarm. I get out and begin to dry off and hear Milton stirring around. I grab my robe and put it on. I walk down the hallway to my spare bedroom, knock on the door, I call out to him to make sure he's ok.

"Hey Milton, you ok man?" I say as I'm peeping in.

"Hey Marcus, when did you get back?" He speaks as he turns over.

"I've been back now for about an hour." I say as I walk in the room• and sit in the lounge chair.

"Wow I didn't hear you come in, man I must have been really tired." he says while sitting up in the bed.

"I'd say so, seeing that you had to stay in a hotel for the past couple days, sleeping on God knows what kind of mattress, that can't be good for you at all."

"Yeah tell me about it but I think it's the stress more from what's going on than anything."

"Yeah I feel you dude so forgive me but tell me again what in the hell is going on with you and Sharon."

"Well lately she has been on me about making more money and getting a house versus renting the apartment we're in. I told her that I'm doing the best I can and she'll just have to be patient."

"Ok so why is she trippin' on you over that. I know you make decent money and she's working too right, so what's the problem bro?"

"Well, what you don't know and I've not told anyone is that she's been diagnosed as a manic depressive and she can't work."

"Oh, Damn man are you for real?" I say with shocked look on my face.

"Yeah I'm sorry to say."

"Man, how and when did this happen?"

"It's been slowly progressing for about a year and a half ever since we lost our last child in the pregnancy. She's getting worse but the thing is she is functional when she's on her meds but she hates taking them."

"Yeah I hate taking medication too but man if it's going to help her then she should take them but I'm not in her shoes so I have no idea what it's like. Man...I'm so sorry, but I don't get it why is she tripping now?"

"Well she feels that since she's up here all by herself with no family to turn too, she wants to go back home and be with them. She thinks that by making a fuss that I'll just let her go and take my kids with her."

"I know you're not gonna have that, so what are you going to do about the restraining order?"

"According to the police and the human service rep, there has to be an investigation before I can go back home. After the investigation is completed and they find that I didn't do anything then I can go home but the thing is they will have to visit our home frequently and sometimes randomly until they feel that things are safe. Man, this is stressing on me and I'm at a loss on what to do."

"Do you have any idea as to when the investigation will be completed?"

"They said no sooner than 30 days but no longer than 60 and I'm to stay away from my kids until it's over. Oh, and I will have supervised visits once a week but for only an hour. Man, I can't go that long without my kids Marcus."

"Yeah I know, I was thinking about you and Braden and what's going on and couldn't imagine being without Jazzmin for longer than a couple days so I feel you bro."

"So now you know why I called on you because I needed somewhere to go and besides the social workers office is nearby where I'll have the visits so I figured it be better if I were close. Plus, my job is closer to you than Braden or Darius anyway."

"Man, it's cool you can stay as long as you need too. Man, I tell you, it seems as though all my boys are going through hell while I seem to be flying high."

"Yeah I know so tell me about the trip and this new woman you met. I'm sure you had a good time."

"Yeah I did, better than I could have expected. Ok first off as I was going to catch my flight I realized that I hadn't eaten anything so I stopped to get me a muffin and some coffee when I sat down and saw this gorgeous woman reading one of my magazines right. Well she caught me staring and asked me if I liked the magazine and I told her I should because I owned it."

"I know she must have been thrilled to meet you then huh?"

"Nah…in fact she wasn't, she thought I was some fly by night brotha trying to take the credit for someone else work."

"Wow really, that's interesting so how did this all work out that you spent time with her in DC?"

"Well after she said that I got up and handed her my card and she began to blush after reading it. Then she apologized for how she reacted. I told her it was ok and that I understood so that's how things started. Now the tripped-out part is and I think this was nothing but Gods doing. We not only happened to be on the same flight but sat across the aisle from one another so it turned out to be a good trip to DC. So after we got off the plane and got our things, I had a car waiting for me and when I got to it I saw her about to get a cab and offered her a ride. I asked her where she was going and it just so happened that she stayed in the hotel right across from mine. So, I was blown away with all of that."

"Wait you mean to tell me that all of that "coincidence" happened and it didn't make you a little fishy?"

"Well, yeah it did at first but I was like no one could be that crazy to go to such lengths in meeting me like that to fake a trip and all. Plus, I had my secretary check her out and make sure she and her business was on the up and up although I told her I was kidding."

"Oh, ok cool yeah I should have known you were safe about things. So, she has her own business and what does she do"

"She has a consulting firm that helps people of lower income, and elderly who's on fixed income budget their money. She not only helps with that but also teaches how to save and invest a certain percentage so their money can work for them. To be real honest with you, that's something that impressed me most about her because you don't find too many people who are into doing something like that. That's why I'm going to work with her and get her business in my magazine to help her get backing so she can grow and help more people."

"Yeah that sounds good so what else happened on the trip?"

"Man, I'll have to tell you the rest later, only because I have to call Braden and meet up with him. I told him I was going to hit him up as soon as I got back to town. But what I think I'm going to do is have a little gathering and tell everyone about the trip and the new business ventures that's about to take place because I really only want to say it once and besides I'm going to see about throwing business in the direction of my boys so be prepared."

"Aww man ok I understand so no worries. Thanks again for letting me stay, I have to get out of here and go to the house and get some cloths while Sharon is out with the kids."

"Oh ok, be careful bro and I'll be here when you get back, hell Braden and the rest of the fellas may be here too because he's gonna need all of us when he hears what I have to tell him."

"Oh, really is it that bad?"

"Let's say it's something that is truly some life altering information that I have to lay on him and I honestly don't know how he's going to take it. So, if you can be back in a couple hours I'm going to see if the rest of the fellas can come over and we all sit down and talk."

"Yeah I can, I don't have much to get so I'll be back by then."

"Ok cool, well let me get myself together and get this meeting set up so we can plan our next moves."

"Ok cool I'll see you later Marcus."

"Ok bruh see you in a few."

I get up and leave out of the room and go into mine. I sit on the side of my bed and my head starts to spin again with the news of what he just dropped on me. Added to the information I already have to tell Braden I guess God allowed me to have such a wonderful weekend because of what hell I had to deal with when I got back home. That's what friends are for right, yep, that's what friends are for. I sent a text to Braden letting him know I was at home and to come over to my place by 4pm and he responded that he'd be there. I then sent out a mass text to Jason, Darius, Justin and Tim letting them know I need them to be at my house by 4:30 no exceptions and that it's an emergency.

Everyone but Jason said they would be there by then but Jason did say he'd be there shortly thereafter. After that I figured I'd just lay down for a little bit to gather myself so I sent one last text message to Kim to tell her that I'm going to lay down and to call me as soon as she gets home. I put my phone on the charger, set my alarm to get up in a couple hours and laid across the bed. Thinking how good it felt to be laying in my own bed. I drifted off.

CHAPTER

28

Braden "Boys Club"

3:30, I wake from a very nice and much needed nap and I must have been truly tired too because I realized that when I grabbed my phone to call and make sure that Kim was home safe I saw I had a couple missed calls from her and messages. I checked my voice mail and she had left me two messages. The first was letting me know she made it home safe and was sorry she missed me and the second one was one of just trying to reach me and check on me to make sure I was ok and to give her a call as soon as I can. I was about to call her back when my door buzzer sounded.

I went to my door to ask who it was and was informed that Braden was in the lobby for me. I informed the desk attendant to let him up and cracked my door so he could come on in. I thought to myself that he's quite a bit early but I'm sure I would be too if I had news like this to find out but I dismissed it. I called Kim to check on her and let her know I was ok and got her voice mail. I guess she was still as tired as I was. I left a sweet voice mail for her.

"Hey baby, it's big daddy wanting to let you know I got your message and that I was knocked out. I must have been more tired than I realized. Anywho. I'm about to meet with Braden and let him know what's going on. Also, the other fellas are coming over for moral support. So, I will check back with you a little later to see how you are feeling. I love you and I'll talk to you later."

As I hung up it just dawned on me what I just said. Damn I said I loved her, wow, could it be I mean it came out so freely and without hesitation. I mean I caught myself almost saying it when I was in DC but I thought it was just the moment. Now I don't know, I mean I never thought of falling for someone so quickly but I've heard of it. Oh well I know I'm not in love with her but I have to admit that I am thinking of her more than I thought I would. Just when I was getting caught up in my own thoughts Braden comes through my door almost in a panic.

"What's up man what's the news that you have to tell me?"

"Uhm hello to you too B and how are you doing?"

"Oh, come on me cut to it what's going on, why did Kandi contact you after all this time?"

"Dude slow down and breathe I'm going to tell you but first I need for you to sit down and breathe because honestly what I have to tell you is something that is going to blow your mind."

"Man just tell me does she want to get back together, is she dying, what, what is it, man I've been going crazy ever since you told me that she contacted you and you had something to talk to me about."

"Ok, ok but come and sit down. Do you want a drink?"

"No man I'm fine, rather impatient but fine."

"Well I'm gonna get you one anyway and me too for that matter."

"Man screw the drink just tell me."

"Ok but I'm going to prepare one for you anyway and have it sitting there because I know you're gonna need it and then some when this is all over."

"Fine do what you need to do but will you just get on with it."

As I get the brandy that I know he's going to need after I lay this bombshell on him I sit down on my sectional across from him with my center table between us and I begin to tell him the story.

"Ok here goes, as you know I was in DC and I received a call from Kandi?"

"Yeah I know, you told me that already, skip the previews and get to the damn movie." he says with high anxiety in his voice.

"Dude will you not rush me on this, it's difficult enough as it is, so chill out."

"Ok man but you have no idea what I've been going through not knowing what's going on."

"Well it's not been easy for me having this information and not being able to tell you until now so it's not easy on me either."

"Yeah I wanted to ask you, why couldn't you tell me then, why did I have to wait to hear this news in person?" he asks very sarcastically.

"Well you see that Brandy sitting there on the table in your face and ready to be consumed?"

"Yeah I do, so!"

"Well just like that Brandy is there for you in your time of need, I knew this is something I had to say in your face and not over the phone so I could be there as you heard it and needed me in your face."

"Ok man my bad, please forgive me but I've not really slept since you told me that information on Friday."

"Yeah I know bro and I'm sorry but I had to do it this way. Anywho like I said she contacted me and it was early in the morning so it startled me and I almost didn't answer the phone because it was an unknown number. But I thought it could be one of you guys or Jazz or Ma so I answered it. That's when she laid it on me"

"What man, what did she lay on you."

"B, you're my boy and I love you so bear with me on this for a minute. So, after she told me who she was and I came out of my sleep to comprehend what was going on. She told me that she wanted to get in touch with you and it was an emergency but didn't know how too nor how you would accept her getting in touch with you after all this time."

"Man you know that I would love to hear from her, hell we just talked about the loves we regret letting get away so what's going on man honestly dude you're scaring me right about now so will you just spill it."

"BRADEN!!!" I said raising my voice at him which is something I don't do.

"Oh, shit it has to be bad because you don't call me by my full name."

"Dude do you want to hear this or not."

"I do man but damn you're taking forever."

"DAMN!!, anyway, as I was saying B, I know you remember what happened almost 20 years ago like you said we just talked about it. Well I'll put it like she told me, remember the bomb you dropped on her or rather she found out, regarding the letter you wrote to Gabriel?"

"Yeah how could I ever forget that day, that was one of the worst days of my life."

Thinking to myself that nope it wasn't the worst but it's about to pale in comparison

"Yeah I know it was hell it wasn't no picnic for me either. Well she told me that on that day the reason why she wanted me to take her home was for the fact she was trying to make you jealous of seeing her with another man."

"Dude you had me wait all this time for that news, man you could have told me that over the damn phone, and you got this damn drink like I was gonna need it after that, come on man you must not know me well."

"My brotha I know you better than you can ever think I do, and no, that's not the whole story. I had to tell you that part because of what comes next. Like I said she told me why she had me drop her off and not you. Also, what I nor anyone else but her knew at the time was she had her own news to drop on you and she had planned on telling you that weekend."

"Man will you come out with it already damn." Braden getting more pissed off.

"B she was pregnant!!"

"WHAT!!!, you bullshitting me" Braden says, with a stunned look on his face

"Nope I wish I was dude, she was pregnant and was gonna tell you that weekend until she found the letter and all hell broke loose."

"So why didn't she tell me and what happened to the baby? Did she keep it or not. If she did keep it why didn't she tell me? If so is it a boy or girl, am I the father, damn I have so many questions?"

"Ok first things first she didn't tell you because of what happened between you and her and could you blame her. Second she did keep him."

"Him, so she had a son." Braden starts to smile.

"Yeah she had a son Braden Jr."

"Oh wow, are you serious, so I have a son and he's a Jr. Damn now I'm pissed. I missed out on all of his growing up and everything. How could she do this man I mean damn I know what happened between her and I was wrong but this is too low even for her." Standing walking over towards my bay window in disbelief.

"Man, I know and believe me you should have seen my face when she told me. I was floored like you are now and hell he's not my son."

"So why now, why you, why didn't she just keep him to herself and never tell me? Hell, she can't come to me for child support now because I know he's what 19, 20 years old. Damn man this is fucked up for real." Braden's voice getting very agitated.

"Well that is the part of what I'm getting too."

"You mean to tell me there's more to this story?" sounding worried.

"I wish there wasn't but unfortunately yes, there is so come back and sit down."

"Man, I'm alright so just tell me."

"Oh, hells no, sit your ass down so you won't pass out when I say the rest."

Braden reluctantly comes back and sits on my chase.

"Ok man I'm sitting now tell me what's going on please"

All this time I was able to hold my emotions and fight back my tears but he could see that this was really getting to me. I decided to take a big gulp of my drink before I opened my mouth.

"B I'm sorry to have to be the one to tell you this but your son Braden Jr. well Braden Thomas Withers II to be exact. But your son is…is…

Tears start to flow and I can see the fear in Braden's eyes as if I'm about to say the worse thing he ever wants to hear.

"Man come on just tell me is my son ok?"

"No B, no he's not, your son I'm sorry to say has Leukemia and is in bad shape and needs a bone marrow transplant."

Just at that moment as I figured he would, Braden takes his drink and gulps it down in one swallow and hands me the glass as if to say "keep 'em coming." I get up to get him another drink and bring the bottle with me knowing this is not the last that I'm going to fill his glass nor mine.

"Leukemia? My son has Leukemia and is need of bone marrow. Man are you sure please tell me you're joking."

"Come on B would I do something like that to you, man this is way too serious for me to do to that. Besides why would I make you wait a few days to tell you if it was a joke."

"I guess you're right but damn man this is a blow." Braden gulping down another glass.

"Uhm tell me about it how do you think I felt waking up to get news like this early in the morning."

"Ok so let me get this right, I have a son who has my name, he's what 20 by now and he has dying from this ailment and needs bone marrow to save his life, did I forget anything?"

"Well yeah but this is what you don't know yet."

"Hold up let me get another drink" As he takes a drink but not gulps it down this time he prepares the best he could for the news.

"He's in a bad way to the point he's may die if he don't get the transplant and soon. Kandi told me the doctors have done all they can do and if they don't find a match and soon there won't be much they can do for him. She said that the therapy has run its course and his body is starting to reject it so the only other alternative now is for a full bone marrow transplant and that's where you come in."

"Me, how do I come in at this point? Why don't she just give her own marrow to save him?"

"Well see that's the thing, she tried to but her marrow is not a match and in these cases the match usually comes from the father. So here we are sitting here now in my living room talking. She needs to talk to you about getting tested to make sure that yours will be a match to save your son."

"Oh wow" Braden stands up holding his head in his hand and walks around my living room. He begins to pace and not say anything for a little while but then stops in his tracks.

"Wait, how does she know the boy is mine I mean I'm not trying to be mean or anything but come on man it's been 20 years?"

"I know and she's fully aware that you'd have to do a DNA test first before anything to make sure you are the father but honestly B I believe her because what reason would she have to lie?"

"Yeah I hear ya man but this is way too much for me right now that's all, I mean with me going through the mess with Gabriel and my other children this is something I didn't expect not now."

"Yeah I hear you bro and believe me I hate to have to be the one to tell you like this but here I am. So are you willing hear from her and meet up so you can get this testing done?"

"Man damn, I mean I've wanted to see her for a long time and see how she's doing but under this circumstance it's different. I mean I'll do it but I don't know how I'll feel and just think if we do the DNA test and come to find out he's not mine, then what, I mean she gave him my name and he has it now and it's too late to change it."

"I know but what's done is done and you have to do what's right now, man think about it if you are the father you could save your son's life and this could be the beginning of something special between you and him."

"I hear what you're saying, so when does she want to meet up?"

"Well, I have her number and she wants me to give her a call to let her know what and how you feel about things and then go from there. So let me call her and let her know that you're willing to talk with her and meet up to get the testing done and take it from there."

"Yeah Ok well let me know as soon as you can, I want to talk to her as soon as possible."

"B you have to be cool with this man don't go off on her. You have to try and look at it from her side of the story ok?"

"Ok man I am I mean I just want to talk to her to see how she's holding up. I'm sure she's not doing well and to have to be forced to get in touch with me couldn't be easy on her. So I'm cool and I won't trip out on her, hell in a lot of ways this is my fault that I wasn't there from the jump anyway so it's the least I could do."

"Yeah I hear ya."

Just at that moment when things were calming down with Braden my buzzer rang and I went to answer it and the front desk informed me that the rest of our friends are in the lobby. I gave the ok for them to come up. As they all came in and sat down I told them the whole story and of course they were all floored by it. We sat there and had drinks and talked and most of all consoled Braden and reassured him that we're there for him no matter what and we all will get through this together as boys.

CHAPTER

29

Braden "Calm before the Storm"

After some time passed and we were pretty much done with the
pow-wow, the fellas leave, leaving Braden alone with me. I knew
that Braden's head was still spinning after the bomb that was dropped
on it. Upon closing the door after the fellas leave, I pause, I knew I
had to face him but it was difficult to see my friend, my brother go
through such an ordeal, I almost couldn't turn to face him, but I knew
I had too. When I did he was staring out into the evening sky not
saying a word, just looking out into what seemed to be emptiness. I
really felt for my brother and also in some ways felt so helpless for what
he is going through now and about to endure. To just now find out
you have a son is one thing, but one who's in a fight for his life with a
debilitating disease is just way too much to handle. I went and stood
next to him, not saying a word, we had one of those relationships
where you don't have to say anything but it seems as though we spoke
a million words. Without looking at him I just simply said…"We'll
get through this bro, trust me we'll get through this together."

He didn't have to say a word but I felt him and my heart began to bleed for him and what he's going through. I knew he was really messed up behind all of this but not fully knowing the head space he was in I told him to chill with me for the night, mainly because I didn't want him to do anything crazy. He reluctantly agreed and I told him that he could crash in my room, since Milton will be in my spare bedroom I was just going to sleep in Jazz's room since she's at my mom's house until I pick her up tomorrow after school. I left him standing there at the window, leaving him to his thoughts and went into my bedroom to call Kim to make sure she was ok. As I entered my room just as my phone rang and it was Kim.

"Well hello there beautiful how are you doing?"

"Hello there yourself handsome, I'm just fine and how is one of the most gorgeous men in Chicago doing?"

"I'm honestly not in the best head spaces but hearing one of the most sweetest voices on earth definitely helps, but I will say that this afternoon has been a little rough."

"Why baby what's wrong?"

"Braden is here and we had the talk about what's going on with him and his son."

"How did he take the news?"

"Hmm, how can I put this, let's just say for someone who's not a drinker, he finished my brandy I had and now he's standing at my bay window just staring out into emptiness."

"Oh, my goodness, babe I'm so sorry, it must be rough on him to find out this now."

"Yeah tell me about it and honestly for the first time in my life I feel helpless. Usually I have something to say some sort of wise advice or comment or something to say but all I could muster up was the fact that we'll get through this together."

"Babe maybe that's all he needed to hear from you right now. So did he go home?"

"No, I didn't let him, I told him to stay at my place until tomorrow at least so he could get his head together. Besides I didn't want him to be alone, not at this moment, especially not in the condition he's in now."

"You are such a good friend Marcus I really see that and he's lucky to have you in his life"

"Thanks babe and I'm the lucky one to have him and all my boys in my life because I didn't have many friends growing up and when I got older and hooked up with them we've been tight ever since."

"Wow that's great I'm so happy for you."

"Thanks, anywho, how are things on your end and are you resting up for work in the morning?"

"Things are good and yes I'm resting. It's good to be home although I had the most wonderful time with you in DC and would love to do something like that again, it's always good to sleep in your own bed, ya know?"

"Oh, don't I know it but I'll have to wait until tomorrow to sleep in mine."

"Oh, and why is that, uhm where are you going to be Mr. Bass?"

"Ha, ha, ha, do I detect a little bit of jealousy Ms. Johnson?"

"Well maybe but more curious as to why you're not going to be in your bed tonight, hell for that matter if you're not going to be in your bed you should be in mine, hint hint."

"Aaahh I see, well that's all fine and good but to be honest with you since I told Braden to stay here I gave him my bed and I'm going to stay in Jazz's room since she's at my mom's until tomorrow."

"Oh, honey that's so sweet of you, wow you know you're just making me fall for you more and more every second of the day. And speaking of falling Mr. Bass I heard the lovely voice mail you left."

"Yeah I figured you did." I said, starting to sweat a little wondering when she was going to bring that up.

"Yes I did especially the ending."

"Ok....is there something wrong with the ending."

"Well kind of but only because I wasn't on the phone or in person to hear those lovely words come out of your mouth. I must say that I am floating on air right now Marcus and honestly I thought I was the only one feeling this way as well as thinking it was too soon for me to feel as strongly for you as I do."

"Well I must say that I too was thinking the same thing about it being too early and believe me I'm not trying to rush into anything but I do feel very strong for you Kim and for the first time in a very long time I feel it's right."

"Wow..."

"What?"

"You just took my breath away that's all I mean here I am thinking I was alone in this but all the while you are feeling the same way I am. I love you Marcus and I'm glad I'm not alone in this."

"Kim, I love you too and honestly I was a little surprised when I said it but I know it's real but we will take it slow and not rush ok."

"Yeah I know and I was thinking the same thing because of how we met and how the weekend went anyone could get caught up and emotions could get out of control so I thought to myself to take it slow and see where it goes but I'll be honest with you Marcus I don't want to and will not fight how I feel for you if this does grow and I hope you don't fight it either."

"Kim look, like I said it's been a long time since I've said those words to another woman and I'll be real with you I'm a little scared by it but I will give you my word on this. You see I've tried dating since Brenda died and on a couple occasions things seemed to go well but just when I thought I could put my heart into it something went wrong and the other person either lied to me about something or they cheated, hell one person tried to set me up to see if I'd cheat on her. So with that it caused me to close up my heart and not try to love again. I just put all my time and energy into my work and raising Jazzmin. But I feel differently with you and I can only give you my word on this, I will do my best not to fight it if the feeling grows, that's the best I can do right now. You have to understand I have to look out not only for me and my heart but my daughter as well."

There's a strange pause in the phone and I notice that Kim did not respond to what I said. This makes me wonder what she's thinking but right now I can't focus on that.

"Kim, are you still there?"

"Yes, Marcus I am, and I do understand, that's why I'm not going to push you on this. I'm just glad I'm not alone that's all."

"Ok good and no you're not alone hon but look let me talk to you later and get my boy straightened out for the night. I have some work to get done before tomorrow when I go into the office so I will say goodnight at this moment but will talk to you tomorrow."

"Ok sweetheart, I'm about to take me a nice hot bubble bath and get myself ready for tomorrow too so it's fine, we'll talk tomorrow, I love you Marcus."

"I love you too Kim, goodnight."

I hang up the phone and found myself staring at it; I couldn't help but wonder what the pause was about though. Maybe it's nothing but my gut was telling me otherwise but I wasn't listening to it at that point. I was thinking to myself that I truly have strong feelings for this woman, another woman outside of my Bren, wow I must say that I'm truly blown away by it.

I get up from sitting on my bed to go into the living room to check on Braden and find him standing in the same spot he was in a half hour ago. I just stand there wondering what he's thinking and how he's truly feeling but not having an inkling of a clue as to what he's going through. I go into the kitchen and get a glass of water, just when I turn to leave out of the kitchen Braden is standing there with tears in his eyes. I walk over to my brotha and give him a hug.

"What am I going to do man?"

"I don't know B, I don't know, but what I do know is this, whatever it will be we all will be here for you no matter what and see you through it 'til whatever end comes."

"Thanks man I appreciate it I really do. Man, this was a blow."

"Yeah tell me about it and shit I had to hold onto it for a few days and it killed me to do that to you bro. I'm sorry about that."

"Man, it's ok I understand why you did it and that's not information that you tell someone over the phone."

"Yeah that's why I did it, I wanted to be here just in case."

"In case what?"

"In case you did something crazy like you were staring out my window, I thought you were thinking about jumping out or something."

"Nah man I wasn't but I was feeling like I was falling off a cliff and kept falling with no end in sight."

"I know we've been through a lot together and we've gotten through it so just know we'll get through this too."

"Yeah we have been through a lot haven't we, man I appreciate you being there for me hell more so than my own brother."

"Speaking of, how is your brother doing by the way?"

"Same old Donte, doing his dirt and not wanting to listen to anyone, especially me."

"Yeah I hear ya but that's how it goes right?"

"Yeah I guess but I just wish he would get his life together and stop doing the things he's doing."

"Yeah I know and after his career in football ended I thought he would finish school and get on with his communications career."

"Yeah me too but he just want to run the streets. Look I don't want to talk about him right now. What I need to know is how am I to get in touch with Kandi about her....my...our son. Wow my son, damn Bass my son is dying."

Braden having a look of anguish on his face and seems to be feeling the pain of it all. First the years that have been lost of not having his son in his life, the struggles his son is facing now and the possibility him not only dying but never having the opportunity to make up for the lost time they never had. It must have hit him hard because he starts to cry uncontrollably. I make him sit down on the edge of the couch. I could tell he is in no shape to talk about anything anymore so I tell him to go lie down in my room and just try to rest and if he needs me I'm in the next room. He gets up and goes into my room and just collapse on my bed and sobs. Again, I pause and feel so helpless as I look at him. I turn to walk into the living room when I realize that Milton never showed back up. I was just wondering what happened to him when my house phone rang.

"Hello?"

"Yes we have a collect call from Milton Carrington will you accept the charges?"

"Charges...what...uhm yes I'll except, Milton what the hell..... where are you?"

"You're not going to believe this but I'm In Jail."

"WAIT WHAT!!, how in the hell are you in jail?"

"When I went home to get some cloths to come back over your place Sharon came home and started in on me and when I was about to leave the police were at the door. Apparently she called them when she saw my car and waited just long enough for them to show up and came in and started yelling at me. So when I was going to leave, I opened the door and they were standing there. They asked who I was and what I was doing there. I told them who I was and I just came to get some cloths but that's when she came and showed them the restraining order and they just took me to jail without question. Man I didn't know what else to do that's why I called you."

"Ok ok...damn....man where are you calling me from and how much is your bail."

"I'm in Cook County Jail, I won't know until tomorrow, because of the weekend they won't arraign me until the morning."

"Damn man something told me not to let you go alone but I thought it would be ok since you said she was going to be gone for a while. Matter of fact what was she doing home early anyway."

"Yeah that's what I was wondering and I asked her about it. She told me that she has her neighbor watching the house just in case I showed up and to call her if I ever did."

"Oh, wow so now she has her neighbor in your business too, damn she's really trippin'."

"Yeah tell me about it so here I am, man you know how my job is, they have this clause in their contract that if an employee is in any illegal activity of any kind they can be terminated."

"Damn man but I'm sure that once you work this out they will understand right, I mean come on this is truly not your fault. Sharon is just on some whacked out shit and once the investigation is completed they will see she's crazy."

"Man, I don't know I can just hope so. I hate to ask this but would it be possible for you to come get me tomorrow, man I'll pay you back as soon as I can that's my word."

"Man look just hold tight 'til tomorrow and I got you and don't worry about paying me back just don't drop the soap homie."

"Man, that's not funny."

"Ha, ha, ha I know but real talk just hold tight and I'll get you in the morning, just let me know when your hearing is and I'll be there."

"Ok and Marcus."

"Yeah bro?"

"Thanks."

"Man, it's cool you my boy so you're good."

"Ok oh and how did things with Braden go?"

"Man, we'll talk about that later because you're costing me money by the minute so sit tight and I'll get you tomorrow."

"Ok my bad, later."

"Later!"

I hang up from Milton I take a deep breath, all I could do is shake my head at what's going on. It seems as though everyone is having their problems. I don't like to think or say that proverbial statement of "what's next" but I couldn't help but think of it. Man, I could use some good news for my boys instead of drama and chaos. That's life right and when that first drop of rain comes you know a storm is yet to follow. How much of a storm is yet to be seen. I couldn't help but think to myself wow what a way to welcome me home. Well since I won't be going onto the office now, I make a call into my assistants voice mail letting her know I won't be in the office in the morning but will touch base with her throughout the day just in case I have to put out a couple fires.

I have an issue about to come out, I can't afford to be gone from the office too long. So I decided to just work from home and contact her by phone if necessary. After that I got me a stiff drink and headed into my spare bedroom since Milton won't be here I figured he don't need it. I couldn't help but wonder what is really going on with his wife for her to flip out on one of the nicest guys I know. But as they say you never know what goes on behind closed doors. I realize that this day has truly drained me and as I lay back to drift off to sleep I think that tomorrow has to be a better day. I hope...

CHAPTER

30

Marcus "Monday Morning Blues"

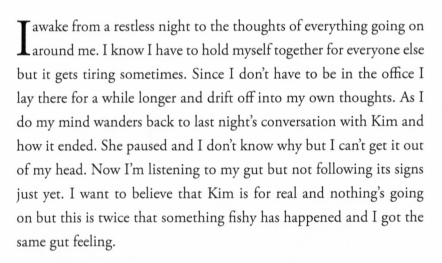

I awake from a restless night to the thoughts of everything going on around me. I know I have to hold myself together for everyone else but it gets tiring sometimes. Since I don't have to be in the office I lay there for a while longer and drift off into my own thoughts. As I do my mind wanders back to last night's conversation with Kim and how it ended. She paused and I don't know why but I can't get it out of my head. Now I'm listening to my gut but not following its signs just yet. I want to believe that Kim is for real and nothing's going on but this is twice that something fishy has happened and I got the same gut feeling.

Oh well I'm sure it's nothing, at least that's what I'm telling myself. Since I can't truly rest I decide to get up and check on Braden only to find him in the same position I left him when he flopped on my bed. He's still asleep so I decide to let him be, besides I need to get on my laptop and look at the layouts for my magazine and check on how it's looking before I release it to the press. I grab my bag and go into my office. I pull out my laptop and open it up where it turns on automatically. I log into my network at the office so I can pull up the layouts of the magazine for this month. I noticed right away that my assistant Genene has added the ads for Jump Athletics to the areas I told her too also I noticed that she put in a "coming soon to Chicago" spot for LUX.

I was truly impressed with how she can complete tasks without me. She's going to be a wonderful publisher one of these days and I'm going to do whatever I can to make sure she gets to where she wants to go. I finish looking through the layout and send her an e-mail letting her know that I love and approve it and to send it off to get it printed up. Also to remind her to have them print just one copy (as usual) so I can see it first before we print up the several thousand's we have to get out. I wanted to especially make this volume a great one since I'm sending copies to Edwin and Charles.

Thinking of them I realized that I didn't contact them to let them know I made it home safe so I pick up my phone and send a text to both of them letting them know how apologetic I am for not doing so and that it has been crazy since I came home. They both responded that they were concerned but glad I made it in ok and hoped that things settle down for me. I responded that they would have a copy of the new magazine in the mail in a few days so be on the lookout for it. They were both ecstatic and happy about the news and couldn't wait to see what I've put together for them. As I finished up with the layouts and replying to a few e-mails that were important I closed out my laptop and got up to check on Braden again.

When I went into my bedroom he was finally sitting up on the side of my bed but I could tell he wasn't right. I sat next to him and we sat in silence for a few minutes. I didn't want to rush him to speak on anything so I waited for him to start whatever conversation we were going to have.

"Tell me that yesterday was a dream?"

"I wish I could, man I wish I could but it's not."

"I woke up in the middle of the night in somewhat of a panic because I didn't realize where I was at first. Also, I didn't feel too good so I went to the bathroom and that's when I knew I was here. Man, what did I have yesterday?"

Laughing a little

"Man, you finished off the Brandy I had and not the cheap stuff either, the one I brought back from Jamaica so you owe me a bottle bro."

"I'm sorry about that man."

"Dude, really, do I look like I'm worried about that. Hell I wasn't surprised that you drank as much as you did but with the news you got and I don't blame you."

"I guess I couldn't help myself at that point and you know I'm not much of a drinker, remember Florida?"

"How can I forget, shoot I still have pictures." remembering when Braden got drunk off two glasses of alcohol after an exhausting drive to Florida for our tournament.

"You still have those pictures?"

"Yep, come on man you know I can't throw away evidence like that.

People would never believe that Mr. Clean Braden got drunk."

"Man, that was a crazy trip but I'm glad we made it back safe."

"Yeah you and me both, I know one thing I'll never do again."

"What's that?"

"Take no-doze with a mountain dew, man I was wired for sound and when I came down I crashed."

"Yeah I remember and you were looking just about how I feel right now. Man, that was nuts for us to drive all the way down there and back."

"It was for the kids' man and I'll do it again if I had to."

"Oh well that was then and this is now and now is a whole lot of mess isn't it."

"I wouldn't say mess but a challenge that you will get through."

"Do you have Kandi's number for me to call?"

"Yeah I do and I told her that I'll be in touch with her as soon as I talk to you. I would have had you speak to her last night but knew you were in no condition to do so. Speaking of calling Kandi let me apologize for not telling you this a couple days ago. Believe me bro, when Kandi called me and laid it on me I wanted to tell you right then and there and wrestled within myself of doing so. I tried to put myself in your shoes and thought if it were me would I want to hear this news over the phone or in person. Knowing the way, I am and you and I not that much different from each other figured that it would be better said in person."

"Marcus I'll admit, at first when you said it I was a bit pissed at you for holding onto the information but in reality I had to realize that you did it for the best. If I had known this a couple days ago I don't know what I would have done. I stayed up late last night just thinking of just that, what I would have done if I'd known a couple days ago. Would I had called Kandi, would I have went to see my son, hell would I had been strong enough to do either. Damn it's been 20 years and although I've wanted to get in touch with her, now it's here I don't know what to say or do."

"I can only try to understand but I'll admit that it's difficult because I'm not the one going through it. All I know is when I get news like this or somewhat on this level I have always hated hearing it over the phone, it seems so impersonal that's why I waited. Hell, if things hadn't gone as well in DC I would have been here to tell you in person on Friday."

"I know and I don't blame you for it, I'm just in a whirlwind right now, there are so many different thoughts and emotions going on that I don't know if I'm coming or going. Don't beat yourself up behind this because in the bigger picture of things I'm glad I was here when you told me."

"Ok I'll let it go but I just wanted you to know and hopefully understand why. Also forgive me for holding it in. Trust me it was eating at me when I was there although I had to put on my business face, inside I was at a turmoil state. Now with that said I'm going to do is give her a call after you get up and take a shower and gather yourself and y'all can talk this out and figure out when and where you'll meet up to get the testing done because time is truly ticking and you can't put this off any longer than necessary."

"Yeah I know, I just hope that things work out and I'm not too late to help him. Bass what if I'm too late?"

"Man don't even begin to think like that. Look you're one of the most positive brotha's I know and hell you even got me to think positive even in negative situations so I'm throwing that back at you. Stay positive and this will work out."

"You're right and I know I have too but this time it's different and harder to do. I guess because I feel like I don't know what to do."

"We'll just take it a day at a time and get it done. Are you up for calling Kandi?"

"Honestly as much as I know I need to right away, my head wont' let me deal with it just yet. I need to do a bit of recovering first."

"Understandable, so let's do this you get up and get in the shower and you can put on one of my sweat suits to lounge around in because you're not going anywhere today. I'm going to go in the kitchen and fix some breakfast, do you want anything?"

"Even though I really don't, but I know with all the liquor I had I need to eat something so yeah whatever you make."

"Ok cool" I state as I get up to go into the kitchen but stop to tell him about Milton and his dilemma, "Oh and by the way your boy is in jail."

"Damn what did Jason do this time?"

"Oh, damn I didn't mean him but you're not wrong for thinking it, but I'm talking about Milton."

"What...you're kidding....for what?"

"Apparently after he went home to get some cloths because he's staying with me for a while Sharon showed up with the police and had him arrested."

"Damn, so when does he get out."

"I'm going to court with him as soon as he calls me to let me know what time it is and get him out. I wish Sharon wouldn't trip out on him the way she did but that's the way it goes."

"Yeah I know, hell I thought they had a great relationship until one day he said she flipped on him. I guess anyone could change on you huh?"

"Yeah I guess so, so here shortly I'll be leaving to get him. Do you want to ride with me or chill here?"

"As much as I love my boy I'm gonna chill, I'm in no mood to really be out in public right now besides I need to get my thoughts together for when I speak to Kandi."

"Yeah I hear ya and it's cool I'll go get him."

"Marcus."

"Yeah B."

"Thanks Bass"

"You don't have to thank me, we're brothers."

With that said I leave out of my room to go into the kitchen and start cooking something to eat. I receive a phone call from Milton letting me know his arraignment is at 11:00am. I tell him I'll be there to pick him up and not to worry. After fixing breakfast Braden and

I sat down to eat, we didn't say much of a word to one another and didn't have too. It was as if we knew what the other was thinking. The phone call he had to make to Kandi. This was going to be hard, harder than the one he did when he contacted her out of the blue a few years ago. After breakfast I told him to just chill out 'til I got back from court with Milton and then we'll make that call. I also told him to stay away from my liquor because I didn't want another episode of last night. He agreed and didn't want another one either.

I went to the courthouse to get Milton and once I got there I found the court room where he was being arraigned. I went in to see him sitting there looking like a lost puppy. He looked up to see me and we nodded in acknowledgement and then his case was called. He looked nervous and didn't know what the judge was going to hit him with but the judge after looking at the record and speaking with the officers surprised him as well as me and let him go on a ROR. I, for one, was happy for him and me since I didn't have to come out of my pocket but I was more than willing to do it. After the judge gave him a few directions and let him go, he turned to me with that big grin on his face as if he just dodged a huge bullet. He walked over towards me

"Man, I'm so glad to see you but more importantly glad to get out of here."

"Yeah I'm sure you are bro and I'm glad the judge saw fit to let you go."

"Yeah me too especially since that's the same judge that's presiding over the investigation."

"Really, well that's a great thing for you."

"Yeah tell me about it and when we first appeared in front of him with the whole restraining order. He actually asked Sharon was it necessary for all of this making me think he was more on my side. But Sharon acted a fool in court, when the judge stated that he was thinking about lifting the order she flipped out. She began stating that she's in fear for her life and ranting and raging being hysterical so much so the judge upheld the order for the 90 days anyway or until the investigation is completed which ever happens first."

"Damn you got lucky on that one."

"Tell me about it, so how's Braden and where is he?"

"He's at my condo now and he's doing a little better than yesterday but he has a ways to go."

"Yeah I'm sure he does."

"Ok so now we have to get your car from your house right?"

"Actually no, the officer, who was real cool, had it towed to the impound lot for safe keeping. He said he didn't want to leave it there and I come back to it all smashed up so he wanted to take the precautions of that not happening and they're not charging me either."

"Wow that is great news, see first you get off on your own recognizance and now you get your car back without paying anything. What a blessing, God is awesome."

"Yes He is."

As we left the courthouse and headed to get his car I couldn't help but think how God answers prayers and I've asked him for something to go right for my boys and here it is. See blessings don't always have to be this big grand type of deal. God sometimes lets you know He's there in the smallest ways. I guess that's what they mean about hearing Gods voice like a whisper. As we got his car and he followed me back to my place. We pulled into my garage and parked our cars. We made it up to my place and I opened the door to make sure Braden was ok. He was sitting there looking through some old photo albums I had and just reminiscing about the past I guess. I thought to myself this may not be good but we'll see. I ask him if he was ready to make the call and nervously he said yes but I could tell that he was thinking he may as well get it over with and not waste more time. So, I pull out my cell phone and look up Kandi's number and hit send. The phone rings a couple times and then she picks up.

"Hi Marcus, I've been nervously waiting your call."

"Yeah I'm sure you have and I didn't mean to make you wait so long."

"It's ok and honestly it's not that long. I mean I know you just got back in town yesterday and you said you had to talk to Braden first so I honestly didn't expect to hear from you for a few more days but I'm glad you called."

"I understand that and I told you I wanted to get this done because time is not on our side right now. So I wanted to let you know that yes I did talk with Braden and told him the whole story and he's sitting here now prepared to talk to you."

Kandi lets out a huge sigh

"Ok, I think I'm ready."

"Ok I'm putting him on the phone."

I hand Braden the phone I tell him to go into my room for some privacy. Although I pretty much know the conversation, he still needs to speak with her alone. He agrees and goes into my room and closes the door. About fifteen minutes later he comes out and tells me that Kandi wants to speak with me.

"Hello?"

"Marcus, I asked Braden to make sure you were there when you come to the hospital is that ok with you?"

"Don't you think it's best if Braden came alone?"

"I thought about that but honestly I don't know how I will feel once I actually see him face to face. I mean talking on the phone just now is one thing but seeing the physical person…well I just don't want to do or say anything that I don't need to say and the truth is I don't know if I can face Braden alone after all this time and I need you like you were there 20 years ago."

"Yeah sure I have no problem with that as long as you both are ok with it" all of a sudden I feel a burning in my heart thinking on what took place that fateful weekend when Kandi and Braden broke up, but I let Kandi know I'll be there. "When is all this taking place and are you coming to Chicago or are we driving to Michigan?"

"Well I told Braden already and now I'm telling you. We've been in Chicago since Friday when I called you because the hospital here is one of the top marrow institutions in the country and they wanted to run some test on BJ. Also they need to perform the transplant as soon as they find out the results of the matching."

"Oh, wow I didn't know that but ok, so when is he to report in?"

"I asked him if he could come today and he said that normally he wouldn't have a problem with it but he had a rough night and don't think it would be good for him to do today."

"Yeah I'll say and I must agree because last night wasn't the best for him and he's not a drinker so I think tomorrow would be better for him. How's your son holding up by the way?"

"He's doing ok, they have him hooked to so many machines it's scary but they have to monitor him very closely so he won't get worse."

"I can imagine but you tell him he's going to be ok and give him a hug from his Uncle Marcus and his Father and we'll see you in the morning."

"Ok I'll do just that and Marcus."

"Yeah Kandi?"

"Thanks again for being there for me I can never repay you for it."

"Yes you can by being there for BJ and doing what you have to do for him that's how you repay me."

"That I have no choice on but I understand. I'll see you two tomorrow."

"Ok bye!"

After getting off the phone with Kandi I look at Braden and he has a look as if he was "falling into emptiness" and there's no one to catch him. The same look that was on his face last night and I just tell him that BJ will be ok, that he has to believe that but Braden doesn't seem to hear me. I get up and head towards my bedroom to get myself cleaned up and to give Braden some space. I go to jump in the shower and try to wash off the worries and problems of the past couple days. I almost succeed too but my mind drifts back to Kim and I don't know why I can't get that out of my head but I guess that darkness will come to light in due time....

CHAPTER

31

Darius "Just When you think you're out of the woods"

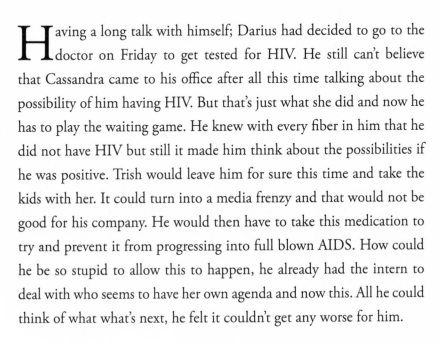

Having a long talk with himself; Darius had decided to go to the doctor on Friday to get tested for HIV. He still can't believe that Cassandra came to his office after all this time talking about the possibility of him having HIV. But that's just what she did and now he has to play the waiting game. He knew with every fiber in him that he did not have HIV but still it made him think about the possibilities if he was positive. Trish would leave him for sure this time and take the kids with her. It could turn into a media frenzy and that would not be good for his company. He would then have to take this medication to try and prevent it from progressing into full blown AIDS. How could he be so stupid to allow this to happen, he already had the intern to deal with who seems to have her own agenda and now this. All he could think of what what's next, he felt it couldn't get any worse for him.

"Damn that bitch, if I have this disease I'm gonna kill her ass."

Darius says out loud for no one to hear, but little did he know Terry, his assistant, was walking through the door and over heard what he said.

"Boss you ok, I heard you say something?"

"I was talking to myself and didn't know you were here yet."

"Well I had to come in a little early to set up some things for Mitch and Zenobia to do since I didn't have them do much over the weekend."

"Oh, ok it's cool, so what's up."

"I just wanted to come in and say good morning and see how you're weekend went."

"Well let's see I had to go to the doctors for an emergency testing, then on Sunday one of my boys got a bomb of information dropped on his head that shook all of us to the core and now I'm sitting here waiting for some results that if come back positive could ruin me. So I'd say I had a not so good weekend overall, what about you how was your weekend."

Making sure to keep the events of Saturday night with Zenobia to himself, Darius decides to just not divulge that information. He doesn't want anyone to know that he truly screwed up literally when he got together with her.

"Well compared to you mine was flawlessly quiet but if you don't mind me asking what test did you have done and are you ok. I mean do I need to start making arrangements to find another job or what?"

"No, you don't and I know I can tell you anything but this one I'll have to keep to myself, sorry man."

"Hey, it's ok we all have to keep some things personal. Oh, before I forget I have to say that Zenobia has been trying to get you alone and she's becoming very persistent with it. Are you sure you're going to be able to keep her here for the duration of the internship?"

"Well, if she continues on this path I may have to cut hers short. I don't know what it is but I get this feeling she's here for a different reason than to learn the music business but I can't put my finger on what it is. If and when I do find out what it is and if she's up to no good I gotta cut her loose."

"Yeah I hear ya, I mean as fine as she is, she could mean nothing but trouble for you and you already dodged one bullet. You don't need any more to dodge, hell, keep it up and you're gonna have to start wearing a bullet proof vest."

Terry starts to laugh and Darius gives him a look as if to say keep it up and you'll be out of a job for real. Terry begins to walk out of the door when he turns around and remembers why he came into Darius's office in the first place.

"Oh, I forgot to tell you that you had a message from Marcus on Friday and he said he needed to talk to you as soon as possible."

"Hmmm I was just with him and he didn't say anything, but I guess with everything going on with my boy Braden that was more important and must have slipped his mind. I'll give him a call in a few. Thanks Terry."

"No problem boss and I'll keep my little bees busy and make sure one in particular doesn't try to come around trying to spread her honey."

"Yeah you do just that because that's the last thing I need. Shut the door please on your way out I need some privacy to make a couple of calls."

Terry leaves Darius's office and closes the door, I pick up the phone and call the doctor to see if any results have come in. The nurse informs me that it will take a few days to get it back and due to legalities she would not be able to reveal the results over the phone and that he would have to come into the office to get the results. Not seeming to happy about that I agreed and hang up the phone. I then called Marcus to see what he needed to talk about and after the news with Braden he wasn't too keen on Marcus and his news lately so he was a little apprehensive over the call.

"Hello!"

"Marcus what's up man?"

"Hey D, what's going on with you bro?"

"Just here in the office getting some paperwork done and received a message that you called on Friday, so what's up?"

"Yeah I did and I really can't talk right now because I'm at the hospital with Braden to see him through this ordeal but I will give you a call a little later on and we'll talk about things then, cool?"

"Do I have a choice in the matter?"

I chuckle just a bit…

"Well since you put it like that no you don't but I will say this, your new female intern, just watch your back on that one bro because she's on some foul shit."

"See you shouldn't have told me anything because now I'm going to be thinking about it all day."

"Sorry man I just wanted to give you a small heads up just in case she tries something with you, but let me get back in this room with B and I'll hit you up this afternoon."

"Alright man but I still say you're wrong for not telling me the whole story now."

"Ok, ok, ok my bad but I can't go into the full details of it just yet."

"Ok, I'll let you go and tell Braden that I'm there with him too and if he needs anything, anything at all to not hesitate to call a brotha."

"Will do."

Darius hangs up from talking with Marcus and feels that his whole life is in limbo right now and there's nothing he can do about it but sit and wait which is something he hates to do. He sits there for a few minutes and everything seems quiet but just as soon as he turns to finish some paperwork on his desk there's a knock on his door. He tells the person behind the door to come in only to regret it as soon as she enters his office.

"Good morning boss!"

Zenobia comes in saying those words in a singing tone of voice

"Morning Ms. Bentley, what can I do for you?"

"Oh, so now it's Ms. Bentley, you weren't saying that on Saturday night."

"Look what happened Saturday night happened and honestly it shouldn't have but we can't change things now."

"Well I wanted to come in and say thank you for a wonderful night Saturday night, I truly enjoyed being with you and I was wondering when we'll be able to see one another again like that."

"Zenobia, again I know what we did on Saturday was nice but we will have to leave it at that just a nice time we had. I can't afford to go on and continue anything with you. I'm sorry if I lead you on and made it seem as if there could be more but I'm just being real with you, there will not be any more Saturday nights."

"EXCUSE ME!! SO WHAT AM I JUST A PIECE OF ASS TO YOU?"

Zenobia begins to raise her voice and Darius knows he has to get this calmed down quickly before someone comes in and finds out what's going on.

"Zenobia lower your voice and we'll talk about it, now look, things happened and honestly got way out of hand for the both of us. You know as well as I do there can never be an "us" that's just the way it is. I'm married remember?"

"Not happily apparently!" said in a sarcastic tone

"Regardless, I am and there's nothing you or anyone can do about that so like I said let's just leave Saturday the way it is. Now from this point forward we must keep things between us strictly on a professional level and that's it."

"Oh ok I see how you want to be, you want me to chase you, well I don't chase men, I replace them, but I will say that you're right and I will keep things between us strictly professional.......Boss!!" Zenobia says in a weird, crazy way.

An uneasy feeling comes into the pits of my stomach as she said that as if that's far from the end of this episode. I know I need to get her out of my office so I let it go at that and said for her to see Terry because he had some things for her to do.

Zenobia reluctantly leaves Darius's office, as she walked down the hallway she decided to make a detour and go into one of the conference rooms and make a phone call. Little did Darius know the phone call she decided to make was to his wife Trish. Feeling as though Darius is playing games, she figures she'll play one of her own. As she made her call she was a bit upset at the fact she got the answering machine but decided to leave a message anyway and tell the story of how Darius was with her on Saturday night when he was supposed to be working with his new group. She knew she was taking a risk for doing so but to cover her base she decided not to leave her name just in case he gets the message and deletes it. As she was finishing her message Terry was walking past and saw her and came into the room.

"There you are, I have been looking for you. What are you doing in here?"

"I had to make a quick call and needed some privacy."

"Well I need you to get to your desk because I have some work for you and Mitch to do and it's a large project so I need for both of you to work on this together and get it done."

"What it is about?"

"Well I'll tell you more in detail but let's just say you'll be spending quite a bit of time with this new female act we just signed and helping them get things in order so this will take a lot of your time up."

Zenobia, sensing something fishy going on, try to get out of it but Terry doesn't budge and she sees that she has no choice but to go along with it but feels confident in the domino she just played on Darius. She feels that all she has to do now is wait for the rest of them to fall and the game will be over...

CHAPTER

32

Braden Jr. "The Fight of His Life"

Braden and I get to the hospital early on Tuesday morning. As we were walking in Braden turns to me and I see this scared look on his face. He looks as if he could faint at any moment so I sit him down in one of the chairs. I go to the service desk to see which room BJ was in and the receptionist tells me he's in room C1302. I turn to get Braden and make sure he can walk ok. We head to the room and as we turn the corner towards his room I realize I'm ahead of him. I take a look back and Braden had stopped dead in his tracks, just simply freezes. I could tell that he doesn't know if he could do this or not and I don't blame him. But I knew he had too. I go back to him to make sure he's ok. He has this deathly look of fear on his face and it scares even me.

"B, you alright man?"

"I...I...I don't know if I can do this Marcus. I mean I know I have to but man I'm meeting my son for the first time in 20 years and he's dying."

"Look, he's not dying or dead yet and you can help him live. Man look, I can't imagine what you are going through and I'm not going to remotely begin to try but all I know is this. That young man is in there fighting for his life and you have the opportunity to help save him. I can only guess how rough this is but you have to do it."

"I know, I know but what if I'm not a match Marcus then what, what am I to do then?"

"Pray my brotha, pray that you are and if not then pray that God works a miracle in your son's life that's all you can do."

At that moment Kandi comes out of the room and sees Braden and I down the hall and just stares as if she's looking at a ghost. Braden and Kandi eyes meet and I think seeing her gives him some sort of motivation to go forward. We begin to walk again but slowly and Kandi comes to meet us.

"Hi Kandi, how is he doing?" I ask

"Hi Marcus, he's holding on, I mean it's rough but he's a fighter and I know somehow he'll be ok." Kandi turns and faces Braden "Hi Braden, it's been a long time and I'm so sorry that we have to meet under these circumstances."

"Hi Kandi and yes it has but it's not your fault it's mine, I mean if I hadn't, well If you, I mean" Braden not being able to find the right words to say.

"It's ok you don't have to say anything. Right now, the focus is on BJ and getting him well. Would you like to go in and meet him? Would you like to meet your son?"

"I do but I'm nervous, does he know who I am?"

"Yes he does, I've told him about you a long time ago and I explained to him as he gotten older why you weren't apart of his life."

"Oh wow, so I'm sure he hates me already?"

"Actually no, surprisingly he feels as though it may have been for the better but now it doesn't seem so because he's going through this. Braden I will tell you that this isn't easy on me either, I mean I honestly hadn't planned on telling you about your son, ever, but now that I look back on things I truly regret it and I want to apologize for that and no matter what or how long Braden will be on this earth I will never hold you two from one another. Although he has his step father who has been wonderful to him, he needs to know you as well. What I'm trying to say is, he needs his father in his life and I'm sure you would want to be in his."

"You're correct I do and I don't blame you for what you did Kandi it was all on me and I'm sorry. All I want now is to do whatever I can to make sure he's ok so we can move forward and get to know one another."

"I'd like that and I know he would too, well the doctor needs to run some test on you before anything can be done so I will go and get him. BJ is resting right now because this takes a lot of his energy but you can go in and sit with him until he wakes up if you want to."

Braden walks slowly towards the room and enters in, Kandi turns to me and reaches out to me and gives me a big hug.

"Thank you for this Marcus, I don't know what I would have done if you hadn't been there."

"Kandi you don't have to thank me but I do understand and I wouldn't be anywhere else than here with you, B and BJ. I told Braden I can't imagine what he or your son is going through so I will do whatever I can to help out."

"Thank you very much and you can go in too, I'm sure he'd like to see your face too."

"Ok I'm confused as to why he would want to see my face. I mean he don't know about me does he."

"Actually, he does, I told him about you a long time ago and said you were his uncle. I even told him about the time when you drove me home on that fateful day so yes he knows all about you. I even showed him a picture of you on Facebook."

"Oh, wow ok, well I'll go in in a bit; I want Braden to have some time alone with him."

"I understand, well I'm going to get the doctor so he can tell Braden what he needs to do and where to go. Just take your time and I'll be back in a few minutes."

Kandi walks down the hallway to the front desk to ask for the doctor to come in. I go and stand outside the doorway directly across the hall, giving Braden time to spend with his son. As I look upon Braden he has a look of disbelief on his face. I look up and see BJ's face and say to myself that yep he's Braden's alright. A smile comes over my face as I look at the two of them. I couldn't help but think of Jazzmin and how much I love her. I don't know how I would be if she was the one laying there in that hospital bed. Just when I was engulfed in my own thoughts Kandi comes back to me.

"The Doctor will be here in a few minutes so he can begin the testing on Braden."

"Kandi can I ask you a question?"

"Sure!"

"Please don't get mad at me for this but I'm just curious to know."

"What is it Marcus?"

"How long has BJ been like this and why did it take you this long to contact me for Braden?"

"Well, he's been like this for a few months but when it first started it wasn't that bad but he got progressively worse. Then when he did begin to get worse that's when they said he would need a marrow transplant. Then they started doing the testing on me and of course asking for donors to see who's a match for him. So, when they found out I wasn't a match and of course his step father wasn't either they asked me about Braden. They told me that I had to get in touch with him right away and had to do the DNA testing on him to make sure he was his father first since it had been so long and make sure that he's a good match so they can go forward with the procedure, so here we are."

"Ok but I thought that you can get marrow from almost anyone, so why does it have to be Braden?"

"In some cases that's true but according to what the Dr.'s said due to the leukemia he has it's something that has to come from the parent and in this case it's from the fathers side."

"Damn, that's truly messed up but at least you got in touch in time hopefully to get this taken care of."

"Yeah let's hope" Kandi says lowing her tone in a hopeful way.

"Wow I mean that's a lot and I'm sorry if I offended or upset you but I just wanted to know."

"It's ok and I don't blame you for your questions, I mean I'd ask them too and it took me a minute to get up the nerve to contact you to even start this whole thing."

"Yeah you should have seen the look on my face when I heard your voice and then you dropped this bomb on me."

Kandi looks down and kind of sad, and says, "I can imagine and I'm sorry for bringing you into this but I didn't know how else to get in touch with Braden and honestly was a bit scared too."

"Kandi, listen, I'm not saying I'm mad or anything because I'm not and I'm glad you did, I was just utterly and completely shocked that's all. I mean to hear your voice after all this time took me back to the last day I saw you that's all."

"Yeah that was a day alright, a day that changed all of our lives. Marcus can I ask you a question?"

"Sure!"

"Have you ever thought about what would have happened if I hadn't found that letter and Braden decided to be with me verses that other woman?"

"Kandi, don't start thinking the woulda, coulda, shoulda's because that's in the past now. But to answer your question, yes I have thought about that and I know Braden has as well because we've talked about it"

"Really, wow, I don't know what to say" sounding surprised.

"Well let's just say that in life everyone has someone they regret letting go and for him…it was you."

At that moment Kandi turns and looks into the room where Braden is sitting there staring at his son that he's seeing for the first time. Her head lowers and I can tell from the look on her face that it's getting to her. I try my best to console her but I don't think I'm doing a good job.

"Marcus what have I done, I mean what if BJ doesn't make it and he never had the chance to know his father. I would hate myself and I could never forgive myself for being so selfish?"

Tears begin to come and I can tell Kandi is having a rough time with this.

"Kandi look, what's done is done and I know you regret it too but the good thing is this he's here now and they have a chance to know one another at least for this time. But just think of it this way when they run the test and find out that Braden is a match, he'll perform the surgery and everything will be fine and Braden and his son can begin anew and from there build a relationship."

"You know Marcus, you're right this will work out, I have to believe that it will. Thank you, thank you for being there and being such a positive person" she says wiping the tears from her eyes that have become to flow.

"Well it's easy to be positive when you're not in the shoes of the one walking."

"True, so very true."

At that moment we share a smile together and as we do the doctor walks up to us and tells us he's ready to run the test on Braden. He says the test won't take long to run; they are going to put a rush on it and will have the results back in a few hours. Do to the fact that a bone marrow transplant is a long process they would like to keep Braden here because as soon as the results come back they are going to get started with the transplant. The Dr. says the good thing is that BJ is stable and as long as he stays that way there's no immediate emergency but does stress that they want to get the ball rolling. At that moment Kandi goes to get Braden and tell him the doctor is ready for him then they leave to go get the testing done. Kandi asks me if I would stay just in case he wakes up while she's gone so someone will be there and I of course agree. The nurse takes Braden off to be tested and Kandi goes with him. I go in and sit with BJ just in case as Kandi asked me to do. As I walk into the room I'm sadden by the tubes and machines hooked up to him and think to myself what a shame for such a handsome young man to be going through something like this. I sit in the chair next to him and just sit quietly listening to the machines beep, toot and hiss. At that moment I think back to the last time I was in a hospital, it was when my Brenda died, and realized why I hated hospitals. To me they are nothing but a symbol of bad news to come. But in this case I could only hope that it's good news for them. Just when I was drifting deeper in my thoughts BJ moved and woke up.

"Uncle Marcus" he says with a small smile on his face as if he's not seen me in years.

"Heeey lil man, well I guess I can't say little huh, how are you feeling?" I'm feeling a bit uncomfortable behind those words only because this is the first time seeing him.

"Very tired, this is rough on me and it's draining all of my energy." he says as he struggles a bit to sit up.

"I can't imagine but I'm sure things will work out soon, and in no time this will be over and you'll start feeling a lot better soon" I say trying to up lift him and give him hope.

"Where's mom, have you seen her?"

"Yes I have and she's with your father getting tests done to make sure that he's a match for your bone marrow."

"He's here, really" another smile comes across his face this time wider and brighter than when he saw me for the first time.

"Yes, yes he is, in fact he was just in the room not long ago but you were sleep." sounding very surprised and a bit relieved that his father is here.

"Wow, I wish I would have been awake to see him."

"Don't worry they'll be back in a little bit."

At that moment a nurse comes in to check his vitals and make sure he's staying stable

"I don't know if I'll be awake because I'm always tired and I drift off quickly. I hope I can stay awake."

"Well I'm sure if you can't, he'll stay here until you wake up again. I don't think he wants to miss out on anything else in your life."

"Good I hope so because I don't want him to go anywhere."

At that moment Braden and Kandi come into the room from getting tested. I tell them I had to make a few phone calls to check on things at the office, with my mom and Milton. So, I stepped out of the room to give them some privacy. I had to go down to the waiting area for better reception and as I entered the waiting area I began to make my calls. I called the office first to see how things were progressing with this month's edition. My assistant informed me that things are right on schedule and will be ready for my approval by morning.

Relieved that I didn't have to go into the office, I then was free to call my mother. She needed to know what's going on besides I needed to make sure it was ok that Jazz stay with her since I'm at the hospital with Braden. She of course loved the idea and said it was fine with her. I tell you I think my mother would rather Jazzmin stay with her permanently but I do understand why though. Ever since my father passed she hadn't had too many people in her life outside of me and Jazzmin so I'm sure she gets lonely at times. After I hang up with my mother I call Milton and check on him. He tells me that his job has found out about the arrest and has suspended him until a further investigation has been completed. I ask him how did they know so fast and he told me that Sharon called them because she knows if he got into trouble they would fire him.

He said all she wants to do is make his life a living hell which will make it easier for her to take the kids away from him. I tell Milton that we'll get this under control and that I know a couple good lawyers that owe me a favor and I'll give them a call to come over and talk with him so he can start being on the offensive instead of the defensive side of the ball. I get off the phone with Milton and sit in one of the chairs to give Braden more time with BJ. A couple hours go past and I hadn't realized it because I dozed off but I was awakened by a nudge from Braden. I jump because I thought back to when I was awakened by the doctor who operated on Brenda but

I'm able to catch myself when I looked into Braden's face.

"Hey man didn't mean to scare you" Braden said, "But the doctor came in and gave us the results of the test."

"Ok so is BJ yours and are you a match"

Braden breathing a sigh of relief

"Yes he's mine and the doctor said that I'm a perfect match for him and the procedure shouldn't take long. The only thing is that his recovery would determine how things go."

"Go, what do you mean?"

"Well he did say that although on paper I'm a perfect match for BJ his body has to accept it and that will determine how he comes out of all of this."

"Aww man I'm not worried about that I'm sure things will work out."

"Yeah let's hope, I'm just glad that I know about him now and I am able to help at least."

"Yeah I feel you and just think about this, when this is all said and done you can start to build a relationship with him and he'll have a part of you inside him to help him live on."

"You're right and I will do whatever it takes to make sure that happens."

"I know you will bro, ok so what now, what do you have to do."

"Well the doctor informed me that the procedure shouldn't take nor more than a few hours to complete and after that the recovery starts."

"What do you need for me to do in the meantime?"

"Just be there bro, I already called my office to let them know what's going on and that I need to take a few days off and they were cool with that so I'm good."

"Cool, oh and you won't believe this but Milton's wife called his job to inform them that he was arrested."

"Dude, are you serious?"

"Hell, yeah I'm serious so I told him it's time to fight back and that I was going to call a couple of my attorneys and have them look into things for him. I told him it's time to be on the offensive and not the defensive all the time."

"Damn she's cold man and I thought she was a sweet person when we met her."

"Yeah I thought so too, hell we all did, but as we see now it's not the case."

"Yeah tell me about it."

"Ok so now what do we do with you?"

"Well they are preparing the operating room now and we'll be heading down in a few minutes. All I need is for you to be there when I wake up that's all."

"Man, I got you on that so that's not a problem at all"

"Cool thanks."

We head down to BJ's room to sit and wait on the doctor to come in and get them I say a small prayer to God to ask Him to bring Braden and his son through all of this and let everything work out for the best. Soon after the doctor comes in to get Braden and BJ and take them off to the operating room. Kandi and I wait in the room for them to return and just talk and catch up on things. I must say it was good to see her again all be it under these circumstances, but she was in good spirits especially after finding out that Braden is a good match for BJ. I'm sure that really took a lot of pressure off of here. Time goes by slow and it seemed to take forever but the doctor and nurses come in with Braden in one bed and BJ in another. He tells Kandi that everything went well and better than expected. Now all they have to do is wait to see how BJ's body reacts to the transplant. If within the next 48 to 72 hours his body responds well then there's a greater chance of a full recovery. She thanked the doctor for all his help and for doing a wonderful job. Braden and BJ were coming around and Kandi went over to BJ to check on him and I went to Braden.

"Hey buddy, how are you feeling?"

"Dude like a mac truck hit me."

I couldn't help but laugh a little

"I'm sure you do but you did a great thing and the doctor said things went well and that as long as BJ's body doesn't reject the transplant within the first 48 to 72 hours then he should be fine."

"That's good, how's Kandi?"

"Well I'll tell you this, she's in better spirits after finding out you were a good match and that the surgery went well. I think that this could be a good thing all around B."

"Yeah I hope so too, Man I'll tell you the pain medicine they give here is the bomb, I can feel them kicking in already. Thanks Marcus."

"For what?"

"Being here/"

"Man you're welcome but you don't have to thank me because I know you'd be there for me and you have always been, so it's my turn now, so don't trip."

"Well, you know as well as I do you're my brother."

"Yeah I know and I'm glad too that way when I kick your ass when you recover you can't get upset with me."

"Kick my ass for what?"

"For not listening to me, hell US, all those years ago."

Braden looks over at Kandi talking to BJ and a tear falls from his eyes

"Yeah man I know but I'm glad I could help him."

At that moment the drugs took over and Braden fell off to sleep as did BJ. Kandi and I sat in the chair talking more about life and about the past 20 years and catching up. She told me that she was married now and a published author. I was happy for her and told her about me and more of my magazine and how I got it started because I always wanted to be a writer too. It was interesting how much we had in common. As we sat there we both began to yawn a little and realized that we were both tired from everything that just took place. I told Kandi to lie down on the couch we were sitting on and I let out the lounge chair and laid back in it and we both dozed off.

Not being able to sleep too long, I look around and see Braden and BJ still sleeping soundly also Kandi was doing the same so I decided to step out of the room for a few minutes to go to the cafeteria. I didn't realize I was as hungry as I was but then remembered I only had something quick to eat that morning before we came to the hospital and seeing that it's in the early evening had to find something to put in my stomach. Also, I wanted to take a moment to call mom and check on her and Jazz. Mom asked how things went and I told her about the whole procedure and how it went well and they are now sleeping.

I asked how Jazzmin was doing and she informed me that she's fine and was doing her homework. I told her to just give her a hug and kiss for me and to let her know how much I loved her and I'll see her in tomorrow hopefully. After hanging up with her I called Milton to check on him, now that was a totally different conversation. He was totally distraught over what was going on and I reassured him that we'll get things worked out. I told him that I will be home in a little bit that Braden had to stay overnight for observations. I got my food and headed back towards the room and realized I hadn't spoken to Kim so I stopped in the waiting room down the hall from BJ's room and called her.

"Hey honey, it's so good to hear your voice." Kim says to me.

"Hey baby it's good to hear yours too, how are you doing?"

"Oh, I'm fine, just been wondering how you were and how things were with Braden?"

"I'm good hon just tired and things with Braden and his son went well. They are sleep right now and Braden has to stay in the hospital overnight for observations. BJ has to be here for at least 72 hours just to make sure that his body accepts the transplant, after that they said he should be able to go home but he won't be able to travel for a little while so they are going to stay with Braden until he's cleared to go back to Michigan."

"Oh, wow well that's a good thing right?"

"Yeah for him and Braden it is, this way they'll be able to catch up and start to build a relationship from here on out."

"That's good, so when are you going home honey?"

"I'll be leaving when they wake up just to let them know I'm gone then I'll go home and start helping Milton get information together for the lawyers so they can start fighting for him. I do want to know when I can see my baby again because it's been a couple days and I need my Kim fix."

"Mmmm I like how you put that and although I know and understand you've been busy I was wondering the same thing. I just didn't want to be selfish and try to monopolize your time."

"You're cute but you're not doing that but I do understand where you're coming from and I know you've been busy since coming back too so I wanted to give you a few days to get yourself together as well."

"Well Mr. Bass I will always have time for you."

"Hmm that sounds like I have an open invitation."

"That you do sir, that you do, anytime you want or like I'll be here."

"That's good to know, now don't get mad if I just show up one day needing my fix."

"Oh please do because I can guarantee that when you need yours I'll have already needed mine so bring it on."

"Hmm I like that in you, well, let me cut this short for now and go check on everyone but we'll talk a little later before I go to bed."

"Ok honey, tell Braden I said hello although I've not met him yet."

"I will do just that and I will talk to you later honey, Love you babe."

"Mmmm those words just shot chills down my spine and I love you too Mr. Bass."

"I like how that rolls off your tongue, ok let me go, I'll talk to you later hon."

"Ok bye for now."

"For now."

I head back to the room I see that everyone was awake and the nurse was in checking vitals for Braden and BJ. Also they were taking their order for their meals. I was glad they were awake so I could tell them I was going home for the night but will be back tomorrow. I gave Braden a pound and told him to enjoy his son then gave BJ a hug and told him it was good go finally meet him and to just get well and lastly gave Kandi a hug and told her to just take it one day at a time and things will be just fine and tell her that if she needs me for anything before morning to just call. I leave out of the room and head to my truck, as I do I think how blessed BJ is right now to have both his parents with him. I couldn't help but get a little choked up at the thought of it and it makes me think of Brenda and how much I miss her in my and Jazzmin's lives. But who knows maybe just maybe Kim is Gods way of giving a bit of her back to me. I don't know but I feel good about Kim and I can't wait to see where things go.

CHAPTER

33

Braden "New Beginnings"

The next day I go to pick up Braden from the hospital. I also check on BJ to see how he's coming along. Kandi tells me the doctor says things are looking good thus far but not out of the woods yet but soon he should be. Braden and I leave and get into my truck and he's smiling ear to ear as he goes home to prepare to have house guest for a while. He seems as though he's like a new kid who just got the latest and greatest toy for Christmas. He tells me that him, BJ and Kandi had a good talk the night before and he's looking forward to getting to know his son. I was wondering though was he happier about his son or about seeing Kandi again and possibly rekindling old flames.

"Hey B can I ask you a question?"

"Yeah sure, oh and thanks again for being there man, this was an interesting ordeal."

"No problem but let me ask you this. I see you walking around now with a pep in your step and I know you're happy to finally meet your son but I was wondering how much of this new step has to do with Kandi?"

"Well I will tell you this, I am happy to know I have a son this is true especially one by her. I'm happy to see her too I cannot lie about it. Seeing her brought back some old feelings that I honestly thought were gone."

"Now see that's what I was thinking. You do know she's married right and happily?"

"Yeah I know and I'm not going to do anything to mess that up but hey I can't help but dream about what could have been right?"

"True, I mean if it were me I would probably be doing the same thing so I can't blame you."

"So what made you ask me that?"

"I don't know really, I guess I just see you smiling a bit more right now and I want to make sure it is for the right reasons that's all. I'd hate to see you get your hopes up for something that's not there."

"Well to tell you the truth, we did talk about things and I did express to her that I'd like to spend some time with her. That's when she told me about her husband and family. I'll admit that it hurt a little but I can't blame anyone but myself right?"

"True, that's why I wanted to know because I thought back to our conversation not long ago about regrets and what ifs. I just don't want you to try and do something that will end up hurting you that's all bro."

"Yeah I know and I'm not, well now I'm not anyway, but it's good to see her though and she'll be staying here while BJ recovers well enough to travel back home."

"Yeah, I was thinking about that and are you sure that's a good idea. I have to admit that it seems as though you have a different agenda in mind."

"Nah man I'm not and besides she did say she was going to stay in a hotel but I told her that she's more than welcome to stay here and save on some money. Shoot hospital bills are expensive and she needs to save all the money she can, right?"

"Oh if you're trying to get me to help you justify all of this you're sadly mistaken but I do know how much it cost for hospital stays but just be cool man and don't try anything. In fact if you get that urge to jump across that pond little froggy make sure you jump over to my place so you won't do anything you're going to regret later."

"Ha ha ha you got jokes and I'm not going to do anything to jeopardize getting to know BJ."

"Alright I just want to make sure of that."

"Speaking of jeopardizing have you talked to Darius since Sunday?"

"No I haven't had a chance to but I know I have to because what Kim told me about her niece, man, this dude is walking into a line of fire and it's not good."

"Really so what's the deal with her niece and when are we going to get to meet this wonderful person you've been talking about."

"Soon my brotha, soon, it's just things have been a little crazy since I got back so I figured maybe this Sunday we can all get together at my place for dinner and have a good old fashioned Sunday meal. That way y'all can meet her and I can talk to you all about a couple ventures I need to tell you about."

"Oh here we go again you keeping secrets."

I couldn't help but laugh at that one

"Nah man it's not like that, it's something great and I want everyone there at one time so I can say it only once and we all enjoy it together."

"Ok that's cool just as long as you have no other bombshells to drop on me I'm good. One is more than I need for my lifetime."

"Well I don't need any more either so we're good in that category. But back to D, I have to give him a call and give him a heads up because this intern has some plans that he needs to know about."

"See we told him after that last debacle to keep his shit together but I guess he'll never learn until Trish takes everything from him."

"Well I hope after what I have to say he'll get it together, but we'll see, hey are you good here."

Making sure that he's ok at home and he's getting things in order for Kandi and BJ to arrive.

"Yeah I'm good, go take care of your business and I'll see you on Sunday, oh and what time?"

"Let's say around 4pm that way I can get to church and not rush coming home to cook."

"Cool, me too, it's been a minute since I've been but I gotta go give thanks to God for bringing Kandi back into my life"

"Who?"

"Braden Jr. who did you think I said?" Braden realizing the slip up and that I caught it

"Yeah ok I heard you and you better keep it straight."

"I will, I will I was just messing with you."

"Yeah ok, but I'm out, I'll see you Sunday unless I talk to you first."

"Ok cool, peace."

I leave Braden's house and jump into my truck. I reach for my phone to call Darius to give him a heads up on his intern. I think to myself that this dude has to learn one day to let that running around go and be faithful to Trish. I keep thinking of that song R. Kelly wrote a few years ago "When A Woman's Fed Up" he's going to suffer that. Hell for all I know Trish is fed up and just biding her time. I hope for his sake things are not too far gone with her to save his marriage. After a few rings Darius picks up.

"Hello?"

"What up D, how you living?" as if I didn't already know

"I'm good Bass how are things with you, haven't spoken with you since last Sunday when you said you had something to tell me"

"Yeah I know but my time has been consumed with Braden and his son"

"Yeah after Sunday I understand, how are things between them now and how is he holding up?"

"Things are looking very positive for them and B is doing great, after they got the results on the test and things came back a match they had to have surgery"

"Yeah I know and I was meaning to get up to the hospital to see him. How's he doing from all that?"

"Oh he's cool and at home getting things ready for BJ and Kandi to come stay with him for a little while."

"Really and how is that going to work out?"

"Well he said he'll keep things cool and for his sake I hope he does. Speaking of keeping things cool, you're not going to believe what I'm about to lay on you."

"Is that so, so tell me what's the deal."

"Well this has to do with your new intern, Zenobia."

"How do you know her name?"

"That's the thing, remember the woman I met when I was going to DC?"

"Yeah I remember you telling me about her and when do we get to meet her?"

"Sunday bro, but that's not the point, the point is she's Zenobia's Aunt."

"Oh damn for real, uhm so what does that have to do with anything?"

"Well let's just put it this way my brotha, I know all about her being up under your desk putting in work that only hookers get paid to do."

"Oh damn how in the hell do you know about that?"

"I just said Kim's her aunt and they talked while I was in DC, duh!!"

"Ok damn, but that's no big deal I got that under control now, so what's up."

"Well the thing is there's something you don't know."

"What, come on man spill it."

"Well apparently while she was under your desk when Tre & Zan came in to talk to you, she had a digital recorder and it was running the whole time she was under your desk."

"Aaww hell nah, you bullshitting me?"

"Come on man you know me too well to come at me like that. Besides what reason would I have to bullshit you?"

"Shit, shit, shit, I can't believe this."

"That's not all either."

"Man come on I don't know how much more I can take."

"Well this is the icing on the cake."

"What?"

"She told Kim she plans on holding on to the tape and using it if she has too to get what she wants out of you. Kim told her to delete it and she said she would but you know as well as I do that she didn't do it so as of right now you gotta play it cool man and do whatever you can to get that recording. AND don't mess around with her again."

"Yeah that's wishful thinking."

"Ah hell what did you do?"

"She was with me on Saturday night in the studio."

"DARIUS..Damn man what in the hell are you thinking, or hell in this case NOT thinking."

"Man I didn't plan on it but we happened to be in the studio and they were taking a break from recording and she came in and one thing led to another and I hit it."

"Damn man, you better hope Trish don't find out about this shit or else you'll be out on your ass this time."

"See that's the thing I told her that it couldn't happen anymore and she got upset talking about I can't use her just to get some ass and think that's all she's about."

"Well hell from what I know that's all she's about anyway."

"I know right but the thing is a couple days after I come home and Trish is flipping out on me talking about a chick calling the house and left a message talking about how she was with me on Saturday."

"See that's the shit right there I'm talking about so how in the hell did you get out of this one"

"I just told Trish I was at the studio, which I was, and to call and ask if I was there. Although I knew she wouldn't do it I made sure that things were covered anyway."

"Man what if she had her little recorder then too recording the whole thing again then what. What are you going to do if that recording shows up at your house in the mail?"

"Damn I didn't think of that but shit I didn't know about her having that damn thing anyway."

"Well you're gonna have to do something before this get out of control."

"Yeah I will, hell I'll have my assistant go through her purse and find it and give it to me and destroy it."

"Now you're being real extra, you're gonna have a dude go through a woman's purse?"

"What else do you expect me to do? I have no other choice."

"Well in this case I guess not but if you do get it back man you better get her outta there and quick."

"Damn I can't right now because she's working on some things with a new artist and if I get her out of there before I get the tape then I'm done and who knows if she has only the one copy or not."

"Damn man you're not gonna learn are you and for your sake you better hope she's not bright enough to have made another copy of it."

"Yeah I am man, hell I already told Terry to keep her busy so she can't get to me"

"Uhm but what happened to Saturday?"

"Ok, ok, damn I slipped up."

"No call it like it is you fucked up."

"Haven't you ever fucked up?"

"Hell yeah, plenty of times, that's why I can talk to you like I am. Man I just want you to chill out and be down with Trish because I know she's down with you."

Darius gets quite on me and I know he knows I'm right although he don't want to admit it. We stay silent for a few more minutes until he breaks it.

"Marcus."

"Yeah bro."

"Thanks."

"Man it's cool, I'm just glad you know her intentions now so that you can do something about it before it gets way too late. We don't want nor need another Cassandra Haywood incident."

"Tell me about it, oh speaking of, she came to see me."

"How, isn't she locked up for another couple years?"

"Well apparently she got out on parole for good behavior or some shit like that."

"So what made her come to see you?"

"She laid some shit on me that you won't believe."

"Right now with you, I'll believe just about anything."

"She has HIV and thinks she may have given it to me."

"You're right I don't believe it, dude I almost crashed my truck behind that shit, let me pull over" getting control of my truck and pulling off the side of the road.

I pull off the road to catch my composure I sit there in awe of what I just heard.

"You there man?" Darius asks

"Yeah I'm here, I'm just flabbergasted that's all, wait did I hear you right. This bitch said she has HIV and that you may have it?"

"Yeah tell me about it, now you can imagine how I felt when she said it to me."

"Damn but wasn't that like two or three years ago and I'm sure you've been making love to Trish since then and I know you don't use protection with her."

"Man yeah it has and no, I better not come to Trish taking about some condom shit, she'd kick my ass for real."

"I know, so now what, did you go get tested."

"At first I wasn't but I couldn't help but think if she was right and did give it to me then I'm screwed for real. So I called my doctor and got tested and now all I'm doing is waiting on the results which should be back any day now."

"Wow can it get any worse for you."

"Man don't say that shit because you know if it can, it will. so don't speak that into the atmosphere."

"My bad man it just came out." Darius believing in what you speak will come true

"Yeah ok if you say so but for real man I'm sitting here sweating bullets behind this shit."

"I bet you are, but wait, if you had something don't you think Trish would have found out by now."

"Yeah I thought about that too but they say it sometimes don't show up for a while, sometimes years, I mean I could have it and gave it to Trish and she not know. I just hope I don't man, hell I'd rather her find out about Zenobia than have HIV."

"Like you said watch what you say."

"I know but it's the truth, hell I don't want either to happen but shit if I had to choose."

"Yeah I know, but hey keep your head up and things will be fine. In the meantime let me get off this phone and head home. I'll see you on Sunday bro, oh and we gotta get together to hoop, I'm in need of some exercise. I haven't had any since I left for D.C."

"Yeah that's cool, will Braden be able to hoop too?"

"Nah not for about a week or so just until his strength gets back to normal."

"Ok cool, I'll give him a call now to check on him."

"Cool I know he'd like that, alright dude I'm out."

"Peace."

I hit end on the blue tooth and drive in a bit of a daze after the conversation I just had. I can't believe that Darius has gotten himself into this much of a mess. HIV, wow that's nothing to play with, I just hope that he don't have it and run the risk of giving it to Trish. Wow more drama I don't know how much more we can take it.

CHAPTER

34

Kim & Zenobia "Trouble in Paradise"

Kim hasn't spoken to Zenobia since she returned from DC with Marcus. She does not know what has transpired between her and Darius since the last time they spoke. Kim decides to call her so they can hang out, do some shopping, and also talk about what's been going on.

"Hey auntie!"

"Hey Zenobia, how are you doing?"

"Oh I'm great and how are you. How was your trip?"

"It was good but I wanted to talk to you. Are you busy today?"

"No I'm not what's up?"

"I'd figure we go to the mall and do a little shopping and hang out for the day, you know catch up."

"That sounds good, what time do you wanna go?"

"Well whenever you can get over here."

"Ok cool I'm just finishing up my workout and I can be there in about an hour ok?"

"Yeah that's fine and I can finish up a couple things for work real quick so I'll see you then."

Kim hangs up from making plans with Zenobia and thinks to herself that she has to talk some sense into her. Not knowing what took place a week ago between Darius and her, Kim is in for a rude awakening once she finds out. Kim finishes what she's doing just in time for Zenobia to arrive.

"Hey auntie, what mall are we going to?"

"Well I have to go get my oils so we'll head to Ford City Mall first then from there we will go downtown and do some shopping and walking around."

"Ooohhh cool I always love your oils."

"Yeah I know you do that's why mine always seem to walk out of my house right?"

"Well you do want your favorite niece to smell good right?"

"Yes I do but you have to get your own, that's part of the reason why we're going there so I can get you a couple of your own."

"Yyaaayyy thank you aunte, I appreciate it. So tell me, how was your trip and your new boo doing?"

"My trip was wonderful, can't wait to go back and my boo "Marcus" is just fine and I'll be seeing him tomorrow for dinner to meet his family and friends."

"Oh wow auntie that sounds like you are serious about this guy?"

"Well honestly I am and I can't help it. He's a wonderful man and from what I can tell a great father."

"He has kids?"

"Yes, just one, a little girl and her name is Jazzmin."

"Oh that's cool, I'm happy for you auntie."

"Thanks hon but this is not the only reason why I wanted you to come hang out with me."

"Uh oh here we go!"

"Yes here we go, did you get rid of that recording like you promised?"

Zenobia gets quiet trying to avoid answering the question and looks out the window as Kim drives down the highway

"Zee did you hear what I asked you?"

"Yes!" trying to avoid the subject

"Yes what, yes you heard me or yes you got rid of the recording?"

"Yes I heard you!"

"Zenobia Zaire Bentley you mean to tell me that you still have that recording?"

"Ooohh I hate it when you call me by my whole name" I said as I crossed my arms and look out the window.

"Forget all of that and answer my question!"

"Yes I still have it" realizing Kim is upset.

"Why Zee, why do you have it and what good will it do for you to keep it?"

"It's just for insurance purposes!"

"INSURANCE PURPOSE!!....what the hell would you need that for and what do you know about insurance purposes anyway?" Kim screams

"I saw it on a Law & Order show once where this woman was having an affair with her boss and then he tried to get rid of her so she told him she has everything they did on video tape."

"Zenobia that's a movie, you don't play with people like that in real life and expect things to just work out, it don't happen that way and besides I saw the same episode and she ended up dead."

"Well what am I supposed to do, I'm trying to get taken care of."

"Use your God given brains and don't rely on a man to take care of you. Look you're smart and you are beautiful so I don't understand why you think it's a good thing for a man to take care of you."

"I just don't want to work as hard as you did trying to get your business off the ground."

"Zenobia listen, I chose to go into business for myself because I knew that in my line of work men don't look at you as an equal and they often time feel intimidated by a woman so that's why I chose this path but as you can see I'm doing very well."

"I know but I'm not you auntie!"

"I know you're not me but you can be like me if you just work at it the right way. Remember what I told you about karma, it will come back around and when it does you won't like it because it will be worse than what you put out there."

"Yeah I hear you but."

"No buts, so where's the tape?"

"It's at home."

"Zenobia, you're lying."

"No I'm not auntie, I promise?" Knowing Kim knows she is and won't give in but she has to try and keep the tape.

"Zenobia don't make me pull over this car and whip your ass, give me the damn tape!"

"Fine" Zenobia reaches into her purse and pull out the tape and hands it to Kim

"Thank you, is this the only copy?"

"Yes, I hadn't had a chance to put it on my computer yet."

"Good, it better be and why did you lie to me, what were you going to do with it anyway?"

"Like I said I was just going to keep it just in case I needed it."

"See that's the thing you don't need it, all you have to do is be yourself and use your brain and you'll go further in life than you ever realize."

I turn on the tape and listens to it to make sure that it's the right one then place it in my purse.

"I'm going to hold onto this until your internship is over and then I'll give it back to you."

"That's cold auntie, that's cold, so since you're making me give up my little insurance are you going to tell Mr. Goody too shoes about your situation?"

Kim now feels her own pressure and sighs heavily.

"I will in my own time."

"Oh now ain't that the pot calling the kettle black?"

"No it's not, my situation is different than yours. I'm not using ammunition to hold over someone's head."

"But you're keeping a secret though, that's just the same thing!"

"You can try and justify it all you like but it's not the same."

"So have you heard from Uncle Larry?"

Kim hating the fact that Zenobia brings up her husband, well ex-husband and now convicted felon. She hates thinking about what he took her through and the fact that it not only cost the child she was carrying but almost her life and freedom as well.

"Not in a while, I told the prison that I no longer want him to be able to call me and I changed my phone number anyway so he can't get a hold of me."

"I'm sorry auntie; I didn't mean to throw that in your face." Zee realizing that she hurt Kim by bringing up the past.

"It's ok, I know you were just asking, but I am going to tell Marcus but right now is not the time because he has a lot going on with his friends and I don't want to add to it burdens. Besides that was a lifetime ago and I'm not worried about it."

"How much longer does he have in prison and aren't you two still married?"

"He is supposed to have two more years and no we're not married anymore. I filed the divorce papers when he went to prison."

"Oh ok I didn't know that you could get a divorce just because someone goes to jail."

"Yes you can and I did, I wanted to make sure I was able to go on with my life and not look back."

"Can I ask you a question?"

"Sure!"

"Is the reason why you treat me so much like a daughter because you can't have any children now, I mean after what happened to you?"

"Yeah I guess that's part of it, I mean you are my favorite niece and I love you so much but I do wish I could have one of my own. I guess that's why I want you to do right and use your head to get to where you need to go and let the ghetto street life go. It's never a good thing and it only has bad endings."

"I hear you."

"You hear me but are you listening and understanding me?"

"Yes auntie I am listening and as always you're right. I'm sorry for the way I've been acting and I promise, no I give you my word that I'll do better from now on and I'm not going to mess around with my boss anymore."

"Good, I'm happy to hear you say that and I know you're going to do it too because you know how I am about when you give your word."

"Yes I know, that's why I changed it from a promise to my word!"

"That's right because promises are made to be broken and words are your bonds."

As Kim and Zenobia headed down the road to have a girls day out she couldn't help but think about Marcus and how he's going to receive the information of her past. She can only hope he's the truly wonderful and understanding man she sees thus far and not end what is starting to be a wonderful thing between the two of them. She can only hope.......

CHAPTER

35

Marcus "The Big News"

Sunday…

Iwake early to a bright and gorgeous day, thankful for all that God has given me. I lay in my bed thinking about this afternoon and what's going to take place. Thinking I'll have all those around me who love and care for me to share in some great news. I must say that things are truly going well for me and it couldn't be better. I get up out of my bed and go into the kitchen to check on my pot roasts that I had slow cook in my crock pots overnight. Taking a fork out of my drawer and sampling the meat, I think to myself mmm mmm mmm oh so tender. I'm glad my mother taught me how to cook early in my child hood. Now all I have to do is cut up the potatoes and carrots and put them in with the meat. I put on my greens so they can cook and make my cornbread and peach cobbler for desert, from scratch of course.

I finish up my meal for the afternoons festivities I take a walk over to my bay window I love. I look out and see the sun is shining extra bright today and I feel so warm inside. I take in a few more moments in my thoughts and then head down the hallway to my bedroom. Before get to my bedroom I stop at my guest room where Milton is sleeping to see if he's going to join me in going to church. I knock on the door and he answers it.

"Good morning bro, are you up for going to service with me?" I ask Milton

"Honestly I thought about not going but then figured that's where I need to be the most right now, so yeah I'll go with you, thanks for asking."

"No problem and I must say I agree with you on going and truth be told I haven't been in a while but I feel with all that's going on for me lately I need to go openly give God some praise. Besides my daughter kinda begged me to go anyway so it's a two for one deal as far as I'm concerned." I chuckled a bit behind that statement

"Yeah I hear ya and I can't wait to see Jazzmin, it's been a while since I've seen her."

"Yeah man it has hasn't it, just wait to see how she's growing."

"I can't wait, damn man what smells good?" Milton catching the aroma from my kitchen

"Oh that's this afternoon's dinner cooking, pot roast with carrots, potatoes, greens and cornbread. With peach cobbler and French vanilla ice cream."

"Wow you're going all out huh so what's the special occasion?"

"I have some news to tell everyone that's why I asked everyone over here this afternoon."

"Oh ok, so what is the news?"

"Uhm didn't you just hear me say this afternoon when everyone is here, so I'm only going to say this once period?"

"Ok, ok I won't push, so what time should I be ready?"

"In about an hour, that way I can go pick up Mom and Jazz on the way to the church."

"Ok cool I'll be ready."

"Bet!"

I leave him be to get himself together and continue heading towards my room. As I approach my door I look at Brenda's picture hanging there looking so beautiful. She looks at me as if to say she's proud of her husband and what God has blessed me with. I smile at her and as always kiss my two fingers and place them on her lips. I continue into my bedroom and head towards the bathroom and turn on the shower so I can get cleaned up for church.

I turn to go get in the shower and get myself together. About 45 minutes later I'm dressed and ready and so is Milton, we head out the door to go pick up mom and Jazz. After picking them up we go to church and have a wonderful time and the ironic thing is the sermon was about God's blessings and how you should share those blessings with others to encourage them to trust and believe that God will do all that He said he would do, I thought that was truly fitting for today and as usual God knows what He's doing all the time.

After service we head back to my house to get ready for dinner. When we get there everyone goes to their perspective rooms to change into something more comfortable. I have my mother change in my room and tell her she could relax there if she liked but my mother being the woman she is had to get into my kitchen to make sure I was taking care of business like she taught me.

"Mmmm mmm Marcus I taught you well, this smells so wonderful." as my mother opens the lid to one of the crock pots with the roast in it.

"Thanks ma I learned from the best didn't I?" smiling at the thought of her enjoying my cooking.

"That you did son that you did and is that peach cobbler I smell?"

"Yes you do and I must say, now I think I can give you a run for your money!"

"Oh do you now well I'll just be the judge of that?"

We have a moment of laughter and it feels good to laugh with my mother.

"Well, all I can say is this, you taught me how do to it but I have perfected my own technique so I think you may be a bit surprised at how good I've gotten."

"Oh I'm not surprised Marcus because you always were a perfectionist and you had to have things done right or not at all. That's why your magazine has done so well because you wouldn't allow any garbage to be put out. So what time is dinner anyway?"

"It's at 4 and I told everyone to be here by 3:30 but I did tell Kim to be here a little early so she could meet you and Jazzmin and y'all can get to know each other a little before the rest of the crew gets here."

"Well from what you told me about her she seems like a lovely young lady."

"She is ma and honestly I was and still am a little surprised of how I feel about her so soon."

"You love her don't you?" that mothers intuition always knows.

"Damn ma, how did you know so fast?" chuckling with her but knowing how she does.

"Well it's the way you speak of her and your tone you use to do it. You seem to float on air when you talk about her. Even through the phone I can hear the smile in your voice, so that's how I know. Besides I'm your mother and I've wiped everything from your roota to your toota."

"Oh wow no you didn't say roota to my toota, mom you are a mess."

"That I am but you can't help but love me?"

At that moment Jazzmin comes into the kitchen to see what we are up too.

"Hey baby girl, how's my favorite lady doing?"

"Hey daddy, I'm great and can't wait for dinner, I'm hungry." looking at me with those deep brown eyes.

"Get a snack but a small one, I don't want you to ruin your appetite."

"Thanks Daddy!"

Jazzmin gets a snack, and I finish looking in on dinner. My mother goes into my living room and watches TV. Everything is looking great and I look at my watch, 2:30, Kim should be here shortly. I go into my bedroom to change cloths and get into something comfortable. As I do that a few minutes later my buzzer sounds for my door. I ask my mother to answer figuring it's Kim. She's early I think but it's ok I'd rather have her early than late. I tell my mother to let her in and tell her I'll be out in a few minutes. When I come out of my room I find Kim and my mother sitting on my couch talking.

"Well I see you two have officially met?" walking in with a big grin on my face.

"Yes we have and she's a lovely young woman Marcus." my mother speaks of Kim.

"Yes and you have a wonderful mother." Kim speaks of my mother.

"Yes, yes, yes you both are wonderful." I repeat in a chuckle.

"But there's one more person I want you to meet hon and you may not be so beautiful once she comes into the room." I look at Kim's expression and she seems a bit frightened at what's about to take place. I give her a wink and reassure her that she'll be fine. I go to Jazzmin's room to get her and have her come out to meet Kim.

"Hey baby girl, come out here so I can introduce you to my friend ok?"

"Ok daddy!"

We come back to the living room and I introduce the two people that if things go well will be the most important people, outside my mother, to me.

"Kim honey, this is my baby girl Jazzmin, Jazzmin this is my special friend Kim."

"Well hello there beautiful." Kim says to Jazzmin.

"Hello Ma'am, it's nice to meet you."

"The pleasure is all mine, you father has told me some great things about you and I couldn't wait to meet you. But I will say one thing though and I'm a bit upset with your father and I hope you don't mind me saying that he didn't tell me that you were such a cutie. He did NOT do you justice" Kim pours on the charm and Jazzmin eats it up.

"Why thank you, but I'm sorry he didn't say much at all about you." saying that with a confused look on her face.

"Well honey we haven't had much time to talk lately that's all." I chime in.

"I know daddy and that's ok, can I go back to my room now?"

"Yes you may, I'll come get you when dinner is ready ok?"

"Ok, it was nice meeting you Ms. Kim."

"It is truly a pleasure Ms. Jazzmin."

Jazzmin smiles at the way Kim acknowledges her and heads back to her room.

"Marcus she's adorable."

"Yeah I know and I thank God for her every day, well, let me show you around a bit, mom are you ok, do you need anything?"

"Child no, I'm just fine watching TV and besides I know where everything is if I need something."

"Uhm mom don't go snooping around in the kitchen trying to take samples of my food."

"Well son you know I have to make sure you did it right, you know how I am."

"Yeah I do it's called greedy." we all laugh behind that statement.

I help Kim up and begin to show her around my condo. I show her the dining area where I have my mahogany table with black accents that seat 10. Then I show her my office where I do a lot of my work. Then I take her down the hallway towards the bedrooms and take her into my bedroom last. This is where I know I can steal a kiss. When we enter my room I immediately take her into my arms and give her a big kiss.

"Mmmm Mr. Bass, I've been waiting on that all day, hell all week." Kim expresses her gratitude.

"Well I've been waiting on that myself, so what do you think, do you like my home?"

"I love it and the view is great. I love your bedroom, it's so spacious and I'd kill for a walk-in closet with an island in the middle." she says as she scopes out my room.

"Yeah that's one of the things that sold me on this place was the closets but I only use this one still."

"Why is that Marcus?"

"The other one is Brenda's well I mean was Brenda's and I just can't open it." Kim could tell I was a little emotional from saying that.

"It still is Marcus, until you want it to be someone else's it will always be hers and no one can take that away and I for one am not gonna try."

"You know something I think that's why I love you, because you don't try to replace my wife."

"It's because I can't Marcus and I'm not gonna try. I can only hope I can have a small space in your heart, that's all."

"Well I thank you for that and just know I do not and will not compare you to her in any way."

The moment becomes a bit tense and I turn and walk towards the window and look out. Kim comes over to me and wraps her arms around me.

"Good I'm glad you won't and I believe you too, now I must say I can truly see that shower being built and we having some fun in there. But uhm I will say though I love your Jacuzzi tub so we'll have to make time for that." Kim says, trying to lighten the mood.

"Yeah I love that too and I love how it's separated from the shower."

"Yeah I do too, uhm Marcus can I talk to you about something real quick before everyone else gets here?" Kim getting a little nervous herself knowing she has to tell Marcus about the conversation she had with Zenobia. She fears that he will blow his top once he finds out what she's up too.

"Sure what's up?" I see that she's tensing up and I suggest we go to sit on the side of my bed to talk.

"Ok, here goes, Zenobia and I hung out yesterday and we had a nice long talk about things." she states with a bit of nervousness in her voice.

"Oh hell, do I really want to hear this?" leaning back away from Kim just a bit to prepare myself for the news.

"Well if things hadn't went the way they did, no you wouldn't but they went well."

"How well?"

Kim reaches into her pocket and pulls out the tape recorder.

"What's this?" I ask in a bit of bewilderment not knowing what's going on.

"It's the recording of your friend Darius and Zenobia that I told you about."

"I thought you said you were going to get her to delete it." starting to get a bit upset at what I'm hearing.

"Well I thought so too but I kind of figured she wouldn't do it so that's when I asked her about it and took it from her and now I'm giving it to you."

"Ok, why give it to me and not just destroy it?"

"Because I wanted you to know that it existed and when you destroy it you can tell your friend that it's done and he has nothing to worry about."

"Yeah that would be a good thing" if that were the only thing he had to worry about I thought to myself. "Ok so what's next?"

"Nothing, you got the evidence so you do with it what you feel you need too. Personally I think you need to just delete it and be done with it."

"I will do one better, when Darius gets here I'll let him know I have it and let him hear what's on it to make sure that it's legit and have him delete it right in front of me."

"If that's how you want to handle it that's fine by me, I just wanted you to know I did my part in making sure that my niece didn't do something crazy."

"Are you sure this is the only copy?" I say with a questionable look on my face.

"Yes I'm sure, I love my niece and she does have some smarts but she wasn't thinking ahead enough to make multiple copies of this, besides I made her give me her word that it was the only copy."

"Good, so at least this will be over for him." I look at my watch and see it's 3:20, "Well, everyone should be arriving in a few minutes, let's go back out and sit with my mom for a bit and I'll check on dinner."

I get up and reach for her to help her up off the bed. We head towards the door. Kim then stalls, pulls my hand, and says

"Marcus?"

"Yes baby!"

"I didn't' do that solely for Zenobia and your friend but also I did that because I wanted you to know I'm a woman of my word too."

I take Kim in my arms and hold her close, I then take her chin and raise her lips to mind and give her a soft kiss.

"Baby, I believe you and you have not given me any reason to doubt your word so don't worry about that."

"I just wanted to make sure that's all." but that wasn't what Kim was worried about and she knew it. She knew she had her own deep dark secret to tell him but truly didn't know how but she knew she had to tell him and soon.

We went out into the living room, Kim sat on the couch not far from my mother and I went to check on dinner. My door buzzer sounded, I knew it was everyone else so I hit the buzzer to let them up. When they got there I introduced Kim to everyone and Braden introduced BJ to our lives and re-introduced Kandi. Just shortly after we all sat down to eat dinner. While dinner was in full swing I stood and told everyone I had an announcement.

"Ok, everyone, you know I went to DC for a business trip for my magazine right?" everyone chimed in saying right at the same time. "Ok now first things first and this is the easiest and not so much of a surprise but I got the account with Jump athletics AND he paid me for a years' worth of advertisement up front." everyone started clapping and congratulating me. "But that's not the best news, the better news well truly the best news of it all was I met this wonderful woman you see sitting here besides me. But I have some news that I want to share and this does or can affect my boys if y'all let it." at this point everyone but Kim was looking perplexed. Jason spoke out and asked

"Spit it out man what is it?" even though he kind of knew part of it and I looked at him crazy like he better not say anything.

"Well while I was out there I had a chance to go to some wonderful spots for dinner, dancing, music, you name it but one spot in particular stood out and I had the opportunity to talk with the owner about running ad space in my magazine."

"Man will you come out and say it already." Jason chimes in and I look at him ready to pop him.

"Man I am just chill out, now as I was saying, this meeting with the owner of this lounge called Lux turned into a business venture but not only for me but I wanted to get all of you who is willing to do so involved with it."

"So you want us to invest in a lounge?" Darius speaks up

"Yeah I do but only if you want too, now I know you don't know anything about it but after we finish dinner I'm going to take you all into my office and show you the lounge and you can make up your own minds if you want to be involved or not. The owner informed me that he has always wanted to expand and come into Chicago but had no contacts here so when he met me I jumped at the chance to bring something classy and upscale to the Chicago land area. I mean let's be real I'm tired of not having a high-class place to go without having to spend sport athletes kind of money to get in and hopes of enjoying ourselves. This is a place where you can come in and enjoy it and not go home wondering how you're going to pay next month's rent or mortgage."

"Well it sounds great my brotha" Braden speaks up "But I'd have to see more of it and think about it but I agree with you, I'm tired of not having a good place to go enjoy myself and not worry about all the youngsters out there with their pants hanging half off their ass."

"Yeah you know I hate that too, cool so after we finish we'll go in and I'll show you." I reply.

We finish dinner and I take everyone into my office where I have a presentation set up so they could see what I see. I had Charles send me a slide show of pictures of the lounge and what it looks like in DC and they were all amazed at the décor. They especially loved the private rooms that you can have, the multiple bars and especially the wood grain floors that were so shiny. I let them marvel in the view and when they were entranced by it I tapped Darius on the shoulder and tell him I need to speak to him alone. We go into my bedroom where we could have privacy.

"Here man, take it." I hold out the tape recorder of him and Zenobia.

"What's this?" Darius looking puzzled.

"It's the recording of you allowing Zenobia perform oral sex on you in your office that's what it is and I heard the whole thing."

"Oh snap for real?" Darius turns on the recorder and sure enough it's him and Zenobia and he chuckles behind it.

"Man that's not funny and you're lucky I have the tape now."

"You're right man and how in the hell did you get it. I was going to have Terry go into her purse or have one of the females do it. Either way I was going to get it?"

"Well Kim brought it to me after she had a long talk with Zenobia about how wrong it is."

"Whew! I'm glad she did, now I have nothing to worry about?"

"Uhm aren't you forgetting something, those little three letters...... the H......the I...and...the V?"

"No I haven't forgotten them, I'm just saying that this is one less thing for me to worry about that's all." Darius stops the tape and hit the delete button.

"So that's it for that and man you gotta be chill from now on and do right by Trish."

"I know, I know and I will."

"Yeah heard that before."

"Come on Marcus, honestly after this and the HIV scare, man I'm scared straight and only want my wife from now on."

"Well I'll believe it when I see it but the words do sound good coming out of your mouth. Now let's go rejoin everyone and have a good evening."

We went back to my office where everyone else were enjoying the slide show. They all said that it seemed real nice and want to look into it further. As the evening wound down and people were starting to leave I asked Braden if he wouldn't mind giving my mom a ride home since it was on his way. He didn't mind at all and I could tell that he was truly enjoying getting to know BJ so I was happy for him. Everyone left but Kim and of course Milton and Jazzmin, I began to clean up and get my house back in order.

"Would you like some help honey?" Kim asked me.

"Oh no babe I'm fine just chill out and relax."

"Well I could do that but I want you to chill out with me and if you let me help you we can get done faster and chill together."

"Well that is true and thank God I clean as I go when I cook otherwise it'd be a hot mess."

Kim helped me clean up while Jazzmin and Milton were in their rooms. After we get my house back in decent order we sit down to watch a movie and relax. While watching the movie my thoughts went over the day and how wonderful it was and I can't wait to see what's around the corner. After the movie was over I wanted Kim to stay but felt that it was a little too soon for Jazzmin to wake up and find her there in the morning. Kim agreed and she reluctantly went home. I made sure Kim called me when she got home so I would know she was safe and I wanted to hear her voice before I went to sleep. Once I knew Kim was safe I did something I haven't done in a long time. I knelt to pray and thank God for His many blessings. Once I finished I got up and got into my bed and had the first peaceful nights rest that I've had in a very long time.

CHAPTER

36

Marcus "Monday! No longer the blues"

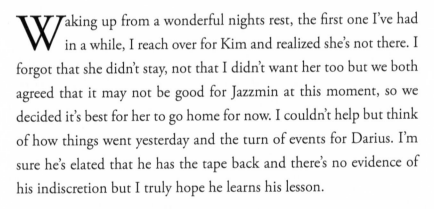

Waking up from a wonderful nights rest, the first one I've had in a while, I reach over for Kim and realized she's not there. I forgot that she didn't stay, not that I didn't want her too but we both agreed that it may not be good for Jazzmin at this moment, so we decided it's best for her to go home for now. I couldn't help but think of how things went yesterday and the turn of events for Darius. I'm sure he's elated that he has the tape back and there's no evidence of his indiscretion but I truly hope he learns his lesson.

Now all he has to do is get past this HIV issue if he can. I get up to start getting myself ready for my day and turn on the radio. I listen to the Steve Harvey show and they are at one of my favorite parts the "Strawberry Letter". It amazes me sometimes how people can get caught up in crazy situations but I know it does happen as I think of Darius. But today's letter is interesting, it's about a woman who recently met a great guy and things are going well for them. The only thing is she has this secret to tell him about her past but doesn't know how to do it. The letter goes on to say how she was once married to an abusive husband who got caught up in the drug game and it almost cost her, her life. It continues to say how he got caught up with a drug lord and was on the run and they came to her house looking for him but he wasn't there so they beat her thinking she was hiding something from them. The bad part is she was pregnant at the time and they beat her so bad that she not only lost the baby but the chance to ever have a child of her own. Her husband was caught and locked up and she filed for divorce but she is scared of the fact that if she tells this great guy she met she wonders how he would see her once she tells him.

Of course Shirley gives some good sound advice but Steve as usual gives some off the wall stuff that has me cracking up. I was thinking to myself that it's a shame that this woman got caught up in her husband's mess and how I feel for her. I thought to myself that hell it's her past and as long as she was able to get the divorce then things should be ok, but what if they're not divorced or even worse he's still wanted by the guy he owed the drugs too. Then that could be a mess once he got out of prison. Oh well I thought I'm not worried about that because it's not me. I go into Jazzmin's room to get her up so she can go over to my mom's house while I'm at work. I know she's happy that her summer school is over with and now she can just play. I go to check in on Milton to let him know that I have to go into the office for a little while and I'll be back so we can meet up with the lawyers to start planning what to do about Sharon.

I finish getting myself together and I take Jazzmin over to my mom's. I then go to the office to check on things and make sure I have nothing pressing for the day. That's the good thing about being your own boss, you don't have to stay in the office all day. It also helps to have a great staff as I do, to handle things when I'm not there. I think that's why I treat them so well when it comes to bonuses each year. I learned from working in jobs where the management treats the employees like shit and they lose money from employees stealing things. I said when I got my magazine off the ground that I would never treat my staff like that.

After spending a couple hours in the office I head back home to get up with Milton. I place a call to one of my best friends from college LaToya Mitchell who has since college become one of Chicago's top litigators. I ask her and her partner to meet me at my house so we can go over Milton's case and strategize just how we're going to handle things. I must say it does feel good to know and have friends in places where I can utilize them, not for free of course, I never believed in getting help from someone and not paying for it. Now if they turned me down cool but I at least offer. I pull into my garage and park my car and head up to my floor. I get off the elevator and head to my place, once in I see Milton sitting on the couch watching TV.

"What up man, what are you watching?"

"Divorce court."

"Uhm do you think that's a good idea considering your current situation?"

"Well there's not much else on that I wanted to watch and besides I figure this gives me a view of what I will be going through once everything is all said and done."

"You're not sure that you're getting a divorce just yet. I mean I know Sharon is trippin right now and sees you as just a bad guy but I'm sure somewhere deep inside her twisted little mind she loves you still."

"Man I don't know, all I know is she's acting a fool and I'm tired of it myself."

"I'm glad you said that because I have one of my close friends from college coming over to help strategize something for you on how to stop her from doing what she's doing at least as far as your job and the kids are concerned. I know they may not stop her from filing for divorce but at least they can stop all the other bullshit she's taking you through."

"Man I hope so, I hope so."

A few minutes later my buzzer sounds and its George from downstairs letting me know that LaToya is there and I tell him to let them up. Once they come I let them into my place and introduce them to Milton. We sit down at my table and discuss what's been going on and what they are going to do from there. Milton is surprised at all the things LaToya has said to him and how Sharon has done things in a way it's not totally illegal but with him not knowing the law did not know she couldn't hold his kids away from him.

The false report she filed to get the restraining order on him would be a bit difficult to get thrown out but not impossible because there was no history of any violence in the home. She went on to say that once charges like that are filed they have to play out in court so it's best for him to stay away from the home for now. She did say that she will file an injunction for him to have visitations with his kids for longer than just an hour a week, but there still has to be a mediator involved right now but he will be able to see his kids for a longer time at least. I sat there while listening to her and her partner go over everything and just shook my head at all that's going on. I often wonder why women treat men that are good to them that way and they always say there's no good men out there.

After some time goes by, they wrap up things with Milton. I thank them for coming by and offer the retainer fee to LaToya and she refuses. I guess she did that because I don't charge her for advertising in my magazine. One good turn deserves another is all I could think.

"So that parts done." I say to Milton

"Yeah, thanks, I don't know how to ever repay you for this."

"It's not about paying be back bro I developed something a long time ago, whenever I do something good for someone and they talk about paying me back or whatever I just tell them to be nice or do something nice for someone else and that's payment enough. So I'm telling you the same, don't worry about me just be nice or do something nice to someone else and that's cool with me."

"Man that's a good philosophy to have."

"Yeah it is, it's called paying it forward and I live by that now. It's something I hear Oprah talk about and I find it very rewarding."

"Well I'm gonna steal that from you."

"You can't steal what's free my brotha." laughing to myself.

"True, so what now?"

"Well I'm done in the office and this month's edition is on its way to the printer so I'm cool for the day. I think I will call Kim and see what she's doing for lunch."

"Yeah that's cool and she seems like a real nice woman. I will say this though when I first met her I couldn't help but think of how much she reminds me of Brenda."

"Yeah I know and that's what I thought of too and I had to catch myself when we first met because I almost called her Brenda's name."

"Yeah you have to be careful with that, cool, I'll just chill out and watch some TV and make a couple calls. Do you mind if I get something to eat?"

"Yeah, I mind"…giving Milton a crazy look then laughing. "Man you're trippin, of course I don't mind, mi casa es su casa bro so you're all good."

"Thanks Marcus."

"No problem let me get up and do what I have to do."

I get up and leave Milton on the couch watching TV and go into my room and call Kim for a lunch date. Unfortunately I got her voice mail and wasn't able to reach her. I leave a message for her to call me back and go back in the living room with Milton until I hear from her.

Hours later

I still hadn't heard from Kim and I'm a bit concerned but not too much because I know she has a lot of work to do but I figured I'd heard from her by now. I send her a text message just to see if everything is ok and that she got my voice message. But after some time goes past I get no response, now I'm getting worried about her. I call her office to see if she's there and her receptionist tells me that she has not been in her office all day. Ok I get this feeling again in my stomach and I don't like it. This is the third time I've gotten it and that's not good. I don't know what to do or where this is going. I think about just going over to her house but I know how I am when it comes to people popping up, I hate it, that's why I live in this secured building and you have to be announced. I try to put it out of my head and just chill with Milton but it doesn't work out well. I pick up my phone and call her and this time it goes straight to voice mail. I leave another message that I'm concerned about her and to give me a call as soon as she can.

"Is everything ok?" Milton asks me.

"No, I've tried to call Kim all afternoon since I told you I was going to see if she wanted to get something to eat but haven't heard anything from her."

"I was wondering why you hadn't left yet but I didn't want to pry into your business."

"Man it's cool and you're not prying but I will say this, not hearing back from her has me concerned and I got this eerie feeling in my stomach and this is not the first time it's happened. The first time was when we were in DC together and she left to go back to her hotel and was gone for a long time and I called her then and she didn't answer. Come to think about it I always get this type of feeling when she's gone and I can't reach her."

"You think something's wrong?"

"I don't know, I hope not but I can't help but wonder."

"I hope for her sake nothing is wrong."

"Me too!"

Milton and I just relax and watch some ESPN but my mind couldn't get off the fact that Kim is MIA. I don't want to think the worse but don't know anything else to think. Yeah she has been a little evasive on a couple occasions but nothing to worry about so I thought. Now I can't reach her at all and she's not returning my calls or text's. I tell Milton I'm going into my office to try and get some work done but in reality I just want to be alone to my own thoughts. When I go into my office I sit at my desk and open my laptop to try to do some work but to no avail. So I shut it down and just sit there in silence and think. *"Damn where are you Kim and what's going on with you."*, I try her number again and get the voice mail, I text her again and no response. Damn this is bothering me. I get up and go to my window and look out, all I can think of is what could possibly have changed in a day's time for her to not communicate with me, I just don't get it. I can only hope to hear from her soon otherwise I'm going to do what I said I wouldn't and take a ride over to her house. I know that's against my better judgment but at this point I don't have much of a choice. I think to myself *"I'll give her until tomorrow and if I hadn't heard from her I'm going over. I just hope everything is ok........it better be."*

CHAPTER

37

Kim "A surprise is not always a good thing"

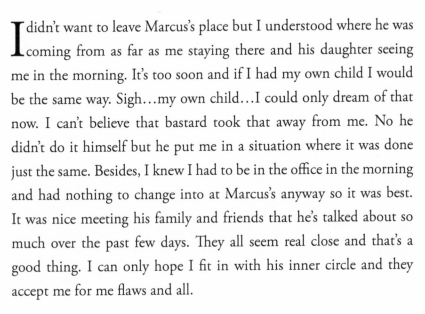

I didn't want to leave Marcus's place but I understood where he was coming from as far as me staying there and his daughter seeing me in the morning. It's too soon and if I had my own child I would be the same way. Sigh…my own child…I could only dream of that now. I can't believe that bastard took that away from me. No he didn't do it himself but he put me in a situation where it was done just the same. Besides, I knew I had to be in the office in the morning and had nothing to change into at Marcus's anyway so it was best. It was nice meeting his family and friends that he's talked about so much over the past few days. They all seem real close and that's a good thing. I can only hope I fit in with his inner circle and they accept me for me flaws and all.

I continue down the Dan Ryan until I come up on my exit which is 87th street. I get off and realize I'm a little hungry again so I stop at Harold's Chicken Shack and get me a 3-piece snack. I get my food and head down 87th to Cottage Grove. I turn right and go to 91st place and turn right and go to my home. It always feels good to be home. I park my car and get out and go into my house. I see I have a few messages on my answering machine and I check them. The first message is a solicitor trying to get me to change my service. The second is one that gives me pause. It's someone looking for Larry stating that he's a probation officer. I think that this must be a mistake because he's not due to be out for another couple years. I wonder why I get a call about that because he's not going to stay here anyway. I try to try dismiss it but it has me concerned. The third call though frightens me because it's from Larry. He says that he can't wait to see me and start to rebuild our marriage also that he never signed the divorce papers. He goes on to say that he'll see me sooner than I think. I delete the message and just freeze. I think to myself *"this can't be happening, not now, not when I have gotten past it and have rebuilt my life all over again. How dare he want to come back into my life as if nothing ever happened, damn him."* Losing my appetite, I put my food in the fridge. I go into the bathroom and take a shower and get myself ready for tomorrows work day. But I know that tonight's rest will not be a good one.

Monday

I get up to get myself together to go into the office. As I grab my food from last night that I didn't eat thinking I'll eat it for lunch. I grab my briefcase and keys and head towards the door only to open it to the biggest shock of my life.

"Larry!!...What in the hell are you doing here?"

"Surprise!! I left you a message saying that I'll see you sooner than you think, what did you think, I was joking?"

"But how did you get out, you're not scheduled to be out for a couple more years?"

"Well just call it good behavior and time served, now can I come in or what?"

Knowing I don't want any commotion out in front of my house for my nosy neighbors to see I had no choice but to let him in.

"Wow I like how you fixed up the place, don't seem as if you're married at all. No pictures of me or anything. What, you don't love your old man anymore?"

"Larry look, I have moved on and we are no longer married so you can just get over that."

"Oh no baby, we are still legally married, you see I never signed those papers. I never want you to be with anyone else and that's that."

"Haven't you caused me enough problems, why would you want me to go back with you after all you've done to me?"

"You act as if all of that was my fault, as I remember you didn't have a problem with all the money I was making and lacing you with Prada and platinum now did you, what you gotta say about that?"

"I'm different now and I've moved on and started my own business."

"Who you think funded your little business, ME! so don't go starting this "I'm different now shit!" hell if it wasn't for me you wouldn't have that damn company."

"Yeah and if it wasn't for you I'd be able to have children too." knowing I struck a nerve with him he backs off a bit. Larry always wanted kids with me but after the gangsters Larry owed money too, beat me trying to find him, I lost the child I was carrying and to top it off found out I could never have a child of my own ever. That's the only reason he turned himself in to the police who was looking for him as well.

"Kim, I'm sorry about that, I didn't think they would come after you I really didn't."

"But they did Larry, they did, and now look at me, no child and no way of having one of my own."

At that moment my phone rings and I see it's Marcus. Knowing I can't answer it with Larry here I just ignore it.

"Who is that and why didn't you answer your phone?"

"Don't worry about who it is and I didn't answer it because I didn't want too. So again I ask you why are you here and how did you get out?"

"Like I said I want you back and I'm not gonna stop until I get you and as far as me getting out I was able to get some time shaved off because I did some work for the warden and it gave me good time so here I am, why, aren't you happy to see me?"

"NO!! actually I'm not, I mean after all that happened and you go off to prison, I had to change my life and move on. I couldn't sit and wait for you to get out and honestly I didn't want too because I couldn't take what you put me through."

"I'm sorry baby and like I said I didn't mean to get you caught up in all of that mess."

"But you did that's the point and now I've moved on and you think you can just walk back up in here like nothing has ever happened?"

"No I don't think that but I do still love you and thinking about you is what got me through prison time. All I could do was think of how I'm going to make it up to you once I got out."

"Well you don't have to make anything up to me and as far as I'm concerned you don't owe me anything. All you need to do is leave and never come back oh and sign the divorce papers so I can truly move on."

"Is that what you really want Kimmy?"

"Don't call me that!"

"Why not, you know that's all I call you, so now I can't even call you my special name?"

I realize that he's getting upset again and I have to calm down the situation.

"It's just that I don't go by that anymore and it brings back to much pain for me that's all so please respect me and not call me that."

"Fine have it your way but can I at least take a shower and get this prison smell off of me?"

"Why don't you go to where ever you're supposed to be when you get out of prison? I'm sure you're on parole and have to have a place to stay when you get out right?"

"Yeah that's right and that's part of the reason why I'm here, I gave them your address and phone number and told them this is where I'll be staying."

"YOU DID WHAT!!!" I screamed at the top of my lungs and also figured that's who called looking for him and left that message on my answering machine. "Damn why in the hell did you do that and how did you get my number because I changed it?"

"Because I had nowhere else to go and nowhere else I wanted to go, is that a problem and besides I got your number one time when Zenobia came to visit me?"

"Yes it is Larry a big problem and damn I'm gonna kill her." I say fuming at the fact Zenobia gave him my number.

"Why is it because you're seeing someone?"

"Whether or not I am seeing someone has nothing to do with it." even though I knew better.

"Then what is it, I mean it's not like you don't know me and we don't have history."

"That's just what we have "history" and I for one would like to leave it right there."

"Wow you've gotten cold on me babe, well if you're not gonna let me stay here I will have to get in touch with my PO and find somewhere else to go but that's going to take a couple days. Can I stay at least until I get that straightened out. Please?"

"Sigh.....damn why are you doing this to me?"

"I'm not trying to do anything; I just thought that you would be happy to see me that's all."

"Well I'm not, I mean I'm glad you're ok but Larry I've moved on."

At that moment my phone goes off. I look at it and it's Marcus again, knowing I want to reach out to him but I can't at this moment because if I answer my phone all hell could break loose. Larry snatches my phone from me and we get into an argument.

"Who is that your little boyfriend and why didn't you answer the phone?"

"Larry give me back my phone it's my personal property and you have no right to it."

"I'll give it back when you tell me who it is that's calling you and you're not picking up."

"Larry it could be my office you don't know that."

"Nahh it's not because if it was you would have answered it and told them you'll call them back so who is he?"

"He's none of your business."

"So you are seeing someone." Larry explodes.

"Yes I am now give me my phone back."

"Oh you want it back huh well take it." Larry throws the phone against the wall and breaks it into pieces.

"You bastard, why did you do that?"

"Because, I told you, I want you back and if I can't have you no one else will."

I see the anger in his eyes and knowing how he is I run into my bedroom and shut and lock the door and just cry. Larry runs behind me and bangs on the door for me to let him in but I refuse too. I can't believe this is happening to me now. Why now, why has he come back into my life just to ruin what I have going on. Now I feel trapped in my own home because he's not gonna let me go anywhere. I go to pick up my house phone only to find him using it. I tell him to get off my phone because I have to make a call. He refuses saying I'm only going to call that nigga and that ain't happening. I feel trapped in my own home and don't know how to get out of this. I have to find a way to get word to Marcus of what's going on and that I'm ok I just don't know how to do it.

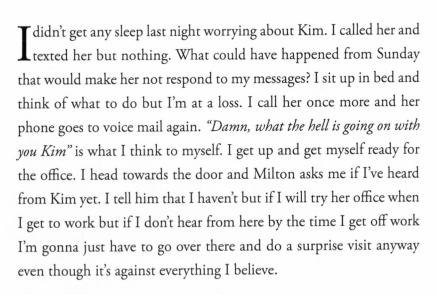

38

Marcus "Tuesday's Dooms Day, All good things come to an end"

❧

I didn't get any sleep last night worrying about Kim. I called her and texted her but nothing. What could have happened from Sunday that would make her not respond to my messages? I sit up in bed and think of what to do but I'm at a loss. I call her once more and her phone goes to voice mail again. *"Damn, what the hell is going on with you Kim"* is what I think to myself. I get up and get myself ready for the office. I head towards the door and Milton asks me if I've heard from Kim yet. I tell him that I haven't but if I will try her office when I get to work but if I don't hear from here by the time I get off work I'm gonna just have to go over there and do a surprise visit anyway even though it's against everything I believe.

After leaving my home and getting into the office, my day goes by in a blur because all I could do is think of what has happened to Kim. I keep thinking about this show I watch called "Find our Missing" and wonder if something has happened to her and keep waiting on the police or someone to call me because of my number being the last one to call her or something.

I'm about to leave work and I call Milton to tell him I'm about to go over to Kim's house. He asks me if wanted him to ride with me and I tell him that I'm good and things should be ok. I guess I was giving myself some kind of false hope about things. I leave my office and head down the Ryan and get off on 87th street. I look at my phone for her address and see that it's 25874 91st place. So, I head east towards Cottage grove and go south to 91st place. As I turn the corner onto her street, I notice her car out front. Now I get worried and that feeling in my stomach comes back strong. I keep thinking of her missing or hurt or something and I can't shake it. I park my truck and sit there watching her house for a few minutes just to see if I see any movement on the inside. After a few minutes I don't see anything, so I get out of my car and go up to the front door. What I didn't know was I was about to be in for the shock of my life. I knock on the door and no one answers, I knock harder all of a sudden Kim comes to the door.

"BABY!! what are you doing here?" Kim asks me in a very nervous tone.

"I'm here because I've been trying to reach you since yesterday morning and you haven't returned my call or text message, that's why I'm here. So, what's going on Kim is there something I need to know?"

"Baby all I can ask of you right now is to trust me and go home and I'll talk to you about it in a couple days."

"A couple days, nah, tell me what's going on because I thought we were starting something special but all of a sudden you pull a no call no show on me, really Kim, what gives?"

Kim not wanting to wake Larry and have him come to the door and all hell breaking loose she asks Marcus to go sit in his truck to talk.

"Baby can we go sit in your truck to talk please?"

"Why can't I just come in and we talk in your house?"

"Because my house is a mess right now and I'm in no shape to have company." Kim looking around to see if her neighbors are watching.

"Oh, so I'm "company" now huh, what's really going on Kim, just tell me?"

"Marcus I can't right now, baby you have to trust me, I'll tell you in a couple days."

"Hmm trust you huh, well trust is earned honey and right now you're not earning any points with me."

"I know, I know but I have something to handle and I promise you that I'll call you in a couple days."

I think to myself "promise" and think back to when she told me she was talking to Zenobia and how she told her she doesn't like promises because they are meant to be broken.

"Is that right, well we'll see if you call me in a couple days." I turn to walk down her steps only to hear the voice of another man.

"Who in the hell is this?" Larry yells out. "Oh, this must be your nigga you're with now huh?"

"Excuse me, who are you calling a nigga" I turn around to see a man standing on her porch.

"YOU!! I'm calling you a nigga that's who."

"Bruh, I don't know who you are and you damn sure don't know who I am so I'd watch who you call that word." I start walking back up the stairs to her porch and Kim jumps in the middle.

"Larry go back in the house." Kim says as she holds up both arms between Larry and Marcus.

"Tell me is this the dude you are seeing or what?" Larry yells at Kim.

"Yeah I'm the dude she's seeing and what of it. Who in the hell are you?" I feel my Taurian rage rising up in me and I make a move towards the guy I now know as Larry.

"I'm her husband mother fucker that's who in the hell I am."

Completely shocked...I'm taken aback and stop dead in my tracks. I look at Kim as she is standing in between her husband and myself waiting on her to say something. Her head just drops and from her reaction I know it's true.

"So, this is why you haven't returned my messages or texts?"

Kim pauses and is unable to speak

"ANSWER ME!!" I yell at her.

"Yo man don't raise your voice at my wife like that."

"Man FUCK YOU!! she wasn't acting like your wife a couple weeks ago now was she." I turn my focus back to Kim "Kim answer me dammit...are you married first of all and is this is the reason you haven't answered my calls?" pointing at Larry.

"YES!" Kim says reluctantly, "But it's not like what you think. It's more complicated than that."

"Oh really and just what am I supposed to think? You know what... fuck it....I'm gone." I start walking back down the stairs again.

"Marcus don't leave." Kim yells after me begging.

"Nah let that nigga go I told you I'm not letting you go." Larry says to Kim.

"Dude I told you not to call me that and if you do it again, you're not gonna like what happens next." I said as I turn back around.

"Oh, so you think you're a big bad ass huh nigga so what are you going to do?"

I run back up the stairs to get at Larry only to have Kim in the middle of us. Trying to keep us separated I lunge forward and connect with Larry's jaw and he falls backward. He gets up and rushes me and tries to pick me up, but I sidestep him, and he runs into the post on the porch. I leap at him and throw a hook into his side and he gasps for air. He stumbles and tries to get to his feet, but I know from growing up in the hood, once you have a dog down you keep em' down. I throw a left and a right, one hitting his jaw and the other hitting gut and at this point Kim is screaming for me to stop and I look at her with tears in her eyes and realize it's not worth my time nor energy.

"You know what Kim...I don't know what's going on here, but you can have it. I told you I have an issue with trust, and I see I can't trust you so I'm gone."

"Yeah leave dude." Larry saying that but saying it from a distance because he realized his jaw and body was hurting bad from the blows I gave him. Kim begs me not to go and tells Larry to go into the house. In fact, she pushes him into the house not giving him a chance to respond. She closes the door, lowers her head, and turns towards me.

"Baby!" tears flowing, "I'm so sorry and I was going to tell you about him."

"OH…REALLY… and just when were you going to tell me about your husband, YOU HAVE A GODDAMN HUSBAND KIM!!!" I yell so loud I shake her windows.

"I know!" Kim starts to cry hysterically now, "But he wasn't supposed to be any more."

"Oh, and how does one not be your husband anymore and you not tell me you're married."

"Because he was in prison and wasn't supposed to get out for another couple years."

"Oh, so you figured you could have fun with me and keep your secret and live high off the hog for a couple years and then just dump me when he got out. So this is what you and Zenobia have been talking about huh. I see the apple don't fall far from the tree. She trying to get her claws in my boy and now you trying to get me hooked up with you."

"It's not like that Marcus I swear it's not. I filed for divorce and sent it to him while he was in prison but just found out that he didn't sign them, and he told the parole board that he would be staying with me. Sunday when I came home, I had a message from him and someone looking for him but I didn't think anything of it but then he showed up Monday morning at my door. When he came in and we got to arguing and you had called he grabbed my phone and threw it and broke it. That's why I couldn't call you back, believe me it wasn't because I didn't want to talk to you because I do."

"That's a bunch of bullshit because you could have used your house phone to call me, so what's your excuse on that one?"

"He wouldn't let me use my phone to call you or anyone, Marcus he was threatening me and I didn't want you to get involved in this and I was going to handle it and get in touch with you in a couple days. That's why I asked you to give me a little time."

"You know what Kim that's the most bullshit story I've ever heard."

"It's the truth Marcus but I understand if you don't believe me."

"You're right, I DON'T, look you have your…whatever it is to deal with and I don't have time for the drama in my life so I'm out. It's been real and it was good while it lasted but I can't do this."

"So that's it, you're going to throw away what we started? I thought you said you loved me?"

That hurt, I mean really hurt because I did love her and was truly falling for her but I know I can't and will not deal with this anymore.

"Yeah Kim I do love you that's why I've stayed to even listen to your story because I wanted to know how someone who says she loves me and then keeps a secret from me like this." at that moment a thought comes into my head about the strawberry letter on the Steve Harvey Radio Show I was listening too this morning and how this seems all to ironic. "You know something I heard this story on the radio about a woman who was in love with a guy but has a secret to tell him and it was about how she has an ex-husband who's in prison. I don't know what made me think of it at this point but it's almost as if this is Deja-vu."

"It was me Marcus, that was my story, I wrote that because I knew I had to tell you but didn't know how you would respond when I did.

I didn't and still don't want to lose you. I just couldn't figure out how to tell you about him."

"Uhm it's called being up front with me, see this is the type if shit you tell me from the beginning and not wait until I figure it out on my own."

"I know but I honestly didn't know I'd fall for you so fast, but I did."

"Well I didn't know either, but I can't do this. This is one of the main reasons why I haven't dated anyone seriously since Brenda died and especially not introduced anyone to Jazzmin. You have too much going on for me right now and I'm not sure if I can be that man who waits while you try to get this mess figured out. Look, I'm not saying never but right now I just can't, I'm sorry."

I turn to walk away, and Kim reaches out to me but I pull away. I get into my truck and pull off. I head down the Ryan with tears coming down my face over what just happened. I didn't want to go home and have a Milton ask me a million questions, so I just took the Lake Shore Drive exit and headed in that direction. I got to the lake front and parked my truck and just sat there. Thinking of what just happened and everything that went on over the past few weeks. I think, just when you think everything is going well and life is good you get the rug swiped out from under you. I sit there for a few hours engulfed in my own thoughts not answering my phone or text messages. By the time I realize it, it was after midnight. I start my truck up and head home. As I drive in the night only one thing comes to my mind. "I'll never trust a woman again!"

Weeks pass by

Another Saturday, I wake up and lay there thinking…just as I have been for these past few Saturday's. I think to myself, I'm glad things are coming back together for me and my boys. Milton has gotten the restraining order lifted. He and Sharon are in therapy about their marriage and her depression. Things seem to be going well for them I hope they make it. Braden and BJ's relationship has blossomed, and he sees him a couple times a month and has even taken him with him on a couple of his business trips. Darius, well, he says he's doing right by Trish and I can only hope he is. I haven't heard much noise coming from his camp, so I guess things are well. I am glad that he didn't have HIV but for a while it was scary for him.

Jason got the job with the CTA and is doing pretty good; the only problem is he's broke most of the time because of back child support but hey when you have a football team of kids they cost. As for me, my magazine is doing well and the project to bring LUX is off the ground. We're scheduled to be open next year, but things may happen where we can open ahead of schedule. Mom is doing well and Jazzmin is great. I think to myself that I have such a wonderful life but wish I could have someone to share it with.

Kim has tried to contact me, but I haven't had the energy to reach out to her since that day, but I do think about her quite often and wonder if she got that mess straightened out. I think to myself, that it's not my problem, well that's what I keep telling myself. I can't help but think of the "what if" factor. I just don't think I could ever trust the fact when someone says they love me and then....... well that's life right.

I get up out of my bed, grab a cup of coffee and go into the office to check my e-mails. Only to find I have one from Kim. As I look at her name and the subject line reading *"Please Forgive Me"* I get butterflies. I wonder if I should even read it or just delete it. I sit there staring at the inbox message... out of curiosity I decide to read it.

Hello Marcus,

I know I'm the last person you want to hear from, and I don't blame you. I tried calling you several times and although I wish you would have answered, I can't blame you. I hurt you deeply and I know it. Marcus, I won't take up much of your time but wanted to clear the air if I possible. Marcus, what I did to you was inexcusable and I know I don't deserve your forgiveness but Marcus, I'm asking…no I'm begging for your forgiveness, and I do hope you can give me another chance. The absolute last thing I wanted to do was hurt you in any way and I definitely didn't mean to hide anything from you. I know you don't believe me but it's true. I was just hoping for the right time to tell you everything about my past. When you showed up at my door that day, I was in complete shock to see your face, so much so… that I had a loss of words and then when Larry came out and made things worse, I knew there was nothing I could say to make you understand or see my side of it. So, after the altercation between you and Larry, with you storming off. I knew then I couldn't say anything that would make sense, so I had to let you go. I was hoping for a time where things would calm down and we talk, but that time just didn't come. Believe me, I regret everything about that situation and wish I could take it all back, but I can't. I know you are a loving and caring man. I saw evidence of that from being around you and watching you with your daughter, your mother, and your friends that's why I hope you can find it in your heart to forgive me and give me another chance to make things right with you. Marcus, I must tell you that I fell in love with you in that short amount of time and truth be told, I still am. I just hope that you see fit to allow me to show you how much I do truly love you. Oh, and I'm sure you're wondering "what about Larry", well he's no longer in the picture… for good. I called my lawyer to speak with him about the whole divorce situation. He stated that even though Larry did not sign the divorce papers initially. When I filed for divorce while he was in prison, he stated that it gave me the right to do so. We were/ARE legally divorced and went on to say some legal stuff about how Larry has no claims on me or our marriage. Also, I was able to get the courts to get him out of my house and he's living somewhere else. Surprisingly, he did apologize to me for everything and said that he wished me well and believe it or not hoped he didn't totally mess things up for you and me. How true he was on that I don't know. I do hope things can somehow get back to where we were. Well I will let you go for now and if you find it in your heart to forgive me and possibly give me another chance you know how to reach me but if not then, I have no other choice but to try and understand. I do hope you choose the former though.

Love always Kim

As I close out the e-mail, I thought about deleting it, but decided the latter and just closed my laptop. As I sat there, looking out the window, I think to myself, wow, how interesting, but I just don't know. *"I do forgive you Kim"* I think to myself, but could I try to go back to the way things were, I just don't know! I mean, I fell for Kim too and thought she was the one who could stand in the "motherless" gap for Jazzmin. Sigh, but who knows what the future holds? I do miss how things were between us but opening my heart again is not going to be easy. Not for her or anyone else, that is if I let someone get close to me again. If I do, whom ever it is, has to truly work hard at getting inside my heart. But, I do wonder if I can ever open it up again. Only time will tell...I wonder....

Thank you...

Thank you for blessing me by picking up and purchasing my very first (of many God willing) novel. I want to say, don't sit on your dream. GO FOR IT, don't let anyone or anything stop you. I've allowed people of my past (and sometimes present) to stop me from pursuing what God has put inside of me. Don't let that be you... because I will no longer allow that to be me. Thank you very much and much love to you. I hope you enjoyed reading it as much as I've enjoyed writing it.

Made in USA - Crawfordsville, IN
15617_9781737373704
02.25.2022 0944